TITILLATED

"What are you defensive about?" His head moved closer to Rhea's than was absolutely necessary. "I just can't understand how someone who was as soft and kittenish in my arms on that dance floor could be so brittle and prickly when she wants to. You really are a . . ."

"I don't want to know what you think I am, Marcus," she began huffily. "In fact, I think it's just . . . improper for you to be speaking to me like that. It was just a dance. I really can't see why you have to dredge it up out of . . ."

"Can't you?"

"No!"

"You mean . . ." he was smiling now, but it wasn't a very pleasant smile. It was the smile a wolf gave a cornered rabbit. "You've forgotten?" He leaned forward, closing in on her like a predator, and in a panic she realised that he would kiss her if she didn't do anything about it. Here, she panicked, in an open field, in front of all the other guests! It was insane but it was about to happen, and there wasn't anything she could do about it. Her mouth opened, partly in protest, partly in crazy anticipation.

BOOK YOUR PLACE ON OUR WEBSITE AND MAKE THE ARABESQUE ROMANCE CONNECTION!

We've created a customized website just for our very special Arabesque readers, where you can get the inside scoop on everything that's going on with Arabesque romance novels.

When you come online, you'll have the exciting opportunity to:

- View covers of upcoming books
- Learn about our future publishing schedule (listed by publication month and author)
- Find out when your favorite authors will be visiting a city near you.
- Search for and order backlist books from our line catalog
- Check out author bios and background information
- Send e-mail to your favorite authors
- Join us in weekly chats with authors, readers and other guests
- Get writing guidelines
- AND MUCH MORE!

Visit our website at
http://www.arabesquebooks.com

NIGHT HEAT

SIMONA TAYLOR

ARABESQUE

BET BOOKS

BET Publications, LLC
www.msbet.com
www.arabesquebooks.com

ARABESQUE BOOKS are published by

BET Publications, LLC
c/o BET BOOKS
One BET Plaza
1900 W Place NE
Washington, D.C. 20018-1211

First Printing: July, 1999
10 9 8 7 6 5 4 3 2 1

Printed in the United States of America

This first novel is dedicated to my agent, Deidre Knight, for taking that leap of faith in me, and for steadfastly singing my praises to any editor who would listen, thus launching me toward the career of my dreams. It is also dedicated to Rawle, for the nights he spent holding my despairing hand and assuring me that I would, one day, be a 'real' writer, and for proving to me that extraordinary love really does happen to ordinary people.

CHAPTER ONE

Rhea could feel the beads of sweat run down her breasts, past her flat brown belly, and soak into the waistband of her jeans. This was not a good thing. She had taken a shower less than an hour ago (although she had to admit that it was a *rushed* shower, what with being more than half an hour late for work). Her short curls clung wetly to the nape of her neck and the heat seemed to rise off her skin, in spite of the huge air-conditioning unit that rattled asthmatically above her head. The afternoon wasn't starting off very well. It was a bad sign.

She did her best to focus on the stream of insults that poured from her boss' mouth. Late again, he was shouting. What was he paying her for? Didn't make sense, his paying her, if she was going to be late all the time.

Rhea tried not to roll her eyes. Ian had a habit of exaggerating. Okay, so maybe she had been late twice this month, but it hardly made her the world's worst employee. But she loved, *needed* her job, so if standing there and swallowing Ian's poison was what it took, so be it. She dug her nails into her palms, clamped her full lips closed, and avoided his gaze.

Ian Hillman was squeezed into a huge overstuffed recliner, behind an even larger glass-topped desk strewn with binders, blotters and chrome executive toys designed more to impress visitors than for any useful purpose. As he rocked from side to side in his chair, Rhea cringed inwardly at the squeaking of the hinges under the onslaught of his considerable weight.

Ian was a short, swarthy man in his fifties, a businessman who ran Tours With A Difference, a travel agency that provided customized, off-the-beaten-track tours. His impressive girth was due in large part to a fondness for fried foods, and the little kitchen, which lay behind the door on his right, was frequently strewn with brightly coloured boxes stained with grease. His straight, thinning black hair was slicked down onto his head, and he ran his fingers repeatedly over it, as though to reassure himself that some of it was still there.

Rhea stood at the desk, behind the plush visitor's chair, head down like a chastened child.

"Miss De Silva," he said, stressing the words to emphasize the contrast between the form of address that he used when he was upset and the less formal "Rhea" when he was in a rare good mood. "Weren't you supposed to be in by two o' clock?"

Rhea nodded, even though as far as she was concerned, they were only going over old ground. She passed her hand over her hot brow. "Yes, Ian, but the traffic . . ."

"If you knew there was going to be traffic, you should have left home earlier. Wouldn't that have been logical?" The rocking of the chair increased in intensity.

"I didn't know the traffic would be so bad until I'd already left home," Rhea replied smartly, although careful to keep her voice calm. She was unwilling to risk causing Ian's attack to become any more spiteful than it already was.

No such luck. He sailed into her again. "Look at yourself!" he waved at her with a pudgy hand. "You're hot and bothered and your face is shiny. You're a tour guide. That's like an air hostess. You ever see an air hostess with a shiny forehead?"

"I've never seen an air hostess run around in this heat either," Rhea snapped. She was fast losing patience. Having this man undermine her confidence by throwing barbs at her appearance didn't help.

Fortunately, Ian seemed bored with the game. He snorted to

himself and gathered a sheaf of papers in a folder. "Here are the details on the group that's flying into Trinidad today. You'll find all their application forms, itinerary, blah, blah, blah, right here."

Rhea accepted the folder and looked down at it. The time of arrival caught her eye. "They're coming in at four-thirty?" she exclaimed. "Four-thirty *today?* I thought they were due in at eight this evening!"

Ian shrugged. "That's another group. Sandra's taking *them.* This is a different tour."

Rhea was stunned. She put one hand on her hip and the other on the back of the chair for support. "This isn't the tour to Las Cuevas, with the three couples with all those children, from Indiana?" She looked down at the folder again, then scowled up at him.

Ian shrugged nonchalantly. "Nah. I gave them to Sandy. This is a tour from the West Coast of the United States. It's a small group: two couples, one guy and a little girl, a daughter or a niece or something. Nature lovers. Nothing difficult, just a bunch of ordinary people doing the Caribbean. No mountain climbing, no marlin fishing, nothing heavy. You should be happy. You should be glad I let you have this one."

He leaned back in his seat and looked smug. "Treat them nice," he went on, "show them around, then send them packing. No problem."

Rhea looked thoughtfully at her itinerary. Their home base would be Mayaro. That meant that after she collected them from the airport, she and the driver would have to take their guests on a journey that would last at least three hours: along the east-west corridor, the main artery that spanned Trinidad, until they arrived at the East Coast, then continue southward until they reached the small coastal village near to the southeastern tip of the island.

She sighed. They would be arriving well after dark, and in her experience, it was the most difficult time to have new guests settle down. They would be tired, cranky, and hungry, and sleep would be difficult.

After a while, she looked up. "I suppose we have the Sinanan

house again, off Hibiscus Circular?'' The Sinanan beach house
was spacious and luxurious, and they frequently rented it for
these occasions. It offered a glorious view of the sea, and the
gently sloping garden was surrounded by pink, magenta, peach,
and white hibiscus, and was protected from the wind coming
off the seafront by rows of sturdy palms. She smiled to herself
as she thought of the small bedroom that she normally used.
Less spacious than the other rooms, it was nonetheless well
ventilated, and had its own deep porcelain bath. She hoped she
had remembered to pack her almond-scented bath oil.

Ian's voice broke through her thoughts. ''No,'' he said, ''not
this time.''

She stood before him, mouth slightly open. ''What? But we
always stay there.''

''Not this time.'' Ian shook his head. ''We couldn't get it.
It's all booked up.'' He fixed his tiny, deep-set black eyes on
Rhea in a manner that sent alarm bells ringing in her head.
''Relax. I got another place.'' He pulled open the drawer on
his left and rummaged through it. Rhea could hear the rustle
of potato chip bags and candy wrappers. Ian had caches of
food all over his office. He pulled out a heavy, jangling bundle
of keys and held them out to her, one finger through the large
brass hoop on which they were strung.

Rhea took them. ''Where's this, now?'' She had to struggle
to keep the irritation out of her voice.

Ian shrugged. ''How would I know? Somewhere in Mayaro.
Holdip Trace. Banner will know.''

Zebo Banner was the driver who was to accompany her on
this particular tour. Rhea was glad about having him assigned
to her, as he was reliable, reserved, and knew every street,
trace, and dead end on the island. She nodded. ''Is it big enough
for all of us?''

Ian smiled. ''Of course. Two double rooms for the couples,
a double for the single guy and the kid, and singles for you
and Banner. Don't worry. No problem.'' He passed his hands
over his hair again.

There he went again, with his ''no problem.'' Rhea hated
his nonchalance. She was particular, even fussy, about her tours,

and read and reread her itineraries and menus meticulously before every assignment. "Are you sure?" She looked doubtfully at the heavy old keys. "These keys look sort of . . . old."

Ian shrugged. "Yes, well, the owner says he had the place redone. It's my brother-in-law's place. Would he give me a lousy place?"

The rhetorical question hung unanswered in the air. Rhea shrugged. "I'd better get going," she said, looking at her watch. There would barely be time to make it. Ian nodded and went back to his papers before she'd left the room.

The stifling Caribbean heat beat down on the long snaking highway, causing hazy, dizzying waves to rise off the black asphalt. The small island capital of Port of Spain simmered with the kind of restless energy that one would normally reserve in one's mind for places like Bangladesh or Tokyo.

Though it was just a few minutes shy of four, it was Friday, and the roads were already clogged with workers who had taken the liberty of leaving their offices early, all eager to get home, go shopping, take in an early game, or simply to indulge in the popular Trinidadian pastime of "liming"—doing nothing in the company of friends. The result was a massive snake of cars that stretched past the city limits to the east and to the west, sluggish, tedious, irritating.

This afternoon, the traffic appeared even more slothful, and Rhea was convinced that something was up, and that she was not simply imagining the delay. She shifted restlessly in her seat next to Banner, craning her neck to try to see around the long line of traffic ahead. "What's the problem up there?" she grumbled. "We haven't moved in half an hour."

Banner was a dark-skinned, hefty man of about forty-five. Stocky, barrel-chested, he moved with ponderous deliberation, like a huge bull. He spoke in a slow drawl, as if carefully weighing each word before it passed his lips. "Relax," he said, as if to an infant. "Listen to the music."

She snorted and leaned forward to fiddle with the radio,

moving from station to station, finding the stimulating beat of
the inevitable calypso too much to handle in her state of mind.

Banner watched her work the controls for a while and smiled
as though she were a child trying to get the tuning right but
just missing it. Then he reached out and slid in a CD of soothing,
low-keyed jazz, the kind of CD they often used to calm their
restless passengers on the way back in from an outing.

The music did little to calm her. She sighed again. "Stupid
rush-hour traffic." Rhea stuck her head and torso out of the
window, trying again to see up the road.

Banner turned his round, balding head to look at her. "You
know," he said evenly, "if you closed the windows and kept
the cool air in, we'd both be a lot more comfortable." Banner
was not the kind of man to raise his voice, whatever the reason.

Rhea smiled a little, acknowledging that he was right.
"Okay." She sent her window up and tried to relax, long brown
fingers beating a tattoo on the dashboard. "Can't you ride the
shoulder?" she asked after a while. It was all that she could
do not to reach out and grab on to the steering wheel.

Banner smiled, and answered without looking at her. "I
could, if I wanted to get a traffic ticket. Relax."

Rhea tried to relax. She turned down the sun visor above
her head and studied herself in the tiny vanity mirror, noting
that the makeup that she had reapplied before leaving the agency
had already begun to blur in the heat. She was pretty in a
healthy, athletic sort of way, with skin that glowed from frequent exercise and vigourous scrubbing. Her skin was a spicy
nut-brown, and her wide-set, inquisitive brown eyes, full lips,
and high cheekbones made heavy makeup superfluous.

The comment that Ian had made about her appearance still
stung. How dare he try to make her sound unprofessional? She
was the best guide he had, and he knew it. Rhea frequently
found herself camping out on the beach with professional pho-
tographers hoping to catch a shot of a sunrise over the water,
tramping through marshy southland with nature lovers, or hiking over the Northern Range with ornithologists. She had suffered blustering rainstorms, held glass jars filled with tarantulas

and been stranded out on jagged northeastern rocks at high tide. All in the line of duty. All without complaining.

If Ian knew what was good for him, he'd stop baiting her, show a little appreciation, give her a raise. This last thought almost made her laugh out loud. Ian would walk across town to save on taxi fare.

It was another forty minutes before they discovered the cause of the heavy traffic. By then, they were well within sight of the turnoff to the airport. Three large police vehicles were parked on the eastbound shoulder of the highway, as were several cars that had been pulled over for various violations.

Rhea cursed in a rush of breath. "A roadblock? *A roadblock?* Don't they know I have work to do? Who in their right minds would set up a roadblock on the highway in rush-hour traffic?"

"The police," Banner laughed.

Rhea sucked her teeth in irritation. "You think they're looking for someone?" The prospect of a criminal on the lam, or a botched robbery, fired her imagination for a moment, distracting her from her anxiety. "You think they'll search us?"

Banner threw her the same indulgent look that her father often had when she gave in to her flights of fancy. "Maybe they're just looking for driver's licenses and insurance," he suggested, always the more rational of the two.

Rhea scowled, brought back to earth with a thud. She folded her arms. "Well, they shouldn't be looking for them *here.*" She looked moodily out of the window. She hoped desperately that her party would be a few more minutes clearing immigration and customs.

Banner took his driver's license out of his faded leather holder and laid it out on the dashboard in preparation. Humming, he pulled to a stop alongside the policeman in his lane.

"License and insurance," the policeman said in a bored voice. Banner handed them over. The young, thin policeman gave the papers a cursory look, as though Rhea and Banner looked so mundane that they did not even merit in-depth examination.

"Anything going on?" Banner asked.

The constable shrugged, handing back the documents. "No,"

he replied. "Nothing." He rolled his eyes to the sky, looking as though he wished that there were.

"Go! Go! Go!" Rhea urged Banner as, free now, they sped along the sharp curves leading to the airport. "Hurry! Hurry!"

"Don't get excited," Banner said slowly. "I'm hurrying."

They drew up at the front of the international arrival hall, and Rhea hopped out even before the van could come to a complete stop.

"Don't go park," Rhea threw breathlessly over her shoulder as she scampered away. "Wait here."

She elbowed her way through throngs of meeters and greeters, family members falling into one another's arms after years of separation, and vendors returning from Miami and New York with suitcases and packing cases engorged with a variety of goods to be sold in boutiques and on street corners all over the city. Aging airport taxi drivers in crisp white shirts hemmed her in, politely offering her taxis. She shook her head, trying to pull herself free of their insistent grasps, yet reluctant to be rude.

Arching her neck to see beyond the crowd, she searched for her party. As she made her way to the Baggage Hall exit, she spotted a small desolate huddle of people to her far right, wedged between the Information office and the huge steel restraining barriers that enclosed the customs exit. A sinking in her abdomen told her that this was her group.

She hurried toward them. One couple, in their sixties, she guessed, were holding hands. They were carefully dressed in brand-new cotton outfits, outlandish versions of what they obviously imagined to be tropical wear. Bright patterned shirts topped pastel drill trousers, and they expectantly held wide-brimmed straw hats in their hands. Dark jackets, obviously used at the originating end of the flight, were slung like huge dead mooses over the metal barriers.

The second couple was a picture of incongruity. The man, a beefy creature with russet hair and a generous sprinkling of equally russet freckles, paced impatiently, glancing at what was obviously a very expensive watch. His broad pale face was scrunched into a scowl. A short distance from him stood a young woman. She was leaning against the wall, her head turned so that Rhea could only see her in profile. She was clad in trendy metropolitan streetwear: off-white leggings tucked into boots of a similar colour, with a hip-length jacket the colour of frosted strawberries. She stood with her arms folded about herself, as though blocking out a cold wind, in spite of the jacket and the warmth of the afternoon. Her half-turned head was beautifully shaped, framed by thick dark hair that was swept up in a heavy knot behind. She appeared to be staring at some imaginary point in the distance, frowning slightly.

As Rhea drew closer, she looked quickly at the last two members of the party. One was a little girl, probably four or five. She was curled into a ball, her thin brown arms and legs almost completely enfolded by the long dark arms of the man who was cradling her. The child was obviously asleep, and for a moment Rhea felt a pang of guilt for having kept such a tiny thing waiting so long.

The man's face was turned away from her. He perched on the edge of a hard metal chair, his entire body curved protectively, seeming to be trying to shield the girl from harm. She had time only to note the breadth of his shoulders and his considerable height before she reached the group.

''Hello,'' she gasped, slightly out of breath, and a little annoyed to hear the hint of desperation in her own voice. ''I'm Rhea De Silva, from Tours With A Difference?'' Her voice rose at the end, as though she were asking a question, betraying her nervousness. She took a deep, controlling breath and held out her hand, not to anyone in particular, but to the group in general. Her placatory smile was met with cold stares.

''Well, it's about time!'' the freckled man exploded. His pale face suddenly flared red with the effort. ''It's about time!'' He glared at her, ice-blue eyes wide with impatient fury.

Others joined him in a chorus of complaints. ''We were told we'd be met,'' the elderly man said, holding his tour brochure out as though to prove it. ''We expected to be met. It's been more than forty-five minutes.'' He waved the brochure under her nose.

Rhea took an uncertain step backward, and steadied herself.

"I'm . . . sorry," she stammered, hating herself for losing her equilibrium. "The traffic . . ."

She was cut off abruptly by the freckle-faced man. "I suppose this is the West Indian manner of doing things," he suggested nastily to the others. "I suppose this disregard for other people's time is some kind of . . . of *island way.*"

Rhea protested hotly. "Sir, we are very professional here at Tours With A Difference. There was a traffic situation, a roadblock. I apologize, but it was unavoidable."

"A roadblock?" The elderly lady looked alarmed, as though she expected to see cutlass-wielding bandits storm howling out from behind the potted palms. "Are they looking for someone?"

Rhea shook her head. "No," she said as soothingly as possible. "It was just a spot-check. For licenses and the like. You're perfectly safe."

The woman sighed and smiled up at her husband for encouragement. They stood for a few moments, uncertain of what to say next. "Well, maybe we should get a move on," the elderly man said at last. He reached across and stuck out his hand. "I'm Fred Stein. This is my wife, Trudy." Rhea took his hand, grateful that the tension seemed to be ebbing.

"Rainer Bainbridge," the freckled man said gruffly, and clasped her hand briefly in his heavy paw. He gestured vaguely in his wife's direction. "Dahlia," he said carelessly, as though he didn't care whether or not Rhea knew her name. Dahlia allowed Rhea to hold her slim languid hand for a few seconds, then pulled it out of her grasp and looked disinterestedly away.

Rhea sighed. This wasn't going all that well. She turned to the long-limbed man who had been observing the exchange silently from the sidelines. "Rhea," she introduced herself brightly, and held out her hand. He rose easily to his feet, as if the little girl weighed barely as much as a large cat, and shifted her, still fast asleep, onto his shoulder. Cradling her with his right arm, he awkwardly offered his left hand to be shaken. As Rhea held it, the hard metal of a wedding ring on the fourth finger pressed into the flesh of her palm.

Although she herself was unusually tall, she discovered she needed to look up to meet his eyes. She did, and froze.

He was watching her unsmilingly, with the deepest golden eyes Rhea had ever seen. They shone like polished amber out of a frame of thick dark eyelashes, giving an effect that was intensely disturbing. The unusual colour of his eyes was thrown into even sharper relief by the smooth mahogany of his skin. His black hair was cropped neatly, close to his shapely head. He took her hand gravely, and as he held it, she got the eerie impression of encountering a strange silent creature, like coming face-to-face with a lion that was none too thrilled. She withdrew her hand, oddly unsettled.

"You must be Marcus Lucien," she said, and smiled broadly to cover her confusion. She remembered the name as that of the single male on her fact sheet.

He nodded. "Pleased to meet you," he said politely, not sounding very pleased at all. The disturbing eyes ran down her in slow appraisal, as if trying to ascertain whether she would be capable of guiding them over the next few weeks. His gaze moved down her face, then down the length of her body, more slowly now. She felt her spine stiffen defensively. The man looked away, as if he had made his assessment and then lost interest. He shifted the small sleeping bundle in his arms again, and turned to gather his things.

She rushed forward to help. It would be an impossible task, lifting two suitcases while holding a child. She lifted the smaller of the two cases easily. He didn't try to stop her, but didn't acknowledge her gesture, either. It was as if he had cast her out of his mind, and then she just wasn't there. She felt a twinge of pique.

"Is the car nearby?" he asked eventually, looking around as if he expected it to appear on command.

Rhea had forgotten for a moment about Banner. She looked around in the crowd, trying to reorient herself to the spot where she had told him to wait. She wished now she had asked him to come in with her. She could have done with the moral support.

She was relieved and only a little surprised to spot him

shouldering his way through the still-thick crowd. He always seemed to be able to read her mind. She turned to the others, who were standing clutching their baggage, waiting for her word. "The driver's right here. Shall we take our things to the van?" She strove to keep the pitch of her voice even.

The tall man turned to watch Banner as he approached. As he did so, something relaxed in his face, his clean-shaven jawline seemed to soften, and Rhea got the impression that he was relieved that he would not be left in the care of a mere woman for the entire hour. She'd seen the same expression on the faces of clients many times before, and each time it hit her in the spot where she was most vulnerable—her professional pride.

She sighed. It meant that her job would just be that much more difficult, as she would have to work a little harder, just to prove herself. The last thing she needed right now was for another man to belittle her professional competence. Disrespect from Ian was bad enough; from a stranger, it was worse.

Banner caught up with them, introduced himself in his usual ponderous way, and easily shouldered the bags held by Trudy and Dahlia. "We're right by the curb," he said reassuringly. He gave Rhea a look that said *"Tough group?"* and she smiled gratefully.

The little gathering followed him to the spot where the large green vehicle was parked, Rhea bringing up the rear dejectedly. It was now well after six, and she felt the stinging embarrassment of a bad start. "It'll get better," she muttered to herself, stoking up her courage. "They'll just need to get a good night's sleep, and it'll all be okay."

CHAPTER TWO

The large van moved swiftly and surely through the dark countryside, like a huge beast lumbering toward its destination. Rhea fanned the sheaf of papers on her lap. They contained all her guests' application forms and general data. By rights she should have had them to study way in advance, but she was stuck with a folder, which was for the most part unread. She cursed Ian for putting her in this position, and made a mental vow not to sleep tonight until she'd read the package through. She peered at the files in the dimness of the interior, but could see very little. Sighing, she stowed it in the glove compartment until later.

"It's true it gets dark fast in the tropics," Trudy said with mild surprise, her nose pressed to the glass window of the vehicle like a child. She seemed awed by her surroundings. "I read that somewhere."

Rhea nodded, pleased that the tension of their first meeting had begun to evaporate. The group was comfortably settled into the wide green leather seats, and was preparing for the long drive ahead. The van had pulled onto the highway, and headed east. The northern mountain range, tall, dark, and somber, loomed on their left. The highway would soon give way

to a simple single-lane country road that would skirt the old
Spanish town of Valencia, wind in a southeasterly direction
into Sangre Grande and continue until it emerged at Manzanilla,
on the east coast. Rhea had distributed road maps to her charges
as soon as they had settled down, explaining in detail the route
that they were to follow that evening, and making sure they
were aware just how long the trip would take.

Fred and Trudy sat close together, two rows back, gray heads
brushing, engrossed in the scenery that flashed past them in
the falling night, while behind them Rainer and Dahlia stared
out separate windows, appearing to Rhea to be blind to the
wide, beautiful countryside.

"Even so, our days are pretty long right about now," she
said to Trudy. "Although I know it doesn't seem that way to
you. You're accustomed to long summer days in the States.
But you should see it around Christmastime. By five in the
evening, it's all over."

"If you haven't got a winter," Trudy said, leaning forward
and draping her arms over the chair seat in front. "What have
you got?"

Rhea smiled. "Well, here in the Caribbean we just have a
rainy season and a dry season. In the dry season you wish it
would rain. In the rainy season, you wish to God it'd just stop.
It's funny that way."

"Just two seasons," Trudy mused. "Don't you get bored?"

This time Rhea laughed outright. "Not when you stop to
consider all that comes with the seasons. With the dry season,
we get earthquakes and bush fires. With the rainy season, we
get tropical storms and hurricanes."

"Well," Fred said, leaning forward to get in line with his
wife. "I don't suppose you can get bored with *that.*"

"Hurricanes?" Trudy's eyes lit up. *"Real* hurricanes?"

"Real hurricanes," Rhea confirmed. "Real howling, ram-
paging, devastating hurricanes. They don't get much more real
than that."

"When do you get them?" Fred asked.

Rhea hesitated for a second. "Oh," she finally said, hoping
to appear nonchalant. "Round about now." Then, seeing a

mischievous grin split Trudy's face, she hastened to add "but we hardly ever get them here in Trinidad, we're a little too far south for that. They usually hit the northern islands, and then move across the sea to Florida. The Caribbean is more of a nursery for baby hurricanes. When they get all grown up, they head for your Eastern seaboard.''

Surprisingly, Marcus smiled in the darkness at her imaginative metaphor. He was sitting in the seat just behind hers, as this was the widest row and the one most able to accommodate his long legs. The tiny girl lay across his lap, with her face cradled in her arms and her thin legs stretched along the length of the seat. Her thick black braids, which Rhea supposed had begun the long journey in impeccable condition, were in disarray.

Rhea felt a pang of sympathy for the little tyke. She supposed that they would have been traveling since the night before, a journey that would be taxing on an adult, much less a little child. Marcus had told her that the girl was indeed his daughter, not his niece, as Ian had suggested, and that her name was Jodelle.

Curious in spite of herself, Rhea's glance kept being drawn to Marcus' face, which she studied covertly in the rearview mirror. The golden eyes glowed warmly in the darkness as he gazed out the window. He seemed to be engrossed in the scenery. She tried to guess his age, and finally settled for thirty-ish. He had a long high nose that for a second caused her a pang of jealousy, as she thought ruefully of her own little snub that seemed to refuse to grow up, causing her to frequently suffer the indignity of being mistaken for a teenager. His wide full mouth drew her involuntary attention more than once, and she was obliged to physically shake her head to dispel the mild jolts of erotic curiosity that they awoke within her.

This man was a client, she reminded herself, and a married one, judging from the shining gold band that he wore. More importantly, he was a client that she had known for less than an hour, and worse yet, one who had just given her the once-over, and had obviously decided she couldn't cut it. Yet her eyes were drawn to the mirror again and again.

The compulsion bothered her. If there was one thing she prided herself on, it was her self-control, her ability to bring everything, her body, her thoughts, even her work, under her will. She had the presence of mind and focus of a woman much older than her twenty-seven years; it was in part this strength that made her such a good guide. And here she was, being tugged at by a stranger . . .

Her impulse struggled against her inner controls and won; she glanced up into the mirror, only to find herself caught in the light of those glowing eyes, trapped for a second like a mongoose in the headlights of a car, and she looked away confused, feeling foolish.

She heard Marcus sigh heavily, and turned around in her seat as far as her seat belt would allow, and caught him passing his hands across his eyes in a gesture of fatigue.

"Tired?" Rhea observed sympathetically.

He nodded. "It's been a rough few weeks. Deadlines."

Rhea was genuinely interested. "Deadlines? What kind of deadlines?"

"Magazine deadlines. I'm a writer." He propped himself up on one elbow, leaning against the side of the vehicle, and turned his gaze upon her. He seemed to be waiting for her next question.

Rhea supplied it. "What kind of magazine?"

He shrugged. "Magazines. Not one magazine. I'm freelance, basically. I do a lot of eco-tourism coverage. Nature trails, travel guides, that kind of thing. So I'm not really on vacation."

"Oh," she said slowly. "So Trinidad is being audited?"

At this, he laughed softly, in spite of his fatigue. "You could say that. So don't let your country get a bad review."

Rhea wondered if he was joking. "I'll try my best," she said with mock gravity. He smiled.

"Your little girl must be tired, too," she observed unnecessarily.

He nodded. "We left Los Angeles on the red-eye last night, and spent most of the day flying across the Caribbean. That's almost twenty hours in the air, and we had to change planes twice."

"Is this her first trip out?"

"Yeah. She's been a real doll about it. No complaints at all. But I guess the excitement finally caught up with her."

"We'll be there in a while," Rhea said, "and then she can stretch out on a bed and get some real rest."

"I think I could do with some of that myself." He smiled tiredly, and there was silence again. It drew out uncomfortably. "Where are we?" he asked eventually, and Rhea got the impression it was more out of a need to say something than out of genuine curiosity, as the scenery outside had now been entirely swallowed up in the darkness of the tropical night. Although the moon was waxing larger, heavy clouds obscured its brightness, throwing a dense shadow over the land.

"We're just coming into Valencia, then we pass through Sangre Grande," she answered. "It's the last big town before we get to the coast. We've got to head east for quite a few miles yet."

He nodded. "Then we get to the coast, and the avenue of coconut trees," he said knowledgeably.

She looked surprised. "The Cocal. It's in Manzanilla. You've heard of it?"

"Of course. I've done my homework. We drive past twenty-two miles of coconut trees, all along the seafront. It must be something to see."

She nodded. "Pity it isn't light outside."

"Pity," he said, and seemed to settle into his seat for a nap. Rhea let him be.

Sangre Grande came suddenly upon them. In spite of the darkness, the narrow, claustrophobic roads of the town were full of people. It was a weekend, and people had been paid. Vendors lined the sidewalks in front of stores that had already closed for the evening. The visitors peered curiously out at the goods that were being offered for sale, which ranged from handwrought leather caps, shoes, and bags to boiled corn, snow cones and rich-smelling blood pudding being fried over clay coal pots. Townspeople loitered on street corners with beers in one hand, tossing shot glasses filled with a curious substance down their throats with the other.

"What are they drinking?" Marcus asked, leaning forward as best he could without disturbing Jodelle, and peering outside. "Those look like whiskey glasses."

Rhea laughed. "Oh, they're whiskey glasses, all right, but they're filled with raw oysters."

"They sell raw oysters at the roadside, just like that?"

"Yep. They serve them with a hot sauce. Each vendor has his own sauce recipe, so each vendor has his regulars, who buy from him just for the sauce."

"Is that healthy? I mean, raw oysters at the roadside? Have they been out in the sun all day?"

"Well," she hesitated for a moment. "I don't know about *healthy*. The health officials are always issuing warnings about preparation and sanitation, but most people just ignore them. It's a national pastime, eating oysters. You can get them on any street corner where there are bars. I suppose they go down well with beer."

"I'm sure they do." He smiled and settled back into his seat.

They arrived at the east coast and turned southward. "Forty-five minutes," Banner reminded her soothingly.

"You have the directions to the new place?" she wanted to know.

He patted his breast pocket. "Of course, Ri-ri. Relax. Take a nap."

She tried to relax. The passengers opened up their windows excitedly, letting in the smell of the sea, rich with seaweed and laced with the faint odour of drying copra from the coconuts that lined the roads on either side. Even little Jodelle seemed to be stirred by the strong smell of the sea breeze, and sat up sleepily to peer outside.

"Well, look who's up," Rhea said softly, and was rewarded by an unexpected, sleepy smile. The girl looked shyly away, slipping the little finger of her left hand into the corner of her mouth. Her father gently removed it, but as she slipped it back in again, he let her be.

The sleepy fishing village of Mayaro drew near, and Banner began peering into the night, searching for the beach house.

"Holdip Trace, Holdip Trace, Holdip Trace . . ." he repeated softly to himself. Suddenly he came down on the brake. "I think we just passed it." He reversed along the narrow road to a small lane and squinted at the dilapidated sign that listed to one side just at the entrance.

"I don't think so," Rhea said doubtfully, looking at the aging houses scattered around the area. Small, unfenced, in varying stages of disrepair, they appeared to be houses belonging to the coconut plantation workers and their families. Mongrels of all sizes gathered in dissolute groups at the roadside, like gangs of idle teenagers.

"That's what the sign said," Banner shrugged. "We might just as well go have a look."

"Maybe it's *another* Holdip Trace," Rhea suggested as they turned into the even narrower, rutted passage. By now the passengers were regarding her with questioning looks. Rhea knew this without turning; she was intensely aware of their eyes trained on the back of her head. The same gnawing anxiety that had held her for a moment back in Ian's office now had her in its malevolent grasp. She prayed silently as the road seemed to get more bumpy with no sight of a house.

"We're supposed to turn right at the first corner," Banner said by way of explanation as he made a sharp turn. "But it looks like we're headed toward the sea."

They were. The smell and sound of the surf were immediately obvious. The vehicle went bumping along the path that was becoming increasingly sandy, until they were on the beach itself.

"For God's sake, Banner," she hissed under her breath, "don't get us stuck in the sand." Banner nodded grimly. His lights shone on a large white object up ahead.

"Car," he said. "Let's stop and ask."

Rhea turned apologetically to the guests. "It's a new beach house that we're looking for," she explained. "We haven't been there before."

They nodded wearily. Rhea tried not to think about the length of time they had probably been up, and that wandering around a dark beach in a strange land was probably the last thing they wanted to do right now.

Banner shone the lights onto the car as they approached. Two round, frightened faces popped up over the backseat, eyes wide with terror, shining in the light of the headlights. With a flood of embarrassment Rhea realised that the couple was naked. They had disturbed a pair of lovers who had sneaked off to the darkened beach for a few hours of privacy. Rainer snorted disdainfully behind her, and a soft giggle escaped Jodelle.

"God," Rhea groaned to herself. This was just wonderful. She threw an apologetic look over her shoulder in Marcus' direction. It was met with a stony glare.

They turned the vehicle around laboriously in the sand and returned the way they had come. "We'll find it soon," she promised them in what she hoped was a reassuring tone. They didn't look convinced.

"This is it, I think," Banner said, turning into a small side street they hadn't seen the first time. A large house loomed ominously out of the darkness. They pulled up next to a wide steel gate.

"I'll check it and see," Rhea said, hopping out. The address that was faintly visible on the sturdy fence post matched the address on the card that she held in her hand. Relief!

She returned to the vehicle, smiling. "This is it," she said as cheerfully as she could. There was an audible sigh from the others. "I'll just open up the gate and Banner can drive in."

The lock on the gate was a heavy old-fashioned one of tempered steel, and as she held it, powdery flakes of rust fell away. She peered down at it, trying to insert the equally old-fashioned key into the keyhole. It penetrated, but as she turned the key this way and that, and jiggled it, it refused to budge.

She felt a presence next to her and looked up, startled. It was Marcus.

"Let me do it," he said brusquely, and tried to take the key from her fingers. As he did so, Rhea resisted, stung by his impatience, and held on more tightly. His long fingers locked around hers, and the two engaged in a silent battle, incongruously, standing ankle-deep in the sand in the middle of the dark track.

"Let me have it," he muttered. "You obviously can't get it open, so hand over the key."

His offhand manner and inflexible tugging only served to make her more determined not to relinquish the key, and she curled her fingers around it like a stubborn octopus.

"I can do it," she hissed. "It's my *job.*"

"I don't care if it's your job. You can't get it open and I can. Give me the key and step aside."

And to think she had allowed herself to stare at him in the mirror like that! Who did he think he was bullying? Rhea glanced up and noticed a row of curious faces looking at her through the side windows, including a tiny round brown one, and realised that she was making a spectacle of herself.

Embarrassed, she relinquished the key, and stepped aside, allowing Marcus to get at the offending lock. She folded her arms and watched as he struggled. Was he always this pushy? It irritated her to remember that if Ian hadn't interfered and switched tours on her at the last minute, she'd be relaxing up north with some couples and a few cute kids. She didn't need this.

"Look," he said, by way of apology, "I'm only anxious to get inside. It's been a long day, and I could do with a bath."

He wasn't joking, Rhea thought. From where she stood his masculine odour was strong, speaking of fatigue and thousands of miles traveled, yet hung in the night air like the perfume of a musky, night-blooming flower. She accepted his apology with a simple nod.

He battled with the lock, cursing, until it finally groaned free, and he swung back the gates and walked into the yard without another word.

Rhea stood aside to let the vehicle pass. The subdued gathering dismounted, and laid their luggage into a single heap before the front porch. None of the lights in the house was on, and Banner had to shine a torch onto the front door to allow Marcus to find the keyhole. The doors swung open eventually, and he reached in and flicked on a light—and gasped.

They had stepped into a huge open L-shaped room in which stood two wooden card tables and nothing else. To the rear of the room they could see a kitchen of sorts; a wide counter separated it from what was evidently the living room, and upon it sat a rusty two-burner hot plate. The five-foot refrigerator yawned open, its door partially unhinged, announcing to all and sundry that it would not be producing ice cubes any time soon. A film of sandy dust covered everything.

The group walked in as of one accord, appalled at the squalor, yet unable to resist seeing it at closer range. Each leg of the L shape seemed to lead off toward bedrooms, and the visitors followed Rhea down one corridor like stunned sheep.

Rhea threw open one of the doors in trepidation, afraid of what lay behind it, and flicked on the light. An ancient metal bed stood in the centre of the room like some torture device in a Latin American prison. A thin sheet of foam that could not by any stretch of the imagination be called a mattress in a civilized society was carelessly thrown across it, unupholstered, bare, stained by fluids that Rhea didn't dare reflect upon. The open cupboard stood empty; there was no evidence of pillows, bed linens, anything.

Wordlessly, they moved on, drawn by a morbid curiosity, past a bedroom that revealed identical squalor, to a bathroom that held a seatless toilet and a small wash-basin, which only had a cold water tap.

"If I'd wanted to rough it, I would have stayed at home and camped out in my backyard," Rhea heard Rainer drawl nastily, and her shoulders slumped. She turned, steeling herself, mortified, to face their angry, repulsed eyes.

"I . . ." she stopped and searched for her voice, found it and began again. "I don't know what to say. I'm sorry. This has never happened before. I had no idea."

"You mean," the owner of two very angry golden eyes barked, "you mean you don't check on these things? You mean you rent your lodgings blind? And you call yourself a *professional?*"

Rhea's eyes sought Banner's, desperate for support. He stood silently at the back of the group, as upset as she was. He pulled his handkerchief out of his back pocket and mopped at his brow, then catching the look that she gave him, held a hand out, palm open, to say, *I don't know what to do, either.*

"No," Rhea said, angry at herself for being intimidated by Marcus' harsh glare. He took a menacing step forward and in spite of herself, Rhea stepped back, pulling up short against the uncovered toilet bowl and banging herself sharply on the calf. "No, I mean we always check our rentals. Always. It's just that, well, this one, was a last-minute thing, I mean I only got the assignment this afternoon, and the place we normally use is taken. . . ." She trailed off miserably.

"My daughter and I booked with your company more than a month ago. Do you mean to say that you waited until this afternoon to start making plans?"

"No!" she protested with a wail. "No, someone else was assigned to you, and then my boss, Ian, he gave you over to me, I wasn't supposed to be here, but he changed my schedule, and then our usual place was booked, and he gave me these keys, and he said it was all right. . . ." She was babbling, and she wished she could shut up.

She heard soft weeping, and looked past Marcus' angry, menacing face, downward, to see Jodelle clinging to the leg of his jeans, face buried in the folds of rough material, shoulders heaving convulsively.

"I w—w—want to use the bathroom," she whimpered in the voice of a miserable kitten. "Daaaddy! I want to use the baaathroom! But it's . . . it's dirrrty!" The mewing heightened into an anguished wail. She could hear the angry breaths become more rapid in Marcus' throat.

Rhea also became aware of a similar need, and looked at the toilet next to her leg doubtfully. The situation could not have gotten any worse . . . until a large gray rat that had apparently been roused by the noise chose that moment to investigate, and squeezed himself through the open, decorative cement blocks that lined the far wall. Curious, it stared at the group, confident that its enormous size was protection enough against the distraught humans. Jodelle's sobs changed instantly into shrill, terrified screams.

"That does it, Miss," Marcus began, swinging the hysterical child into his powerful arms. He was almost shouting, and the anger in his voice made her recoil. "We are turning around, right now, and I don't care if you have to drive us all the way to the airport, I am not letting my daughter spend another minute in this hovel."

Rhea looked at him in helpless misery. She hated the way he was speaking to her, but God knew, he had every right. The filthy surroundings closed in on her, robbing her of her very breath, preventing her from speaking.

"And, in the morning," he went on, more loudly than necessary, "we shall talk about a refund. Or a lawsuit, if you're not careful."

She looked at him, not knowing what to say, cursing Ian again and again.

"Ladies and gentlemen," Banner stepped forward, made his way through the small group and stood to face them. "I think that we are all very tired. And I am sure that we are all very hungry. There are other beach houses in Mayaro. Why don't we just find an open restaurant, find ourselves a place to spend the night, and then in the morning, we can all sit down and discuss what we are going to do?" He bounced on his toes in that manner that he had. "Does that sound fair?"

There were reluctant nods of assent, and finally, silently, they retraced their steps to the living room where their bags sat forlornly. Marcus, still with the keys in his hand, shifted the girl's weight to one shoulder to allow him to hold the heavy front gate open as the others drove out. Having learned her lesson, Rhea stood aside as he snapped the huge lock shut and, tight-lipped and unsmiling, returned the heavy iron keys to her.

Rhea was hot with mortification. This . . . disaster couldn't really be happening to her. She was always so careful, always so meticulous—and now this. It made her feel helpless, out of control, and that was the thing that Rhea most hated to feel. She avoided his gaze, and followed him to the waiting van.

CHAPTER THREE

Seascape was unusual, to say the least. The old establishment was a hodgepodge of architectural styles, boasting a restaurant front that was typically touristy, with its palm-thatched roof and rough-hewn wooden furniture; a pool hall; and bar that were the stomping ground of the young men in the area, and a country snack shop where children stopped on the way home from school to buy bubblegum and candy. It had the air of a few bits and pieces thrown together by a proprietor who couldn't make up his mind what he wanted it to look like, but still it managed to be charming and insouciant, a part of the countryside.

Along the length of it stretched a massive wall, built from huge boulders stacked upon one another as protection against the pounding of storm waters. Beyond it the sea heaved restlessly, a mere suggestion of black against the slightly lighter backdrop of sky.

Their first mission upon arrival was to locate the lone bathroom round the back, and to take turns making hurried visits. Jodelle had scurried in first, telling her father quite primly that no, she did not in fact need any help. When she emerged, she contented herself with chasing a skinny white cat up and down the length of the building. While she found the little game quite amusing, the cat didn't look so sure.

Rhea stood impatiently outside the bathroom, allowing all the others to go first, wishing they would hurry—she was *bursting!*

The night air was filled with the strong smell of dried sargasso, a fern-like olive-coloured weed that grew in massive clumps that could be as wide as several miles, and which drifted aimlessly, floating upon the surface of the water with the aid of thousands of tiny round air-filled balloons which dotted the weed like grapes. If a clump of seaweed should happen to be dashed up onto the sand, it would soon wither and dry out, sending its own unique, pungent odour wafting across the sea breeze. As a child, Rhea had enjoyed squeezing the little balloons until they collapsed with a satisfying pop, over and over, walking great lengths along the beach in search of the dark green strands.

In spite of her body's urgent need, she smiled at the memory. Maybe she'd do a little popping herself in the morning. Then she remembered that it was more than likely that they'd be back on the road after dinner, northward-bound, if she and Banner were unable to find suitable accommodations. The thought wiped the smile off her face. Curse Ian a thousand times.

"What's going on in that head?"

She jumped, startled, and spun round. "Excuse me?"

"What are you thinking?" The voice was unmistakably Marcus'. She could feel him inches away from her. She turned to him, surprised that he was speaking to her so pleasantly after their disagreeable exchange a half-hour earlier. Well, she decided, she would take his placatory gesture with a grain of salt.

"Oh," she said vaguely. "Nothing much."

"What do you mean, 'nothing much'?" He answered, coming round to face her. "You were grinning like an idiot, then all of a sudden you looked like you were brought back down with a bang."

He was much too astute. She shrugged. "I was inhaling the smell of sargasso. The seaweed."

He sniffed the air appreciatively. "Oh, is that what it is? Sargasso?"

She nodded.

"Smells like fish."

She smiled in spite of herself. "Well," she reasoned, "I guess it *would.*"

He smiled too. "I guess it would," he echoed, nodding. Then, after a pause, "So why were you smiling?"

"Well, it's got these little air bladders on it. Like little balloons. And when I was a kid I used to run along the beach and pick up huge clumps of it, and pop the balloons. I could keep it up for hours."

He looked at her for a long time, then swiveled his gaze to the cold dark beach. He seemed to be imagining her, six years old, running along its length, gathering the sandy little bundles into her arms.

"Jodelle will like that," he said. "I hope she gets to play with some."

"I'm sure she will." The words *if you decide to stay* went unspoken, but hung heavy in her heart.

Marcus seemed to hone in on her thoughts. "Maybe things will seem better after we've eaten," he offered comfortingly.

Rhea didn't look at him. She almost resented his offer of a truce, so embarrassed was she at the goof she had made. Besides, his ability to veer between stony anger and pleasant, almost warm conversation was a little too much for her to handle at the moment. She tried to pass the time by staring at the frail wooden door of the bathroom, willing it to open.

Obediently, it creaked ajar, and Trudy came out, rolling her eyes in exaggerated relief. "Whew!" she exhaled, and smiled.

Rhea looked around to see if there was anyone else in line, but she and Marcus were alone. Her need had reached critical mass. She looked at him apologetically, embarrassed.

"Please," he gestured toward the door in his most courtly manner. She scuttled in, grateful.

When she emerged she went round to the front to join the

others. They were seated around the largest of the tables, a round teak object, which was encumbered by big potted plants that had been placed there by the proprietor in a moment of whimsy.

"I'll just get dinner ordered," she called out to them, and went to the kitchen in search of the waitress, a pretty but bored-looking young girl with a head full of fine braids, each tied off with a colorful piece of string.

The girl smiled and rose to her feet as she spied Rhea. She recognised her on sight as a frequent customer who usually brought a brood of Americans, big tippers, with her.

"Ready to order?" she asked as perkily as she could after thirteen hours on the job.

"What have you got tonight?" Rhea asked, knowing that in small eating places such as this one there were seldom more than two or three dishes on the menu.

"You can have roast beef or fried shark," the girl said.

Rhea wondered whether the visitors would be in enough of an adventurous mood to try the shark, drenched in spices and batter fried as it was normally served here. She didn't think anything that exotic would be advisable for a group of tired, hungry travelers, fresh off the plane. "Beef all round," she decided. "And cut up a piece into small bits for the little girl, no pepper on that one, and give the men really large steaks."

The waitress nodded and bustled into the kitchen, and Rhea went out to join the others. "Half hour!" the girl called after her.

Rhea hoped it would be no more than that, and prayed that her guests would understand that the pace of a country eating house would not be anything that they would expect in a California restaurant.

Evidently too short to see over the high table, Jodelle was ensconced in her father's lap, and regarded Rhea's approach with bright black eyes. Rhea put on her brightest hostess smile and sat down with the others. The little girl smiled back. Even in the dim light, Rhea could see that she was a beauty, with fine dark features, a tiny mouth and a round face that was nothing like her father's. Obviously, the girl resembled her mother. For a moment, Rhea wondered where Marcus' wife was, and why she had not joined the little family on the trip, but dismissed it as none of her business.

A large dark shape fluttered past their table, swooping dangerously close to the fat candles that sat on the table in their country-made clay dishes. It was a huge brown moth, with swirls the colour of tigereye in its feathery wings. Anxious that it might fly into the naked flame, Rhea caught it deftly, cupping it lightly between her hands.

"A butterfly!" the little girl said, eyes now fully awake. She leaned forward on her father's lap.

"It's a moth," Rhea corrected.

"Moth?" The child was puzzled.

"A night butterfly." Then, impulsively, she held it out over the table. "Do you want to hold it?"

Eagerly, Jodelle held out her tiny hands. Rhea gingerly transferred the delicate creature, who, surprisingly enough, did not seem too perturbed by the arrangement. It sat in the palm of the child's hand, wings stretched flat out, vibrating gently.

"It's beautiful," Jodelle breathed in awe, and looked up, eyes aglow, at Rhea. Then, suddenly, her face split into a smile of such sudden adoration that Rhea was taken aback. A light seemed to rise out of the tiny face; it was like the sudden parting of the clouds from in front of the sun. The child was thunderstruck—she had fallen into sudden, powerful, childish love.

Marcus, who had been watching the interaction with parental indulgence, saw the light that suddenly burst forth from his daughter's face, and recognised it for the impulsive crush that it was, and threw Rhea a sharp, surprised glance. Unsettled, she avoided his look. The moth rose, tired of all the attention, and disappeared into the darkness.

After thirty-five minutes, with her own stomach growling and her guests lapsed into a sullen, hungry silence, Rhea was relieved to see the young girl emerge from the small kitchen with two steaming plates. These she placed carefully before the Steins, showing respect for their status as the eldest among them. They smiled gratefully and inhaled the richness of hot, fresh steaks. The girl returned to offer plates to the younger couple and a small one to Jodelle, and then again to place huge meals in front of Banner and Marcus.

The air was dense with the smell of hot beef, and Rhea, pleased to note that Marcus' steak was even larger than the others, looked up, a wide smile on her face, certain to find it returned with one of pure pleasure at the sight and smell of a hearty dinner after such a long day.

The furious glare that met her smiling glance was enough to make her stomach clench. Her mouth fell open as she searched his face uncomprehendingly. She looked anxiously down at his plate, eyes frantic—what could be wrong? What did she do this time? Was there a caterpillar in the salad? She had angered him once again, and for the life of her, she couldn't understand how.

He pushed the plate away from himself with a firm, definitive gesture, and turned his angry eyes upon her again.

"What?" she asked tremulously. "What's wrong *now?*" She felt like a chastened child. Her eyes stung.

"Miss," he said quietly and evenly, with great effort. "Don't you read your client profiles? Don't you do any reading up on your clients before they arrive?"

By now the others, in spite of their hunger, were sitting up and listening in unabashedly.

"Why?" Rhea asked, still perplexed. "Why? We *do* read the profiles. Of *course* we read the profiles. Only I got yours at the last minute and . . . and I was late . . . and you weren't *supposed* to be my group. . . ." She trailed off, knowing that she was sounding foolish. Besides, she'd tried to explain the whole awful story before, and it hadn't worked then. "What's the matter?" she asked finally, knowing that she had done something terribly wrong, but unable to figure out just what. "Is there . . . a problem?"

He pushed the plate even further away from himself, across

the table onto her side. "The problem," he said slowly and carefully, as though she were mildly retarded, "is that I'm a vegetarian." He took a deep breath, and added for good measure, "I don't eat meat."

"My Daddy don't eat meat." Jodelle echoed, though she wasn't allowing her father's predicament to spoil *her* dinner. She was stuffing hot fries into her mouth by threes and fours.

Rhea was aghast. What a terrible faux pas! She tried to steady the sudden, sharp rise and fall of her chest, and nodded, feeling foolish. "I'm sorry," she said, embarrassed once again. The others were listening carefully to the exchange, gobbling up the little scene as greedily as they were gobbling up their dinners. "I didn't know."

"Obviously. You would have if you had done your homework," he said tightly.

"Look," she began heatedly. She'd admitted that she was in the wrong, but he didn't have to harp on it. She'd had enough of being embarrassed by situations that weren't her fault. "I'm really, really sorry. But I've told you over, and over, you had been assigned to someone else, not to me. This is not how I do business. I know I've made some mistakes, but . . ." she threw up her hands, helpless. The way that he was glaring at her, she knew that it wouldn't make any sense trying to get through to him. "I'll go order something else for you." She was about to rise, but stopped. "What about your daughter?"

"My daughter eats what she pleases, and that includes meat. I don't impose my own dietary restrictions on her. She can make her own decisions about that when she's good and ready."

She nodded. "So it's just you, then?"

"*Just* me," he mocked.

Rhea got up and turned abruptly toward the kitchen, only narrowly avoiding a collision with the waitress who was bringing the last plate, Rhea's plate, out.

With the maddening scent of piping-hot beef in her nostrils, she explained the situation. The girl peered curiously at Marcus over her shoulder, puzzled as to the reason that anyone would choose not to eat meat. She looked at him skeptically. These Americans were truly curious creatures.

Rhea eventually negotiated for a large salad and a plate of fries, the only non-meat items on the menu, and walked slowly and apologetically back to the table. She waited staunchly, eyeing the two plates of food before her, wanting to ensure that Marcus got his dinner before she began to eat. Her hunger, fueled by the smell of the thick gravy, made her giddy.

"Eat," he said with surprising gentleness, and her eyes flew to his face, searching for irony or malice, but found only resignation. "You go ahead. Don't wait. You must be starving."

She didn't have to be told twice. She delved gratefully into the steaming food, pausing only to note with satisfaction that the girl returned within five minutes with a large bowl of salad and a generous plate of fries, which she laid gingerly before him. She shot him another cautious glance, as though afraid that anyone insane enough to forego good meat might certainly be prone to other irrational acts. He took the plate from her with a polite nod, and the waitress receded into the shadows. They ate in a silence broken only by the steady rhythmic sound of Jodelle's small feet as she kicked the leg of the table.

Tempers seemed to have cooled by the time the meal drew to a close, and the exhausted group sat around nursing cold local beers and murmuring among themselves. Almost unnoticed, Banner slipped quietly away from the group. Rhea sat miserably over her now-empty plate, wondering just how she was going to go about trailing a group of tired, irritable tourists about the sleeping village in search of a hotel.

She felt a light hand on her arm and spun round to see Banner's round, smiling face close to hers. "Rhea, a minute, please," he said in discreet tones. She rose to her feet and followed him to a corner out of earshot of the table.

"What? What is it?"

"I got us a house. A good house."

"A house? Where?"

"Not too far, in Guayaguayare. A good house." Guayaguayare was a small settlement just fifteen minutes away, peopled chiefly by expatriates and locals working with the many petrochemical and servicing companies along the coast. It was comfortably upscale, with pretty houses perched right at the edge of the shore. That wouldn't be too bad.

"Are you sure it's a good house? How did you hear of it?"

He smiled triumphantly. "I talked to the bartender. It's his sister's house. She rents to visitors."

"Big enough for all of us?"

"Yeah, sure. Five bedrooms. Fully furnished. Linens and everything."

Things were looking up. "Well, I guess I'd better negotiate a price and get the keys." She squared her shoulders, preparing to haggle over price with the bartender. "Although at this point I'll give them anything they ask, it would serve Ian right if he loses money on this deal."

With a swift movement Banner held his hand before her face, palm up. A ring of shiny new keys lay in his hand. "Got it already. Good price, too."

She almost kissed him. "Thanks, Banner. I owe you one."

"Nah," he was a little embarrassed at the open admiration in her eyes. "It's okay. Let's gather the troops."

They returned side by side to the table and explained their find.

"Well, I hope it's not too far," Rainer said gruffly. "We've been on the road long enough as it is."

"I just hope it's clean," Dahlia sighed, gathering her things.

They followed Rhea in an untidy bunch to the van, and climbed in wearily. As the van nosed into the quiet night, headed southward once again, Rhea explained briefly that the village they were going to had grown up around the oil and natural gas industry, and that they would be able to look across the bay and see clusters of oil rigs and gas platforms out in the Atlantic. She gave the information as a matter of duty, even though she got the distinct impression that her audience was barely listening. They were just anxious to get there, wherever they might be going.

They turned off the coastal road and into a wide well-paved cul-de-sac, which extended a few hundred yards toward the beach. Banner pulled alongside a sprawling white house and checked the address he had scribbled on a scrap of notepaper.

"This is it," he said, relieved. The group peered anxiously out at the structure that sat silently in the light of the moon.

"Are we here, young lady?" Fred called out to her.

"Yes," Rhea put a brave smile on her face and climbed out. "This is it. I'll just let us in." She located the padlock on the gate. This time she needed no assistance from Marcus to open it.

The van swung into the wide two-car garage and shut off. Rhea fumbled along the walls for the light, found it, and switched it on. Once again she easily unlocked the heavy wooden door that lead off from the garage. It swung noiselessly open. Holding her breath, she located and flicked on the switch.

The interior was beautiful. They were standing in a long entrance hall that led to a spacious living room. Doors on either side of the corridor suggested bedrooms. She could feel the proximity of the others standing behind her, impatient to see the rest of the house, so she moved a little farther in. Now she could see the kitchen beyond the living room to her left, and straight ahead, large glass doors hung with curtains screened a wide front porch from view. Weak with relief, she moved through the house, flicking on lights until the entire structure was ablaze, as though she felt the need to dispel the darkness and distaste that still lingered in her from the last disastrous house.

The wood-paneled kitchen housed a gleaming white stove, microwave, and refrigerator. Glass-doored kitchen cupboards revealed more than adequate crockery and glassware. Rhea was so relieved, she was smiling.

"Relieved, huh?" Marcus said softly close to her ear. She jumped in surprise. The others had long begun poking about in the bedrooms, making a selection, and moving their things in for the night.

"Yes," she admitted honestly. "Yes, I am relieved."

"I guess you weren't looking forward to another tongue-lashing from us tonight."

She wondered if he was being cruel, but there was only sympathy and fatigue etched in his handsome face. Even his eyes, so unusual against the darkness of his skin, held genuine compassion, and even a little humor at their predicament.

She took heart, glad for a brief moment that someone else seemed to understand. Then she straightened awkwardly, trying to be as professional as possible under the circumstances. It was close to midnight, and in her fatigue, she ran the risk of indulging in self-pity. "Don't you want to select a room for you and your daughter? The others are moving in already."

He shrugged. "Then it makes no sense selecting one, if the choice has already been made. Besides, any one will do. I'm sure it'll be all right."

She nodded, unsure of how to respond. "Shall we get our gear, then?" she suggested finally.

He turned to his daughter. "I'll be back in a minute, okay sweetheart? I'll just get our things from the van. You just wait here."

Jodelle was looking around with wide-eyed curiosity. "Is this a hotel?"

"Well, it's kind of like a hotel. Only smaller."

"Okay." She accepted this with equanimity, and stood with her small red cotton jacket hanging idly from one hand, prepared to wait until her father returned.

To Rhea's discomfiture, he turned and walked almost companionably alongside her out through the back to the van.

"I'll help you with your things," he offered as she shouldered her kit bag with some effort.

Rhea refused politely. "No, thanks. It's okay." He'd already showed her up with the padlock at the other house. She didn't need him treating her like a weakling now. She was woman enough to carry her bags her own sweet self.

He already had his bag, a large canvas one, and another that appeared to hold photographic equipment. "Sure?" He juggled his things to free his left hand, and held it out in an offer of assistance.

"Yeah. Sure. I can manage." She hefted her gear onto the other shoulder, doing her best not to look as if she were straining under the weight.

"Okay." He smiled and waited until she locked the van. He was humoring her, she was sure of it.

They returned inside and laid their things in a heap in the corridor. The Bainbridges had already snapped up the room with the best eastern view, the view of the sea, and the Steins were ensconced in the room right next to them. Banner, as usual, had taken the smallest, more of a child's bedroom actually, round to the back. This left two rooms. Both were fairly small, and both had two single beds.

"Which one do you want?" She figured as hostess, it was her duty to give him first choice, even though the rooms appeared identical.

"Which one do *you* want?" he countered. They stood just outside the two rooms with all their luggage scattered at their feet.

She was about to answer when a strange buzzing caught their attention. They looked around, puzzled. The buzzing sounded again.

"Phone, Daddy!" Jodelle piped up.

"Not mine, honey." He pointed to Rhea's kit bag. "You got a phone in there?"

Foolishly, she looked down at it. The ringing was definitely coming from in there. "Oh, yes, of course. I'm sorry." She fished out the slender cellular and opened it. "Hello?"

"Where the hell have you been?" a voice bellowed on the other end. "You were supposed to call me at ten. I've been calling and calling." God. Her heart sank. It was her boyfriend, and she'd forgotten all about him. With her bags stowed away in the van, she hadn't heard the phone ringing.

"Brent," she began, but was interrupted by the angry voice.

"Look, Rhea, I told you to call at ten. Remember? Do you remember? I told you, didn't I?"

"Yes, well, we had some problems. . . ."

"So big that you couldn't take ten seconds to call me?"

"Brent . . ."

Two questioning pairs of eyes were on her, one of glittering black, one of amber. She was sure that Marcus could hear the tone, if not the words, of the voice on the line. Her eyes caught his for a second, and then she looked away, embarrassed. Without a word, he bent and gathered their things, and ushered Jodelle into the room closest to where they were standing, leaving Rhea to her privacy. Relieved, she stepped into the room that was left.

"Brent," she said as firmly as she could, "I didn't call because I was busy, okay?" Then, timidly. "Okay, honey?"

He appeared to be mollified by her placatory tone. "Okay. You know I was just concerned. I worry about you, you know that. I need to know if everything's all right."

She nodded, even though he couldn't see her. "Yes, I know."

"So you're okay."

"Yes. We had a problem with the house, so we had to find another one."

"When am I seeing you again?"

She was a little taken aback. Hadn't he heard what she'd said? Didn't he want to know what the problem with the house had been? She answered slowly. "I don't know when I'll see you. Maybe late next week, when the tour moves up north."

"I hope so. Find the time and see me, okay? I miss you already."

"Miss you, too," she said automatically, and the line went dead in her hands. Brent was one of those busy young men who worked hard, but demanded a lot of her time. It was difficult, on her schedule, to see him as much as he would have liked, and he let her know that at every opportunity. She tried not to think about it and carefully folded the phone with a soft click and laid it down on the small table between the beds.

She put her hands on her hips and surveyed the room. It was quite comfortable, with built-in closets and a dressing table with a mirror. The house had really proven to be pleasant, and she made a mental note to get the name and number of the owner so that they might use it next time there was a tour.

She plumped herself down gratefully onto the bed, yanking off her shoes and wriggling her tired toes to get the blood running again. The sheets on the bed were crisp; the beds had obviously been made just that morning. Rhea wondered if there was someone who came in to do the cleaning daily.

"Not that it matters," she said to herself. "The others will probably still be so upset that they'll want to head back up north in the morning." She sucked her teeth in frustration. This tour could have worked.

Just above her head, through the walls, she heard the soft humming of water rushing through the pipes, and deduced that Marcus was probably having his much-longed-for shower. The Steins' and the Bainbridges' rooms were equipped with private baths, she'd noticed, and it seemed to her that she would be sharing one with Banner, Marcus, and Jodelle. She wasn't sure if she liked the idea of sharing a bathroom; sharing with Banner was one thing, she'd done that before, but sharing with this disturbing stranger was another. Somehow it felt a little too . . . intimate. Still, she reminded herself, it would just be for one night.

The water was silenced, and soon she heard a knocking on the door. She half sat up, startled. "Yes?"

"I'm out," he said softly through the door. "The shower's free."

"Thanks."

"Don't mention it. Have a good night."

"You, too." She waited until she was sure that he was in his room, and gathered her things and slipped into the bathroom. It was filled with steam that was scented with a man's bath soap. As she showered, the warm odour of the man filled her nostrils, and for a moment she could not deny that it was pleasant.

"You must be crazy," she said irritably to herself. This was a man who was threatening to make her turn the whole tour around in the morning, worse yet, to sue, and here she was sniffing his soap in the *bathroom!* It was really too ridiculous. Angry with herself, she splashed liberal amounts of her favourite cologne onto her skin, as if the action would eradicate every scrap of Marcus' odour from her nostrils, and every thought of his tall, imposing presence from her mind.

Clean and perfumed (smelling of herself, and no one else, she noted with satisfaction), she crawled gratefully into bed. The rest of the house was silent, except for the faint hum of

Banner taking his turn in the showers. It was well past one in the morning, and she would have given anything to just be able to roll over and go to sleep, but the stinging humiliation of the dinner foul-up with Marcus still sat uneasily upon her. She had been determined to examine her client fact sheets before she went to sleep tonight, and this was exactly what she was going to do. Resignedly, she spread open her folder on the bed next to her, and began to read.

CHAPTER FOUR

Rhea woke to find herself sprawled across the bed with her face buried in a sheaf of crushed documents. She recalled her firm intention to read through her clients' files before the night was out, and it was a while before she was able to clear the mist in her head and remember whether she had or not. She sat up groggily, smoothing out the forms under her hands. Yes, she'd done it; it was coming back to her in bits and pieces, all those details.

The Steins, from San Diego, both retired, he a former physics teacher, she a head matron of a day-care centre. Both in their early sixties. The Bainbridges, from Laguna Beach. Both in their early thirties, no children. He owned two jewelry stores. She had been an artist but had stopped painting after she was married. Rhea recalled noticing Dahlia's hands, how well shaped and beautiful they were. So that was it; hers were artist's hands. Yet she also remembered how limp they were, how ineffective her handshake, how they hung disinterestedly at her sides. Artist's hands, yes, but hands that no longer housed the glowing energy of hands at work.

And Marcus, yes, she had certainly gone through his files, carefully, more than once. The embarrassment of her gross mistake returned again to mock her, but at least, armed with the necessary information, it would not be happening again. She would make sure of that. Marcus was thirty-three, and Jodelle, six. The girl's age was mildly surprising, as Rhea has put it at four or five. She certainly was a tiny thing.

The space on the form that was to list marital status was enigmatically blank, and yet the man wore a wedding ring. Curiouser and curiouser, Rhea thought to herself. The form also told her that he was originally from New Orleans. That didn't surprise her—she had worked with Americans long enough to know that his soft, musical accent wasn't West Coast. Yet he was a resident in Los Angeles, and wrote for several big-name nature and travel magazines. She remembered what he had told her about writing a piece on eco-tourism in Trinidad. It must be quite a big piece if he had come all the way here, no doubt at great expense, in order to gather the information for the article.

What did that mean to her? Surely it meant that what he saw, what he experienced, would find its way into his article, and that could impact significantly on her country's image abroad. Tourism might be a small part of the country's econ-omy, but the movement was growing, and the livelihoods of thousands depended on it.

And after his experience last night . . . talk about getting off to a bad start! Damn! She would have to be careful, ensure that what he saw from now on would show the country in the best light possible. It was a heavy responsibility; she would have to whisper a little in Banner's ear when she got him alone.

As for Marcus' dietary habits, he was truly vegetarian: no meat, no fish, no shellfish, though he did eat eggs and dairy. That was something, at least. Since she would be responsible for cooking many of their meals, she had a horrible vision of herself planning meals for someone who wouldn't even eat dairy, and, worse yet, sourcing the necessary grains and other foodstuff here in the little village. God, what a nightmare! Imagine running into a Mayaro grocery and asking for tofu and alfalfa! She couldn't contain a chuckle at that image. She'd

have to have a word with Banner about that, too, since she and
he often took turns seeing about the breakfast.

Then she shook her head. She was thinking as if they would
be staying. She couldn't be so sure; depending on what the
group decided, they could well be on the northbound road by
midmorning.

"Time to get up, Ri-ri." She got to her feet and took a quick
look around to re-orient herself. The overhead light was still
on—she'd fallen asleep without bothering to turn it off. The
sky outside was just beginning to pale. They were on the east
coast, and would therefore be the first to enjoy the orange rays
of the early sun that had already begun creeping across the sky.

She decided to take a quick walk out into the yard; the others
wouldn't be up yet, not after the kind of night that they'd had.
She'd just sneak out for a while, without having to put on her
uniform or her hostess face. That would be great. Quickly, she
slipped on her jeans and tucked the T-shirt in which she had
slept into the waistband, and tiptoed into the bathroom to brush
her teeth and splash some cool water onto her face. The stream
was powerful, stronger than the water pressure that she could
have expected in the city, and the water had the characteristic
sweet, cool taste of a seaside water supply.

Barefoot, she padded past Marcus' and Jodelle's closed door,
glad that her feet made no sound on the tiled floor. It wouldn't
do to wake them up; they'd both had a rough time the day
before. Besides, she reasoned, the more Marcus slept, the less
likely he would be to hold the events of the previous night
against her.

She crossed the living room to the wide glass doors that
separated her from the porch. They were unlocked, and slid
open easily. Someone had obviously let himself out earlier. So
much for solitude, she thought.

The smell of the sea struck her with full force: clean, relaxing,
full of salt and sand, seaweed and coconuts. The chilly early-
morning breeze whipped her uncombed curls about her face
and pressed the T-shirt against her body. Across the yard, in
the pale early light, a figure sat silhouetted against the sky. It
was Marcus.

''Figures,'' she said wryly. No moss growing on *him*.

She hesitated before approaching, but then shrugged. She was entitled to watch the sunrise, too, wasn't she? Surely the sky was wide enough for both of them. She crossed the wide expanse of grass purposefully. The spiky grass was heavy with dew, and cool to her feet.

As is the case with so many houses on the coast, the yard was separated from the beachfront by a solid storm wall of boulders and mortar that was at least two feet thick, and about four feet high. There was no telling how deep it extended into the ground. The overall effect was one of reassuring solidity and silent strength—it was like living within the walls of a small fortress. It served not to keep anyone out, but to protect the houses from the deadly capabilities of an angry sea.

Marcus was sitting atop the wall, knees drawn up, with a sophisticated camera lying idle at his side. He was staring out to sea. Right on the skyline, a cluster of oil rigs and gas platforms loomed out of the gray sea mist. They stood on sturdy metal legs, some more than two hundred feet tall.

''They look like a bunch of young girls wading across some deep water, with their skirts raised above their knees, so as not to get them wet,'' he said as she approached.

Rhea looked sharply at the cluster in the distance, taken aback. She'd never given them so much as a second thought, far less bothered to wonder what they looked like. ''I never thought of that,'' she admitted. With their broad platforms set on wide-spaced solid legs, they did, in fact, look just like a group of girls with their skirts up. Trust a writer to come up with an image like that!

She drew to a halt close to the wall, a short distance from him. Maybe she was invading his private space.

He seemed to read her mind, as he had already displayed a capacity to do. ''You aren't bothering me, you know.'' He gestured for her to come closer. ''Sit down.''

Gingerly, she sat next to him and let her legs dangle over the edge of the wall. Out of the corner of her eye, she watched him warily. The night before, he'd swerved wildly between cold anger and almost courtly concern for her, and she wasn't quite sure which of his faces he'd be showing her this morning.

As he looked forward, mind lost somewhere on the pale horizon, she continued her covert examination of him. His profile was sharply etched against the rapidly brightening sky, and she was able to clearly follow the line of his forehead, his long straight nose, and, she hated to admit it, his fine-looking pair of lips. It was quite irritating, the way her eyes were drawn to his face again and again, since the previous evening. Rhea sharply turned her head away, and forced herself to concentrate on the awakening waters.

They sat in companionable silence, allowing the morning to wrap itself around them. Seagulls, who had been up long before they, were already going about the business of searching for breakfast, swooping over the water, quarreling like children out of school. The tide was at its lowest, and the wide expanse of beach was crisscrossed with the footprints of sandpipers that haunted the shallows for almost invisible morsels.

"How do you feel, having those so close by?" he said finally, snapping her out of her reverie.

"Excuse me?" She didn't have a clue what he was talking about.

"The girls in the skirts. The oil rigs. How do you feel having them so close by?"

She was baffled. "I don't understand."

He turned his golden gaze fully on her. "Pollution. I'm talking about oil pollution. Don't you have spills? They look awfully close to the shore."

"Oh . . . yes." Like a well-oiled machine, she slid back into hostess mode and began rattling figures she had learned by rote. "Some of them are as close as ten or twelve miles, some as far away as fifty miles." Then, more thoughtfully, she added "But you're right. I guess that's close. I don't know about the degree of pollution, though, or if there is any at all."

"Wherever you have an installation like that, you're going to get it. Has there been any drop in the fishing industry around here? What about marine life?"

She nodded, reluctant to reveal anything so negative. "Yes,

I suppose so. I remember when I was a child, we used to come here around Easter to dig for shellfish, they were all over the place. We practically used to walk on them. There're hardly any, now.''

"Maybe that's it, then.''

"Maybe. I don't know.'' Then she turned toward him, as if a thought was suddenly dawning on her. "You're really concerned for the environment.''

He looked surprised at the observation, as though it were a given. "Of course. Aren't you?''

She felt her face grow hot. "Well, yes, of course. But I have to admit I don't really think about it. I mean, I don't look at something and wonder if it's polluting us. It doesn't really enter my mind. Not that I'm insensitive or anything,'' she hastened to add, "I just don't spend a lot of time thinking about it. Maybe it's more of a California thing, save the whales and all that.''

His face grew stern, and Rhea immediately felt like a chastened schoolgirl. "No, Rhea, it's not a California thing. It's a world thing. Maybe it's time you realised that.''

God, she'd gone and done it again, spoken off the top of her head and made herself sound like an idiot. How embarrassing! She resisted the urge to gnaw on her thumbnail, a habit to which she often succumbed under stress. "Sorry.''

"You don't have to apologize to me. Apologize to the water.'' He scowled like an old schoolmaster, but she could see he was only half serious.

She could barely suppress a smile at that. She turned to the gently breathing ocean. "Sorry, water.'' Then she turned to him. "You think it accepts my apology?''

"I think it will, if you make up for it.''

"Make up for it how?''

"Pledge not to eat fish for a month. That'd do it.''

"Oh, yes. Really.'' *Not a chance*, she thought privately. Then, aloud, "Is that why you don't eat meat? You're atoning for the sins of man?''

He smiled at the way she put that. "Atoning for my own sins, maybe.''

She covertly studied his handsome profile once again, and wondered to herself what sins this intriguing man could have to atone for, and for a second, the devil within her rose up with an urge to explore them. Then her little angel slapped the devil down, and she turned to him and asked: "And Jodelle? How come she eats meat, if you don't?"

"Well, like I said, she'll have all the time in the world to make her own decisions. All I can do is help her understand the situation, I can't make up her mind for her. Besides, I won't let her even think of it until she's a lot older. I don't want to interfere with her nutrition. And she's a bright kid. She'll decide when the time is right, not me."

Rhea listened carefully, digesting this. "She's a tiny little one, isn't she?"

"Yes, well, her mother's just about as high as my armpit. I hardly think Jodie's going to be very tall."

So, there *was* a wife in the mix somewhere. Rhea's curiosity pushed her beyond the edge of discretion. "But it's er . . . just the two of you traveling?"

The air around them seemed to grow several degrees cooler. Realising she'd stepped on a corn there, she bent her head to hide the embarrassed flush. Stupid, stupid, stupid.

"We're divorced." He said crisply, and brought his heavy camera to his face, focusing with what seemed to Rhea to be undue care.

She shifted uneasily, wondering how she could gracefully remove her foot from her mouth and slink away. It was peculiar, though. He was divorced, and yet a wedding ring still gleamed on his finger. Why in the world would he want to keep it on?

After a few painful minutes, he took mercy on her discomfort and offered a red herring. "I've been doing my own photography for my articles, just a few dawn shots of the rigs out there."

"Well," she said, a bit too brightly. She grasped the change of subject with the desperation of a dying man clutching at a placebo; she knew it didn't help the situation, but it was better than doing nothing. "You'll get lots to photograph here. There's a lot to see."

"I'm sure," he said.

"Do you always use your own shots in your articles?"

"I usually do. That way I get to choose exactly the right image for it. I can write about it just as I see it, and the photos that I take can back up whatever I write, from my point of view. Of course, the extra income from the photos isn't bad, either."

She nodded. "You've been writing long?"

"Eight years, maybe nine. Before that, I wanted to be a vet."

She supposed that wasn't all that surprising, given his interest in animals. "Why did you stop?"

He shrugged. "At the time, I thought it would have chained me to one place. I would have had to open up a practice somewhere, get stuck in one spot. I was restless. I wanted to see the world. So I quit before my final exams. Call me a coward."

"So now you roam the earth."

He laughed at that. In the quiet of the morning, the deep, pleasant sound was snatched away by the salty breeze. "So now I roam the earth. Trying to save the planet, in some little way, I guess. A crusader with a pen instead of a sword."

"Does it work? I mean, do you think you reach people with what you write?"

He thought for a while before answering. "I think so. I mean, I get letters from people who have taken my advice and visited places that I recommended, who've had their lives touched by seeing creatures in their natural habitat. Then there are people who weren't aware that their water was being poisoned, or that there were companies in their neighborhood who were dumping waste in the wrong place."

"So you don't just do tourism."

"I don't just do tourism." He paused for a moment and added "Of course, I've been sued a few times." His warm eyes gleamed. "By people who thought that I was stepping on their toes. But I take it as a compliment. It means I'm doing something right."

Rhea watched the wicked grin on his face. He seemed to be enjoying the image of himself, like some kind of modern-day knight righting environmental wrongs. She wondered what that would mean for his article on Trinidad. She watched him shrewdly. "So, what kind of ax are you here to grind?"

"No ax . . . yet. For now, it's just a travel article."

"But that could change?"

"It could. Depends on what I see."

"Oh." She sounded crestfallen.

"Don't worry. I've forgotten last night. You get to start off with a clean slate today."

"I'm grateful," she responded dryly.

"My pleasure," he answered, just as dryly. They turned to watch the last of the early morning mist dissolve in the full glare of the sun. By silent agreement, they said no more, sitting quietly in appreciation of the freshness of the new day.

"Are we supposed to go looking for breakfast, or is it part of the package?" A night's rest had done nothing to lessen the irritating note in Rainer's nasal voice. The spell broken, Rhea leaped to her feet, almost guilty at being discovered in this moment of simple intimacy.

"No, of course not. I hadn't expected you up yet."

"Well, we're up." He stood in the open doorway clad in a deep maroon bathrobe that Rhea could see was expensive. She hurried toward the house.

Marcus followed, camera in hand. "I suppose I should see if Jodie's up. She fell asleep without a shower last night." He disappeared up the corridor into his room.

She made for the kitchen, calling out to Rainer over her shoulder. "Did you have a good night?"

"Good enough," he responded gruffly. "Considering."

She didn't bother to ask considering what. She entered the large white kitchen to find Banner already there, unloading the contents of a sturdy cardboard box onto the table. There was a large brown-paper bag of fresh country bread, the crisp dark loaves that Rhea loved. A tray of eggs followed, with butter, cheese, milk, and a plastic bag filled with tomatoes.

"Banner to the rescue," she sighed with relief.

He smiled. "I thought you'd be tired, so I didn't bother you. I popped up to Mayaro to get a few things."

"Thanks, Banner."

"Don't worry, my lady. Let's get these people their breakfast."

They worked quickly. Soon the house was filled with the aroma of cheese and tomato omelets. Drawn by the smell, the others emerged from their rooms.

"Mmmm! Something smells good!" Trudy chirped as she entered the kitchen. She looked ready to hit the beach in a light cotton outfit with flowered shorts. Bright red plastic bangles picked up the floral patterns in the material, and were echoed by cheerful hoop earrings that swayed as she moved. "Need help in here?"

Rhea shooed her out. "No, no, just have a seat."

"Thank you, dear." She floated out again, yelling to her husband, Fred, to come sit with her. Rhea smiled. Trudy seemed to have completely forgotten the upset of the night before, and was all excited about the new day. Maybe things would work out after all.

Marcus arrived with a squeaky-clean Jodelle in tow. She was fresh from a good night's sleep, and made a beeline for Rhea.

"Hi!" Her small face was split with a wide grin.

"Hi, little one," Rhea smiled back. The child had a smile that warmed the whole room. "Did you have a good sleep?"

"Oh, yes," she said gravely, and clambered up onto a chair next to Rhea. "And a *long* one, too!"

Rhea laughed. "That's good. I bet you were pretty tired."

The girl shrugged. "A little." Losing interest in the conversation, she began eyeing the hot breakfast on the table eagerly.

Everyone settled around the heavy wooden table and dug in. Once again Rhea was relieved that Marcus hadn't made her life any more difficult by refusing to eat eggs and dairy!

Finally, as they finished off their meal, Rhea decided that it was time to broach the uncomfortable subject. She pushed her plate away and took a deep breath. "I think we have to decide what we are going to do now. I mean, you had a pretty disappointing night, and I apologize for that. I'm truly sorry. But now I need to know from you what you want to do. Would you like to stay at this house instead, or would you like us to take you back?''

There was silence around the table.

''It was more than just *disappointing,* young lady,'' Rainer spoke up. A trail of butter rimmed his fat mouth, and Rhea felt a wave of revulsion. She knew in her heart of hearts that no matter what, she was never going to like this man. And his insistence on maintaining his hostile stance made her heart sink. She was hoping to get through this without a confrontation.

''Oh,'' Fred began. His cheeks crinkled as his deep-blue eyes looked kindly at Rhea. ''It wasn't so bad. Just think of it as one of those things. A little adventure.''

''Not so bad?'' Rainer countered aggressively. ''The place was filthy. Taking us there was unprofessional.''

A chorus of voices rose. Rhea sat quietly, enduring the discussions. On the other end of the table, Dahlia sat, looking as uncomfortable as Rhea herself felt. Her face was ashen in spite of her careful makeup, and the jet-black hair that was pulled sharply back from her face only served to throw her pallor into further contrast. Rhea got the impression that Rainer, whose voice was growing louder and more disagreeable, was embarrassing the woman. Still, the conversation was leaning toward staying at the house, and even Rainer did not appear to be opposed to this. He seemed more bent on venting his spleen, getting his money's worth for last night's fiasco through humiliating her.

Her best defense, she decided, was silence; let the storm pass. She caught Dahlia's eye for a moment, and the woman flashed her a sympathetic, embarrassed smile. Rhea nodded in understanding. Dahlia looked away.

''It was just negligent, that's all. That's all I'm saying.'' Rainer folded his arms across his chest, his voice peevish. He sensed that the others were turning against him, and set his fat jaw determinedly, like a stubborn schoolboy backed into a corner.

''Look, Bainbridge,'' Marcus snapped so sharply that Rhea's

head whipped toward the sound of his voice. "It was a mistake. The girl explained it to us last night, more than once. It was a mistake and it's over. It's done. Forget it. Trudy and Fred are staying. My daughter and I are staying. You and your wife make up your minds."

Rainer glared at him. Dahlia's voice was soft, almost timid. "I'd like to stay, Rainer." She said this without looking up, arms clasped around herself. Rainer opened his mouth, then shut it. All eyes were on him. He turned to Rhea, the belligerence in his tone somewhat lessened. "Fine, young lady, we're staying. This house will do."

Rhea nodded, throwing Marcus a grateful look. "Thank you for understanding." He nodded and gave her a warm smile that made her turn away, flustered. His kindness made her almost as nervous as his anger had. She had not expected to find an ally in him. Used as she was to fighting her battles on her own, she had to quell the flaring independent spirit that rose within her, threatening to scream, like a willful child: *I can do it myself! I don't need any help from you!*

Ignoring the impulse, she spoke as brightly as she could, all business now. "I just know you'll find it enjoyable. You have your itineraries, and I'm sure you've gone over them. Today, we'll be taking it easy, to let you get over your day's traveling. We'll just pop into town to allow you to change whatever currency you would like at the bank, and we will be spending the day at the beach. Lunch will be served at one, and this evening we'll take a drive back down into Mayaro for dinner. Now, is there anything you would like to ask?"

"No, dear. I'm sure everything will be all right," Trudy said comfortingly.

The others nodded in agreement. Rhea stood to her feet. "Thank you again." A loud buzzing drew her attention. She was thrown for a moment. It seemed to be coming from her bedroom.

"I think it's your phone again," Marcus said dryly.

God. That had to be Brent. The phone continued to buzz, manifesting the impatience that was Brent's most notable trait.

"Excuse me," Rhea said through gritted teeth. Brent never failed to do this to her. He was the kind of man that just couldn't understand that anything else might just possibly be more important than he. He would swear upon the heavens that he was not sexist, oh no, he was as liberated as you could get. Yet he walked around boasting about how he "let" his girl-friend work long hours, like it was a gift that was his to convey.

She reached her bedroom and snatched up the phone.

"Rhea!" the angry bellow was distorted by static. "Where have you been? You were supposed to call me this morning."

"It's still morning," she said evenly.

"I know that. I mean you were supposed to call me *early* this morning. What's going on down there?"

Rhea felt the walls around her draw in a little closer. Was it her imagination or was the room getting hotter? "I know, honey, but I've been working." It was an effort to keep her voice as soothing as she could.

He seemed to calm down. "Listen, baby," he said softly. There was no trace of the impatience that his voice so recently held. "Listen. You know I miss you. It's hard for me, you know, with you so far away. So sorry if I sounded impatient. Okay?"

She felt her shoulders relax, but the room somehow still felt hot. "Yes," she said softly, "I miss you, too." She tried to sound convincing. For the first time, it struck her that she hadn't given him a second thought since she started on the tour. She tried to pour conviction into her voice. "I'm sorry I haven't called. I meant to." *Liar.*

He laughed softly. "When am I seeing you, then?"

She shrugged. "We'll be here for two weeks or so. Then we'll move back up north. I'll still be working, though. We'll just be doing the north run." Hadn't they gone through this conversation just last night?

"Can't you steal away and see me for a few hours? Send them to the zoo or something." His voice was almost coquettish. He really could wheedle when he wanted to.

"I can't leave my people, Brent. You know that."

"Try, baby."

"I'll try," she said without conviction.

"Miss you." His voice was like velvet.

"Yes," she said. She hung up. Slowly, the room began to expand again.

CHAPTER FIVE

Rhea always liked to let her group have the first day to themselves. It allowed them to settle in and get used to the climate, get over their jet lag, and take a few naps if they wanted to. It turned out that today was just right for that. It was brilliantly sunny, without the merest threat of rain that usually marred rainy season visits to the beach. For this, she was grateful. She wryly recalled the many times that she had taken northerners on tour only to encounter gray beaches distorted by cold slashing rain and having to endure protests of "I thought these were the tropics! Isn't it supposed to be *sunny*?" As though they expected the year-round greenery to maintain itself without the contribution of the rain!

This time she was lucky. By mid-morning the sparkling stretch of beach looked so inviting that even she herself was excited by the prospect of a swim. She dressed modestly in a deep green one-piece swimsuit as required by company rules. She left the porch doors wide open and strode out onto the beach. Round the side of the house, she saw Banner doing what he loved best—buffing the minibus to a high gloss.

They were in an area where quite a few of the houses were occupied during the day by the wives of the oil company executives. One or two of these had taken up their positions on the narrow strips of lawn between their houses and the seawalls that ran along the front of every house.

Once on the beach, Rhea looked quickly around for her charges. Her group had spread itself out along the beach. Rainer and Dahlia wandered farthest away, just within view. To Rhea they seemed to be arguing, but she couldn't be sure. She could see Rainer's arms gesturing widely. Dahlia's face, its features barely visible at this distance, seemed to bear no expression.

Rhea sighed. They were a difficult pair, all right. Rainer seemed bent on imposing his will on everyone, not just his wife. He seemed like a man who was so spoiled by his own personal power at work that he expected the same response in other spheres of his life. Dahlia seemed like a woman who realised too late that she had sacrificed too much for too little, but had given up any effort to make things right.

Neither of them seemed too interested in the group's itinerary, or in anything that Rhea had told them about the country. So what were they doing here? Just getting away from it, she guessed. They didn't care where. Maybe they were just buying into the myth of the tropical paradise where all wrongs could be righted. Rhea had seen too many couples come down to the Caribbean expecting two weeks of sunshine to repair the years of damage that they had done to their marriage. As if Nature were a marriage counselor that would do all the work for them, and their marriage would progress right along with their tans.

Fred and Trudy had gone walking in the other direction, loud Hawaiian shirts and all. They followed the curve of the beach, knee-deep in water. They were holding hands. Now and then they would stop and pick something up off the ground. Rhea guessed that it would be a shell of some kind, a pebble, or a piece of glass frosted by the surging action of the ocean. She herself liked to indulge in that activity, collecting little things that the sea had tossed up onto the sand. Sometimes she took them to town to have them made into jewelry. Other times she kept them until her visit was over and returned them to the sea before she left, to let someone else have the joy of finding them.

Marcus was standing at the water's edge, feasting his eyes on the water before he ventured in. Jodelle stood next to him, one hand clinging to his fingers, the other holding onto a pair of goggles, complete with snorkel. She was wearing a tiny turquoise and white swimsuit, and her crazy braids were tied back with a ribbon.

Marcus had his other arm raised, and he seemed to be pointing out things up on the horizon. Jodelle was listening intently, but instead of letting her gaze follow in the direction of his pointing finger, she was staring upward at his face with an expression of awe.

Rhea sat back and watched them. The two obviously adored each other. She couldn't help but wonder once again about the little girl's mother, Marcus' ex-wife. It was peculiar, this working man, traveling with his daughter, when in most cases, women left a marriage with their children in tow.

Then her mind shifted to more down-to-earth, more interesting things. . . He stood outlined against the bright sky, tall and brown. In spite of herself, she noticed (and appreciated, if she had the courage to admit it) the smooth length of his legs, with their generous sprinkling of dark hair, and the muscled broadness of his back that narrowed sharply inward to his waist. *Damn*, she thought. *He looks good.*

Rhea snorted. She was sure that he knew this. Well, there wasn't anyone around for him to show off his physique to. The beach was practically empty, and she herself was hardly interested in anything more than a cursory glance. Jamming her sunglasses up on her nose bridge, she marched up to him. Somehow, the fact that he looked so fine irritated her, but it looked like he and Jodelle intended to hit the water, and it was still her responsibility to warn them about the hazards of the East Coast.

"The currents are tricky," she told him sternly. "Don't underestimate them. This isn't the North Coast. You aren't dealing with the Caribbean Sea here. The Atlantic is unpredictable and vicious." She gave him a stern, schoolmarmish glare over the tops of the sunglasses, which just wouldn't stay up on her well-oiled face.

He grinned. "Yes, Ma," he said solemnly.

Rhea felt her face go hot. She hadn't realised she was coming off like a picky parent. It occurred to her then that she was echoing exactly what her mother said over and over during her childhood visits to Mayaro. She apologized grudgingly. "I didn't mean to sound like that. I just wanted to warn you."

He gave her a funny look. "I was only joking," he said finally. "I'm glad for the advice. Hell, I'm glad for any advice that could save my life. Why are you so uptight? Relax. You don't have to have your back up all the time."

"I don't have my back up," she said shortly. Who did he think he was, calling her uptight? "I'm just doing my job. I can't let you drown out there. It just wouldn't be professional."

He let his golden gaze rest on her for an uncomfortably long time. "Thank you for caring," he said with the same solemn tone.

Just as she was about to begin squirming under the warmth of his examination, Jodelle provided a welcome distraction. "My Daddy's gonna teach me to swim like a doll-fink!" She beamed proudly up at him and squeezed his hand.

Marcus tore his gaze away from Rhea's flushed body and smiled indulgently down at the child. "Dol-*phin*, honey."

"Doll-fink," Jodelle agreed, and nodded vigorously. She looked up at Rhea, eyes squinting in the sunlight. "That's a fish."

Rhea nodded gravely.

"Well, *kind* of like a fish," Marcus said.

"Are you coming swimmin', too, Rhea?" Jodelle asked.

Rhea glanced across at Marcus, who was standing there in his close-fitting cutoffs, grinning at her, and decided that the ocean wasn't big enough for both of them. She feigned a yawn. "Oh, you know what? I think I'll just lie around here and get me some sun."

"Aren't you brown enough already?"

Rhea didn't know what to answer.

"She's got you there, you know," Marcus said smugly. "I personally think you've got a fine tan."

"Well," Rhea huffed, "a little more sun won't hurt it." She

tried to ignore his hearty laugh at her discomfort. To Jodelle, she said: "You go on in, little dolphin. I'll probably take a swim later, okay?" The girl nodded brightly, and began impatiently tugging her father in the direction of the glittering water.

Coward, he mouthed at her. She pretended she didn't understand. He tossed his towel down next to her and walked toward the water with the gait of a man who was relishing every footstep on the warm sand.

Rhea watched him as he went. The short cutoffs hung low on his hips. For a moment she wondered what they would look like on him when they were wet. The fact that she had indulged herself in the thought annoyed her. Still, she watched as Marcus entered the rhythmically pounding waves, letting the water rise along those long legs, up to those strong, solid hips . . .

"That's enough!" she pulled herself up sharply. She was shocked by her own voyeuristic impulses. As Marcus snatched his daughter, who was squealing with excitement, up into his arms, well above the waves, she returned to the little nest she had made for herself in the sand, rolling over onto her belly. She never bothered with beach towels; she preferred to have full contact with the warmth of the grains that clung to her skin. She didn't need to watch them as they swam, she was certain that Jodelle was in very good hands.

She only realised that she had drifted off to sleep when she felt a few droplets of water splash onto the backs of her bare legs. Marcus flopped down beside her like a big happy dog, reclaiming his towel from by her side.

"Are you really not swimming?" he asked.

She flipped over onto her back and looked up at him. The sun was fully over-head. It made her squint. She shook her head.

"Why not? Don't tell me you're one of those islanders that takes the sea so much for granted that you don't even bother to go in."

She grinned at that. If he only knew why she'd decided not to go in! "Nah, I just don't feel like it right now. Maybe later. Maybe tomorrow." *Maybe any time you're not around, you sexy creature*. The last silent thought made her pulse skip a beat.

"Sure, as long as *I'm* not in the water, right?"

She was stunned. The man had a mind like a blade. "Excuse me?" She pretended to look puzzled, thanking God for the shelter afforded her by the dark glasses.

"I mean, there's a lot of ocean out there for you to worry about bumping into me. I wouldn't have bothered you. Besides, my hands were full."

How did he keep doing that? Was her face that transparent? She answered as politely as she knew how. "Oh, no, not at all. You're not a bother."

He lowered himself down onto his elbows next to her. Gleaming beads of water ran down his perfectly molded face and onto the sand. He hadn't done a very good job of drying himself. "You're doing it again, you know."

"Doing what?" This time she was genuinely puzzled.

"Doing your hostess thing. Putting on the mask. If you could see yourself do it, you'd know what I mean. It's really something."

"Marcus, I really don't know what you're talking about."

"You fall into this hostess routine whenever you get uncomfortable. Like you're quoting from the Official Tour Guide Bible or something."

"I *am* a tour guide," she countered, although she felt stupid just saying it.

"Yes, but you're not a *plastic* tour guide. You act like you feel you need to say just the right thing, and that if you say it, and wear your tour guide mask all the time, then you don't have to give anybody a genuine response to anything."

What was he doing, Rhea wondered, psychoanalyzing her within a day of meeting her? She didn't have a response.

He nodded to himself in a way that said "Say what you like, I know I'm right" and looked away down the beach. She closed her eyes and pretended to be dozing, hoping that he'd let the conversation drop.

Marcus wasn't having it. "My daughter's really taken a

liking to you, you know. She spent a whole lot of time in the water just gabbing on about you.''

That brought an involuntary smile to Rhea's face. Instinctively, she cast her eyes around for Jodelle, and spotted her, right at the frilly edge of the water, digging in the sand like a small, enthusiastic dog.

"I think she's a real darling," Rhea confessed.

Marcus accepted the compliment and went on. "It's not often that she gets to spend time with other people. Usually, it's just her and me, and when I'm away, she stays with my parents. And they mean well, but she just doesn't have the opportunity to get out and play like this."

Rhea nodded, genuinely interested. "She seems to really like the water."

"Oh, yes, she's a regular fish."

"Doll-fink," she corrected. They both laughed.

After a while his face grew serious again. "I'm glad that she's getting old enough to travel with me, now. I think it would be good for her to see a little of the world, when she's not in school."

Rhea propped herself up onto her elbow and looked at him, encouraging him to go on.

"And I'm glad that her first trip is to the Caribbean. This is where her roots are, you know."

Her eyebrows rose. "Really? Yours?"

He shook his head. "Her mother's. She was from Barbados."

"Oh." There it was, the mention of the ex-wife again. She waited for him to elaborate, but he said nothing, and instead lay on his side, eyes fixed on her face. Her gaze was trapped within his, and she could see the hurt welling up within him, but unable to spill out, unable to pass some invisible barrier, which he had set up within himself. She was moved with compassion, and had to struggle bravely against the impulse to reach out and touch him on the arm, do anything that would bring the light back to those amber eyes.

Finally, she was forced to break the silence. "Little England," she said.

His brow furrowed. " 'Scuse me?"

"That's what they call Barbados. Little England. Of all the British West Indies, they are the ones who've most adhered to the British lifestyle, and retained most of the mannerisms and the systems. We, here in Trinidad, tend to think of ourselves more as part of the Americas, rather than part of the Commonwealth."

"Oh," he didn't seem to be listening. His gaze returned to Jodelle, who was running excitedly up toward them across the hot sand.

"*Oooh! Oooh!*" she squealed as the pale flecks, now superheated by the sun, stuck to the soles of her feet.

Marcus sprang into action, meeting her halfway across the sand, and taking her into his arms. "Come, honey. Sit on Daddy's lap. Let me get your sandals on."

As Jodelle allowed Marcus to buckle on her little blue rubber beach sandals, she twisted fully around to hold out her hand to Rhea. "Look! Look at what I got, Rhea! Look at it!"

Rhea bent over to peer into her little hand. She picked up the flat, round object and examined it. "It's a sea biscuit, Jodelle."

Jodelle peered at it. "Can you eat it?" She wrinkled her nose. "It's all gray and cold and stuff. It doesn't look good to eat at *all*!"

Rhea laughed. "No, you can't eat it, not unless you're a bird. It's a little sea animal. Look, if you turn it over, you can see hundreds and hundreds of little legs. See?"

"Yeah."

"And if you touch it, you can see all the little legs wriggling around."

"Ohhh!" Jodelle gasped in awe. "Can I put him back in the water?"

Rhea handed the little animal over. "I think that would be a good idea. I don't think he likes it on dry land. Just make sure you put him down with his legs facing downward, or he'll just lie there."

Feet clad safely in her sandals, Jodelle trotted off to the shoreline again, holding her hands cupped before her, as of she were about to make a precious offering to a sea goddess.

She turned to find Marcus' eyes on her face once again. "Was that the boyfriend this morning?"

His rapid change of subject threw her. "What?"

"The phone. The way you scooted out of the room, I gathered it was the boyfriend."

Rhea said nothing. What business was it of his?

"I bet he misses you."

"Marcus," she began. She wondered how to best tell him to mind his own business and still keep her job.

He raised a hand in surrender. "All right, all right. I'll withdraw my nose."

Good, she thought. *And keep it that way.*

In the cool of the evening, the group dressed casually for dinner. Rhea promised that they'd go looking for some kind of entertainment, although, as she said, it would hardly be a black-tie affair. The group seemed excited at the prospect of a country evening, and spruced up in clean jeans and shirts.

Even Rainer seemed more relaxed. He held the door open for his wife as she left the house, and stood aside to allow her to climb into the van. Her face radiated gratitude. Rhea watched them as they sat together and felt a pang of pity for the beautiful, pale woman. She was so desperately unhappy that she seemed to be licking up any crumb of decency that fell from her husband's table.

As they drove out of Guayaguayare into the darkening evening, Trudy chattered on with Rhea, recounting in detail every scent she had smelled and every sight she had seen during the day on the beach. Rhea listened, grateful that with Trudy's constant stream of information she wasn't called upon to make much of a contribution.

Marcus had decided to sit up front with Banner; Rhea relinquished her seat gracefully at his request. She could hear the two men's voices during Trudy's infrequent pauses. They were talking about fish, sharks especially. Marcus was saying that he wanted to get some photography done at a nearby fishing settlement.

"I thought you didn't eat fish," she heard Banner say.

Marcus gave a low laugh. "I don't eat it. Doesn't mean that others don't have the right to eat it. I'm here to observe, not to preach."

Jodelle, all dressed up for dinner in a bright cotton dress, and shiny patent-leather shoes, opted to sit with Rhea, much to both Marcus' and Rhea's surprise. She sat close to the window, staring intently out at the trees as they whizzed by, pausing from time to time to beam up at Rhea.

The child's attention was both flattering and disconcerting. As if the appreciative, disturbing golden glances of the father weren't bad enough, she was now finding herself the object of the onyx-eyed, adoring glances of the daughter! She loved children, especially children as bright and good-natured as Jodelle obviously was, but while she always tried to make their visit as enjoyable and educational as possible, it would never do to become too attached to them. Countless tear-filled scenes at the airport at tour's end had taught her that. Still, she succumbed to the urge to reach out and touch the heavy black braids, and was rewarded with a wide smile.

Her thoughts were drowned once again by a breathless account of a family of pelicans that Trudy and Fred had seen bobbing in a group on the water. "They were so huge," Trudy was saying. "And swimming together, like a family. It was so exciting!"

To Rhea's surprise, Dahlia turned her head and joined in the conversation. It was the first voluntary words she had spoken since the group had set off the night before. "I saw them, too. They really were big."

Even Trudy seemed a little taken aback at this sudden decision to speak, but quickly recovered. She agreed enthusiastically.

Dahlia continued. "I sculpted a pelican once. Larger than life-size. It had a wingspan of six feet. I sold it to a collector in Malibu."

"Oh," Trudy leaned forward and lightly placed her arm on Dahlia's shoulder. "Are you an artist?"

Dahlia flushed in the dim light. She nodded proudly. "Yes. I am. The collector mounted it outside of this marine zoo."

It was Rainer's turn to surprise everyone. He turned and joined in the conversation. "Yes," he joined in, "my wife was a terrific sculptor. Really terrific." He squeezed her arm almost affectionately. Rhea wondered if Dahlia had caught her husband's reference to her art in the past tense. With a quick look at the woman's face she knew, by the flicker of pain, that she had. Dahlia turned frontward and was silent for the rest of the journey. Rhea let Trudy ramble on.

Appaloosa was one of those incongruities of West Indian life: a Trinidadian dude ranch. It sprawled more than 30 acres of land north of the village, a horse farm nestled amongst coconut trees where tourists could spend a pleasant hour or two riding horses in an area where the biggest hazard for the horse was tripping up in a crab hole. Because of the lack of entertainment in the area, it also found itself doubling as a hotel, motel, restaurant, bar, and party ground. Every month or two some slick Port of Spain party promoter would come down in a wave of brightly coloured flyers and cardboard notices nailed to lampposts. He would bring with him a popular deejay and a live performer or two, and youths from within a twenty-mile radius would flock to the site for the rare party.

The entire sprawling building stretched one's credulity. It looked like a building patiently copied out of an old spaghetti western, complete with saloon doors and tethering posts and watering troughs at the side. The group couldn't resist a surprised giggle as they walked into a narrow corridor that smelled of varnish.

"I don't believe this," Trudy breathed.

"Yeah," was all her husband could say.

"Cowboys and Indians, Daddy!" Jodelle enthused. She was still sticking close to Rhea, declining Marcus' offer of a hand to hold on to, but ensuring that she kept him well in view. He accepted her decision with raised eyebrows, but said nothing.

The interior was decorated with bamboo posts, rough wooden tables, brass ornaments, and wildly coloured paintings of buffalo and American prairies. The walls and the roof were fes-

tooned with dried coconut branches, which swept low enough
to brush Marcus' head lightly as they walked toward a table.
Rhea considered for a moment letting him know that coconut
branches were a haven for all manner of insect, but thought
better of it.

The meals were served with surprising swiftness, and they
ate hungrily, without much conversation. A day on the beach
could really raise an appetite. The local Carib beers were cold
and went down well.

The other diners were mainly tourists. At the far end of the
dining room, a small space had been cleared for dancing. The
wall that ran along that far side only came to waist high, and
through the space, the lights in the yard could be seen glinting
off the nearby sea.

The music blared scratchily from a huge heavy pair of speak-
ers. A young boy, dreadlocks pulled back from his face and
tied with a shoelace, was earnestly spinning old vinyl records
for the meager two dozen guests. He wore a T-shirt that lauded
the skills of the Chicago Bulls, and his long narrow feet were
bare.

"Think he's got a record there that was cut after 1980?"
Marcus asked with amusement.

Rhea smiled. The tinny music that had been assaulting them
all evening was an incongruous mixture of Bob Marley, Percy
Sledge, the Drifters, and the Carpenters. "It's a Trini thing,"
she explained. "A kind of cultural recolonization. We have
our own music, and we listen to all the stuff you get on the
pop charts, especially since communication is opening up with
satellite services and all that. But you'll still hear this kind of
music playing on the radios and in bars, especially out in the
country. It's quaint, but the golden oldies please more people
than anything else."

"You're kidding," he said. "People listen to this all the
time?"

She nodded. "Pity you can't get the chance to go to a Trini
wedding. You hear everything but the eight-tracks."

"Pity," he agreed.

"I kind of like it," Dahlia said. She closed her eyes and

tilted her head back. The deejay was playing an old reggae number, low and rhythmic. "It's kind of old-fashioned. It's honest."

"Reminds me of doing grass in the seventies," Fred said wickedly. His wife hissed at him to shut up. He protested. "I'm not all that old, you know," he countered.

"I *know* you aren't" she said just as wickedly. They laughed at some secret joke.

"Let's dance," Rainer said suddenly. He held out his hand to his wife. She wasn't the only one surprised at the gesture. She took his hand and they both rose and crossed to the floor.

The Steins thought it was a good idea, and followed suit.

There was an uncomfortable silence at the table. It reminded Rhea of her teenage forays into public parties where she and her girlfriends would stand around looking nonchalant, terrified that they'd never be asked to dance and even more terrified that they would. Marcus sat across from her with his long legs stretched out before him, arms folded, watching her with a mischievous gleam in his eyes. She wouldn't doubt that, given his remarkable ability to figure out what she was thinking, he knew exactly what was going through her mind and had decided to let her suffer. Banner seemed unaware of any such undercurrent and rocked backward in the dark mahogany chair, puffing on a cigarette.

"Well," Marcus said after a while. "I guess that leaves us, then."

Rhea pretended not to hear him. The sultry reggae beat gave way to another old classic from the Eagles, "Hotel California." Rhea groaned.

"I don't believe that," he said, with mock amazement.

"What?" She couldn't help but ask.

"They could still *find* that record?"

She shrugged. "It's got to be one of the most-played pieces in the country. I kind of like it myself."

"Let's not waste it, then." He held out his hand.

Panicked without fully understanding why, she looked around wildly. "Oh," she floundered. "I wouldn't want to leave Jodelle alone."

Jodelle was oblivious to the discussion, still drawing designs in her melting ice-cream with her spoon. Marcus turned a querying glance at Banner, who was contentedly puffing and staring out the door.

"Mr. Banner?" Marcus asked with mock politeness. "Will you keep an eye on my daughter while I dance with Rhea?"

"Oh, yeah." He waved a hand. "Sure, sure."

Marcus turned to her with the kind of smile that a Venus's-flytrap reserves for a fat moth. "She won't be alone."

"Well," she began. She wondered what to say next. "It really wouldn't be fair." She hoped *that* would work.

Fat chance. This time Banner himself did her in. He plucked the cigarette carefully from his mouth between the tips of his forefinger and thumb, and turned to face them. "You kids are joking. You forget I have four children of my own? Look girl," he swatted at her with the hand that held the cigarette. "Go on and enjoy yourself, okay?" He sucked his teeth with manifest impatience and put the butt back between his lips.

"You heard him," Marcus said with the cockiness of someone who has won a surefire bet. "Let's go."

Rhea uncurled her legs and got to her feet. "Okay," she said with all the grace she could dredge up, and followed him to the tiny floor.

She held her hands up and out for him to take, but instead he slid both arms around her waist and pulled her to him. "This isn't a waltz," he said humorously. "And that certainly isn't a twenty-piece orchestra."

Her first instinct was to protest. That instinct was immediately squelched by the sudden awareness of him. He smelled woodsy, like some quiet mossy place. The scent threw Rhea; it seemed to fill her nostrils yet elude her, causing her to lean even closer to pursue it. She was a tall woman, so in spite of his height, she didn't feel squashed against his chest and unable to breathe. Instead they seemed to fit perfectly; his mouth reached just to her ear and she could feel his breath against the nape of her neck.

He danced with precision and grace, and in spite of her

mental resistance, she felt her body relax and fall into time with his.

"Now you've got it," he said approvingly.

This man disturbed her. Yet, her body seemed to soften as they moved together, and she realised just how much she was enjoying their rhythmic motion. She didn't want his sly taunting to intrude on the moment, so instead, she concentrated on the music.

As they danced, an uncomfortable sense of wonder came over her as she felt the smooth, toned body that she had admired earlier pressed against hers. Without any direction from her, one hand slid up to his shoulder, and her fingers tingled with the movement of the bunched muscles under his rough linen shirt. This was a man who worked out, she decided appreciatively, and as far as she could feel, the effort did not go amiss. The song changed. He didn't let her go. Marcus began humming along softly in her ear and she smiled. Obviously, he enjoyed moving to music.

This is good, she thought. *So good. It's been such a long time since I danced like this.* Her boyfriend, Brent, hated dancing. He didn't see the point. He saw it as a social skill, like making good conversation, or being able to tell one wine from another, and he used it as such. His dancing was good but without feeling, just another trick that he pulled out of his little bag to impress bored corporate wives at company dinners. As a result, Rhea never enjoyed dancing with him. *She* didn't see the point of being whirled stiffly around a dance floor while his body had nothing to say to her. The change was refreshing. She closed her eyes.

"I see the sisters are out tonight," Marcus said softly.

The sound of his voice had her confused for a moment. She'd been lost in the echoes of the music. She lifted her head reluctantly from his shoulder and her eyes flew open. "Huh?"

"The sisters. Our little girls across the water." He spun her around so that she was looking beyond him and out to sea. The scattered oil rigs were quite visible, lit up by hundreds of lights that glittered and winked in the distance. "They've got their ball-gowns on this evening," he mused softly.

He was right. The powerful lights glittered brilliantly against
the dark sea, and the plain little girls in their dowdy gray skirts
were now festooned with gaudy sequins made of stars. Instead
of looking like girls wading in across the water, they looked
like fine young ladies gliding across a ballroom floor. He did
have a way with images.

She nodded. "They're beautiful. Especially when you look
at them like that, like girls dancing."

He didn't answer. She laid her head on his shoulder again,
indulging in the scent of him and in the rise and fall of his
chest as he breathed. It was like being lulled into a state of
total relaxation, cradled halfway to sleep. One of his long-
fingered hands—Rhea had already come to think of them as
writer's hands, sensitive and thoughtful—came up to rest lightly
on the back of her head, nestled in the short thick curls at her
nape.

Then a disturbing thought struck her: What about the others?
Were they watching her as she allowed herself to be seduced
by the rhythm of the music? She tried to turn her head discreetly
to one side, looking out to see if the two other couples would
glide by.

He sensed her discomfort. "What's the matter?" he said
into her hair.

"I . . . nothing." Still, she was uneasy.

"Are you wondering what the others must be thinking?
They're still dancing, Rhea. They aren't paying any attention
to us. Besides, there's nothing wrong with a little dance, is
there?"

There was *lots* wrong with this dance, she wanted to say.
She was being sucked down by a very disquieting undertow,
pulled under by the scent and the feel of him, and the waves
were closing in over her head. She was afraid she would never
be able to come up for air.

Then suddenly, she became very afraid that the music would
stop, and that the dance would end. When the song changed
again, she half expected him to release her, but was relieved
that he didn't. Instead, he pulled her even closer, impossible
as it would seem, firmly grasping her wrist and winding her

arm around his waist. She didn't move it away, but instead prayed hard that he wouldn't speak and jar her into brutal reality. He seemed to feel the same way, enjoying the peaceful bubble in which they were enclosed, and simply allowed her to nestle close to him, saying nothing.

It wasn't until the rhythm shifted to a louder, more frenetic piece that the spell was broken. When he released her, he thanked her with a polite nod that she could only construe as being mocking. As he pulled back, she was disoriented for a few seconds, and more than a little embarrassed at having leaned all over his shoulder like a wilting vine. They walked back to the table with exaggerated nonchalance, keeping a good distance between them.

Dahlia glowed like a thousand-watt bulb. Rainer had his arm around her and his face held the softest expression that Rhea had seen on him yet. Banner was holding Jodelle in thrall with a couple of his magician's tricks, making the caps off the beer bottles disappear and reappear seemingly at will. Luckily for Rhea, no one seemed to be aware of her discomfiture.

They returned home in good spirits. Up front Rhea could hear Banner expansively reiterating his promise to take Marcus on an early-morning visit to the fishing area. Next to her, Jodelle dozed lightly, small mouth open, head thrown against her shoulder. By the time they pulled into the driveway, pins and needles had taken up residence along Rhea's entire arm, from the pressure of the sleeping girl's body, but Rhea didn't mind at all.

The group split up quickly and went to their respective bedrooms. As had become the pattern, Marcus used their shared bathroom first, and knocked softly on her door as he emerged, letting her know it was free. She gathered up her towel, soap, toothbrush, and washcloth and made for the door, only to find him still standing there.

Droplets of water rolled out of his short hair and down the sides of his face, like beads of perspiration. The man was wearing a plush bathrobe of moss green, and wafts of some warm soapy smell seemed to rise off his freshly scrubbed skin. He hadn't pulled the robe completely shut; the wide lapels fell open to reveal a nest of fine dark hair that clung wetly to his chest. Her eyes were drawn unbidden to the dark thatch, and she tore them away.

This was too much. First, he had invaded her senses out there on the dance floor, humming softly in her ear, and feeling so good against her body, and now, here he was, half naked and dripping wet, standing in a puddle at her bedroom door. She hoped desperately that no one would choose this moment to pop out of their bedroom and find them there together, alone in the narrow, intimate corridor. "Can I help you?" she said pertly.

"Don't give me the hostess voice, Rhea," he said in amusement. The fine laugh lines around his eyes crinkled. "I don't buy it."

"What do you want, then?" she asked more sharply. *That* wasn't her hostess voice.

"Nothing. I just wanted to tell you good night, and thanks for the dance. It was . . . enjoyable."

Enjoyable! He must be joking. He had almost pulled her apart out there. She bit back an irritated retort—he was still, after all, a client. It wouldn't do to be rude. "Good night," she said as mildly as she possibly could. With her bundle of clothes and toiletries clutched to her chest like a shield, she eased past him and up the corridor.

"Don't forget to call the boyfriend," he said to her receding back.

Wouldn't you know it? She *had* forgotten. She halted for a second, surprised at herself, then continued on. She didn't thank him.

CHAPTER SIX

Rhea sat on the edge of her bed with her day's itinerary spread out before her. As she pored over her road maps, trying to decide on their best course of action for the next trip, she listened to the sound of Marcus moving about his room. Irrationally, she found it almost irritating how meticulous he was about being up and about by dawn. He'd given Jodelle her bath and dressed her, showered and changed, and there she was, just getting up. Didn't he ever sleep late?

She couldn't believe that ridiculous scenario that had gone on last night at the club, the two of them dancing at the window, looking out over the water's edge at the Christmas-tree glitter of the oil rigs in the distance. *Little sisters in their ballgowns!* Ridiculous. She was letting her imagination run away with her, that was her problem. Letting a tall, handsome man with a sonorous voice and extraordinary eyes sucker her into swallowing his childish imaginings as poetry.

And to think he'd made her dance through three of those awful old numbers! Didn't he know when to stop? She accepted as part of her role the duty to make her guests feel at ease, and if it extended to exuding a little charm during their evenings out, and to stepping in as a dance partner when the occasion warranted, well, so be it. But that stubborn, selfish man had gone a little too far! She cringed as she remembered how she'd danced in his arms, almost languorously, feeling his breath as he exhaled against her nape.

She stood abruptly to her feet; time to get breakfast going. Let Banner sleep late for a change. Meals were her responsibility, too. He'd already gone out again the afternoon before to buy more substantial groceries. She pulled on her regulation jeans and green T-shirt and went to see about her face.

In the bathroom, the air was warm and steamy from the shower Marcus had taken. The warm spicy scent of the aftershave jolted her, and for a second she was back in his arms, dancing at the window. She shook her head and the image cleared, but not before she became startlingly aware that much of her irritation over the dance with Marcus—which was, after all, just a dance—was due to the fact that she had truly enjoyed it.

"Don't be an idiot," she snapped at her reflection. Sometimes the woman in the mirror could be so stupid! Embarrassed by the memory of the pleasure that the simple dance had brought her, she wrenched open the bathroom door and stomped into the kitchen.

There was still some bread left, but she thought that her guests would enjoy a little Trinidadian breakfast specialty. With practiced ease, Rhea set about with her bowls and spoons, measuring out flour and oil, adding a liberal mountain of fresh grated coconut and kneading it to a soft dough, which she patted into a huge flat round mass and popped into the oven.

Slabs of boiled salted cod came next. These she stripped into small pieces, carefully removing the fine, needlelike bones that ran throughout the entire cut. She shuddered at the idea of one of her guests choking on one of the sharp, invisible filaments hidden within, and redoubled her efforts. When she was done cleaning the fish, she doused it in vinegar and olive oil, laying it attractively out onto the biggest serving platter in the house and decorating it with tomatoes, avocados, and slices of boiled egg.

She was surveying her handiwork with her hands on her

hips, congratulating herself on her skill as a cook, when she remembered with a start that there was a vegetarian in their midst. Sure, there were vegetables on the plate with the fish, but how much of a purist was he? Suppose he refused to eat food that had been tainted by contact with flesh? That would be a disaster. Quickly, she set about getting the ingredients for a tomato omelet ready for Marcus. They would be eating in no time; already the house was full of the sounds of life.

"Smells good in here."

Rhea spun round to encounter Trudy and Fred, who were standing in the kitchen doorway, holding hands and smiling. They were dressed in cheerful cotton shirts and matching khaki shorts, with leather sandals and straw hats. Rhea resisted the urge to laugh at the sight they presented; naive, outrageously touristy, almost comical. Straw hats in the house!

"What are you cooking, young lady?" Fred came fully into the kitchen and sniffed the air.

Rhea smiled broadly at the obvious compliment. "It's called a coconut bake, and it's ready to eat." Slipping bright padded oven mittens onto her hands, she pulled the hot tray out of the oven and set it onto a cooling rack. "It's a coconut bread, very popular in this country."

"Well, I know I'm going to be having some of that," Fred laughed. He and his wife sat close to each other at the table, eyeing the hot bread like eager children.

By then Rainer, Dahlia, and Banner had joined them, lured into the kitchen by the wonderful smells that filled the room. "Sit down, please," she waved a hand at them. Her eyes drifted to the doorway as she set out the fixings for coffee and tea. Marcus and Jodelle hadn't turned up yet. She wondered idly where they were. She wouldn't get the omelet going until he got there.

Rhea began cutting the round bake into huge slices, which she slit with the long bread knife and slathered in butter. As she reached out to offer it around, she happened to encounter Rainer's ice-blue eyes trained on her. They held a studied innocence, and some other unidentifiable thing, something which jarred her. She almost recoiled, but dismissed the slight chill that ran down her spine as a figment of her imagination, and cranked her hostess smile back up a notch.

Dahlia seemed oblivious to Rhea's discomfort. "What's this?" she asked, a look of pleased wonder on her face. She indicated with a long slim finger the fish salad that took pride of place in the centre of the table. "It looks amazingly good."

Rhea smiled. The compliments were really coming thick and fast this morning. She determined to ignore the unpleasant chill that the woman's husband had sent down her spine; after all, if there really had been something in those pale blue eyes, surely his wife would have sensed it! Instead, she answered Dahlia's question about the dish in her warmest tones.

"It's called *buljol*. It's a salad of salted fish, onions, and garlic with a vinaigrette sauce. Most Trinidadians consider it one of our national dishes."

"Lovely," she said. Eagerly she picked up a bit on the end of her fork and tasted it experimentally. "It's delicious!"

Rhea's "thank you" was interrupted by a voice in the doorway. "It's cod, isn't it?"

Rhea looked up to see Marcus standing with his daughter, both their faces flushed by the early-morning sea air. They must have gone for a prebreakfast stroll to work up an appetite.

She cringed, wondering if they were in for a lecture on the sanctity of piscine life. "Cod, yes," she nodded, and rushed to the kitchen counter to start Marcus' omelet. "But I'm getting a few eggs ready for you."

He set Jodelle down on one of the empty chairs, and with a few steps, he was at her side, and his long fingers tried to prize the spatula from her hands. "Relax, I wasn't getting on your case. I was just a little puzzled, that's all. And I can make my omelet myself, thanks."

Rhea's fingers refused to release the spatula. "It's my job," she hissed. "I'm *supposed* to get you breakfast."

"Well, I kind of like getting my own, thank you." He pulled even harder on the spatula. Rhea let go, realising how ridiculous they looked, squabbling over a kitchen implement. Let him cook his own breakfast, she thought, if it was so important. She returned to her place at the table, where the others were digging in, oblivious to the little power struggle that had just taken place at the stove. Patiently, she began buttering small slices of bake and placing them on Jodelle's plate.

Then a thought about what he had just said struck her. "Puzzled about what, Marcus?" she asked.

He carefully flipped his omelet before answering. "Oh, about the cod. Cod isn't indigenous to the West Indies. It's a cold-water fish. How does a cold-water fish become such a popular dish on a Caribbean island?"

"He's right, you know," Fred said, pointing at her with a chunk of tomato speared onto the end of his fork.

"Yes, dear," Trudy said, "We're curious. Tell us."

Rhea hadn't thought of that before. She'd just grown up knowing it as one of her favourite dishes, refreshing and filling. But he had a point. Why on earth would a northern fish, which never even ventured this far south, become such a popular local dish?

As she watched Marcus settle himself down at the table with his hot omelet and help himself to a buttered slab of coconut bake she thought: damn that man. Always putting her on the spot. Now she was going to have to struggle with trying to decide whether to come up with something off the cuff and maintain the illusion of being the all-knowing host, or whether to admit that she hadn't a clue. Marcus was watching her, smiling impudently. "Gotcha," his smile said.

She silently vowed her revenge. He knew she didn't have an answer, but he'd asked the question anyway. He was playing with her, and they both knew it. She stared at his face for several heartbeats, wondering half seriously if a swift kick under the table would make her feel avenged.

"It's a relic from the days of slavery," Banner said lugubriously. Rhea's head snapped in his direction. Until then he had been silently and swiftly consuming large portions of the meal, with little more than polite greetings to everyone else. Banner took a swig from his mug of hot country chocolate and went on. "You're aware that the West Indies was largely populated by land developers and planters during the four hundred years or so after their discovery by Columbus?"

"Well, I didn't know that!" Trudy put her cup down and leaned in toward Banner, as if she didn't want to miss a word. All the others watched him silently, urging him to go on.

"Well, as happened in most of the New World, the Europeans began to import slaves from the West African coast to work on the land. And of course they had to feed all those slaves."

"So they fed them on cod? Why?" Fred wanted to know.

"Well, it was a supplement to the fresh fish that they caught here. Cod was cheap and abundant in Europe, and it could be salted and shipped to the West Indies, where it would last for years, if they preserved it right." He shrugged elaborately. "That's how a foreign dish passed into the local cuisine."

The others looked at him admiringly. "That was a good story, Mr. Banner," Trudy said encouragingly.

"I might even put it in my article," Marcus nodded. "I think my readers would like that."

Rhea relaxed in her chair. *Disaster averted*, she telegraphed to Banner across the table. He just smiled.

With breakfast over, Rhea shooed her charges out of the kitchen so she could wash up. There was very little to pop back into the fridge, as everyone had devoured most of the meal. They rose from their chairs with exaggerated groans of satisfaction, and filed out.

"Let me help you with the dishes, Rhea," Rainer said loudly as the others filed past. Dahlia's surprise was as obvious as Rhea's, but the other woman lowered her eyes and left the kitchen silently.

A little flustered, Rhea waved away the offer. "Don't be silly. I can handle it. You go on out and get yourself some sun."

Rainer began stacking the dirty plates at the end of the table without answering. Not willing to take it any further, she accepted his help with grace. They worked quickly. The stocky, florid man stood next to her at the sink with a large white dish towel, drying as fast as she washed. For a man who had obviously not done his own dishes in a long time, Rhea thought, he was pretty efficient at it.

"Nice evening we had yesterday," he said conversationally.

She agreed pleasantly. "I'm glad you enjoyed it. Maybe we'll manage to squeeze another one in before we leave."

"I hope so, my dear. I certainly do. I mean, after seeing just how much you like dancing, I certainly wouldn't say no to the opportunity to experience the pleasure first-hand."

Rhea stiffened. So that was his game! Her soapy hands paused over a large dish, then picked up their rhythm once again. Rainer had been watching them, her and Marcus, dancing by the window last night! Her face and neck ran hot with guilty embarrassment. She thought of how close she'd allowed that man to hold her, and about the large hand that had moved caressingly along the small of her back. God, she'd made a spectacle of herself, even though Marcus had assured her that nobody had been watching! She could find no answer.

Determined to press home his point, he leaned closer to her and said, softly in her ear, "So don't forget to put me on your dance card next time, okay, dear? We know you wouldn't want to show any favouritism."

The pointed barb about Marcus made her flinch. Unable to find a suitable response, she concentrated on the dishes for another torturous five minutes, during which Rainer chatted pleasantly on about the most pointless of matters, the weather and the tide.

This is a dangerous man, Rhea realised as he handed the folded dish towel back to her with a flourish. Not just impolite, not just cruel, but *dangerous.* She'd have to be careful. As the realisation sank in, she felt a heaviness descend upon her.

First, there was Marcus, who was bent either on making her mad or on making her blood quicken. That, in itself, was a unique and difficult situation. But this . . . cold predatorial threat from a man who seemed to consider no one but himself, this augured trouble. And more trouble was the last thing she needed right now. She stood in the kitchen for a long time after Rainer left, struggling to regain her composure.

"It's tomorrow," Marcus said to her, with a grin like a shark.

"What?" she looked at him as if he were mad. What non-sense was he speaking? They'd only just gone outside into the sun, and she was still reeling from the nasty feeling that Rainer had given her. Now this man was hanging around, seemingly doing his best to get on her nerves. Why couldn't he leave her to read in peace?

"It's tomorrow. Yesterday you promised you'd go swimming with me tomorrow, and now it's here. So how about it?" His teeth were gleaming. The man looked mighty pleased with himself.

Rhea sucked her teeth. She couldn't believe he was being so childish. He didn't really think she'd been serious, did he? Surely he was just trying to get her back up. "I never said I'd swim *with* you," she argued. "I said I'd swim. And maybe I will. Later."

"Com'on." He tugged insistently at her arm. "everyone else is in the water. Don't be a spoilsport. Besides," he threw his trump card at her, "I already know you're a coward. You don't want me to add fibber to that list, do you?"

That did it. He really knew how to press her buttons. Irritated, she sat up and tossed her book onto the beach towel. Her sunglasses, slippery with suntan oil, followed. "Fine," she snapped. "But stop tugging at me. I can make it into the water on my own."

He'd gotten his own way, so there was no need to push the point. He helped her to her feet and then let go of her arm. (Why did she feel so let down when he released her?)

"Race you to the water?" he asked hopefully, innocently.

The request flattered her, and the "What's gotten into you?" that she tossed at him was not as angry as she intended it to be. In spite of herself, she found that she was smiling.

"That's better," he said. "Let's go."

They swam in silence, doing slow laps along the beachfront. What initially began as a swimming contest of sorts, in which each tried to show off their superior skills to the other, soon became a leisurely swim. They fell into each other's rhythm, arms and legs leaving and entering the water with barely a sound.

"Glad I made you come in, eh?" he said presumptuously when they stopped for breath.

She was about to confess that he was right, and to follow it up with an irritated *"You're pretty sure of yourself, aren't you?"* when without any warning the water began to boil.

Rhea looked around her in horror as the cool sea escalated to a hundred, no, a thousand degrees, looked to see if it was bubbling on the surface, and if steam was rising. Then she realized that it wasn't the water that was on fire, it was her own flesh. The searing pain that overwhelmed her blazed along her legs, up to her hips, engulfing her, and a pressure that she had never felt before began to build at the backs of her eyes.

"Hot!" she gasped, mouth twisted with horror.

Marcus stopped dead and stared at her aghast. "What? Rhea, what's wrong?"

"Fire, fire!" she was screaming now, because the pain was so bad. In her shock, she began to sink below the water, but she was glad for that, sure that the waves that slapped her in the face would cool her blazing skin.

Marcus sprang into action, snatching her up into his arms, and began pulling her frantically to shore. "Not fire, baby, jellyfish. A big one. Stay still, let me take you in."

But Rhea couldn't hold still, not while she felt like the flesh below her hips was being torn from her body. In her panic, she clutched at Marcus, held on to his ears and pulled him toward her. The water closed in over both their heads, and the burning of the water as it poured into her nostrils and open mouth almost rivaled the agony of the vicious sting.

With all his strength, he tore free of her grasping arms and dragged her to the surface. "I'm trying to help you, Rhea!" he sputtered, but she was beyond rational thought. As she began to pull him under again, Marcus slapped her, hard, across the face.

Rhea was stunned. She stared at him uncomprehendingly for seconds, before retaliating on instinct. Her closed-fisted blow landed across his nose with a loud crack, and then she went limp in his arms.

Reeling from the force of her punch and from a lungful of

water, he somehow managed to lift her and carry her out. By this time, everyone else had realised that something was wrong, and with her venom-numbed brain, Rhea could perceive a blur of faces and hear their garbled shouts.

Marcus knelt to lay her on the dry sand, and as he did so, a spurt of blood from his wounded nose sprayed her green swimsuit like a crimson pattern of embroidered flowers. She leaned forward to see where she had been stung: a series of tortured red marks ran the length of her right leg, from hip to ankle. The swelling had been massive and immediate, and already the broken skin was turning purple.

The horrific sight, and the mad pumping of her blood within her made her dizzy, and as Marcus held her forward with gentle, anxious hands, she vomited, loudly and copiously, into the sand. When her awareness faded, shutting out the humiliation, the noise and the terrible sunshine that burned her eyes, she was grateful.

The doctor had come and gone—or so they had told her. Rhea remembered little of his visit. She remembered voices, whispers, and a soothing cold cream being rubbed gently into her hot wounds. She was sure that the cream had come straight from heaven, so comforting it had been, and positive that they had swathed her leg in bits of cloud.

She also remembered something else, a shadowy presence who seemed to be always there. The presence was always accompanied by the scent of musk and spice, and this was vaguely familiar, and deeply comforting.

The curtains in her room were drawn, but even so, Rhea could tell it was night. Everything around her was damp—the sheets, the pillows, everything. She passed a curious hand along her forehead and it came away wet. Surely she couldn't be sweating that badly!

''You have a fever, Rhea,'' Marcus' voice came from somewhere behind her head, but she was too tired to turn to look at him. He sounded concerned . . . and weary. ''You were a hundred and three, but it's going down now. The doctor gave you something for it.''

She tried to remember why she was in bed. It was hard at first. She knew she was wounded, stabbed, maybe. It certainly felt like she had been stabbed, slashed with a long, thin knife all the way down to her foot.

Then she remembered the jellyfish, with its horrible filaments that had wrapped themselves around her leg and sent its venomous barbs into her blood.

''You were lucky,'' he was saying. He had moved closer, and now his voice was right by her ear. She felt his fingers stroke her wet hair, and felt the cool rag that he passed gently along her heated brow. The coolness against her hot skin was welcome, and she hoped he would never stop.

Lucky? If her face didn't hurt so much, she'd have given a rueful smile.

Marcus read her mind. ''I know you don't think so, but you were. It was a Portuguese man-of-war that stung you, Rhea. You only brushed against a few of its filaments. If you had run smack into the whole thing, you could have gotten enough venom into your system to send you into shock. It could have killed you. You *were* lucky.''

The rhythm of his touch was hypnotic. She felt so helpless, so grateful that he was there with her. Then she remembered how she had come to be in the water in the first place: it was he who had taunted her until she gave in. Anger surged.

''It was you,'' she told him testily.

''What?'' he leaned closer, as if her were not sure that he had heard her right.

''It was your fault. You made me go in. I told you I didn't feel like it, but you badgered me and badgered me. Why didn't you leave me alone?''

Marcus was quiet for a long time. Then he let his breath out with a rush. ''I'm so sorry. I was just playing with you. *I'm sorry!*''

She knew she was wrong, and she knew it had been an accident, but she needed somebody to blame, and right now, he was it.

"I told you I didn't want to swim today." She whined plaintively, like a wronged child.

"Yesterday," he corrected automatically. His stroking of her brow had not ceased.

"What?" He wasn't getting into that yesterday-tomorrow thing again, was he? That was how it had all started. She scowled.

"Today is Saturday, Rhea. It's Saturday night. You were stung a day and a half ago."

She sat upright and twisted round to look at him for the first time. He must be lying! It had to be another one of his jokes. Before she could dispute him, or speak further, she saw his face, and gasped.

A large white bandage covered his nose bridge. For a while, she wondered if he'd been stung, too, in the face. Then she remembered that in her delirium she had hit him—hard.

"God!" Her hand flew to her mouth. "Is it broken?"

He touched his own nose gingerly. "No, just a little banged up. The bandages come off tomorrow. You pack a heck of a punch there, lady."

Rhea felt ashamed of herself. There she was blaming a rare and unpredictable jellyfish sting on him, and she was guilty of busting his nose when he had tried to save her! She hung her head. "I'm so . . . I don't know what to say. 'Sorry' just doesn't seem good enough. Marcus, I . . ." She didn't know what she could do to adequately apologize.

He came round to sit at the edge of the bed and took her hand. "It's okay. You were in a panic. It happens."

She continued to protest. "But I hit you. And your nose, it was so . . ." She was about to say *beautiful,* but stopped. Saying that would mean having to admit she had noticed.

"Well," he said lightly, "if it makes you feel any better, when you're up and around again, you can let me take a swing at *you.*"

The incongruity of Marcus hitting any woman was enough to make her laugh, even though the effort made her chest hurt. He joined in, and in the dark stillness of the room there seemed to be perfect peace between them. She was glad he was with her.

After a few moments of silence, he stood up and began to pull her sheets back.

"What are you doing?" she protested in surprise.

"Don't worry. I'm just going to put a little cortisone cream on your leg. The doctor's instructions were to put it on every four hours." He laid her wounded leg bare. "Lie still," he commanded when she tried to curl forward to take a peek. She ignored him, and kept on looking.

His large gentle hands ran the length of her leg, long sensitive fingers just lightly touching the puckered wounds. Although much of the swelling had gone down, the wounds looked pretty bad.

"You think they will scar?" she asked anxiously. The thought of spending the rest of her life with a series of uneven stripes adorning her leg was unbearable.

Marcus held her foot thoughtfully in both hands, one thumb idly stroking the round bump of her ankle. "The doctor said probably not, if you keep it clean and use the right creams and lotions. The wound is already healing, so your chances seem good." He looked down at the expanse of brown leg and added "it would be a shame to mark such pretty skin."

At his remark, she pulled modestly away. Sensing that he had said too much, Marcus began to apply the cortisone in light but detached strokes, as any nurse or doctor would do. He completed his task and stood up. The naked male admiration was replaced by cool efficiency.

"I'll just help you into the other bed so that I can put dry sheets on this one, and then you can get some sleep."

She glanced across at the second single bed in her room. She didn't like the idea of being helped into it; her independent spirit rebelled against the thought, but in her weakened state, the bed next to her might just as well have been a mile away. Reluctantly, she allowed him to gather her in his arms. *Just because it's necessary,* she reminded herself. *He's only being a Good Samaritan.* But as he wrapped his arms around her and pulled her to his chest, there was a stirring within her that had nothing to do with her present incapacity.

Marcus laid her down carefully, and pulled the sheets up around her with something close to indifference. There was nothing on his face to tell her if he had sensed her quick response to his touch.

Good, she told herself, but the relief was tinged with pique.

She watched as he quickly changed the sheets on the other bed, making crisp hospital corners that surprised her. She shouldn't be surprised by anything he did, she thought. In the short time that she had known him, he had already proven himself to be a quick thinker and a resourceful man.

He straightened up with her damp sheets in his arms. "You try to sleep now," he told her softly. "I'll look in on you in a bit. Get some rest."

"Thank you," she said. She was truly grateful. Something inside her wanted to hold out her arms and beg him not to leave her alone all night. She struggled to silence that something.

He was silhouetted against the light of the corridor. "Good night," he said.

By the time she said "good night" in return, the door had clicked shut.

In the morning, he brought her breakfast, and he was glad to see that she was strong enough to eat it. When he took her tray away, he drew back her sheets once again to tend to her leg. Again, she submitted to his ministrations, holding her lips tightly closed to prevent the sigh that threatened to escape. Then, as she watched his quick hands move along her legs, something struck her as odd.

She looked down at herself, and realised that she was clad only in an oversized T-shirt and a pair of panties. Hadn't she been wearing a swimsuit when she'd been injured? "Marcus?" she began tentatively. "How did I get out of my swimsuit? How did I get into these clothes?"

His hands didn't stop moving. "I helped you into those." He didn't look up.

"You did *what*?" Rhea was scandalised. She pulled her leg away.

Marcus lifted his head to meet her eyes. He had taken his bandages off, and a large purple bruise was clearly visible across his nose. She had to forcefully shove her guilt aside to continue her attack on him. "You undressed me? How could you?"

"Rhea, don't be ridiculous. You were sick. You were in a wet swimsuit. You needed help. What did you expect me to do?"

"Yes, but . . ." She was sputtering, unable to find words to express her embarrassment. A total stranger had seen her naked, no, had undressed her while she was unconscious.

"Besides, Trudy was with me every time. Don't worry, I didn't take advantage of the situation. I was properly chaperoned every time." His attempt at humor told her he still wasn't taking her umbrage seriously.

"So why didn't she do it on her own?" Rhea raged, even though deep down she knew he was making sense. "Why did you have to help her?"

Now Marcus was getting defensive. "You have any idea what you *weigh*? Trudy is not a young woman, and I wasn't letting her handle the situation on her own. Let me tell you, even with the two of us, it wasn't easy. You were thrashing around like . . ."

Something else that he had said hit her. "What do you mean, 'every time'? What do you mean by that?"

He seemed to be trying hard not to lose his patience. "You've been ill for two days. So you've had two baths. Not to mention the half dozen or so trips we made to the bathroom together." He added this last almost maliciously.

Embarrassment hit her hard. "You mean you took me to the bathroom, too?" She wanted to pull the sheets up over her face to hide the fierce blush. *God,* she prayed, *don't let it be true.*

"*We* did." He was obviously angry. "Trudy and I did. It was necessary, so it had to be done. It seems like your boss was barely willing to spring for your medical attention, much less to provide a nurse to look after you, so we stepped into the breach. So if you're suggesting any impropriety . . ." He trailed off, too upset to continue.

He handed her the large tube of cream, thrusting it out to her roughly. "Here, Rhea. If you're well enough to be such a pain in the butt, you're well enough to put this on for yourself." He moved with long, angry strides to the door. "If you need anything more," he threw at her as he stormed out, "you just shout."

Then she was alone with her guilt.

CHAPTER SEVEN

Throughout the day, Trudy came in to serve Rhea her meals and to see about changing the bedsheets. She saw no more of Marcus, and even though the older woman was gentle and cheerful in her mothering, Rhea couldn't shake the terrible guilt that weighed upon her. How could she have behaved that way? All he had wanted to do was help. *Sometimes you make me sick, Ri-ri,* she chastised herself bitterly. She struggled to stay awake until well after midnight, waiting for him to look in on her. He never did.

The next day she was just able to walk. Limping just a little, she made it out to breakfast, to rousing applause from her guests.

"Welcome back," Banner greeted her warmly with a kiss on the cheek. "You had us kind of worried there for a while!"

She was grateful for, if a little embarrassed by, all the attention. Marcus seemed to be putting a good face on it for the sake of everyone else, but the looks that he threw her were carefully guarded. Rhea took her courage in her hands and asked to speak to him in private after breakfast. An apology for her behavior was certainly overdue.

He nodded gravely, and as the dishes were all cleared away, he met her on the sunlit porch.

"I'm sorry," burst from her lips as soon as he came to stand beside her. "For the way I acted yesterday. I was just a little embarrassed, that's all."

Marcus accepted gracefully. "Okay. Don't worry about it."

But Rhea was still anxious. "I mean I'm really, really sorry. I never meant to suggest that you would . . . that your motives . . ." She struggled to continue.

He decided to put her out of her misery. "Don't worry about it. It's forgotten. How are you feeling?"

She sighed. "Okay, I guess. I think I'm well enough to do a tour today."

He held out a restraining hand. "Oh no, you don't. Not for a few days yet. You've been through a traumatic experience. You have to get your rest. You have to give your body time to heal."

She protested. "But I have responsibilities, and these people have been cooped up on the house for days! It isn't fair to them."

Now he was laughing outright. "Come on, Rhea, do you really think they've been cooped up all this time?"

She was puzzled. "What do you mean?"

"They've been out and about. Every day. On tour with Banner."

Rhea was aghast. "What do you mean, out? They can't go out without me. I'm the guide!"

"Don't worry. They did fine. They've been joyriding, they've been sightseeing. I stayed home with you, and Trudy kept Jodelle for me. It was okay."

Somehow, it wasn't nice to know that life had been going on as usual without her. That really stung. "Why? How could they just *leave*?"

"Because, just like you said, it wouldn't have been fair to leave them house-bound. I told Banner that I thought it would be best, and he agreed with me."

"Oh. You *told* Banner it would be best." Her voice was

sarcastic. She forgot that mere minutes ago she was struggling to apologize to this man.

"Yes, I did. You were out of your mind with fever. Someone had to take charge."

"Oh, and that someone *had* to be you, I suppose?"

"It usually is. Why are you behaving like this?" The expression on his face was half angry, half puzzled.

She herself didn't know. Why *was* she behaving like this? She knew he'd been trying to help, and knew that he had made the right decision. But somehow the idea that the reins had been taken from her hands was difficult to handle. She was the one who made the decisions about where they went and when. It was *her* job. She was unable to stop herself from continuing to attack.

"So tell me, Mr. Tour Guide, where did *you* decide they were going today?"

He answered as if her nasty tone passed him right by. "To the Ortoire River. Up the river, in a boat. And *they* aren't going. *We* are. I'm in on this one. Trudy'll stay home and take care of you."

"The river? Why in God's name are you going up the river? We haven't done a tour there in years. It's polluted and it's ugly. It's not the kind of thing you show tourists."

"Well, I want to see it. I'm a journalist, remember? There could be a story there."

"A dirty, polluted river?"

"In my profession, that's the best kind."

"And the others? You think it's okay to just drag them up there behind you?" She stared at him in amazement. He was really insufferably overbearing.

He dismissed her astonishment with a shrug. "It'll be an interesting trip. I told them about it, and they said they wouldn't mind."

"Oh, that's just great. You *told* them. You always *tell* everyone what you want, and you get it, right?"

Marcus got up out of the porch chair and turned angrily toward the short gate that led to the beach. She knew she'd pushed him too far. "You know what your problem is?" he asked in a voice that told her he was struggling mightily to keep his rage in check.

"People who run around telling other people what their problem is?" she shot back.

He accepted her barb grimly. "No. You're a control junkie. *That's* your problem. You're so insecure, and so scared that if you let someone else make a decision, or if you're not always the one in charge, all the time, you'll lose control forever. Look babe, I'll tell you what. I didn't ask for control. I didn't want to have to make any decisions for you. But you were incapacitated and I was trying to help. Sorry if I stepped on your pretty toes. You want to be in charge again? Abracadabra." He waved his hands over her head with a broad, exaggerated gesture, "You're in charge again. Happy?"

She watched as he stalked down the steps and onto the beach. She could tell by his ramrod posture and long strides that she'd really pushed him beyond the limit. He stopped a short way off and turned. Her hopes rose; maybe he was coming back.

"Boy, gratitude sure isn't your strong suit, is it?" he commented, almost resignedly, and then he walked away.

The small group stood on the banks of the river in Mayaro and looked dubiously into the dirty water. The river, once wide and majestic, had dwindled to a sluggish trickle that was the menacing colour of discarded motor oil.

She had insisted on joining them, in spite of their chorus of pleas for her to stay home at least one more day. Her pain was pretty bad, and she had to be helped into and out of the car by Banner, but she wasn't going to let them go without her. Her job was her job, and that was that.

She and Marcus had not exchanged a word, mainly because she was too embarrassed to approach him after their conversation, but also because, although she hated to admit it, he had been right. It was sheer cussedness that forced her to join them. If the decision to go there had been made without her, she felt, the least she could do was take the tour.

Painfully, she allowed Banner to help her into the small open boat that was piloted by a huge muscled boatman. She wouldn't have to move about, at least. All she would have to do was sit there and answer questions.

"All aboard," Banner said cheerfully, helping first Trudy and then Dahlia into the small wooden craft. Then he stretched his arms out and lifted Jodelle into the boat with ease. The girl stood in the middle of the boat with her hands on her hips, refusing to sit where Banner pointed.

"I want to sit with Rhea," she insisted loudly. "Rhea, I'll sit next to you, okay?"

"All right," Rhea said. She'd missed the kid's cheerful presence. Jodelle clambered hurriedly over to where Rhea sat, setting the small boat rocking.

"Now, don't go tipping us over," Marcus admonished, steadying her with a hand on her shoulder.

"Then a crocodile might come around and try to eat me, huh?" Jodelle said cheerily, oblivious to any fear of becoming a crocodile's dinner.

"Yeah," Rhea said teasingly, "and believe me, the crocodiles in this neck of the woods are always on the lookout for a snack."

Jodelle gave an exaggerated shiver, knowing that Rhea was joking. "Daddy, I want you to sit next to me!" she bawled out. Her high voice echoed across the water.

"I thought you wanted to sit with Rhea, honey," her father called back.

She was adamant. "I want to sit next to you *and* Rhea." She pointed at the seat next to her. "Come *here,* Daddy!"

Marcus seemed to hesitate for a moment, then clambered heavily forward, weighed down by his equipment. "Seems you got another seatmate for the rest of the morning, Rhea," he said ironically. "Sorry if we Luciens seem to be crowding you."

"Oh, no problem at all," she answered with automatic hostess politeness that drew a smirk from him. Next to her, Jodelle looked up at each of them in turn and beamed, suddenly less interested in the dark waters than she was in the company on either side of her.

They moved swiftly upriver, away from the muddy delta and the pockmarked shore to a place where the ribbon of brown became dark green glass, reflecting the deep colours of the trees that stretched above them. As soon as they were well away from the coast, the boatman cut the engines, allowing them to drift in precious silence.

The dark green mangroves loomed overhead. Their trunks, unlike most others in the plant kingdom, did not consist of a single column but of many, each as thick as a forearm, which twisted their way downward from the parent tree into the earth. The plants grew close together, and each plant's peculiar downward-growing stumps co-mingled with the others, forming a dense wall along either side of the river.

Too intimidated by the quiet majesty of the river to speak in tones any louder than a whisper, Rhea explained to the others that the mangrove was essential to the survival of the river, and all the creatures in it. It acted as a buttress for the riverbanks, its strong tangle of stumps preventing the erosion from which many coastlines suffered. In addition, she went on, it was home to an amazing range of creatures.

They peered eagerly over the sides to get a closer look. Crabs swarmed along the branches of the trees to the water's edge and back, like busy women at the marketplace. Many of the crabs were a humble brown, some dark gray with pale speckles that allowed them, when motionless, to pass for just another bump on the branch.

Closer to the water's edge, larger, deep-blue crabs could be seen. These darted at a startling speed out of their large round holes in the muddy banks, looking fierce as their milky blue eyes waved around on the ends of short stalks. Those, Rhea whispered, were the famous blue crab, one of the most delicious local dishes available. She promised solemnly that they would be sampling some of them before they left.

The crabs, Rhea explained in embarrassed tones, were just about all that was left alive in the river, as the fish population was now being seriously threatened by pollution, and the manatees, which once populated the depths were being forced to seek cleaner waters farther afield, often as far as South America.

Marcus busied himself with his more professional camera, and made detailed notes on a thick pad in his broad, sprawling handwriting. Rhea eyed him warily, wondering just what he could possibly be writing. She guessed that with his journalist's instinct, he was carefully cataloguing every detail, right down to the filthy water and the dying aquatic life. After all, that was what he'd brought them here for, wasn't it?

A burning resentment rose within her. Just who did he take himself for, coming to sit in judgment on them, carrying all their dirty laundry back with him to the North so that he could wash it in public? What would the repercussions be once the level of pollution in the rivers became known within the tourism industry abroad? Damn him, taking advantage of her weakened state to go muckraking, just so that he could get a better story.

She shot him a dark glance that was filled with unveiled hostility. He looked up suddenly, with a spontaneous smile that froze when it encountered her resentful glare. He paused for a moment, sure that he could not possibly be the target of such a venomous look. When the realisation sank in, the smile died on his face, and he bent his dark head abruptly, concentrating once again on the task at hand. Flustered, embarrassed at having been caught offguard, Rhea looked away.

It seemed that a quick tour of the coconut plantations was also on Marcus' jury-rigged itinerary. Mulishly, Rhea refused to allow them to drop her off at the beach house and go on without her. She knew she had to keep a sharp eye on the man, or next thing she knew she'd be relegated to the sickroom while he gallivanted about doing as he pleased, with the others in tow. She should have known that a reporter couldn't be trusted once he was on the scent of a story!

They did not have far to drive, as the entire Mayaro coastal region used to be dedicated almost exclusively to the cultivation of coconuts. The estates had once thrived, as the dried flesh provided oil for lamps and for cooking, the rough brown husk was a filler for mattresses and could be woven into articles such as rope and floor mats. Even the dried branches of the trees were useful for brooms and brushes.

But the advent of plastic had been the death knell to the industry. Man-made fibers caused coconut ropes and mattresses to become almost extinct, and greater health consciousness caused the coconut oil industry to suffer as well.

The group surveyed the sad-looking estate, shaking their heads. Huge piles of rotting coconuts cluttered the hard-packed earth, never to be used. Many of the trees were marked with a white or orange X.

"Those Xs," Rhea explained grudgingly, wishing they had never come, "mark trees that are suffering from a contagious disease called Witch Broom. It means that they're slated for destruction."

"A lot of this paint is old, Rhea. These marks are flaking off the trees. Shouldn't they have been destroyed right away?" Marcus had his dreaded notebook open, and his pen hovered hungrily over it, waiting to consume the information.

"Well, unfortunately, a lot of frustrated owners have abandoned their estates, so the infected trees are just allowed to stand where they are."

"Passing the disease on across property lines?"

"Well," she admitted miserably, "yes."

The group left for home, a little subdued. "It's such a shame," Marcus said softly in her ear as he fell into step next to her. Jodelle tagged along between them, oblivious to their conversation, but overtly happy at simply being close to them both.

Rhea nodded, unable to deny it. She cast a sidelong look at his journalist's paraphernalia, aching with curiosity to know what he had been scribbling all day, and even more anxious to find out just how damning the final article would be.

Sharp-eyed, he saw the look. He slid his hand around her upper arm, gently pulling her aside as the others took their places in the van.

Jodelle moved to follow them, but Marcus held up a restraining hand. "You stay there for a second, honey," he instructed softly.

She stared at him in puzzlement. "Why? I want to come with you!"

"I'm not going anywhere. I'm right here. I just want to talk with Rhea for a second. Okay, dumpling?"

The girl pouted, but didn't move. She stood watching them, arms folded across her chest, as Marcus drew Rhea into the shade of a clump of trees. Unwilling to make a display of herself by snatching her arm away, Rhea was obliged to listen solemnly to what he had to say.

"I'm not here to condemn or to destroy, Rhea," he told her softly. "I'm just looking for information. I'm not seeking to make your country look bad. Maybe what I write can even help a little. Maybe if I create an awareness . . ."

This was too much. Who did he think he was, the caped crusader with a mission to save the planet? "But we don't need your help," she blurted hotly. "We're doing fine!"

One wave of his arm encompassed all the diseased plant life around them. "You call this fine?"

As surreptitiously as she could, she twisted her arm out of his grasp. "All I'm saying is that your article might discourage tourists from coming here. That's all. You go spouting off about pollution and dead coconut trees and who will want to come?"

"It's the truth," he said patiently.

"Tourism isn't always about truth," she hissed. "Sometimes, it's about fantasy. You don't go on vacation looking for reality. You go to leave reality behind, suspend disbelief. You come for beautiful beaches, sunshine, sand. That's all. You don't want to be reminded about anything dying." It was an effort to keep her voice low. "Marcus," she went on, squaring her shoulders in determination. "I'm asking you not to put any of this into your article."

His thick eyebrows flew up to his hairline. He stared at her, unsure that he'd heard right. "What?" he asked.

Rhea didn't seem to have heard the note of warning in his voice. She went on resolutely. "No, I'm telling you. I'm *telling* you not to put any of that stuff into your article. Nothing about the dirty river, nothing about the manatees."

He met her demand with a harsh, barking laugh. "Have you been hitting those painkillers a little too hard? You're *telling* me?" He was incredulous.

She nodded resolutely.

"On who's authority?" He looked as if he wasn't sure whether to be amused or outraged. "Has the concept of a free press trickled this far south, or is your country still living in the dark ages?"

"On *my* authority," she snapped, a little too loudly. "And on the authority of all the people you might be putting out of work, once your . . . your *rag* hits the stands!" She knew that she was stepping onto dangerous ground, but she was driven by some internal fire that she couldn't quite name.

Marcus took a step toward her and bent lower, so that he could speak slowly and softly into her face. "My rag," he began, "the rag that has already paid for my story, has been in circulation longer than you've been alive. This . . . *rag* . . ." he drew a furious breath, "is one of my major sources of income. It has an international reputation for truthful and unbiased reporting. As have I." The nostrils of his bruised nose flared with anger. Rhea knew that she had gone too far. She could feel the blast of his rage, and, with sudden fear, stepped back.

They eyed each other hotly for a long time until, with great effort, Marcus seemed to have regained control of his temper. "Rhea," he said softly. His hand reached up halfway to her shoulder in a placatory gesture, but he stopped as he seemed to think better of it, and his hand dropped to his side. "Your island *is* beautiful. The beach is beautiful, the water's gorgeous, and the food has been lovely. There's no reason why my article would make anyone not want to visit here. It's a glorious island. But the apple has a worm and it's my responsibility to ensure that I report it as I see it. It's for the greater good, believe me." He bent even closer. "Will you trust me on that?"

His luminous eyes hemmed her in; she couldn't tear her own away. She felt an uncomfortable flush come over her body. Her behavior embarrassed her, but obstinately, she refused to respond. She didn't trust him an inch. But, eventually, as he seemed to be growing impatient, demanding a response, she nodded grudgingly.

"Good," he said, satisfied, patting her almost paternally on the shoulder. By this time the others were peering curiously out of the windows at them, wondering what could possibly be taking them so long. The many pairs of eyes on them, and Rhea thought with an inward groan about one pair of ice-blue eyes in particular, caused her to pull away from Marcus a little too sharply.

Jodelle, who had been watching the interchange intently from the sidelines, tilted her small face up toward Marcus' as they approached. "Daddy?" she questioned, "are you and Rhea mad at each other?" Her face was about to crumple.

Rhea felt sharp pain at causing the child any hurt.

Marcus bent forward and pressed his lips lightly against his daughter's forehead. "Of course not, honey. Everything's okay." The girl did not look convinced.

Rhea decided to intervene and bring this uncomfortable scenario to an end. "I think it's time we got going," she said briskly in the hostess voice she was so good at. He nodded wordlessly, and they followed her in.

That evening, as her guests sprawled out on the wide porch, digesting the huge dinner that Banner had prepared, Rhea slipped out onto the still-warm sand with her cellular phone. She slipped into the shadows of the palms and dialed Brent's number. The phone rang and rang and rang. There was no answer. She shut the phone with a decisive click and slipped it into her pocket. Maybe he'd grown tired of her broken promises to call, and had gone out for a while. Not that she blamed him. She hadn't been all that attentive to him lately. For some reason, he wasn't on her mind as much as he usually was.

But even during the time that she was sick, he hadn't called. Banner had been certain about that. The older man explained that he'd called Brent immediately after the accident with the jellyfish, and that his only response had been an exasperated "Trust Rhea to do something like that." As if she had deliberately gone looking for trouble! Sometimes, she just couldn't understand him. He veered between an almost overbearing craving for attention and something that was almost indifference.

She sighed and folded her arms around herself as she paced back and forth between the front porch and the thick seawall. Being up and about was doing her wounded leg a world of good, she thought. What she needed was exercise, not rest. Besides, it was better than being cooped up in her room, alone with her thoughts.

The night was quiet, with no sounds other than the gentle breathing of the sea and the sharp cries of the owls that circled watchfully overhead. Rhea should have been soothed by the mildness of the evening, but instead she felt only a gnawing disquiet, the source of which she was only partially able to identify.

Her behaviour toward Marcus had really been unforgivable. He had been right, he was only trying to help while she was ill. But even in his kindness, he drew her fire. Why?

Then there was Jodelle. The little girl was bright and pretty and full of fun. And Lord knew, Jodelle really loved her. That, Rhea mused, was part of the problem. In her innocent adoration of Rhea, she seemed bent on keeping her close by as much as she could. This, Rhea didn't exactly mind. She loved having the opportunity to show new things to such a bright young mind.

Unfortunately, Jodelle wasn't prepared to sacrifice time with her father, either, and thus seemed bent on ensuring that they *both* were within her view at all times. Rhea groaned miserably. It was hard enough having to tolerate his proximity as it was (especially knowing of the intimate tasks he had performed for her during the past two days) without having to suffer under the tender mercies of a six-year-old dictator.

As far as Rhea could see, there was little that could be done without hurting such a sweet little thing. This was a little girl, she reminded herself, who evidently didn't have a mother, and who obviously craved female attention. Unfortunately, she thought wryly, the father didn't seem averse to some female attention himself. . . .

Or was she imagining it? Could it be that she was laying the blame for her own attraction (okay, she admitted that she was attracted) at his feet? In spite of the obvious pleasure he had derived from their dance those few nights ago, he seemed almost oblivious to her charms. More interested in that damn article than anything else, it seemed to her.

As she approached the house for the umpteenth time during her restless pacing, her eyes were drawn upward. Silhouetted against the far window, Marcus sat at a small table, banging on his laptop. His head was bent close to his work in concentration, the back of his neck curved. The light drapes in the window undulated in the mild breeze. She was sure that he would look up, look out of the window and see her staring at him, so intense was her gaze, but he seemed swallowed up in the world of his own words. Rhea tore her glance away from the window and continued pacing. When she was tired, she went in.

CHAPTER EIGHT

After a day of taking it easy, Rhea was well enough to tackle a long trip across the island. They left for the jaunt right on schedule, and Rhea was pleased at that. The Devil's Woodyard was more than an hour away, she explained as they pulled onto the road.

"Hmm. Devil's Woodyard?" Ever interested in the unusual, Trudy's curiosity was piqued.

"It's an area full of volcanoes. . . ." Rhea began, before the older woman interrupted her with widened eyes.

"Real ones? With lava and all?"

Rhea hastened to reassure her. "Oh, no," she couldn't hold back a laugh, "Trinidad doesn't have any of those. I'm afraid if you were looking for a Vesuvius type adventure, you'd have to look to one of the other islands. All we have to offer you," she said mock contrition, "are mud volcanoes. Nothing dangerous, I assure you. Interesting to look at, though."

Before she could continue, she became aware that her phone was ringing. She pulled it out discreetly and put it to her ear.

"Rhea?" The soft voice belonged to Brent. She was relieved to hear him, as she'd tried without success to get him until quite late the night before. "Brent?" she whispered.

"You haven't called. . . ." he began.

Rhea was amazed. She was the one who was sick. *He* should have called *her*! "You heard I was sick. Why didn't you . . ."

"Oh, sure, Banner told me, but it was just a little sting," Brent said dismissively. "It wasn't so bad, was it?" He spoke as if he was trying to patronize a small complaining child. Rhea thought of the days of agony, delirium, and dependency, and said nothing.

When she realised that he was not going to speak, she continued her hushed conversation. "I thought about you a lot, though," she said honestly. Last night, in her confusion, she'd really missed him, out there on the lonely, dark beach. And she wished he could show a little more concern about her accident!

But it was the wrong time to tell him—not here, not in front of so many people. She sighed. "I think I must be going," she told him in a crisp voice, still struggling to keep up the charade of this being a business call. She could feel Marcus' eyes on her, and knew that he could sense her discomfort. This embarrassed her even more.

"Why? Can't you talk to me? Don't you know how much I miss you?" He was beginning to sound agitated, not wanting her to hang up just yet. "Rhea? Is everything all right?"

She tensed. "What do you mean?"

"I don't know. I just feel . . . something. You just seem a little distracted."

Distracted? There she was with enough jellyfish venom to stun a mule coursing through her system, burning with the knowledge that one of her own guests seemed more concerned for her well-being than her own boyfriend, and he thought she seemed distracted? Rhea didn't trust herself to answer that.

Hating herself, she began wildly to improvise. "Brent, this is a bad time to talk. Besides, the cell phone keeps fading in and out when we turn the corners."

"Tell Banner to stop the van and let you talk."

Rhea couldn't believe what she was hearing. He was actually expecting her to stop the van full of paying clients to indulge in a private phone call! "I can't make him do that!" she said, unable to hide the shock in her voice.

Now his tone became agitated. "You're the one in charge. He has to listen to what you say, doesn't he?"

She nodded, even though he couldn't see her. "Yes, but I can't make him do that. I'm working. We're *both* working. We've got a *job* to do." Her frustration was becoming too much for her. Sometimes, Brent just didn't seem to understand. "I'll talk with you later, okay?"

"Rhea . . ."

"I can't hear you so well," she lied. "I'll call you later."

"Okay," he gave in at last. "Tonight, Rhea."

"Thank you for calling," she said loudly and clearly. She hung up.

They stood on the slight rise that overlooked the Devil's Woodyard, an expanse of gray claylike mud that at first glance looked like nothing in particular.

"I thought it was supposed to be a *volcano*!" Jodelle exclaimed. She was unable to hide the disappointment in her voice.

Rhea couldn't help but smile. "It isn't a hot fiery volcano, sweetie. It's just a little muddy one. But the good thing is, you get to walk right up to the edge and look in, and you don't have to be scared."

"It don't blow up with smoke and stuff?" She looked disappointed.

"Weeell . . . you might hear a little plop, but no explosions, kiddo." Rhea led them along a path toward the huge expanse of soft clay. It was an ugly pit that looked like a lake on the moon's surface, one of several that dotted the landscape. Upon her urging, and with the assurance that they would be perfectly safe, they moved gingerly toward it. The smell of sulfur was heavy in the air. The mouth of the mud geyser was about a foot across, and as they watched, the peculiar land formation spat mud a few inches into the air, splashing the clothing of the curious.

Jodelle squealed. Nature's little display was making up for her disappointment.

"All these little volcanoes are constantly churning up cold mud," Rhea explained to the others. "They're harmless, but interesting to watch. The mud is pretty good for your skin, if you dare smear it on." She said this last with a mischievous smile. Nobody dared.

The group began to dissipate as the couples wandered off around the site to find their own little volcano to look into. Banner returned to the van, where he sat behind the wheel, drumming his fingers on the dashboard.

Rhea remained atop the huge mud pile with Jodelle and Marcus, watching the girl's face as she amused herself by making a game of sneaking up on the mouth of a crater, timing the frequent spurts, and darting excitedly out of their way. The delight that Rhea herself felt in watching the little girl took her by surprise. It was, in part, simply pleasure at watching someone so young and full of energy enjoy herself, but there was something else, a kind of protectiveness and pride that was almost . . . motherly.

Rhea snapped sharply to attention as the thought entered her mind. There she was, doing it again. She was getting far too attached to this child; she knew this. As a professional, she knew the difficulties that it might pose once the time came for Jodelle and her father to leave the island. Still, that ray of light that had shot out of the girl and into Rhea's soul that first night, the moment she let her hold the moth, still remained with her. There was a caring here, an emotion, which was growing. She gave herself a hard shake. She'd have to watch that.

When she dragged her mind back to the present, she became aware that Marcus had joined his daughter in her little game of volcano baiting, and the two of them were capering about around the lip of the crater, daring it to spit up on them. With the wild laughter filling the air, they looked both like little kids. Marcus' tight blue jeans were as spotted as his daughter's, and his face was split with a boyish grin that made Rhea's chest contract. There she was, worrying about what she would feel when the child was due to go back, but suddenly she had a

suspicion that bordered on a premonition that the departure of
the father, the man, would be just as hard.

It was stupid. She and her premonitions. She knew better
than to rely on the whims of her undisciplined inner mind.
This man was intriguing, yes. Sexy? Definitely! But she was
a professional, a woman with a perfectly good boyfriend waiting
for her when she got back to the city. Why would she possibly
dread Marcus' leaving? Especially since he seemed to get on
her nerves all the time!

His deep-throated laugh drew her eyes to his handsome face
once again. In spite of the irritation that she felt at her unwel-
come thoughts, she indulged in the simple pleasure of looking
at him.

Her pleasure was cut short by a noise that came from a spot
a short distance away from where they stood. She spun round
to face the source of the sound. Jodelle and Marcus, out of
breath from their games, stopped short in alarm.

Dahlia and Rainer standing at the edge of the mud field,
close together, having a heated argument. Dahlia was shrieking
words they could just hear. "Just try, Rainer. Just *try*! Why is
it that every time we go somewhere you start . . ." Then her
words were lost in the wind. They watched as Dahlia began
stomping her foot into the soft earth, pounding on Rainer's
chest in obvious anger.

Jodelle stared, black eyes wide and round, little mouth falling
open. Then, to Rhea's surprise, her face began to contort with
what she quickly recognised as the onset of tears. "They're
. . . they're fighting! They're *arguing*!"

Rhea was perplexed. Why would a little spat between a
couple she didn't even know upset the child so?

Marcus seemed to have no such problems understanding. He
was on his knees at her side in an instant, ignoring Rhea's
proffered handkerchief and pulling out a large one of his
own. He swabbed gently at his daughter's face. "It's nothing,
honey. It's just a little quarrel. We don't even know what it's
about." He looked around distractedly. The fighting couple
had moved farther along the perimeter of the field, and could

now still be seen, but not heard. "Don't worry about it, okay? It's noth . . ."

She interrupted with a bewildered wail. "But they're *married*! They're married and they're fighting and it's not nice!"

Realisation hit Rhea like a cold wave. That was it! The girl didn't like seeing the married couple quarrel because it reminded her of her own parents' broken marriage. Pity intermingled with open curiosity. A thousand questions rose in her mind about Marcus' marriage. So strange, this man, so bright and attractive, such a good catch for any woman, yet who was divorced, toting around a young daughter who, because she obviously bore no resemblance to her father, most likely was to him a constant reminder of his wife. And, as if a living, breathing reminder wasn't enough, a broad gold band still flashed on his ring finger, as if he hadn't the courage, or the conviction, to remove it.

She wondered about the girl, and how many arguments she must have heard in her young life, and had no doubt that the sight of the two guests shouting loudly at each other on the other side of the field would bring back memories too painful for one so young to bear.

Moved by compassion, she dropped to her knees beside Marcus and drew Jodelle toward her. "Jodie, sweetie," unconsciously, she used Marcus' own pet name for the child. "It's okay. Sometimes people argue. It doesn't mean anything. They'll be alright in a minute. You'll see."

Marcus shook his head up and down vigorously in support of Rhea's claim. "Yeah, baby. Sometimes . . . sometimes married people argue and it doesn't mean anything bad." His voice caught in his throat. The scene had obviously brought back memories that were unpleasant for him, too. Rhea had to fight the urge to put her arms around him as well.

After a while, the whimpering stopped. Jodelle seemed content to snuggle within the circle made by two pairs of arms, and soon she was smiling again, in spite of the drying, telltale streaks that ran down her cheeks. With surprising good spirits, she prized herself free and plodded down the side of the hump, obviously enjoying the loud squelching sounds of her sneakered feet as she pulled them out of the clinging mud. "I'm goin' explorin' " she advised her father, as if nothing untoward had happened.

"Don't go far, Jodie," Marcus called after. His face held relief, tinged with a little concern.

Jodelle answered without turning around. "No, Daddy!" She began stomping heavily around at the base of the volcano, sending more splashes of gray up around her ankles and onto her dark blue jeans.

"She'll be okay," Rhea assured him. "She can't get into too much mischief out there. It's pretty safe for a kid."

Marcus watched Jodelle indulgently for a while, then turned once again to Rhea. "Thanks," he said in a voice thick with emotion. They both rose off their haunches and faced each other.

She waved away his gratitude. "Okay. No problem."

He held out a hand to stop her from going on. "No, really. I mean it. I'm grateful."

Still uncomfortable, she said nothing. He was too close for her liking, she realised. Since moving away abruptly would have been too obvious, she peered into the mouth of the volcano as if she had never seen it before, rather than look up at him or be forced to continue the conversation.

Marcus, too, seemed to struggle for something to say. After a while, he spoke. "Have you had any serious eruptions?"

Always the reporter, Rhea thought. She was filled with contempt; how predictable. No matter what the situation, the wheel of their conversations spun around and the needle always pointed to his work. They were a self-indulgent lot, these writers. She supposed he was hoping for a nice juicy story about whole villages being buried under tidal waves of mud. That would have been good for his royalties, she was willing to bet. She was glad to disappoint him.

She shook her head vigorously. "It depends on what you call serious. We've had a few houses swamped by mud in the past, but they're hardly *dangerous*." She tried to keep the contempt out of her voice.

He smiled ruefully, obviously picking up on her hostility. "Are you always this defensive?"

She didn't look at him. "What do you mean by that?"

"I mean you just don't give an inch. You've got defenses built so high, it's a wonder you can even see over them."

An exasperated snort escaped her. "Oh, for goodness' sake! What would I have to be defensive about?" Really, he could be ridiculous. Talk about an ego!

His eyes were fixed on her lips, so much so that she licked them nervously. "I don't know. You tell me. What *are* you defensive about?" His head moved closer to hers than was absolutely necessary, considering that there was nobody near enough to warrant the whisper in which he spoke. "I just can't understand how someone who was as soft and kittenish in my arms on that dance floor could be so brittle and prickly when she wants to. You really are a . . ."

"I don't want to know what you think I am, Marcus," she began huffily. "In fact, I think it's just . . . improper for you to be speaking to me like that. It was just a dance. I really can't see why you have to dredge it up out of . . ."

"Can't you?"

"No!"

"You mean . . ." he was smiling now, but it wasn't a very pleasant smile. It was the smile a wolf gave a cornered rabbit. "You've forgotten?" He leaned forward, closing in on her like a predator, and in a panic she realised that he would kiss her if she didn't do anything about it. Here, she panicked, in an open field, in front of all the other guests! It was insane but it was about to happen, and there wasn't anything she could do about it. Her mouth opened, partly in protest, partly in crazy anticipation.

Before their lips could touch, there was a piercing shriek. Rhea's heart leaped into her throat. Several yards away, a small figure flailed about in one of the mud pits, arms waving frantically, panicked face a smear of mud.

"Jodelle!" Rhea's scream was torn from her throat. Before her stunned body could react, Marcus was running headlong across the mound on which they stood, skidding in the slippery

clay, sending splashes of water up around his crashing feet. He
was shouting Jodelle's name, and in his voice was a terror that
clutched at Rhea's throat.

The others ran in from wherever they had wandered, Fred
and Trudy from the far end, Banner throwing wide the van
door and closing the distance with remarkable speed, even
Rainer and Dahlia, forgetting their argument. All were gathered
around the pit by the time Rhea gathered her fear-scattered
thoughts enough to dash forward.

Marcus had thrown himself down on his front, into the wide
pool of mud. He was unable to find purchase in the slippery
mess, and flopped around like a beached fish. In an effort to
hold him steady, Banner caught him in his strong grip, bald
head shining with the effort, teeth gritted with concentration.

Up to her shoulders in mud, churning with terror, Jodelle
threw her head back, eyes wide open, and out of her mouth
came one unending wail: *"Daaaaddddyyyy!"*

"I've got you!" Marcus shouted in response, but the girl,
in her distress, was bucking and throwing her arms up, and he
was having a devil of a time grasping her slippery arms.

In control of herself once again, Rhea dropped to the ground
beside Marcus, stretching out toward the girl, urging her to
stay still. But her efforts were unnecessary, as with one desperate lunge, he had Jodelle, and was drawing her to him, out of
the sucking mouth of the earth, which obstinately resisted giving
her up, and which succumbed only to Marcus' stronger will.

"Got you, Jodie," he gasped, and held her high in his arms,
trying in vain to wipe the mud from her face and mouth with
his own muddy hand.

"Let me take her, Marcus," Trudy stepped in and took the
child from him. Exhausted, Jodelle made no protest. With the
ease of a woman who had worked with children for years,
Trudy deftly stripped off the cold sticky clothes and proceeded
to clean Jodelle's face with a large flowered bandanna and
bottled spring water from her cavernous purse.

Marcus knelt at the edge of the mud pit, chest heaving. His
own raw emotion defied his efforts to catch his breath. Rhea
put a hand on his shoulder. He grasped it by the wrist and

tossed it roughly aside. Uncomprehending, she stared at him, brown eyes wide with hurt.

"Don't touch me, Rhea," he snarled.

Her belly grew cold. "Why?"

His harsh laugh was a surprising sound compared to the happy sound of a mere few minutes ago. "Why? Wasn't it you who just told me that this . . . this wasteland was a safe place for a child to play? Isn't it what we pay you for, ensuring that we're safe? You could have killed my daughter! Where's the professionalism you so pride yourself on?"

All those who were within earshot averted their eyes in embarrassment. Rhea was mortified. He was right. She had failed in her duty as a guide. How could she have done that? She wet her lips and tried to explain. "Marcus . . ." her first attempt was stillborn. She tried again. "Marcus, I didn't know. I truly . . ."

"Didn't know what?" he snarled. "What didn't you know? That this mud hole had cracks in it big enough for a child to fall into?"

She nodded emphatically. "Yes! Yes, exactly. I had no idea . . . I've been here dozens of times, and the ground has always been perfectly safe to walk on. The flatland has never been more than a few inches deep. I've never seen anything like this . . ."

His furious, stony face told her that he wasn't convinced. She threw her hands up in frustration. Tears of shame, and the aftermath of such blind panic, stung her eyes. "I'm sorry," she said meekly.

"Sorry's not good enough, lady." He stood to his feet and stalked off.

She had to wait a few minutes to regain her composure. When she thought she could face the rest of the guests, she walked slowly to the van. They parted to allow her through to the open door. She peeped in at Jodelle, who was lying on the front seat, limbs streaked with gray, bony chest still heaving from the ordeal. Her father knelt in the aisle next to her, stroking her mud-encrusted braids. He didn't look up.

Rhea hesitated, wondering if she dared speak to the child.

Again, her shame assailed her. Though Rhea had stopped short, Jodelle seemed to sense her presence, and lifted her head to peer out the door at her. "Rhea!" she said with undisguised pleasure. "Can you hold my hand?" She held a skinny hand out before her.

Rhea stole a darting look at Marcus. The girl, thank God, was happy to see her. She supposed she was too young to try to ascribe blame to anyone for the accident. But Marcus! Oh, Marcus was an entirely different story. Rhea decided that she would rather walk past a hungry lion than squeeze past Marcus to get to his daughter. She threw him a nervous look and racked her brains for an excuse for not complying with the little girl's request.

"Jodie . . ." she began, and stopped. That pet name was Marcus' privilege, not hers. "Jodelle . . . darling . . ."

Her attempt was not necessary. With a contemptuous snort, Marcus squeezed himself into the seat behind her, and sat there, watching her with cold, unbending anger as Rhea sat next to Jodelle and allowed her to lay her head on her lap.

Subdued, they moved off. Jodelle couldn't ride all the way home in that condition, Banner insisted, so in the village they picked a house at random and explained their position to the smiling, heavyset elderly woman who came to the gate. Full of concern, and amid much clucking and fluttering, she let Rhea and Marcus into her simple wooden house, where they were able to bathe away the mud from Jodelle's skin. Throughout the entire procedure, Marcus addressed Rhea only when necessary, and with the most clipped of syllables.

The woman even lent them a blanket, which Rhea promised faithfully to return on her next tour south. The kindly samaritan waved away Rhea's protestations and saw them to the gate, even stopping to present the others in the van with a brown paper bag filled with ripe mangoes from her yard.

On the way home, the entire group was quiet.

"I think we'll turn in early," Fred said, as he and his wife rose to their feet. It was barely nine, and instead of lounging

out on the porch after dinner as would be expected on such a
pleasant, warm night, everyone seemed restless, their spirits
dampened by the scene that had played out earlier.

Jodie was none the worse for wear, and even seemed to
enjoy the concerned ministrations of the grown-ups. By late
evening, the little devil had been milking it for all she was
worth, accepting gifts of candy bars from Fred, and letting
Trudy read to her from the big book of stories that she'd brought
along on the trip. She'd fallen asleep just after dinner, exhausted
from the excitement and the thrill of being the center of attention. That took care of the daughter, as far as Rhea was concerned. She knew very well that it was the father that she would
have to be worried about.

Marcus brooded throughout the meal, eating with his long
arms wrapped around his plate and his head bowed, like a
defensive dog who wouldn't let anyone near his dinner. Rhea
couldn't watch him. She couldn't bear to look into those elo-
quent eyes of his and see the contempt written there. Even the
others sensed the tension between them, and treaded lightly.

She felt ashamed, utterly incompetent. Marcus had been
right. They were paying her to look after their interests, and
she had failed. Failed because for a brief moment she'd been
too befuddled by the disturbing proximity of this man, out there
on the top of one of the volcanoes, to attend to the youngest
of her charges.

A nasty voice whispered in her ear that maybe she wasn't
as good at her job as she'd always thought. Maybe she should
get a grip, or pack this career in before someone got really
hurt. She couldn't remember when last she'd felt so low.

When the dinner dishes were finally cleared away, Rhea was
relieved. She rose painfully to her feet, with her dinner sitting
heavy in the center of her chest, and dropped into one of
the heavily padded armchairs like a weighty bundle of rags.
Listlessly, she leafed through a magazine that, typically, had
little more to offer than makeup tips she'd read a thousand
times before. At any other time, this would have irritated her.
Tonight, she could barely read the print.

She got up restlessly, walked through the wide glass doors,

and stood barefoot on the sand just outside the porch. The water stretched out beyond the seawall, looking dark and inviting. Oh, if only she could head for that dark mysterious water, keep on walking until it was up past her breasts, letting it lap up around her and wash all this heart-weariness away! A sigh forced itself up out of the depths of her spirit. It was a fragile sound, like something breaking.

"Rhea?" The deep voice behind her made her spin round. Marcus was standing in the shadows at the side of the house.

Her eyes grew wide with fear, and something else . . . delight that he was speaking to her again? Then reason stretched a hand up from within her and dragged her spirits down back to where they belonged: on the ground. This man blamed her for endangering his daughter's life. If he was indeed addressing her, he was probably just setting her up for the kill.

She began to discreetly back away. He held up a hand to stop her. "Don't go. . . ." he began.

In her fear, she kept inching backward until she encountered the glass door behind her. "I . . . don't want to disturb you." She searched for an excuse. "It's time to turn in. It's late." *It's not late*, her logic said nastily, *it's another two hours until your bedtime*. Her own cowardice embarrassed her.

Marcus' hand was still suspended in midair. "Rhea," he took a deep breath and let his hand fall to his side. He looked pained. "I need to talk to you."

Stop him right there, she decided. She shook her head. "You don't need to say anything, Marcus. I'm sorry. I'm dreadfully, terribly sorry. I was wrong."

"No, Rhea. *I* was wrong. To blow up at you like that, I mean. It was a simple mistake. The ground looked solid to me, too, and I know how these land formations are. One month they're there, hidden beneath the surface, the other, they're gone. I understand that. And Lord knows, I should have been watching her. It was *my* responsibility."

Rhea was sure she'd stopped breathing. She inhaled sharply and let the air back out through her mouth in a rush, just to remind her body of its job. He couldn't be apologizing to her! It was unbelievable. Not after the looks of black resentment that he'd been throwing at her all evening! She struggled for something to say. Even insisting that she was wrong seemed a more comfortable option than enduring the look of pain that had taken over his face right now.

"Really, Marcus, you were right. I should have been watching her. It was my job."

He went on as if she hadn't spoken. "I was out of line to challenge your professionalism. You've proven yourself to us many times over, so far, with your knowledge of the area and your love for the island. It's just that," he drew a deep breath, "I was out of my mind with fear. I love her so much. The idea of losing her just . . . threw me."

Her resistance weakened by the sincerity of his words, she stepped forward again. "Of course you love her, she's your daughter. How could you not?"

His golden eyes were deep pools in the shadows in which he stood. He seemed to hesitate, then went on as if he hadn't heard her. "Lord knows, I'd let myself be distracted just at that moment. . . ." His eyes dropped to her mouth and the ripple of pleasure that she'd felt out in the field sped through her again, cutting a deeper track this time. He'd been thinking of kissing her, she remembered. That's when their minds had become focused only on themselves, as if only they existed. That's when the accident had happened.

It was dizzying, the realisation that she was so enthralled by his personal magic that she had been willing to let him kiss her, no, correction, she was willing to kiss *him* in a public place, at the risk of her own reputation. What kind of madness was this?

To her chagrin, Marcus diverted his attention to the sea, his mind seemed to be out there on the dark horizon, with the oil rigs. She took advantage of the opportunity to take a good look at him. He had changed from the clothes that he had muddied, and was now wearing an ancient pair of Levi's that was worn white in some places from contact with his body. In deference to the warmth of the evening, he wore a thin white cotton vest that left large areas of his chest intriguingly (dangerously!) bare. Rhea let her eyes flicker over him (just for a second, she assured herself). For such an irritating, stubborn man, he looked pretty good. Like her, he was barefoot, savoring the spirit-soothing feel of warm sand in the nighttime.

She tried to stifle her pique at his seemingly short attention span where she was concerned, and sought to make small talk.

He beat her to it. "Funny how the sand keeps its warmth this late at night."

She nodded, glad for an innocuous topic of conversation. "When you have a really hot day, like today, the sand stays nice and warm until about midnight. Even the water's warm."

He surveyed her with an inscrutable smile. "Is it?"

He was smiling again! After the scowls and glares that she'd endured all day, it was like the silver night clouds scudding out from in front of the full moon. She couldn't help but smile back. "Yes. As long as it isn't overcast or windy." The weight that had settled somewhere within her chest grew several pounds lighter.

"How about a swim, then?" He moved slightly closer. Instinctively, she flinched. She hoped he hadn't noticed her self-protective movement. One quick look at his face told her that he did; he was smiling like a serpent. What a strange man this was, a man of so many moods!

She searched her head wildly for a good reason not to go swimming with him. She didn't exactly relish he idea of getting into the water with this disturbing man. "Well, I don't know if it would be such a good idea. The tide's high right now."

He quirked an eyebrow. "So? We'll just stay closer to the shore. You've done it before, haven't you?"

She acknowledged this. "Yes, but ... "

He waited, amused. "But ... ? Do the sharks come out at night?"

She shook her head.

"Sea monsters?" He'd moved even closer, and was grinning at her.

To her chagrin, Rhea found herself grinning back. He really could be charming when he chose to be. "I haven't seen a sea monster around recently," she confessed. "Especially not at night."

"They're probably asleep," he suggested.

She nodded, smiling broadly. "Probably."

"So there isn't much of a risk, then. I think we'd be pretty safe."

"I think we would," she admitted.

"Do you think you're well enough? Are you tired or in pain?"

Her curls bounced as she shook her head. "No, I'm fine. It hurts just a little, but I can walk just fine."

He patted her on the shoulder. "Good. We won't do anything too strenuous, and when you get tired, just say so, okay?"

She nodded.

"Run along and get your gear, then. Meet me back here in five."

She scurried to her room and dressed quickly in her green regulation swimsuit, and topped it off with a brief pair of shorts and a T-shirt, strangely excited by the prospect of sharing the silent dark sea with him.

Childhood memories came swiftly to her; she remembered splashing in the shallows on moonlit nights with her brothers while her parents slept. They chased crabs by the light of the moon, and played games, darting in and out of the foam that the sea threw up onto the sand. Vacations at the beach had always been good times for her, and she attributed her eagerness to join Marcus in a late-night dip more to a desire to relive those good times than to anything else.

She was back outside in three minutes, armed with a towel, which she had coyly wrapped around her shoulders. He was already waiting, having exchanged his jeans for his cutoffs. His empty hands hung at his sides. He didn't seem inclined even to take along a towel with him. She wondered if he was planning to share hers. The small intimacy made her tingle.

"Ready?" he whispered. His eyes were bright. He, too, seemed to be feeling some adolescent excitement at running away to play while others slept.

She answered with a whispered "yes."

"Good." He put his arm lightly around her shoulder. "Let's go, then."

They made their way down to the edge of the water. Many sand creatures were out, as the moon would soon be full. Huge blue crabs scuttled past, their legs audibly clicking. Less visible, almost translucent sand-coloured crabs, some barely two inches across, got hurriedly out of their way as they walked.

"Those are *cirique,*" she said, pointing. "Sand crabs. They're all over."

"There really are a lot of them tonight," he observed.

"Crabs love the moonlight," she explained. "The bigger the moon, the more they come out. On full moons you have crab runs, where you just get all the family together and go to the seaside or out to the swamp to catch them. There are more than you can ever eat."

He turned his dark head to her, interested. "Really?"

"Really." She nodded with pride.

"We'll come out when it's full moon, then, and watch the crab hunters."

Rhea smiled, forgiving him just this once for appointing himself director of itineraries. "We'll do that," she agreed. They had reached the water's edge, and instead of entering the water, he steered her northward, parallel to the frilly line that the waves etched in the sand. He still hadn't taken his arm from around her shoulders. It just rested lightly there, carelessly, as if he'd forgotten it. She realised with sharp surprise that she didn't mind.

They walked past brightly lit beachfront patios from which emanated music, food smells, and snippets of conversation.

". . . met her in the market yesterday. She looked awful. She was wearing this . . ."

". . . almost brand-new! For five hundred dollars. It's really a bargain if you . . ."

"Let your sister play with it for a change! I'm warning you. . . ."

The voices carried far in the still night. "They sound so lively," he said softly. "They sound so happy in there."

"Yes, they do. Why shouldn't they be happy?"

He shrugged. "I don't know. It's not that I think they shouldn't be. I'm just glad they are."

There was a brief silence. Rhea felt herself relax, felt the tension in her shoulders dwindle under the warmth of his arm. He walked slowly, allowing her to keep step with him without rushing her. Although she favoured her injured leg just a little, the walk was more stimulating than taxing. From time to time, Marcus threw her anxious glances to ensure that she was alright, and for this she was grateful.

Overhead, the coconut trees rustled softly in the wind. Night birds flitted back and forth, crying. It just felt good to be out and relaxing, she thought, not worrying or mommying or looking out for anyone. Marcus certainly did not seem like a person you had to look out for.

"Rhea, can I tell you something?" He was almost timid.

She wasn't sure if she wanted to hear whatever he could possibly have to tell her. "Yeees," she said hesitantly.

"About Jodelle and me . . . we've been alone a long time. I mean, there's my parents, I told you already. . ."

Rhea nodded.

". . . they take care of her while I'm traveling. But the two of us, as a unit, we've been alone for a while. Almost as far back as she can remember. My wife . . ." he removed his arm from around her shoulders, and by the light of the moon Rhea saw him twist nervously on his broad gold wedding band, "my ex-wife, Yvette, left a long, long time ago."

Rhea said nothing, silently encouraging him to go on.

"Jodie was a baby, when Yvette left for the first time."

"First time?" She turned to look up at him. His dark handsome face was taut with pain.

He shrugged. "Well, we had our ups and downs. Lots of ups, lots of downs. It was good at first, though. She was so tiny, so beautiful. And we were sure that even with the two of us doing a lot of traveling, we could make it work."

As they kept on walking side by side along the powder-soft sand, he returned his arm to its position on her shoulders. The grip of long fingers was tighter than before, almost hurting, but she knew that talking was cathartic for him, so she didn't protest.

"Why did you both have to travel?"

He sighed deeply. "Yvette, well, she's a dancer, a ballerina."

Rhea's curiosity rose. "A *real* ballerina?"

He smiled ruefully at this. "A real ballerina. A classical ballerina. And a very talented one, too."

Suddenly Jodelle's small stature made sense. Ballerinas tended to be very small-framed, and Marcus had said that the child had gotten her tininess from her mother. She listened intently as Marcus went on.

"She loved the stage, loved to dance. We met at college. I'd just given up veterinary medicine for journalism, and she was studying dance. She was a foreign student, from Barbados . . . I told you, remember? I'll never forget the first time I saw her; she was this tiny, exquisite creature with a West Indian accent. I think I fell in love with that accent first. I was so intrigued by her. And the way she walked, she was so graceful. So . . . perfect."

Marcus had said that his ex-wife had only come up to his armpit. She stole a glance across at him—she was tall enough for him to lay his arm around her with ease. With her five-foot-eight-inch frame, she began to feel like a clumsy giraffe.

Marcus was still speaking. "We were married before we even got our degrees. It was good, at first, even with all the studying and the exams, we both found time for each other. Then we got out into the real world and had to work for a living. I decided to do freelance travel writing, because I've got this curiosity for the world, and besides, I thought my writing could make a difference to how people saw things."

Then, his tone grew bitter. "Strangely enough, she wasn't as put out by my being away so often as you'd expect from a newlywed. I think, well, sometimes I think she was glad when I chose to travel for a living, because my absence gave her time to . . . dance. Her career took off fast, and, well, I guess our marriage had to suffer for it." He made a bitter grimace. "It happens to the best of us, I suppose."

Rhea was touched. Her pleasure at this simple walk alongside of him, the feeling of just being close, was swamped with a more powerful emotion—compassion.

"And she left Jodelle with you?" This still puzzled Rhea.

She lived in a society where the mother was the focus of the home, and the fact that a woman could leave a marriage and not take her child was alien to her.

"Well," Marcus ground out, "you can't dance in *Moscow* with a *child* in tow!"

"Moscow?"

"She got a contract to dance at a large theatre in Moscow. By that time, Jodelle was about three, and even then, the marriage was a shambles. So Yvette didn't find it difficult to leave all her unwanted baggage—Jodelle and me—behind."

"And she never came back," Rhea anticipated the end of the story.

He snorted. "Oh, she came back, whenever she felt in the mood for a fight. It wasn't enough for her that her career was booming. She just couldn't stand the idea of me not missing her. So she made her appearance every now and then, just to satisfy herself that I was sufficiently miserable."

Those must have been the arguments that Jodelle remembered from her infancy, Rhea guessed. The quarrels that had caused her to be so horrified at the sight of Rainer and Dahlia arguing earlier today. It made sense.

Marcus was still talking. "So finally, about a year and a half ago, I decided I'd had enough. She and her troupe were performing one weekend in Texas. I flew over, and bulldozed her into going across the border with me for a fast divorce. It was all over in a weekend. Eight years of marriage."

The bitterness and hurt in his voice made her want to curl her arms up around his neck and pull his face down so she could kiss his brow in an attempt to comfort him. She didn't know what to say to console this man, who showed such manifest bitterness at his failed marriage, but who still wore the woman's ring.

He gave a shrug of finality. "So there you have it. The love story of the century. And now you know, my dear."

Rhea couldn't get a word past her dry throat. She still wasn't sure why he chose to tell her. It could be that he just felt the need to confide in someone. That had to be it. She continued to walk silently beside him.

His toned lightened a little, but still held a sharp edge. "So what about you?"

She was truly puzzled. "Me? What about me?"

"The boyfriend. How are things with you?"

She bristled with knee-jerk loyalty to her relationship. Really, it was not his place to ask, even if he'd just chosen to unburden himself to her. "Fine," she said grudgingly. It was peculiar, though, that all she could say when queried about her relationship, was "fine." What about "terrific?" Her brow wrinkled as she pondered on it, but she had to admit that all she could honestly say was "fine."

"He wasn't exactly put out by your accident, was he? I mean, if I had a woman as beautiful as you are, and if she was going through what you are right now, I'd be down here in an instant."

Rhea looked at him sharply. She was right. He had noticed Brent's indifference. How embarrassing!

"Sorry," he said, looking at her solemn face, which she was sure was flushing, even in the moonlight. "I didn't mean to step on your toes."

She waved it away. "It's good between us. Really."

"I'm glad," he said quietly. He sounded like he really meant it.

Rhea looked around. They'd been walking for a long time, and their house had long disappeared from view round a curve. All around them, the night stretched out. There were no houses close by, only wide belts of coconut trees that rustled in the wind. Even the crabs seemed too awed by the silent beauty of this peaceful place to scurry about. They were utterly alone.

She drew to a halt, and Marcus stopped beside her. "Maybe we should have that swim now," she volunteered.

The dark water glittered invitingly. "You know this section of beach?"

She looked around to get her bearings. "Yes, I know where we are."

"Is it safe to swim here?"

"Most of this stretch of beach is fine. Just don't go out too far, because you might fall into a trough, you know, one minute you're standing and then you take a step and there's nothing under your feet. And if you suddenly feel a pocket of cold water round you, move to warmer water. It might be a current, coming in from offshore. You don't want to get caught in that."

"No, I don't," he agreed vehemently.

She unwrapped her towel from around her shoulders and laid it over a coconut tree that sloped downward, running almost parallel to the sand. Then she peeled off her thin cotton shorts and T-shirt and laid them next to the towel. Suddenly, she felt naked and unprotected. Her arms flew up around her breasts in an unconscious bid to hide them from his view.

Marcus noticed the gesture. His eyes dropped to the arms that strove to hide her shapely curves from his view, and the flame that rose swiftly to his eyes convinced her that she'd been right in feeling the need to protect herself from his intoxicating gaze. Here she was, alone on an unending stretch of beach with the most bewildering, enticing man she had every met—and she was practically nude. Was she mad?

She struggled for control as he peeled off his vest and tossed it beside hers on the tree trunk. His dark skin looked like the hide of an exotic night creature, smooth and supple, and she had to slap down the urge to reach out and touch him to see if his incredible skin was real. He stretched, arms up above his head, sighing as he tried to ease the tension in his body. As he did so, his musky scent assailed her nostrils, and was answered by a sudden warmth between her thighs that took her completely by surprise.

The water, was her only rational thought, *the water will ease this desire*. She made her way with untoward haste into the ocean. Marcus followed silently behind. At the water's edge, she hesitated. She hadn't been anywhere near it since her encounter with the jellyfish. All of a sudden their earlier bantering about sea monsters didn't seem so funny.

Marcus knew what she was thinking. He held her hand encouragingly. "That was a one-in-a-million accident, Rhea. You may never meet another jellyfish like that in your life."

She knew that, but still . . .

"Come, we'll go in together." He led her in gently. The

warmth of his hand and the gentleness with which he seemed to understand her fear made her less nervous, and she allowed him to help her into the water. It slid silkily up around them, up along their legs to their hips, and past. It was like being caressed by warm, soothing, liquid hands, like stepping gradually into a deep comforting bath. The contact with it relaxed her, but did little to take her mind off the violent physical reaction she had had back on the beach.

"It's like a bath," he said softly.

"I was just thinking that," she said and looked up at him with a delighted smile. His answering smile softened the eyes that were until recently so full of pain. They had taken on a darker luster; the smooth amber gemstones were rimmed with dark halos. Rhea was taken aback at the sudden depth that they added to his handsome face. Instead of looking out at the world, sharp and inquisitive as ever, they allowed her to look in . . . no, they drew her in, tugging relentlessly at her, in spite of her staunch resistance.

Then the seed of companionship that his shared confession had planted between them disappeared, leaving a discomfort that they both acutely felt. She withdrew her hand from his and struggled to disentangle herself from the deadly intensity of those eyes, shivering in spite of the soothing warmth of the water.

Turning away from each other, they moved out to the depth up to their chests and stopped, feeling no need to go farther. They were not there for athletics, not to go swimming out into the night but to enjoy the regenerative powers of the quiet water. Maintaining a fair distance between themselves, they floated on their backs for a while, looking up into the clear bright sky that went on and on forever.

"Perks of the job, eh?" he chuckled nervously.

"Yeah." She didn't dare to glance across at him.

"Makes up for the bad times," he said, returning to his feet.

"Yeah." She didn't want to think about the bad times. Not now. She remained floating, closing her eyes against the turmoil of pleasure that being in his company on such a beautiful night had wrought. The water lapped up over her body.

She could feel his proximity; nevertheless, his light kiss took her completely by surprise. She immediately lost her buoyancy, and sank like a rock. Swiftly, he thrust a hand under the water and helped her to her feet. She came up coughing and spluttering, outraged. "Are you crazy?"

He thumped her on the back as she spat out the salty water that she had swallowed. "Sorry," he told her, but he wasn't sorry at all; he was laughing like a child that had pulled a schoolyard prank. He patted her on the back while she regained her breath. "Are you okay?"

"Fine," she snapped.

"Your face is all red," he told her solemnly.

She ignored his teasing. "Why did you do that?" She scowled fiercely up at him.

"Do what?" he said, feigning innocence very badly.

"You know what," she snapped.

He was standing in front of her, too close for her own liking, trying to cup her face to turn it toward him. She resisted him irritably. "That's not a trick to pull in the water, you know."

"I thought the water was a fine place to pull it," he told her. "I mean, you were just floating there next to me, all laid out like Ophelia, with your eyes closed. . . ."

"That's *sick*! Ophelia was *dead*!" She didn't want him to make her laugh. Laughing would have broken down the last of her defenses. Instead, she scowled.

He was undiscouraged. "Okay, like a little mermaid, then."

"Whatever. It's still dangerous. I could have drowned." Well, she admitted to herself, she felt like an idiot, but she had to concede that she wouldn't have drowned.

"You know I wouldn't have let you drown, my sweet," he said in a perfectly villainous stage whisper. He wriggled his eyebrows at her. All he needed was to throw a cape around her and snatch her up into the night on preternatural wings.

He might have found it funny, but she was not amused. "Well, there's no telling," she said irritably. "And it's still a stupid thing to do. Didn't anyone ever tell you not to play games in the water?" It was disturbing how her lips throbbed from such a light kiss.

"So let's get out of the water, and try it again," he murmured. His face was so close she could feel his breath on her cheek.

She looked at him from under her lashes. Water ran out of his hair and down his face, clinging to his lips. The film of water that adhered to the hair on his chest and fore-arms seemed to glitter eerily in the pale light. The proposition seemed annoyingly tempting. "Don't be ridiculous," she snapped, and barely finished speaking because his mouth was on hers, still light, still teasing.

She raised her arms instinctively to wind them around his neck, but thought better of it and began to drop them. Marcus took them by the wrist and wound them firmly round his neck again. This time, she didn't take them away. Instead she allowed them to stroke the corded muscles of his neck and shoulders, her fingertips sensitive enough to feel the fine powdery salt that was already being left behind by the evaporating water.

"Come closer," he whispered against her mouth. She realised she was holding her torso and hips away from his, just tilting her head forward, afraid of the shivers of pleasure that might rise from coming into fuller contact. Her mind whizzed with indecision. He repeated his request, more urgently now. She realised that he was not going to be the one to move, that he was going to leave it up to her to move toward him, if she wanted to. The realisation embarrassed her, because although it left her with a way out, her movement toward him would be an undeniable admission of desire. The few inches between them seemed like a chasm. Suddenly, the water seemed to chill.

"Rhea," he tore his mouth away and stared at her. His eyes were as black as the water around them. He pleaded silently.

Strictly without her permission, Rhea's feet moved forward, and Marcus was clasping her against him. He brought his hands up to her face again, stroking her throat with his thumbs, moving along the base of her jaw to her ears and temples. Giddily she realised that his mouth was following the heated trail left by his fingers. All she could hear was the pounding of the surf. All she could feel was the rise and fall of his chest, keeping time with it.

His hands dropped to her waist, roaming like curious children, along her back and hips, seeming to her to move very slowly under the water. He slid one hand between them, forcing it in between their two bodies, which were pressing eagerly against each other. He pressed his palm flat against her belly, feeling how the solidity of her upper torso gave way to soft roundness. All of a sudden the thin material of her bathing suit seemed to be too much.

''Marcus,'' she began as his insistent fingers tugged aside the material that covered the tops of her thighs. The inquisitive hand that invaded her suit became entangled in the fine curly hair that it found there. Despite the water all around them, she could feel her own wetness and heat on his fingers, and the knowledge that he had driven her so swiftly to sharp, painful arousal made her desire grow even more.

She struggled again to call him back to reason. ''Mark . . .'' but his tongue was mimicking the gentle probing of his fingers, and the shudder that coursed through her made it impossible for her to continue. It was then she realised that her urgent repetition of his name was not a protestation but a cry of hunger.

Somehow, they made it to the shore, high up above the waterline, at the edge of the row of coconut trees. Somehow, she found herself lying in the sand looking up at him. Eyes glittering, he tugged at her dark, wet swimsuit like a hungry man tearing away at a cellophane-wrapped meal, slowing down only when he remembered the raw skin of her injured leg.

''Oh, Rhea,'' his words came in a rasping whisper, ''you don't know how beautiful you are. If you could see yourself like this . . .'' He managed to free her of the offending suit, and his taut, hard body hovered above hers as if she were the place where it belonged, hiding her arching naked breasts from the view of the moon.

''You've seen me naked before,'' she reminded him breathlessly, ''when I was sick, when you . . .'' She remembered how angry she had been at his revelation, but this intimacy made that other time pale in comparison.

''That was different. I tried to be careful, I tried not to stare. But this time, now . . . you look so . . .'' He didn't seem able to gather his thoughts long enough to finish the sentence.

Instead, he lowered his body down upon hers with a pained sigh.

His hardness pressed insistently against her belly through his rough, wet cutoffs; the steel rivets along the zipper seemed to transfer the heat from within, rubbing against her naked skin, almost cutting her. The tiny pain whetted her appetite, so much so that she ground against him, desperately desiring the little pieces of metal to leave their permanent mark on her belly and thighs so that she could look down at herself and remember how roughly, yet sweetly, she had been caressed by this devastating man.

She reached up and explored him through the rough denim, stroking, kneading gently, and her action drew an exclamation of pleasurable shock from deep inside him. She let her fingers slide along the inside of his waistband, feeling the coarse crinkly hair that plunged down from his navel, yet not daring to venture further. The tiny area of her mind that still remained rational warned her that to take that risk would unleash a response that neither of them would be able to control.

When he pulled away from her, her body seemed to deflate suddenly, like a balloon that had been stuck with a needle. She lay back against the sand in total shock, unable to still the erratic rhythm of her breathing. The fact that his breath was as ragged as hers was no comfort to her; she felt a bewildering sense of abandonment.

For his own part, Marcus seemed to need to steady himself, half-sitting, half-kneeling, supported by both hands against the sand. Still only inches apart, they regarded each other silently, eyes wild and dark, as though each was waiting for the other to speak first. But after such craziness, what could you say?

"Sorry," he said finally.

Rhea felt a surge of disappointment. Sorry? That wasn't exactly on her list of the top ten things she wanted to be told after she'd been so thoroughly kissed.

"Maybe that wasn't such a good idea," he muttered, this time more to himself than to her.

Her heart plunged. She felt suddenly embarrassed, exposed. He rubbed her cheek with his knuckles, in an almost brotherly fashion. "I think I'd better help you back into this, Rhea." He struggled with her suit, trying to slide it up over her breasts without touching them, as ludicrous as that might seem, considering that a few moments ago they were explored by his fingers, and tortured by the rough hair on his chest. The exaggerated chastity of his actions stung. She brushed his hands away and dressed herself.

She felt like a chastened child. Her body was aching deep inside, and his abrupt halt left her bewildered. What did she do wrong? Maybe she'd kissed him back too hard, reached out for him too hungrily, seemed too available. She *wasn't* available, didn't he know that? But still, perhaps she'd shocked him with the heat of her response. Hell, she thought wryly, she'd shocked herself.

He was taking her by the hand and helping her to her feet, and leading her, as if she were too young to help herself, to the water. Solemnly, he scooped up water in his cupped hands and tried to wash away the sand that encrusted her body. Tiny grains of sand had penetrated the unbandaged wounds that ran the length of her leg, and these he removed carefully. This she allowed him to do without protest. When he was done with her, he plunged under the waves, to rise again a few seconds later, freed of the sand that had covered him.

Numbly, she followed him back out of the ocean. On the beach again, she retrieved her towel from the tree and began to pat herself dry. Marcus was at her side at once, solicitous. "Are you cold?" he asked with concern.

She realised that she was. She nodded. Gently, he took the towel from her hand and began rubbing her down, briskly, starting with her back and arms, then dropping into a squatting position to dry each leg in turn. She looked down on him as he worked, thinking that he was touching her lightly, with no hint of the heated urgency of just a few moments before. She was reminded briefly of her father, drying her when she came in out of the rain, so she wouldn't catch a cold.

"Okay now?" he asked softly when he was done.

"Thank you." She found her tongue at last. He handed her clothes to her, and she turned her back on him as she stepped into them. He arranged the towel over her shoulders like a cloak. "Don't you want to dry off?" she asked. She remembered that he hadn't brought a towel.

"I'm fine." He gathered his own clothes and rolled them into a tight bundle, which he tucked under his arm. "Let's go," he said decisively. Rhea nodded. They fell into step. Somehow, the walk back seemed a lot longer than it had on the way out.

The beach house was a welcome sight. She climbed the front steps quickly, anxious to part company from him. Marcus seemed equally intent on getting away from her as soon as possible. In their haste, neither of them noticed the slight movement in the corner of the patio, and the faint glow of a cigarette as Rainer stood, cloaked in darkness, watching them come in.

CHAPTER NINE

Better not to think about it, Rhea advised herself the next morning. *You kissed him and then it was over.* No big deal. Nobody was hurt. Nothing but her pride, she amended wryly. How could she? There she was, in a stable relationship for almost two years, and some handsome stranger comes along and she ends up clinging to him, naked, on the beach at night. Was she out of her mind?

Stable relationship. Her mind turned to Brent. She'd never cheated on him, never felt the need for it. And she was sure (well, she never had a reason to *suspect*) that he'd never cheated on her. That meant they were satisfied with what they had with each other, didn't it? *Didn't it?*

The little devil inside her snorted scornfully. *Then why,* it said, *did you respond the way you did? Why were you so ready to give yourself up to this man out there? And how come, in the two years that you've been dating, Brent has never, not once, made you feel like that?*

She thought of Brent, with his ordinary habits, his ordinary jokes, his ordinary kisses, and was truly bewildered. She had come to accept their perfunctory embraces as the norm. *This,* she'd always told herself, *is enough for me. He's a fine man and he's good to me and we hardly ever fight, so we're okay together.* So how could one insane encounter with an alluring stranger, with the ability to mesmerize her with his touch . . . how *could* he awaken in her so much doubt?

And with a client! A guest! Was she crazy? It was against every rule in the book. The pitfalls of such an encounter were legendary within the tourist industry, not just here, but everywhere throughout the world. The single, unattached tourist, the attractive guide, cruise director, hotel clerk, whatever, and a quiet unguarded moment. It had happened before, and it certainly would happen again. But not to her. Never to her. She had never thought of herself as prone to such reckless romantic impulses.

And as for him, she should be ashamed of himself. Surely he should have known that she was tired, weakened by her ordeal of the past few days, not entirely herself. If she was in her usual good health, and fully in control, it would never have happened. Of that, she could be sure.

Don't think, Ri-ri. Just go about your business. You have a job to do. It never happened, okay? Armed with her own good advice, she plunged into the day's activities, glad that they allowed her to put the shameful incident on the back burner for the time being.

Jodelle was up with the gulls, full of life, and now that the fear associated with her accident was behind her, she was only too eager to regale everyone with the gory details.

"It was so *squishy*," she squeaked over breakfast, "I had mud all *over* me!" she began an inventory of her affected body parts, "I had mud in my ears and on my neck and my hands and my feet and my knees and my elbows and my hair and . . ."

Rhea, at whom this long recital had been primarily aimed, listened indulgently, glad of the opportunity to ignore Marcus' silent presence across the table. The few times she glanced, against her will, across at him, he was staring studiedly at his cereal, and didn't seem to be aware of her. Her ego was really taking a bruising, she thought wryly. Here she was, thrown into turmoil, and there he was, picking raisins out of his granola. Would she ever really grow to understand men?

She listened to the girl, nodding encouragingly throughout the meal, glad at least that nobody else at the table seemed to be aware that anything was amiss.

After breakfast, the group drove out to Mayaro to catch a glimpse of the daily life of the villagers, and Rhea thought it would be nice to stop in at the market. As she usually did there, Rhea let them wander about on their own, with instructions to rendezvous outside the bank at eleven. The market was a place of chaos: there was no sense even trying to keep a semblance of order, no need for a guided tour. Besides, she was sure that they would enjoy the opportunity to wander about unaccompanied for a change, while she, for her part, was glad for the chance to be away from eyes that might engulf her once again into their golden glow—or worse, further bruise her already wounded pride by holding nothing but nonchalance within their depths.

It was a typical market scene, as is found in any small village in the country. Ramshackle stalls lined the area, piled high with a colorful collage of fruit. There were the dark green and bright orange papayas, oranges, grapefruit, limes, watermelons, and a few dozen varieties of mangoes. Vegetables, not to be out-done, also worked hard at catching the eye. There were dark, leafy lettuces and pak choi, paler cabbages, bright striped cucumbers, deep-red tomatoes, rows of herbs and seasonings, celery, scallions, fine thyme, fat thyme, and bay leaves tied up in bunches.

Along the roads, fishermen laid out their catch of the morning: long gray sharks that looked ominous even in death, red snapper that retained their brilliant colour, silver-gray kingfish, carite and cavalli, prized in the culinary world for their incredibly sweet, flavourful white flesh. Rhea purchased a large kingfish, sure that fish steaks, seasoned in lavish amounts of ginger and garlic, would go down well that evening. She had the vendor chop it into fat slabs and put them into a bag.

Her eyes, traitors that they were, searched out Marcus' tall figure among the crowd. He was down at the end of a row of

rickety stalls, engaged in a conversation with a young East
Indian boy who couldn't have been more than twelve. The boy,
barefoot and in threadbare shorts that were obviously part of
an old school uniform, held a string of blue crabs in his hand.
A dozen or so of the unfortunate creatures had been trussed
securely with strong blades of grass, their vicious claws immo-
bilized. Thus bound, they had been tied together on long pieces
of string. The creatures were still alive—in fact, crabs were
always sold alive. It was foolhardy to buy a dead crab, as you
never knew how long it had been dead, or what had killed it.
The malevolent things all seemed to be glaring at them with
their long stalk eyes.

Marcus held Jodelle high in his arms, allowing her to lean
forward to indulge her curiosity by actually *touching* (this made
Rhea flinch) the hard shells. At the same time, his strong arms
offered the girl a safe harbor, if her curiosity about the ugly
creatures grew into intimidation. The boy was obviously pressing for a sale, while Marcus, she assumed, was busy looking
for an angle for a story.

As if to prove her right, he set Jodelle down and began
fiddling with his camera, positioning the boy against a background of brightly coloured bolts of cloth that were draped
over a counter for sale. The boy, soaking in all the attention,
grinned broadly, holding his string of hapless crabs up beside
his face while Marcus clicked away.

Huh, she thought to herself. Can't let a story slip by him,
could he? At least there's no scandal here, nothing exciting to
report like tainted meat or . . .

At that precise moment Marcus happened to glance up from
his camera and, as if guided by some secret knowledge, his eyes
met hers across the busy, crowded market. Her contemptuous
thought must have been written in her expression, because he
halted, puzzled, before returning to his work. A few moments
later he handed the boy a folded local bill, the denomination
of which she was unable to see at this distance, even though
the national currency was colour-coded. It seemed sufficient to
induce a brilliant ear-to-ear grin from the boy, who immediately

offered Marcus his entire collection of crabs in return. Marcus held up a hand in polite refusal, and shooed the child away.

In spite of his obvious generosity toward the boy, Rhea was still inclined to be uncharitable toward Marcus. "Should have known that a ... a *vegetarian* like him would turn down a perfectly good bunch of crabs," she was grouching to herself when he raised a long arm and imperiously waved her over.

He wasn't serious. He couldn't be trying to get *her* to move toward *him*! If he wanted to speak to her, she decided pigheadedly, he could find his way across the market himself! She developed a sudden and overwhelming interest in a pile of small green mangoes on the counter at her elbow, and maintained this interest until Marcus, in exasperation, stomped over with Jodelle in tow.

"I was calling you, Rhea," he said, mildly irritated.

Of course he was, she thought pettily. And like a good woman she was supposed to pick up her heels and scuttle on over to him. Not likely. She drew a hand up to run it through her thick dark hair. "Oh, Marcus," she murmured with feigned surprise. "I'm sorry. I didn't notice." She bared her teeth at him in her patented hostess smile and asked with manifest meekness. "What can I do for you?"

An obscenely fat woman, dressed in a brilliant yellow cotton dress and matching head scarf, chose just that moment to squeeze past, forcing Marcus to step out of her way, pinning Rhea against the stall. As he did so, Rhea caught the scent of his aftershave, that scent of unidentifiable but heavenly spices that had become so familiar to her in their shared bathroom, but of which she never seemed to tire.

On top of that, like the high note in an exotic blend of fine cologne, she could smell the sand and the sea and the coconut trees, all memories of their encounter of the previous night, and all, she was sure, more a product of her imagination than anything else.

Her olfactory hallucinations were interrupted by a delighted squeal from Jodelle. "Oooh, Daddy! That lady! She's so fat! She's hooo-mongous!"

They were both taken by surprise, and tried to smother guilty laughs as the woman in question spun around glaring. She looked down toward the source of the voice and was about to let some choice West Indian epithets fly when she stopped, mouth open, obviously disarmed by the tininess of her aggressor. Instead, she smiled broadly, revealing a fortune in gold teeth, shook her yellow-wrapped head and waddled away.

"Jodie," Marcus began, "you can't talk about people like that. It's not nice." His smile belied the severity of his words.

Jodelle scowled. "But it's the truth! She's . . . she's bigger'n *Grandma*!"

That set Marcus off again. He laughed loudly, the same gloriously full-throated, deep laugh that had so entranced Rhea the day before. The child always brought out the best in this man, she observed with a kind of awe. Whenever she was around, he became a happy person.

He reached out to tug at her hair. "My dear, I wouldn't advise you to mention your grandmother's weight when she's around." The laughter made the corners of his eyes crinkle, and Rhea's hand itched to reach out and touch the side of his face to see if his skin was as warm as his smile.

Jodelle, ever practical, put her hands up on her skinny bejeaned hips and looked ready to defend her position. "But Grandma's fat, too! She's real, real, real . . ."

Marcus put a hand playfully over her mouth to silence her. "Listen, girl. Let me tell you, Lucien to Lucien. My mother's not fat. She's well-padded. Okay? Them's the rules in that lady's house, and we all just have to live with 'em. Okay, honey?"

Jodelle was unconvinced, but nodded resignedly.

Marcus straightened up and turned to Rhea. "Ri," he began, then corrected himself, "Rhea, I want to wander around a little. Take a few shots. Can you do me a favour?"

"Sure," she said, thinking *why is there nothing of last night in your eyes? Have you forgotten? Did it matter to you?* She waited patiently for his request.

"Could you take care of the little beastie for me for half an hour or so?"

Jodelle squealed with childish laughter at her father's newest sobriquet for her. She released her grip on her father's hand and held on to Rhea's, looking up at her with a grin of undisguised pleasure.

"Yeah, Rhea! I get to stay with you!"

Marcus seemed to accept the transaction as ended, and handed over the girl's little straw bag, which she seemed to have grown fed up of carrying, and entrusted to his care. "Good. I'll see you girls back at the bus, then. Eleven o'clock, right?" And he was off, head visible above the crowd as he moved in the direction from which he had come.

If Rhea had any inclination to be miffed at his presumptuous manner, it melted in the warmth of Jodelle's gaze. The girl really did want to be with her. Both warmed and flattered, she asked "Thirsty?"

Jodelle nodded vigorously.

"All right, then, let's find a nice place where we can sit down and have something cold. Okay? This heat is killing me."

"Killing me," Jodelle echoed as Rhea led her through the throng of vendors.

They found a small quiet shop that sold a little of everything, and which had two or three small tables round the side. Rhea ordered two glasses of ice-cold coconut water and led the way round the wooden counter to the tables. They selected the chairs that seemed least likely to collapse under them and sat. The wooden table was spread with a bright plastic tablecloth covered with an incongruous pattern of garish apples and grapes.

Sometimes, you didn't realize just how hot it was until you actually came in out of the heat. They sipped their drinks gratefully. Jodelle amused herself by dipping her finger into the glass and tracing over the outlines of fruit on the plastic tablecloth. Bored with this game within a few minutes, she raised her head and looked inquisitively around the shop. The shelves were lined with every imaginable item, many of them covered with a thin film of dust. Open-mouthed gallon bottles filled with sweets and chewing gum lined the counter. The few patrons that were in the store leaned idly against the counter, chatting with the shopkeeper, obviously more in the mood to socialize than to make any purchases.

Suddenly, the child turned round to hold Rhea's gaze in her sharp black one. "I like how you talk, Rhea."

"What?" Rhea was confused. She had been silent for quite some time.

"I like how you talk. Like music. Like the sun."

Ah, she was talking about her accent! The girl liked her Trinidadian accent! "Oh, thanks, darling." Funny how children think. Ideas pop into their heads without warning. She wondered what she must sound like to the child, and decided that her accent must indeed be noticeable.

She was basking in the glow of the compliment when she remembered the last person she's heard make a comment about a West Indian accent—Marcus, the night before when he was telling her about his ex-wife, Jodelle's mother. What was it that he'd said? He loved her accent. He'd fallen in love with her accent first, he'd said. Trust a man to do that.

Maybe that explained Marcus' sexual curiosity (dare she call it attraction?) about *her*! This man with the failed island fantasy, who still wore his ex-wife's wedding ring as faithfully as if she were still there with him by his side. Maybe he was seeking, once again, to be lulled in the arms of another woman with a sun-kissed Caribbean accent. The thought was sobering.

Stupid of him. Fool. Could he really be a sucker for a voice, an inflection, a manner of speech? If he was, he was deaf into the bargain, if he couldn't tell the difference between a Barbadian accent and a Trinidadian accent! Or didn't he care? Was one island-girl fantasy as good as another? Damn the man!

"Are you mad at me?" Jodelle's plaintive voice brought her back to the little room in which they were sitting. Suddenly Rhea realised she was scowling.

Hurriedly, she struggled to smooth her brow, and chase away her dark thoughts, for the girl's sake. "No, no. Just thinking."

"Thinking what?"

"Thoughts." Really, there was no explanation she could offer right now.

"Bad thoughts?" Jodelle was concerned.

Rhea sighed. "No, just thoughts." She tried to divert her

attention. "I'm glad you like how I talk. I like how you talk, too."

The girl's face became sly. "You like how my Daddy talks?"

Rhea was taken aback. Now, where did that come from? She became aware of those sharp, older-than-they-should-be eyes fixed on hers. She floundered, thinking again—and again and again and again, what was *wrong* with her?—of the sound of Marcus' hungry voice as he groaned out her name against her throat. Rhea took a healthy swig of her coconut water and managed to croak, "Oh, yes. I like the way your Daddy talks, too." *God help me, don't you go telling him that,* she added silently. *I'd just die.*

The girl looked smug, and seemed about to belabor the point further when a heavy hand fell on Rhea's shoulder.

"Well, now," boomed a too-hearty voice in her ear. "How's the little one doing?"

Rhea didn't have to look around to know it was Rainer. He came to stand at the end of the table, and looked from one to the other with a grin that did not stretch from his fleshy lips to his eyes. "Having a little drink?" he stated the obvious.

Rhea nodded politely, glancing around for the man's wife, who really seemed to be absent at the most inconvenient times. The beautiful, dark-haired woman was nowhere in sight. After their conversation over the dishes the last time, she wasn't keen on chatting with him when the others weren't around.

Jodelle craned her neck back to look up at him, watching him with the mistrust a child holds for a Santa Claus with a beard that's coming unstuck. Children have a way of recognising fake bonhomie in people who constantly chucked them on the chin or patted them on the head but didn't really mean it. The child obviously didn't trust him. *Smart kid,* Rhea thought.

Rainer was going on. "Pity about yesterday. The fall in the mud and all that."

Aw, Rhea groaned inside. *Don't go there. Please, don't go there.*

The heavyset, florid man was oblivious to (or ignoring) her reluctance to discuss it. "I couldn't help thinking . . ." at this he leaned forward conspiratorially, "I couldn't help thinking that it could have been avoided, though. That little accident. I mean, you, and the girl's father, of course, would probably have been able to keep a better eye on her if you hadn't been, er, distracted.''

She could almost smell his malice in her nostrils. They flared as if they detected a bad odour. The slimy man had seen them! Oh, he'd been arguing with his wife, she recollected bitterly, but obviously he was not so deeply engrossed in the conversation that he hadn't noticed the kiss-that-almost-was up on the volcano! She ground her teeth in order to keep a growl of absolute vexation inside.

Rainer straightened himself, and beamed at Jodelle again. He reached out to tug at her braids but the girl, no longer able or willing to conceal her dislike for him, yanked her head out of the way. *Good for you, Jodie,* Rhea thought. *I wish it was as easy for me to avoid his little digs.*

Rainer laughed heartily at the rebuff. ''Oh, kids are so cute.'' He fished around in his pocket and came up with a wad of money, from which he peeled off a brilliant emerald local five-dollar bill. He proffered it to Jodelle. ''Why don't you buy yourself a candy bar? Maybe you could find an American one. I bet you're missing American candy.''

Jodelle regarded him impassively, and when it became clear that she would not be reaching out to take the money from him, he laid it carefully on the table before her. When he left, he was humming to himself, and smiling like a crocodile.

A dark cloud hung over the girl's small face as she watched the man disappear out the door. How much of the conversation did she follow? What had she understood? Rhea sucked her teeth in irritation. He could have done better than that. If he'd had a bone to pick with her, he could have waited until they were alone, as unpleasant as that experience would have been. Why sling his barbs at her in front of a six-year-old?

''He's a stinker,'' Jodelle announced with conviction, and nodded vigorously to back up her declaration. ''I don't like him.''

Hear, hear, Rhea thought, but did not say. She looked at her watch. It was almost eleven—time to meet the others.

"Up, up, kiddo," Rhea said cheerfully, and began to gather Jodelle's things about her. "Time to get going."

Jodelle smiled, all good humor again. "Up, up!" she echoed. Together they walked out into the brilliant sunshine to meet the others, leaving the five-dollar bill on the table.

Rhea missed Brent. This surprised her, because she never thought of herself as being one of those clinging women who just couldn't be away from their men, couldn't stand on their own two feet for short periods of time. But for some reason, she missed him. She was honest enough with herself to admit that it was not his touch that she missed. Their physical relationship was okay—*just okay*? she thought wryly as soon as the word came to her head.

It was almost enough to make you cry. Two years of knowing someone, and the only word that leaps to mind when you think of the way someone makes you feel is . . . *okay*. She could never claim that she left his bed with regretful longing, wondering when they would next come together. Sex was all right, she and Brent agreed, but it was never a pillar of their relationship. Most times, going without was just fine with them both.

The reason was obvious; even she couldn't pretend to overlook it. She needed Brent close by to remind herself that there was a reason why she shouldn't be feeling what she was feeling for Marcus.

It was ridiculous. She'd never been this way with anyone, and certainly never with a client. The few past relationships that she'd had developed slowly, with specific, well-defined intervals of attraction, exploration, and finally, culmination. It was easy that way. She could enjoy male companionship and still remain in control.

The word *control* almost made her laugh. Marcus had called her a control junkie, and he was right. But what was wrong with that? Who said you had to run around throwing caution to the wind, getting knocked about by this sudden sexual fascination like a leaf on the waves? That kind of stuff didn't belong in her life. She preferred her emotions to remain nicely in check, thank you.

Calling Brent seemed like a good idea—a very good idea. So, after a lunch of fresh-from-the-market fish and vegetables, she made her excuses and left everyone to their dessert of coconut custard and fresh pineapple, and stepped out round the back of the house, into the brilliant sunshine. Somehow (and God knew, she had no reason to), she felt guilty, as if she needed to sneak around where she shouldn't be seen.

Stupid, the idea of having to hide to call her own boyfriend! Still, she defensively wedged herself between the gleaming dark green van and a row of brilliant purple and fuschia bougainvillea plants. Avoiding assault by the thorny branches, she dialed his direct number at the office.

His voice came as a relief to her. "Brent!" she said happily, almost as if pleasantly surprised to find him on the other end of his own line.

"Rhea, how you doing, baby?" He sounded distracted. Somewhere in the background she could hear muted office chatter, and she could have sworn that she heard him shuffling papers on his desk.

Her disappointment was tangible. "Did I call at a bad time?"

"Oh, no," he said absently. "You know I'm always glad to hear from you. How are things going?"

How are things going? She wanted to say "Oh, things are going fine. I'm falling hard and fast for a tall, irritating, sexy man with yellow eyes whose little girl follows me around like a duckling, and who kissed me last night and made me feel things that I never felt with you, and think things that you never made me think, and if you don't step in fast, if you don't give me something to hang on to I'm going to be washed out to sea before I even know it. But apart from that, things are just *great*!"

Instead, she shrugged and said, "Oh, pretty good. We had a bit of an accident with the little girl yesterday, but she's just fine now ... "

"I closed a hell of a deal today," Brent breezed on, as if she hadn't spoken. "A *hell* of a deal. Baby, you'd have been proud of me ..." To her shock, he began regaling her with the intricacies of a his latest financial coup, how he'd managed to convince a gun-shy corporate client to invest heftily into a new financial package his investment company was putting together, and how slyly he'd stalked them, primed them, and massaged them, "... set them up for the kill!" he crowed exultantly.

Rhea listened, appalled. It always seemed to boil down to this, him being convinced that his prowess in the negotiating room was a source of as much fascination to her as it was to himself, while her own career, her own little anecdotes, were just fodder for small talk.

Had she only just discovered this, or had she always known, but was never prepared to let her dissatisfaction step to the forefront of her consciousness, where it could stand up and be recognised? And why now?

As she listened to him gleefully detailing the size of the commission package due to him as a reward for his latest exploit, she felt her hands grow cold, despite the heat of the afternoon. After a few minutes of lackluster conversation, she said her good-byes.

"Miss you, baby." His voice dropped to an intimate whisper that somehow made her cringe.

"Miss you, too," she sighed, and clicked off the phone. She stood under the waving branches of the thorny hedge, fingering the keys of the phone, as if she had a call to make, but couldn't for the life of her remember the number. She realised, not with any pleasure, that the owner of the only voice she really wanted to hear was inside the cool white house behind her.

"What a mess," she groaned, and slid into a squatting position on the low wall that separated the garden from the driveway. Disinclined to go inside anytime soon, she sat and stared at her toes. She was just deciding that a self-administered pedicure wouldn't hurt (and at least it would give her an hour or so of something to do to take her mind off you-know-who), when you-know-who rounded the corner with his hands in his pockets, humming to himself as if he were not wreaking havoc in her previously unruffled life.

Marcus' appearance did not surprise her. The man had radar, she was sure of it. He had some kind of sensory device that was able to let him know whenever she thought of him, and then, nonchalantly, he would appear. It couldn't be an accident. It was all calculated to annoy her.

She lifted her head and threw him a black look.

"Whoa!" he stopped short of her and threw up his hands in surrender. "Where did that come from? Was that glare for me, or did an innocent man step into the line of fire?"

She would hardly call him innocent, not after the way he'd touched her last . . . *Let's not go there, Rhea,* her defenses told her. She tugged idly at her wild brown curls and waved away the thought. "Oh, no. I wasn't glaring at you, Marcus. It was the sun in my eyes." *Liar, liar, pants on fire.*

"Oh, yeah." He agreed wryly. "Damn that vicious sun." The fact that he didn't believe her didn't prevent him from settling down on his haunches next to her. She tried to ignore his presence, and returned to her intense examination of her own toes.

"Nice toes," he observed casually, is if they were detached from her, pieces of sculpture on display in some small-town museum.

"Marcus," she began to protest, but he didn't let her finish. "Okay, okay. . ."

Undaunted, she pressed on. "You shouldn't be telling me that. I mean, it's not the kind of thing you should say to . . ."

"Alright, Rhea," his eyes were gleaming. "I'm sorry. I take it back. You don't have nice toes. As a matter of fact, you have really ugly toes." He bent closer to examine them. "You know, if I'm not mistaken, those have got to be the ugliest toes I have ever seen. How do you live with yourself?"

She was laughing in spite of herself. "That's enough, now. I get your point."

"Good. I'm glad to see you smiling. You've been skittish as a cat all day." His sunshine eyes came to rest on her smiling mouth.

Did he wonder why she was nervous? Or was he just playing with her again? "I was just calling Brent." She waved the phone around as evidence. That was a good touch, she told herself. It was good to mention the boyfriend. It let them know where you stood.

A flicker of God alone knew what passed across his face and he straightened up and stepped away from her. "I hope I wasn't interrupting," he said shortly. "Don't let me bother you, then."

She got to her feet, glad that her wild blow in the dark had found its mark. It brought a small smile of triumph to her face, but she was quick to subdue it. "Oh, no. We're done." Then, to avoid any confusion, she amended her statement. "Talking, I mean. Done talking."

He nodded. He seemed to have wrestled his negative response to the ground, and mastered it, because he was smiling again. "I need you, Rhea," Marcus said, and her spine was suddenly ramrod straight. "Jodelle and I want to go sargasso hunting, and since you're not doing anything, I thought maybe you'd come along and point it out to us."

"Sargasso?"

"Yeah. Don't you remember, that first night, back at the restaurant, you were telling me about how much fun it was to pop the little balloons on the sargasso weed when you were a kid. And I said I'd like my daughter to try it. Remember?"

"Yes."

"Well, we're ready to try it."

She relaxed once again, but still, she wasn't inclined to spend any time with him right now, even if it was broad daylight. "Umm . . ." she racked her brain for a credible excuse.

"Are you doing anything right now?" he pressed her.

She had to admit that she wasn't.

"And we're free for the rest of the afternoon, aren't we?"

"Technically, yes, but I really don't see why you need me to show you what sargasso looks like. It's green, it's wet, and it's all over the beach. Trust me, you'll know it when you see it."

He was already on his feet, and hauling her playfully along by the arm. "You have to come, missy. It's your job."

The sneaky wretch was using her own pet argument against

her! "Alright," she said ungraciously, in a voice that was definitely not her hostess voice. She tugged her arm free. "And you don't have to drag me, just let me get my sandals."

"And your swimsuit," he called behind her.

She stopped. "I am *not* swimming. We're looking for sargasso. There'll be more than enough of that on the sand. We won't need to go hunting for it in the water."

"All right! All right!" He was grinning like a wicked child. "Jodie and I await you outside, your guideness." He gave her a courtly bow, and disappeared into the house.

Talk about a man of many moods! Once in her room, Rhea rooted around under the second, unused bed for her beach sandals. This morning Marcus was polite, almost disinterested. And now this afternoon he was a ten-year-old prankster. If she'd had pigtails, he'd have pulled them. It made no sense trying to figure him out. She changed into her shorts, keeping on her green uniform T-shirt, and slicked her arms, face, and legs with sunscreen before stepping outside to meet them.

The two married couples, and, surprisingly, Banner, were out on the beachfront lazing in the afternoon sun. As they passed, Trudy called cheerfully out to them. "Going swimming?"

Jodelle bawled back enthusiastically. "We're looking for weeds!" She waved her bright red plastic pail as evidence.

A veteran at caring for small children, Trudy seemed to understand perfectly. "Weeds! Wow! Really? Are we going to have them for dinner? Are you going to make us a weed salad?"

Jodelle snorted loudly. "You don't eat seaweed! It's not lettuce!"

"Oh, I see." Trudy nodded her head wisely. "You enjoy yourselves, then."

Jodelle was not about to let anyone get the last word in. "We will! We'll bring back lots and lots, and I'm going to plant them in the garden!"

That stirred up some laughter, but not, Rhea was quick to observe, from either Dahlia or Rainer, both of whom were staring at them unsmilingly. A double chill went down her spine. If it wasn't bad enough that Rainer seemed to monitoring her activities, Dahlia seemed to be watching her husband watch Rhea! The sensation was not pleasant.

She wondered if she should tell Marcus about the nasty encounter with Rainer, especially since he'd made his most recent comments in the presence of Marcus' daughter. Unwilling to stir up a hornet's nest, though, she thought better of it, and kept it to herself.

Deliberately, she led Marcus and Jodelle in the opposite direction from the one which they'd taken the night before. If Marcus had any comment to make on this action, he didn't voice it.

They let Jodelle run along ahead. The girl was taking the concept of hunting very seriously. She followed the water's edge, hunched over, peering downward at her feet, as if she had to take the seaweed by surprise before it darted out of her grasp. From time to time she would grab at something green and come trotting back to them.

"Is this it?" she would ask, but it would either be a seaweed of a different type, or a branch or leaf that had fallen into the water.

"Not exactly," Rhea would say indulgently, "Try again." And the girl would trot obediently back to the water's edge.

They walked in silence, just listening to the waves. "You must feel very lucky," he said at last, "to be able to come out here so often, and take in beauty like this."

She turned to him in surprise. She hadn't expected that. "Yes, I guess I do. I feel really proud of it. I mean I think it's a privilege for me to be able to show it off to new people all the time. That way I don't run the risk of becoming bored, as so many people do. I always get to see it again and again through other people's eyes. Then it's all fresh and new again. It's like a vacation for my eyes."

"A vacation for your eyes," he repeated slowly. "I know what you mean."

"You must have been to the Caribbean before," she couldn't believe she was actually bringing this up! "I mean with your wife being from down here and all . . . '' She feigned nonchalance.

"Oh," he hemmed and hawed a little before answering, as if the mere mention of the woman was uncomfortable for him. "I've been as far as Barbados, of course, but just twice. Yvette, she ah . . . didn't get along well with her family, my in-laws, so . . . it didn't make much sense coming, I'm afraid."

"You missed out on a lot," Rhea said gently.

"Yeah. I missed out on a whole lot." He forced a heavy sigh through his nose, like a horse.

The brief silence that followed loomed, threatening her, so Rhea rushed to fill it. "Did you get any good shots today?"

He accepted her attempt to fill the silence graciously. "Oh, yeah, some really great ones. The market was so colorful, and so alive. Thanks for taking Jodie for me."

"Oh, it was a pleasure, really."

"She likes you a lot, you know." He didn't look at her.

Marcus had said that to her already. What was the point of repeating it? Why was it so important to him? Instead of dwelling on it, she just said "uh-huh" and lapsed into silence again.

After about twenty minutes' strolling, the girl struck pay dirt. "This is definitely it," Rhea said approvingly, holding up the clump of weed that Jodelle had handed her, pretending to inspect it with great care. "You're a pretty good detective."

Jodelle beamed as her father added his praises to Rhea's. "Now," Marcus said, "we let the resident expert on seaweed show us what to do with it."

Jodelle eagerly turned to look at Rhea.

"Well," Rhea stopped and sat heavily in the sand. The other two followed suit, one on either side of her. With their heads all bent close, she grasped one of the small air bladders that helped the weed to float and popped it between her fingers. It burst with a satisfying sound. "You just pop the little balloons, like this."

"And then?" Jodelle prompted her eagerly.

Rhea was taken aback. She'd always just popped for popping's sake. "Then nothing. You just pop all the balloons, throw it away, and go find another bunch."

Jodelle looked crestfallen, but seemed determined to make the best of it. She retrieved her precious weed and settled herself down where the waves lapped at the sand, a few yards away, and began popping with a sincerity that made her father laugh.

"The Nintendo generation," he shook his head. "I think they've missed out on some of the simple pleasures of life."

Rhea agreed ruefully. "Like drawing in the sand with sticks."

"And frying ants on the sidewalk with a magnifying glass." He was being mischievous again. When he was like this, approachable and warm instead of piercing or cold or angry, it was impossible not to like him.

"You know, it's nice when you look at me like that." The sun made the shadows of his long thick lashes look like fringes on his cheeks.

"Look at you like what?" she asked, and looked away.

"Not like a schoolmarm or a dragon lady, scolding me for my wrongdoings. Or not like you're afraid of me. Do I frighten you so badly?"

"Hey, give the ego a rest, okay?" Frighten her? He must be joking.

"Or do you just frighten yourself?"

She gave him an arched brow look that she hoped was convincing. "What's there to be scared of? You're being ridiculous."

"Oh," his voice was exaggeratedly casual, "I don't know. Maybe the fact that you let your hostess mask fall off last night. Maybe you're worried about how much I enjoyed kissing the woman behind the mask, and how much that woman enjoyed kissing me back."

Her embarrassed flush betrayed how close to home his words had hit. She glanced sharply across at Jodelle, just in case she was getting any of this. The girl had abandoned her weed and was digging energetically in the wet sand.

"She can't hear us, Rhea."

Pity, that would have made a pretty good excuse. *Not in front of the kid, dear.* She tried to tune him out. It was too hot for such a serious conversation.

"Rhea," he said. His voice was suddenly soft. "Just give me one minute. There's something I have to say."

She squared her shoulders and looked at him. "Yes, what is it?" She tried to make her voice sound as patient and as martyred as possible.

"Are you all right about last night?"

She was surprised. A few moments ago he was needling her, casting bait in her face and daring her to rise to it. Now the teasing boy was gone, and the pensive man sat in his place. He was almost tentative. "What do you mean by 'all right'? What does 'all right' mean?"

"I mean, I said I was sorry. Are you still upset?"

She shook her head. "No, I'm fine." And if he bought that, he'd buy anything.

"I just need to hear that from you. Like I said, I enjoyed it. Very much. But I'm not a poacher. I don't hunt on any other man's territory. I know you've got a boyfriend, Rhea. You don't need to remind me of him. I feel like a skunk, doing what I did."

"Oh, please!" She wasn't having any of that. "That's so sexist! I don't belong to anybody. Not to Brent, not to you. What you do, you do to me, not to him." "Hunting" on someone else's territory! Was he for real?

"Hey," he protested softly. "I'm trying to apologize here. Cut me some slack, will you?"

"Fine, then, Marcus. Apology accepted. Let's just put it behind us, okay?" Then for good measure, and in an attempt to comfort herself, she added. "Really, it was nothing."

His eyebrows shot up, male ego bruised. "Well, I hope it wasn't *quite* nothing."

He sounded so hurt that she began to laugh. He joined in, and it broke the tension. "Well, if you want the truth, I wasn't really sorry," he confessed. "I was sorry I *stopped.*" His face was serious once again. "But I never meant to offend you. Okay?"

"Okay," she said softly. She got to her feet and dusted the sand off her bottom and thighs. She was restless now, and wasn't keen on staying still much longer, especially next to him. "You want to head back in?"

He shook his head. "That's okay. Jodie and I will be fine out here a little longer. Thanks."

She tried to hide her disappointment. Strange, how she wanted to be alone and far from his magnetic influence, yet his apparent disinterest in keeping her cut deep as she walked swiftly back in the direction of the beach house and sanctuary. Sharp memories of those few breathless moments with Marcus were flooding her brain, and refused to leave, even when she commanded them to. She was embarrassed, furious with herself, but was loath to admit it, because, if the truth be told, she was sorry he'd stopped, too.

CHAPTER TEN

The Bainbridges were going to be trouble. There was something about the way that Rainer looked at Rhea, and the manner in which he behaved whenever she was around that filled her with an ever-present sense of dread. It seemed as if he were weighing her up with every look, measuring her, and biding his time. It was a nasty feeling.

His sly smiles and long unabashed stares had not been lost on his wife, either, and she, in turn, responded with a cold, studied indifference to anything that Rhea had to say. It made Rhea's job all the more difficult. Their visits to places of interest were becoming painful.

On one hand, she was avoiding too much contact or discussion with either Marcus or Rainer, for vastly different reasons, while on the other, Dahlia was avoiding her. The only people who seemed to simply enjoy the pleasure of being there and soaking up the experience were Fred and Trudy, who were either oblivious to the underlying tensions, or didn't care, and Jodelle, who, God bless her, was having the time of her life.

The overnight trip to the northeastern village of Toco was a welcome change from the lethargy of quiet Mayaro. Instead of gently sloping miles of sand, there were craggy cliffs and wild crashing waves. The savagely beautiful scenery was, for Rhea, a source of strength, and strength was something she was particularly in need of right now.

Their arrival at the northeast coast was heralded by the strong smell of the sea. The little pockets of beach were embraced by gray boulders and rocks, as though the cliffs above were jealously guarding them from intruders. The smell, the entire feel of the coast, was different from the one that they had left.

"It even smells different," Marcus observed, looking outside in awe.

She looked at him in surprise. They hadn't had much to say to each other since the seaweed-hunting expedition a few days ago. She decided that wherever the conversation was leading, it would be innocuous enough. "I was thinking the same thing."

"Yeah?" He held her eyes for a little too long. "What do you know," he said slowly, "We have psychic connection."

Rhea was glad (hoped!) he was joking. She already half suspected he could read her thoughts, judging from his uncanny ability to turn up and bug her at the most inopportune times. If he could decipher her thoughts, if he could read the endless uncomfortable stream of images (all involving him!) that had been invading her mind over the past few days, she would be in a tight spot indeed. She shrugged his comment off with a forced grin.

They checked into a hotel just past the town of Toco. Rhea had been nervous about this part of the proceedings; the stinging humiliation of the first night at the Beach House From Hell still lingered in her memory. Even though she had used the small family hotel many times before on such trips, she was still a little anxious, and had called the hotel manager up three times to ensure that everything was in order.

To her relief, the rooms were impeccable, and even Rainer seemed content. The hotel was well-kept, with a garden of lush oleander bushes that were in full pink bloom, brilliant hibiscus of every imaginable colour and hedges of sweet lime bush, whose leaves and tiny white blossoms perfumed the air.

They had lunch on the patio: fried flying fish with coo-coo balls, a thick spicy yellow paste made of cornmeal and okra.

"Fish looks good," Marcus commented slyly to her out of the corner of his mouth. She flushed. She somehow could never shake the mild embarrassment that she felt whenever she ate meat in from of him. She looked up to see the gleam in his eye.

"Just teasing, darling," he whispered again. "Don't be so sensitive. I used to be a great fish lover once, you know."

"Oh, yes?" somehow she'd always seemed to think of him as being perpetually and conclusively vegetarian, as if he were born that way.

"Yeah."

"So you still feel like eating it?"

"Of course I feel like eating it. Just because you can't have something doesn't mean you never long for it. I'm not *dead*, you know."

The remark made her flush.

The evening should have been cooler, but somehow, it was not. "Funny heat," Banner said to her. "Strange, this heat," he said again, this time to himself.

They were on their way to the lighthouse, an old but functional monument that stood at the crest of a cliff a mere five minutes' drive from the bay. In spite of the fairly heavy tourist traffic and the fact that the lighthouse was still in use, the single approach to it was overgrown with vines and high razor grass. A small wooden bridge, which had no protective barriers along the sides groaned under the weight of the van, causing her passengers to catch their collective breath. Rhea always cringed when they crossed this bridge; the shrunken wooden slats would not hold out much longer, and she hated the vision that she had each time she crossed it; the vision of herself and a vanload of passengers being the unfortunate ones to finally break the camel's back, and plunge into the shallow river below.

But, as always, they made it across in one piece and parked safely within the lighthouse compound. As they gathered around her, she explained briefly that although it looked like something out of a Robert Louis Stevenson novel, the lighthouse was in fact functional and served to guide ships passing through the notorious stretch of sea between Trinidad and its sister island, Tobago.

"We'll stay until sunset," she promised, "That way we can see the lights come on. But while we're waiting, there's something I want to show you."

They followed her down the narrow trail that led past the lighthouse and onto a breathtakingly beautiful rock face. The expanse of rock jutted out into the water, ending in a sharp drop to the sea several yards below. Although the rock was jagged and a little scary, Rhea assured them that it was perfectly safe to walk across the forty or fifty feet of it that was flat. They walked out, gingerly at first, but more confidently once they became used to the eerie feeling of danger that was not entirely absent.

The sea breeze roared about them like an infuriated beast, whipping at their hair, forcing them to squint against the stiff salt wind. It was like standing on the back of a huge sleeping creature, and knowing that if you were to wake it, it would be very angry.

"I can feel the sea breathing," Jodelle whispered. Her eyes were wide with wonder. "It's like a monster under my feet!"

"The sea has cut its way under the rock that we're standing on," Rhea told them. "There are channels and passageways running through the entire rock face. Come, let me show you something." She led them farther down the slab of rock and pointed to a hole the width of a basketball in the surface of the rock. The hole led all the way to the sea, and on peering down it they could see the furious surging of the frothy water.

The waves were slamming hard against the rock in a hypnotic rhythm; a series of small waves were inevitably followed by the sudden assault of a huge one. As they stood around the hole, looking down, a big wave came. With the roar of an awakening giant, and with a rush of air, the water surged up through the small hole, forcing its way up and out until it shot up at them, splashing their arms and faces, leaving them laughing like delighted children.

"Oh, that was wonderful," Trudy smiled, "Let's see it happen again!'' They waited patiently, trying to listen to the rhythm of the sea, trying to predict when the next surge would come. Finally it did, spraying them all over, and they laughed.

Rhea loved this spot. She loved seeing the simple delight of her guests at the little trick of nature. Leaving them peering into the lungs of the earth, she walked to the very edge of the cliff. With her arms wrapped tightly around herself in a bid to calm the queasiness that this action always gave her, she looked down into the surging water that beat against the rock as though there was a personal vendetta between them. She liked peering over; it was for her a test of courage, trying to outstare the sea. The fear was almost an erotic thrill, a mixture of power, splendor, and danger. Nothing that plunged over that seductive edge could live.

''Magnificent.'' Marcus' voice in her ear made her start with fright. So close to the edge, the effect was giddying. He shot out a quick hand to steady her. ''Step back a little,'' he advised.

She stepped back before glaring at him. ''Don't you know you shouldn't do that? What if I fell?''

''Then,'' he said soberly, ''I would've had to leap after you, my dear.''

''Don't be silly.'' She returned her gaze from the water. He still hadn't let go of her. She tried to ignore the warmth of the hand that curled around her arm, and pretended not to notice that the backs of his fingers brushed against the curve of her breast, which was covered only by the thin material of her swimsuit.

Unsteadily, she pointed toward the water, ''See, over there, that frothy white line in the water? Like waves coming from different directions, colliding?''

Marcus nodded.

''That's the meeting of two currents, each one going the opposite way.''

''And when they collide,'' he added softly, ''it must be really dangerous, with the two of them being drawn together, yet struggling to pull themselves apart. It must be hard to be caught in that, with the water and sand being churned up from the bottom, getting sucked under, getting tossed about.'' As he spoke, his fingers stroked the soft inside of her arm in a hypnotic rhythm.

Rhea didn't trust herself to answer. In the unusual heat of the evening, his caresses were causing an uncomfortable warmth, which originated not at the point where he touched her, but from somewhere deep inside. It flowed up and out of her, suffusing her entire body. She shifted uncomfortably, embarrassed at her body's leaping response to such a minor touch.

"Look at those two," he said and pointed across the way with his chin. With pique she realised that he was not even looking at her. There she was, getting her insides all twisted into moist knots, and he didn't seem in the least bit affected! She turned her head in the direction that he indicated. Dahlia and Rainer had found one of the smaller blowholes, one which was no larger than a grapefruit. Instead of shooting water with the surging of the waves, it sent a column of cool air up the channel. Dahlia was straddling the hole barefoot, and with each surge of air her bright pink and orange cotton sarong unfurled around her like a sail, whipping up about her hips with an audible snap. Rainer was holding her sandals in one hand; the other grasped Dahlia's tightly.

"She looks like Marilyn Monroe with her skirt flying up like that," Marcus said. He brought his camera up to his face and squeezed off a few quick shots.

"Yeah," Rhea said dryly, "Marilyn Monroe." Funny how even those two, with their continued unpleasantness, could actually relax long enough to be enjoying themselves. The North Coast air must be working overtime. They hadn't so much as smiled, either at each other or at anyone else, in days.

"There's something seriously wrong with that couple," he frowned slightly. "They just don't seem to participate, and there's this tension . . . like a cold front. Have you noticed?"

She sighed, but didn't answer.

"Of course you have. How stupid of me. It must really make things hard for you, having to make sure that they have a good time and all, when they seem to be wishing that they were anywhere else but here, at least with each other."

Or with anyone else as their guide but me. She wanted to

tell him just how hard they were making things, just how difficult the tour was becoming for her, but held her tongue. Marcus was a guest, just like them. Complaining to one paying client about another just wasn't right. She murmured something vague and inaudible, and hoped he'd let it slide.

"Rhea?" His sharp eyes missed nothing. "Are they giving you any trouble?"

"Don't be stupid," she snapped. *Not half as much trouble as you've brought into my life!*

She cast anxious eyes around the rock, looking for Jodelle. He saw her panic and guessed the reason behind it. "Don't worry," he said reassuringly. "She's gone into the lighthouse with Fred and Trudy. They're chatting with the lighthouse keeper."

"Well, I've never seen anyone do that before. I don't even know if you're allowed."

"Well, you know my daughter. She just marched right up to the door, banged on it until he opened up, and demanded to see the inside of the lighthouse. I think she intimidated him. I wouldn't be surprised if he's giving them the full tour," he said.

To Rhea's relief, he seemed to have let the Bainbridge matter drop, and finally saw fit to release her arm. They stood for a while contemplating the sea. The sun was getting low, and the tide was coming in, making the scenery more wildly beautiful than ever. "That leaves you and me," he told her after a while.

It wasn't what she wanted to hear, so she pretended she hadn't.

He wasn't prepared to let her off easy. "Is there any way to get down there?" he pointed downward to the base of the cliff that was already being lashed by the rising tide.

She stared at him, aghast. "Are you crazy? Why?"

He shrugged. "Just to see what there is to see. I don't know. I thought you were adventurous."

That rankled. "I am. But I'm not stupid."

"Look, there's a broken fishing rod on one of the lower rocks. That means people go down there to fish, doesn't it?"

She was forced to admit that it was indeed a popular fishing spot.

"So if other people make it down there, why are you afraid to go?"

"I'm not afraid to go down there. I've been down there lots of times, with fishing parties."

"So what makes today any different?"

"The time does. And the tide. The sea isn't something you play with, Marcus. Sometimes the time is right; when the sea is gentle and the tide is low, and you've got sunlight. But this isn't one of those times; it's getting late and the tide is coming in. I won't do it."

"I thought the customer was always right," he said petulantly.

He'd hit a nerve. Her pride in her career and her professionalism was one of her tender spots. "It just doesn't work that way. I'm responsible for all my clients. And I won't let you take any risks."

"I'm a journalist. I've put my skin on the line before, you know. I know how far to push it. And I'm a grown man, Rhea; I'll take all the risks I like."

She got the feeling that her refusal to take him down was more responsible for his insistence than any desire or curiosity to get down in the first place. "Look," she said, trying to keep her tone even. "I'll show you a way down, but not this cliff, okay? There's a safer slope round the side."

He looked pleased at that. "Good. Let's go."

With exaggerated reluctance she led him back up the rock, past the big blowhole, round the side of the lighthouse to a cliff face that sloped more gently toward the sea. On the way, they passed Dahlia and Rainer, who both stared but abruptly looked away. Rhea gritted her teeth. Just what she needed. She hoped she didn't have to regret letting Marcus needle her into this!

"Here it is," she said gruffly, and pointed to a track that had been worn down the side.

He peered over the edge. "Huh! A boy scout could make it down there! And you said it was dangerous!"

She bristled. "I never said *here* was dangerous. I said the *other side* was dangerous."

He patted her patronizingly on the shoulder. "Chill out, darling. I'm just teasing you. Gosh, you're sensitive!"

Instead of wasting her breath on an answer, she began feeling her way over the edge. Marcus abandoned the idea of needling her and followed close on her heels. The rising tide had reduced the already narrow spot of sand at the bottom of the sloping cliff to a strip that was just two or three feet wide. Fallen stones and stubborn tree roots made easy handholds, and they were at the bottom in minutes with little effort. The curve of the rock cut them off from the major face on the other side. They were utterly alone, and Rhea didn't like it.

"Happy now?" she asked sarcastically.

"Very," he told her.

She put her hands on her hips and scowled at him. "Well," she demanded. "You wanted to come down here. I brought you down. What now?"

"I don't know, Rhea," he said. "You tell me." He was standing close to her, closer than was required even by the limited dry land around them. His voice was soft and low, and as she perceived some indefinable tone in it, she looked up and was startled to see how wide and dark his pupils had become. Their pale gold had given way to a darkness and depth that was infinitely more disturbing. She recognised his intention, and to her own horror something inside her leaped with delight.

This time, she was the one that moved first. As she tilted her face upward and closed the space between them, she had one last rational thought: that she would hate herself later for being the one to cross that fine line between indecision and decision, and that this time she would not have the luxury of blaming him.

The taste of salt seemed destined to be forever a part of her memories of their kisses. She could feel it on his cheek, in a light powder, and taste it on his lips. But inside, in the depth of his mouth and along the uncanny softness of his inner lips there was only sweetness. The shock of contrast made her shudder, and for the second time that afternoon, he had to steady her from falling.

The relentless slamming of the waves against the cliffs was nothing compared to the pounding of her heart in her chest, and the throaty gush of air driven up the blow-holes nothing next to her gasps as she fought for air that her body simply could not seem to acquire. The rising tide surged around their feet now, frothing between their bare toes and swirling round their ankles. Her lungs were screaming for air, begging for it, and yet at that point she would rather die for lack of air than break the kiss, in case once she tore her lips away he would never kiss her again.

Marcus pulled away at last, suffering from the same need, and they leaned against each other, gulping in deep shuddering breaths. He took one dizzy step back, and Rhea felt a sudden panic that he would walk away from her, turn away, and begin his ascent to the top of the cliff, leave her alone with her humiliating desire. ''Mark, please,'' she put a restraining hand on his arm.

''Don't worry,'' he said gently, ''I know.'' He put his hands up to her face, cupping her chin firmly, searching her eyes, but she didn't want thought or logic or reason to intrude and return either of them to sanity. She took one of his hands away from her face and placed it over her breast. She wore only her jeans over her damp swimsuit, and her nipples were straining painfully through the clingy material, pointed and hard. He let his hand rest there, staring at her, his eyes full of questions. She waited, impatient, willing him to bend his head once again and press those full, firm lips against her mouth so that she could taste the sweetness inside him once more.

In her anxiety, a full, high-pitched vibration began rising from her depths, like a single note on a fine violin, threatening to erupt from her mouth in a cry of hunger and anguish. Finally, like a sand dune collapsing into the sea, Marcus sighed and surrendered.

He began covering her face and throat with kisses, and seemed torn by indecision between the pleasures to be derived from her mouth and from the rest of her face, as he moved back and forth between them. His sharp teeth inflicted quick nips along her ear and jaw, bites which would in a sober moment have been painful, but which now only had the effect of forcing her to grit her teeth to prevent herself from crying out in delight.

He struggled for a brief moment with the straps of her swimsuit, hands clumsy from impatience, but soon the upper part of it lay down around her waist. He cupped her aching, swollen breasts lightly for a second, feeling their weight, and then moved his large hands down to her waist, stroking her torso in wonder, as though astounded by the softness of her skin. Her own hands explored his body, running along the sharply defined planes of his chest and shoulders. The sand that clung to his chest hair was rough under her fingers.

When he lifted her abruptly to stand her on a thick slab of fallen rock, she was surprised at the ease with which he had done it. She was not exactly a tiny woman. The fleeting conscious thought was obliterated by sheer excitement when she realised his purpose in making her taller than he. His head was now at the level of her breasts, and as he began his assault on them, Rhea had to grasp his shoulders for support, digging her short nails into that wonderful chestnut skin of his, knowing she was hurting him, but unable to stop. His mouth was awakening dormant areas on her tender skin, every tiny nerve was suddenly and fully aroused, and to Rhea they seemed to join in a collective roar, like the creatures of a jungle being disturbed by an intruder. Their voices sang in her ears.

Her own voice joined them, and she was crying his name into his hair when he stopped. The shock was like a sudden cold wind. "Marcus!" she couldn't believe he was stopping. She couldn't believe she was begging him not to.

He was pulling her swimsuit up over her breasts, and the constricting fabric was the last thing she needed to feel against her heated skin. She turned her flushed face up to him in confusion, her mouth opened to speak his name again, but her tight throat could release no sound.

He kissed her again, on the cheek this time, like she was a child. "Shush, don't say anything. I know, honey. I know how

you feel. I know what you need, but this is just not the place,''
he said gently. "It's not *right* here."

She couldn't believe the extent of her need and disappointment. "Why?" she wailed, her voice high and petulant, like a
little girl being prevented from playing with her favourite toy.

"It isn't right. Not here. Not now. Look up, Rhea. We can
be seen. And we're facing the open sea."

Her mind told her he was right, but her body was not about
to give up that easily. Her skin and her face, her hair, her
mouth, her breasts clamoured their disappointment. There was
a heat running through her which the water that now coursed
around their calves couldn't cool. A sharp groan of frustration
exploded past her gritted teeth.

To her surprise, he laughed. The sound rumbled in his chest
and she could feel it under the outspread palms of her hands.
Infuriated, she considered hitting him. "I'm not laughing at
you, Rhea darling," he said. "I'm not. Do you really think I
want to stop?" He took her hand and placed it flat against the
bulging front of his jeans. "Does this feel like I want to stop?"

She let her hand rest there awhile, stirred by the feel of him,
hard under the damp, coarse material, curious, wanting to slide
her hands under the waistband to feel again the crisp crinkly
hair that grew there. She blushed and snatched away her hand.
Good sense was returning, and with it, the sobering memory
of her own behaviour. She turned her head away. He reached
up to stroke her cheek. "Rhea," he said, "Beautiful Rhea. We
have all the time we need. Okay?"

She nodded, but creeping resentment began to fill the spaces
within her left by unfulfilled desire. Once again, she'd allowed
herself to lose her control, and once again, he'd been the one
to stop. Like he was the only one with any common sense, or
any self-control. The heat in the pit of her belly made her
nauseated. She turned her back to him, hoping to hide the range
of emotions that raced across her face.

The sky had begun to take on the violet hue that warned of
the sudden night that was closing in around them. "I think we
should get back," he said. He laid a hand lightly against her
dark curly hair. She flinched, and he withdrew sharply. She

heard him sigh deeply, but she didn't turn to face him. Let him suffer like she was suffering! It was a while before he spoke again. ''The others will be waiting.''

She was flooded with embarrassment. ''I can't,'' she moaned. ''I can't face them. They'll just look at us and know.''

''No, they won't.''

''They will,'' she insisted. She could visualize all the staring eyes. How could she have done something so stupid? Was she mad?

''They won't,'' he said decisively. He tugged at her limp hand. ''Come, let's climb back up. You just stay calm, okay?''

Stay calm. He wasn't serious. Her career was on the line, along with her reputation, and he was flip enough to simply tell her to stay calm. As he prepared to ascend, she stood behind him, resenting him to the point of hatred. It seemed that ever since he had arrived, her life had begun to come unglued. Her tour and her professionalism were slipping between her fingers, and she just couldn't seem to find a way to prevent it. He'd muscled in on her territory by taking over her tour while she was sick, he'd muscled in on her country's privacy, and now, he was muscling in on her mind and soul.

She followed him up the face of the cliff, concentrating on her handholds more than she needed to. As she looked up at him moving swift and agile above her, she was sorry she couldn't just wish him away, blink twice to clear her vision, and he'd be gone like he was never there. If only the magic that he made her feel when he touched her could be transmuted into a more malevolent, powerful magic that could obliterate him from her life!

The climb was quick and easy, but the few moments it took to get to the top were enough to allow her time to come to the frightening, sobering realisation that she was falling into something that she knew she was not prepared for.

There were feelings there that she could not rationalise, and couldn't contain, and they were coming too thick and too fast for her to catch a breath and say to herself, *Relax, Rhea, this is just curiosity,* or *this is just fear,* or anger or desire or excitement or wonder or rage or joy or guilt or pleasure, or

any of the unending range of feelings that this man seemed
capable of awakening in her. She had skidded somewhere along
the way and was falling into something deep and wide and
perplexing—and it was going to be a long, hard fall.

CHAPTER ELEVEN

He was right: at the top of the cliff, around the other side of the lighthouse, the others were indeed waiting for them. Banner was calmly leaning against the hood of the van, puffing on a cigarette, listening indulgently to Jodelle's breathless account of the tour of the lighthouse.

"You can see all the way across the sea to Tobago," Jodelle were saying. "That's an island! Over there!" She pointed across the wide blackness of sea to the northeast. "You can just see the light of the lighthouse over there, flashing back at us! It's like they were saying hello!"

Rhea and Marcus approached, the conversation came to an abrupt end.

"Daddy! Rhea! Where you *been*? I was looking all over for you!"

The party turned of one accord and regarded them curiously. *Damn*, Rhea thought, and felt herself flushing to her scalp, *just what I need*. She began to wonder frantically if there was any visual evidence of her encounter with Marcus. She just knew that she looked very much kissed. Her breath was still a little uneven, and her eyes, she was sure, held the bright glitter of frustration. Would the exertion of the climb have been sufficient explanation for her high flush? She was realistic enough to know that the chances of that were slim.

As Jodelle broke away from Banner and raced toward them, Rhea drew her courage around herself like a cloak and stepped forward, not even looking at Marcus.

"Sorry, sweetie" she said, loudly enough for everyone to hear. "We were rock climbing."

"Really?" Rainer asked, his tone dangerously noncommittal. "All the way down to that wild sea?"

She nodded hard, and something in her belly tightened. She tried to keep her voice as level as possible, hoping that she could diffuse the insinuations in this odious man's voice—or at least, hoping that she was the only one to hear them. "Yes. Uh . . . there's a spot where it's easy to scale down the cliff face. We climbed down it and just . . . lost track of the time." She felt Marcus' eyes on her face and thought *he'd better not be smirking at me!*

"Ah," Rainer nodded and smiled congenially. "I'm sure it was quite an experience. I hope I get the benefit of one of your private tours next time!" He laughed congenially while his wife looked daggers at Rhea. Fred and Trudy shifted uncomfortably. Someone coughed discreetly.

Rhea didn't have to look up to know that Marcus' astute eyes were on her face. She busied herself by ruffling Jodelle's hair and insisting cheerily that she tell her everything that she'd seen and done in the lighthouse. Grasping the small willing hand, she led her into the van, hoping that the others would follow suit. As they moved along the winding, unlit road back to their guest house, Rhea listened determinedly to Jodelle's breathless ramblings, determined to ignore the inquiring glances that Banner occasionally threw in her direction.

Turtle watching was one of the highlights of this particular tour package, and tonight was the night. They ate out on the patio of the hotel, as it was a bright clear night. They had a hearty meal, their appetites sharpened by the hectic day at the beach and the strong smell of the sea air. Rhea was surprised at the amount that she ate. Her life had changed dramatically for the worse in a few short hours, with this hideous realisation that this handsome, annoying stranger, had barreled into her life, and somehow, indefinably, changed it, and there wasn't a thing she could do about it.

She was sure that the sickening upheaval that she was feeling would have rendered her unable to swallow a bite, but she consumed her hot meal almost as though she was relying on it to provide her with the strength to resist the folly into which she was now being drawn. She thought of just how sweet that folly could be, and the blood raced to her face.

"You look real pretty tonight, Rhea." Jodelle's sudden assertion was enough to stop conversation around the table. "You look like the sun."

Rhea flushed even deeper. Somehow this thing that she felt for the girl's father was showing on her face, flashing out of her skin and her eyes like a light from the beacon that they had just visited. She wished she could pluck one of her handy hostess masks from out of the air, and cover it up with ordinariness and schoolteacher cool, but when she reached for it, it wasn't there.

"Ah, well," Banner began slowly. He put his shrimp-laden fork down onto his plate and surveyed Rhea's face, which was now blazing more with embarrassment than with anything else. "It must be the wonderful sun we had today, little one. It was enough to put a glow into anyone's cheeks, if they didn't stay in the shade. Maybe tomorrow, you must see to it that Rhea takes better care of her skin."

Jodelle swallowed that explanation, but she was probably the only one who did. "I'll lend you some of my Coppertone tomorrow," she offered generously. "It smells real nice. And you won't burn no more."

Rhea thanked her and returned her attention to her food, grateful to Banner for his intervention, for what it was worth. Dinner seemed painfully long. Before dessert was served, she got to her feet, scraping the chair along the wooden floor as she stood.

"I think that after dinner we should all try to get two hours' rest. We'll need it for the turtle watching. It will probably be a long night.'' With this, she made as dignified an exit as was possible under the circumstances, and went quickly to her room.

She lay uneasily in her bed unable to take a nap, thinking again about Marcus, and wondering what she could possibly have done to merit her current predicament.

This couldn't be love, could it? She twisted her lips in self-mockery. It would come as a shock to her if she was capable of recognizing the phenomenon. Her past experiences with men had never been anything like this.

Before, there had simply been gradual admiration and attraction, which progressed at a safely sedate pace from there. Nothing like this sudden gut-wrenching emotion that assailed her now. As for her sexual response to this man, she was appalled! Could that really have been her, so swiftly and completely driven out of her own sexual comfort zone that she found herself stripped to the waist on an open cliffside, exposed, driven to beg a man she barely knew to touch her, and keep kissing her with that sweet chocolate mouth of his? *In full view, Rhea,* she chided herself miserably, *you were in full view of anybody who cared to come along at that moment.* She didn't know what to think of herself.

The image of Brent came to her mind, suspended before her mind's eye like Bob Cratchet's ghost, chiding her. *What about me?* it said.

Rhea was thrown even deeper into despair. What about him? What about honesty and fidelity, and all the pillars of a relationship that she believed in so deeply? In the two years that they had been together, her eye had never even wandered. She was reasonably sure that the same could be said for Brent; although she had to admit they'd never discussed it, she had simply taken it for granted that he had felt the same.

As for feelings, all of a sudden she was assailed by the horrible realisation that she was no longer sure how she felt about Brent. Wasn't it safe to assume that the mere fact you could love another man (there, she'd admitted it to herself, that made it true, didn't it?) was an indication that the relationship you were actually in was hardly rock-solid in the first place? She tried to think, tried hard to analyze her situation, but her head was full of dense clouds.

She was embarrassed to admit that their relationship was low-keyed, comfortable, predictable. They'd never actually said "I love you." Brent had said early in their dating that those words were too theatrical, too overused, too commonplace to be valid anymore, but there had always been "an understanding." She accepted Brent's self-centeredness, his possessiveness, his love of things routine, as just part of a normal relationship. That was love, wasn't it? Being comfortable and steady? Maybe a little bored?

Who said there had to be fireworks? Who said you had to feel this lurch in the pit of your stomach when the man's face came to mind? Who said you had to want, to crave, to burn for a kiss or a touch or the feel of a hot tongue along the side of your neck. . . .

This wasn't working. What, did she think this train of thought was going to make things any better? She rose from the bed (a bed was the last thing she needed on her mind right now!) and stepped hurriedly into the shower and let the powerful stream of water hit her in her face. She stood under the forceful white gush, hoping to wash the scent of him from her skin and hair, but twenty minutes later, when she finally came out again, she had to admit to herself that the scent that followed her around adhered to her mind, not to her physical self. By pressing, grinding, clinging (stop!) against her, he'd gone and made an imprint of his smell, this wild nightflower/animal/hungry-man smell, on her mind. And that was a place that water could not reach.

She pulled her phone out of its thin leather case and dialed a number, but her hands were so nervous that she had to hang up and redial twice. Then, after only a few rings, the call was answered.

"Brent," she said, glad that he was home. She needed to hear his voice, remind herself that it was he that she loved. "Hi."

"Rhea, honey, how you doing?" He sounded glad to hear her voice.

"Oh, fine," she lied. She hoped that her treasonous thoughts could not manifest themselves into sound waves and travel cross the lines to him. That would be disastrous. *Hold on to his voice*, she advised herself, *get him talking and try to get some of his voice down inside of you, so you can carry it around for protection*. "What about you?"

"Oh, you know. Kind of busy at work, running around doing this and that. Things are okay. Where are you now?"

"I'm up in Toco. We're going out to see the turtles tonight."

"Good. Dress warm."

Dress warm, he'd said. He was concerned for her well-being. That meant he loved her, didn't it? "I will," she said. She wondered what else there was to say. "Anything exciting going on in Port of Spain?"

"Nah. It's the middle of the week. Things are pretty dead around here. And it's getting hotter, even out of the city. There's a concert going on at the Queen's Hall, but I'll wait until you get up to this side again. We can go see it together."

"You can see it, if you like," she told him. "You don't have to wait on me, if you really want to go." Now why did she say that?

"Maybe I will. I'll think about it."

"Okay." She waited for the conversation to take a turn for the better, waited for the tiniest of sparks to shoot across at her over the line. With Mark, she never had to wait, the threat, the promise of sparks was there in every conversation. But with Brent, now, tonight, she realised there was only . . . dullness. The unidentifiable, niggling characteristic of their relationship, for the first time had a name: boredom.

It was as if she'd been having the same thin watery soup as her only meal for such a long time that she could no longer identify it on her palate, until she tasted strawberries and champagne, bringing her mouth alive. Now, tasting that soup again, she could identify that old pervasive flavour, and its name was boredom.

"Okay."

There wasn't much else to say. She was tempted to break their self-imposed rule, and say "I love you," more to afford herself the sense of comfort that she would derive from saying it, but the sounds would not come out. Her unaccustomed lips could not even shape the words. Instead, she simply promised to call him when they returned to Mayaro the next day.

"Good night, babe," he said softly.

"Good night," she said, and folded the phone away. She got up and began pulling on her deep green company cardigan and her sturdy hiking boots. It was time to go see the turtles.

The group arrived at the small community of Matura and climbed out onto the dark beachfront at ten-thirty, waiting to be met by the guide who was obliged by conservation ordinances to accompany them.

They stood in a small huddle on hard-packed earth, close to a rough wooden shack with a thatched roof. It was here that campers spent the night, and the wardens sought shelter under it while they took a break from patrolling the beaches. The dirt road that led into this dead end was unlit and quiet, and the sky stretched overhead, curved, dark and blue, like an upside-down bowl. The stars were like brilliant pinpricks.

"Daddy!" Jodelle's squeaky voice pierced the air. She stood in a clearing, head thrown so far back that she looked in danger of falling over backward. She pointed upward to a cluster of stars. "Look, Daddy! O'Brian!"

Everyone looked upward to the constellation at which she was pointing. Above them, the hunter ignored them, pulling solemnly back on his bow. Marcus humored her. "Yeah. That's him. But you know, some people call him Orion."

She gazed up at her father in wonder. "They call him that, too?"

Fred and Trudy laughed loudly. As usual, they were dressed almost theatrically, both in khaki shorts and shirts, with sturdy hiking boots and long socks, even though most of the night would be spent on soft, powdery sand. All they were missing was a pair of pith helmets to make the picture complete.

As usual, Rainer and Dahlia seemed subdued. Rhea was growing almost accustomed to their sullen silence. Still, she noticed that Dahlia had walked with a small sketch pad, and in spite of the discomfort that she always felt in the woman's company, she was glad that Dahlia was prepared to do a little art again. To hear her speak, she was regretting letting her art fall by the wayside because of stresses on the marriage. This little excursion might have some benefits for the Bainbridges after all.

Restlessness soon began stirring within the group. Marcus, who hadn't addressed a word to her for the evening, poked idly around in the nearby shrubbery, searching for God knows what. Fred and Trudy began playing with their expensive designer canteens, sipping what smelled like strong local coffee. Rainer stood with his hands deep in his pockets, pursing his lips and staring upward as if examining the heavens, although Rhea was prepared to bet that he was hardly much of a stargazer. The guide better come fast.

Sand flies and mosquitoes were delighted by the scent of fresh warm human, and launched an attack. "Remember," Rhea said as she hurriedly passed around a can of repellent, "there are no guarantees that we might see a turtle. They're difficult to predict. We might sit around for four hours and the most we will see might be other turtle watchers."

They all laughed, but Rhea's answering laugh was forced, and died on her lips. Usually, she loved doing the turtle run. She loved the excitement of being out in the cool night air, of waiting, whispering in hushed tones, wondering whether a turtle or two would appear. But tonight she wanted to be anywhere else but here, near him. As long as Marcus was around, there would be the risk of her frightening, tumultuous feelings being discovered. It was too soon for that. Rhea was sure that if their eyes connected, even for a second, he would look right down inside her and recognise the feelings she was harboring for him. And that would be a humiliation that she wouldn't survive.

An old black pickup rattled as it made its way across the rough dirt road. Rhea stepped forward and stood at the door as their guide descended. She and Albert had worked together

several times before. He was a man with a true passion for the
animals over which he watched. Rhea shook hands warmly
with the small, dark young man, and introduced him to the
others.

"Albert knows everything there is to know about turtles,"
she boasted on his behalf, causing him to smile shyly behind
his mustache. He whispered briefly into a heavy, old-fashioned
walkie-talkie that he was holding, notifying the other men with
whom he worked that he was about to proceed toward the
beach with a party. It was important to know where each warden
was; anyone seen unannounced on the beach would be pre-
sumed to be poaching.

The Matura turtle reserve had been established in an effort
to stem the wanton killing of the leatherback turtle along the
coast, Albert explained. The tight security around this particular
area was all in the best interest of the animals whose numbers
were decreasing at an alarming pace. As the female turtles
came out of the sea to lay their hundreds of eggs on dry land,
they were at their most vulnerable. The huge, heavy-bodied
creatures were slow-moving, and an easy target for poachers
who stole their eggs, which, soft, yolky and flavorful, were
highly valued on the black-market. They were also butchered
for their meat. In the worst possible act of barbarism, poachers
often captured a hapless turtle and cut off her flippers, leaving
the bleeding animal to suffer a prolonged and hideous death
in the sand.

As Albert spoke, Rhea sensed Marcus close at hand, listening
to his every word. She ventured a glance at him. What she saw
bore no reference to their encounter earlier this afternoon. He
was all reporter, all animal activist, and the golden eyes that
had so confounded her with their passionate darkness were
wide with horror at the ugly story that Albert was recounting.

She felt a rush of pique that she tried immediately to quell—
no lovelorn looks coming from his direction, no indication that
their abruptly truncated embrace had left him with the same
nagging frustration that it had her. He listened silently like a
professional, gathering material for his story. That was all.

It was like a swift kick in the ego. That he was more able

to shunt aside the memory of their encounter down by the cliff, and concentrate fully on his work while she was barely capable of doing the job that she was there to do really bugged her. Was it that he was better able to bring himself back under control than she was, or was it that he was simply less affected by her than she was by him?

The feeling of rejection was quickly translated into a rehash of her old resentment of his purpose for being here—his article. She knew she was overreacting, and knew that his story, as explicit as it might be, could hardly be as damaging as she had first assumed it would. But in spite of this reminder from her more rational self, her anger spurted up and out of her. She glared at him, hating his curiosity, hating him for his do-gooder instinct. Seething, she tried to ignore him as he fell into step beside her.

"Horrible story," he whispered. His voice was heavy with emotion.

"Yep," she said curtly. If he noticed any sharpness in her voice, it would have been impossible to tell because of the darkness that enveloped them. Her own irrational response made no sense to her. First, she was piqued that he wasn't paying her any attention. Then, when he did speak to her, it upset her as well. Was she losing it?

The man seemed undaunted, and whispered some question or other about the turtles' plight in her ear. "Hey," she snapped, "you've got someone else to answer your questions this time." She jerked her thumb in Albert's direction. "Why don't you ask him?" She lengthened her stride to move to the head of the party, and away from him. He was stunned, and stopped in his tracks, staring at her as she hurried away. Rhea couldn't care less. Why couldn't he learn to leave her alone?

The party trekked forward in near-silence, using the light of the moon for guidance, as it was best to reserve their flashlights for emergency use. The turtles hated bright lights, and nobody wanted to scare them off. They found a spot where they could sit quietly, unnoticed, and wait. There was a little shifting around to get comfortable, and then the group settled down.

Rhea felt a tiny hand slip into hers. "Jodie," she said softly, looking down.

The little girl was bundled up like an Eskimo in jeans, a sweater, and an anorak, in spite of the mildness of the night. Marcus wasn't taking any chances with any sudden nippy sea breezes. The sight of the small excited face peering out at her from the dense pile of clothing almost made her laugh out loud. Marcus was a good father. You had to give him that.

"It's kind of like Camp Fire girls," Jodelle whispered happily. "I've never been anywhere like this!"

Rhea bent down and kissed her round nose. "You like it?"

Jodelle nodded vigorously, and snuggled against Rhea's arm. She was silent for a while, drinking in all the drama of the late night and the hushed waiting. After a while she dug her small sharp elbow into Rhea's ribs. "Are they here yet?" she hissed.

"Honey, when they're here, you'll know."

"Okay." She seemed to be satisfied with this, and settled down again. Moments later, though, she prodded Rhea again. "Are they here *now*?" she asked loudly.

Marcus answered before Rhea could. He plopped himself in the sand and gave his daughter a playful shake. "They won't come if you keep making all that racket! What did I teach you about patience?"

"Patience is a virtue," she parroted, smiling at her father.

"And that's a good thing, right?"

She gave him the thumbs-up. "Right!"

Rhea had a Lucien on each side of her; she was outflanked. As Jodelle again settled into silence next to her, she stared at the small face, and realised that there was another dimension to her newfound problem that she hadn't thought about before: Jodelle. As if the turbulent emotions that she was feeling for the father were not enough, there was also the love that was growing inside her for the daughter. It was a sweeter kind of love, a gentle thing that posed no threat, and awoke no fear. There was just caring and compassion for this motherless creature who seemed to make Rhea's day brighter just by being nearby.

What about her? Rhea had grown to enjoy the company of

many of the children who came on tour, but this was different. Somewhere inside her was a growing instinct—no, urge, to care for her, be with her ... that was wrong, wasn't it? The girl (and her father!) would be returning home in ten days or so, and if the attachment between them was allowed to grow and strengthen, the sensation of loss might be too great for her, as an adult, to bear, much less for a child. It wouldn't be right, leading her on like this. Loving her, and showing that love, would be just setting her up for a fall.

She wished she could get up and walk down to the sea. She could leave them in Albert's hands and stand there at the spot where the water met the sand and let them watch their turtles until it was time to go home. But Jodelle was curled up against her, drowsing, and she wouldn't disturb her. Sighing, she give in to her fate and decided to wait her predicament out. The wait wouldn't be long.

The crackle of the walkie-talkie in Albert's hand was a welcome distraction. He held it close to his ear, as the poor quality of the reception made it impossible to understand the incoming message from a distance.

"We've got one coming out of the water just a little farther up ahead," he announced with satisfaction.

With renewed vigor, everyone rose to their feet and followed Albert along the beach. Awake again, Jodelle trotted alongside Rhea, clasping her hand tightly. The feel of the small soft hand in hers sharpened and deepened Rhea's pain.

A huge dark shape could be seen emerging from the surf. It was an older female, easily more than five feet across the back, and weighing at least a thousand pounds. She came slowly and painfully out of the dark water, pausing shyly on the beach, wondering if it was safe to proceed. The group stood a respectful distance away so as not to frighten her. As her courage grew, she continued forward with stoic determination, her huge dark flippers leaving a crisscross trail on the soft sand.

"She'll just go a few feet above the high-water mark," Albert whispered, "and then she'll start digging her nest."

As he had said, the giant began digging hard with her strong hind flippers. She would burrow determinedly until she had a hole about three feet deep into the hard-packed sand before beginning to lay.

Rhea whispered a warning to an overexcited Jodelle not to go running up closer to get a better look, as this would frighten the beast. Instead, she managed to convince her to settle into the sand just out of the path of the flying sand being tossed up by the turtle, where the girl sat and watched happily.

Marcus knelt a good distance away and set about preparing his photographic equipment. Some devil, some niggling need to confront him even in the face of her own reluctance to spend time with him, drove her over to the place where he stood. Tight-lipped, she squatted next to him and snarled into his ear, warning him about the use of a flash on the beach, which might frighten the animal enough to send her lumbering back into the sea, eggs unlaid.

"I know what I'm about, Rhea," he said crisply. "What is wrong with you? You've been impossible all night!" Immediately, he relented the sharpness of his response and demonstrated the light-sensitive equipment he'd brought along for night photography. He promised her sincerely that the last thing he wanted to do was hurt the animal. She nodded curtly, accepting this to be the truth.

Although the resentment burned within her, Rhea stayed nearby, irrationally seeking an excuse just to be close to him. Hating herself for acting like a teenager with a crush, she remained rooted there, watching him work. It was bizarre, this new feeling, these conflicting urges to be physically close to him and as far away as possible at the same time. She searched her mind desperately for something to distract her from these disturbing thoughts.

"Marcus," she took a deep breath, "are you going to write about what Albert just said? About the poaching?" She bit her lip nervously and watched him with vain hope.

He did not look up from his work. "I'm writing the truth, Rhea, that's all I can write. I told you that before. Why do you keep bringing this up?"

"But Marcus, do you really have to portray us as barbarians who butcher our own wildlife?"

"Rhea," his voice was calm but stern, "I'm not painting a picture of the entire population of your island. That would be impossible. There are just a few people committing this act, and that's what my article will say. No more, no less."

"But there will be a public outcry!"

"Good," he said firmly. "It's a crime, what they're doing, and it must be stopped. And I'll try to stop it the only way I know how." For a change, he set his equipment down and gave her a hard look, bending so close that she could feel his warm angry breath on her face, in spite of the cool sea breeze. "And let me tell you this: I don't want to hear anything about my article. Not another question. Not another word. You are here to do a job. So am I. I respect your professional integrity, and as one professional to another, I expect you to respect mine. Am I making myself clear?"

She nodded sullenly. She had the grace to feel ashamed of her behavior. It really did amount to bullying. Why? Why did she keep coming back to that stupid, stupid magazine article over and over? He must think her such a fool! She struggled to frame an apology. "Marcus . . ." she began, and stopped, suddenly remembering all too clearly the way she'd called out his name into the wind just a few hours before.

He heard the note of despair and remembered, too. He rose to his feet and looked down at her anguished face. "Why don't you think about what's really bothering you, Rhea?" he suggested softly. "It has nothing to do with the turtles or the tourists or my article. You know that as well as I do."

Eyes wide, she stared at him. "What?"

"You know exactly what I mean."

"No," she lied, stammering. "Marcus, I don't . . . I . . ." She felt the blood drain from her face and a fear rose within her. He *knew*!

His look changed to one of concern.

"Are you okay?" he asked softly. "Rhea, baby . . ." She shifted under his sudden scrutiny—it was better to mask what she felt for him. There would only be complications, complications she did not need. She nodded dumbly.

"Forgive me? For this evening?" His eyes were still on her.

She wished he'd look down at his damn work instead of burning her face with his stare. She was getting tired of this nonsense; first he would kiss her, next, he would say he was sorry. He was beginning to make it a habit.

"Of course," she said curtly. She hoped the matter would drop right there.

He nodded. Rhea contemplated going back to join the others who were stooping in a semicircle in the sand round the turtle. There she could just settle down and wish the evening were over, thank her stars that Albert was there to lift the burden of guideship off her shoulders for one night. She was about to get to her feet when Marcus spoke again. "We need time to talk, you and me," he said.

"What?"

"We need to talk. We need to find some quiet time when we won't be disturbed and talk this thing through. Soon."

"Talk about what, Marcus? What do we have to talk about?" Her best strategy was to stonewall, she decided. Be strong, don't let him in. Don't let this new and threatening love take root. If you strangled a sapling, cut it off from light and air, it would die. Then everything would be okay again.

"I think you know what, Rhea. Don't be stupid. Don't try to convince me you didn't feel what I felt down there. And don't try to convince me that you haven't been feeling it since we met. Don't take me for a fool, Rhea."

Her face was burning furiously. She felt so ashamed, that he could see straight through her. "As I said, we don't have anything to talk about. It was no big deal."

He snorted. "No big deal? You mean it was nothing for you, what we did down there?" The harsh, grating tone of his voice made her glad for the covering noise of the surf. He let a short, bitter laugh escape his throat. "And there I was, thinking you were some kind of naive child, walking around like you *thought* you knew what being with a man was all about, but that you didn't know the first thing. Listen, when I touched you, I felt there was something deep down inside of you that was sleeping, and I thought maybe I might be just the man to wake it up. . . .

But now you're telling me you didn't feel anything? Well, you sure had me fooled!''

She felt as though she had been punched in the gut. He was right. The experience of touching him, and wanting him, had gone deeper than anything she had ever experienced before. He had sensed that, and knew that it would hurt her to admit it, but his intention *was* to hurt. He'd known exactly where she would be the most vulnerable, and was taking careful aim. "I don't believe you said that!" Her voice was strangled with emotion.

"I don't believe you tried to convince me that the woman who was clinging to me just a few hours ago, with her whole body begging me to throw caution to the wind and make love to her on a open cliffside, is the same woman who's standing here in front of me saying that it didn't matter. As I said, don't take me for a fool."

She was humiliated, ashamed at the way he was throwing her own weakness and hunger for him back in her face. She regarded him with dark, angry eyes. He never saw the expression on her face; he had returned to his work. Snubbed, she decided to get as far from him as she could. "We'll talk," he said threateningly. "Don't bother trying to weasel out of it. I'll find you when I'm good and ready for you." She pretended she had not heard him and got up, dusted herself off, and walked away.

Even the coast was mocking her. The group was close to the very tip of the island, and on one side, she could see the intermittent white flash of the lighthouse. On the other, in the distance, was the steady orange glow of the oil rigs, miles away on the horizon. Little sisters in their ballgowns. Everywhere she turned, there were reminders of him and of what was now coursing between them. She didn't need this.

She gathered by the gasps of awe coming from the group that the turtle had finished her careful excavation, and was gently depositing her eggs into the hole. Although she had seen the wonderful phenomenon many times, she was usually as enthralled by it as anyone else. This time was different: tonight, the sickness deep in the pit of her stomach would not allow her to stand around and watch. She walked away, not in the direction of the water, but close to the dark row of bushes that lined the beach. It was dark there, and the privacy was comforting. She paced restlessly, wishing again that it were all over.

"Not interested tonight?" The voice near to her shoulder was the last one she wanted to hear right now.

"Rainer," she sighed.

"Yes," he murmured in an oily tone.

She didn't need to turn round to know that he was close to her, and staring at her hard. She struggled to keep her tone pleasant. "You're missing all the good stuff."

"Yes, I am, aren't I?" His words were thick with innuendo. Rhea froze. The odious man went on. "You know something? I hadn't realised that this tour package of yours had so many delightful things to offer. I didn't know that you included so many . . . little perks." His malice encircled her ribs and began to squeeze the breath out of her lungs.

"I don't know what you're talking about." Rhea struggled to keep her answer low, praying for him not to make a scene. Nothing would be worse than someone else overhearing them talk. *You mean*, a nasty voice in her head pointed out, *nothing would be worse than having Marcus experience your embarrassment.*

"Oh, yessss," Rainer whispered in a voice full of snakes. "I think you know what I mean. What makes you think I haven't seen what's going on between you and Lucien there? Do you think I don't see the way he looks at you? What do you think you looked like this evening, when you came back from your little 'private tour'? Do you have any idea what your face looked like? What your mouth looked like?"

His eyes, pale and cold as melting frost, dropped to her lips, and Rhea felt befouled. She wished she could kneel and scoop up a handful of sand and scrub away at her mouth until she had rubbed away the bitter, nasty taste of his implications. She said nothing.

"Now," his voice became even more secretive, "what I want to know is this: are your fringe benefits limited to single guests, or are they available . . . upon negotiation? Because you know, I think I might be interested in one or two of those private tours of yours."

She felt the acrid taste of her own bile rise to the back of her throat. She knew if she did not get away from this man soon, she would find herself in the shameful position of being seen throwing up into the bushes. She hadn't been this sick since her encounter with the jellyfish. She tried to inhale, but the breath just wouldn't come. She cast around desperately, looking for an avenue of escape, but found none.

"Mr. Bainbridge," she struggled for the control of her tongue.

"Rainer," he corrected almost humorously. Now that he had her backed into a corner, he could toy with her at his leisure.

"Rainer," she amended miserably, "It's not what you think."

"Enlighten me," he was smiling and nodding pleasantly, the sly bastard, making sure that anyone glancing in their direction wouldn't dream that they could be talking about anything other than turtles.

"There's nothing going on." Her eyes burned.

"No?" His mocking tone said *I don't believe you.*

"No." She shook her head vigorously to underscore her emphatic denial.

He shoved his hands deep into his pockets, and she could hear the suggestive rustle of bills. "I don't mind some extra . . . compensation. I can be very generous, you know. *American* dollars," he added this last with the studied arrogance of one who believed that the whole of the third world was willing to kill or be killed for his country's currency.

Rhea's nausea grew worse. She looked around desperately.

The man kept smiling, and put what at a distance would seem to be a light, friendly hand on her arm. "Now you listen carefully. You smile, and look at me like we're just chatting. Do you hear? Because if my wife sees that look on your face, my God, if she calls me on it, I'll kill you."

"No," her chest rose and fell, hard. Although the air was pleasantly warm, she wished she had brought a jacket.

"Don't doubt me, Rhea. Now if you're smart, you'll think about this very carefully." He let go of her arm suddenly. "Think about it. And let me know the deal. I can make things very hard for you, my dear. I don't think you know just how much I'm capable of."

She might not know what he was capable of, but she knew him enough to be determined never to find out. She watched him as he walked casually away to rejoin the group, whistling softly. Her chest hurt, and she had to struggle for air. It took a lot of effort for her to force her lurching stomach to settle down again. Hunched over, she rested her palms on her knees and closed her eyes until she was able to bring her breathing back to its steady rhythm.

In the center of the beach, the huge turtle was gently packing sand onto her nest, covering her eggs to keep them safe from predators. With her task done, it was now safe for Albert to shed limited light upon her, so that the others could have a closer look at her, and perhaps touch her to discover why they were called leatherbacks.

"She's crying!" Rhea heard Jodelle say in awe, and for a moment she wondered if she were referring to her, if the anguish she was suffering had spilled out of her eyes without her knowing it. She put an instinctive hand up to her dry cheek before realising that Jodelle was pointing to the turtle. The large female was indeed shedding copious tears. On seeing her, you would think that giving birth to such a large number had caused her great pain.

"She isn't crying," Rhea heard Albert explain. "Not out of grief, anyway. Her eyes are accustomed to the water, so when she comes up on dry land she has to keep them moist by secreting fluid. Besides, that's how turtles get rid of salt in their bodies. Don't worry about her. She's not really crying."

And neither will I, Rhea reminded herself. *My life has suddenly fallen to bits. There's a man who's teaching me how to truly feel love, and another who seems bent on teaching me how to feel fear and loathing. But I won't cry. I'm a professional. I know how to do my job. All I have to do is be strong. So I'll just walk back along the beach with the others, back to the van, and I'll get in and smile and chatter on and on about the miracle of creation and what a wonderful time we all had tonight. I'll pretend none of this is really happening. I'll soon be home, and then, if I like, I can cry and cry and cry until I get all that salt out of my body, too. But don't be afraid. This, too, shall pass.*

CHAPTER TWELVE

"Do you love me?" she asked. She felt foolish even asking, like an uncertain little child asking her father for reassurance; *Daddy, do you love me?* It was absurd. Love was something you got for free, you didn't have to ask for it or deserve it or earn it. You couldn't save up points and then send them off in the mail and sit around waiting for your package of love to show up. Professions of love, too, should bubble up out of the heart, unsolicited. Still, in her desperate need to anchor her unwieldy emotions in reality, she asked the question again. "Do you love me?" There was an uncomfortable silence.

"What kind of question is that?" Brent sounded genuinely puzzled, as though he could not for the life of him understand why she would need to ask.

Rhea's heart weighed heavy in her chest, causing her to slump in her chair. She propped the phone between shoulder and ear and looked outside her hotel window onto the neatly kept lawn. Everyone else was having breakfast, but she knew she would never have been able to stomach it, and she'd remained in her room.

"Brent, I'm just asking if you love me. What do you mean

what kind of question it is? It seems like a perfectly straightfor-
ward question to me.''

"Sweetheart,'' he said in the tone of a harried but benign
doctor trying to calm a mental incompetent. His voice crackled
on the line, ''is something wrong?''

"No,'' she said, a little too shortly, ''nothing's wrong. I just
want to know, that's all.''

"But you do know,'' he hedged. ''Don't you?''

"How would I know, Brent?'' Agitated, she got to her feet
and began to pace back and forth between the door and her
bed. ''How would I know? You never tell me!''

"I treat you well, don't I? Don't we have fun together?''
His mild response was not what she wanted to hear. What about
passion? Why couldn't he protest too much? He couldn't bring
himself to say it. He was bracing from it. But why? Would it
have been so hard? It was just three little words, each only a
simple syllable long. Easy to say. And there was so much riding
on them, those three words. Didn't he know? Couldn't he tell?

"Brent,'' she spoke slowly, to make sure that she got the
words out right, ''Brent, I just need you to tell me you love
me, that's all.''

"They're just words, Rhea. They aren't important. People
use them all the time. They love ice cream. They love the blues.
They're just words. You want to base our entire life together
on words?''

Their entire life together. He'd never even made such an
assumption before. Whereas at one time she would have found
it pleasing, even flattering that he would assume that they would
have a life together, now the mere concept sounded empty,
pointless. What life would there be if there were no love, if he
couldn't even articulate it?

One last time, she told herself. She'd give it one last try.
Carefully enunciating each word, separating them for emphasis,
she asked again. ''Brent, do . . . you . . . love . . . me?''

"I suppose so,'' he said after a moment.

"Good-bye,'' she said, and folded the phone. She tossed it
carelessly aside on the starched institutional white bedspread.
Her shoulders ached, and her neck was simply not strong

enough to support her weary, confused head. She let it fall
forward into her hands.

What was happening to all the men in her life? On one hand
she was seeking support, reaching out to the man she had
believed she could rely on to provide her with the emotional
nurturing that she desperately needed. It had seemed the only
way for her to cling to her own sanity. But his coldness, his
cluelessness, left her wanting. Two years. She'd put two years
into that relationship, and still the man was incapable of sensing
her confusion, and stepping forward when she needed him
most.

And talking about need, there was Marcus. Was what she
felt need or simply desire? That she wanted him, there was no
doubt. Her body didn't lie. It spoke the truth in a way that
made it abundantly clear to her just what it wanted from him;
there was something inside her that reached out, yearning to
be touched or even just to be close, whenever he was nearby.

This fresh new miserable love was nothing like they said it
would be. No roses, no drifting off to sleep in a happy cloud.
Last night, sleep had been elusive, and when she did attain it,
her dreams were full of sadistic taunting. If this was love, then
it was overrated.

And Rainer. That bastard! Him and his evil innuendo and
gloating stares. In one night, two men had questioned her virtue.
The one whom she loved had implied that she bestowed her
kisses lightly. This, she knew, he'd said in anger, and she didn't
find it difficult to forgive him. But this other man—no, this cold-
eyed, evil *monster* had treated her like some whore, offering her
money, and making light of those moments that she'd stolen
with Marcus. He'd reduced her precious encounters alone with
Marcus to the basest of trades: money for her favours.

The memory of it made the sour taste race to her mouth
once again. Never, not once in her six years with the company,
had anyone ever dared to treat her like this. Sure, there had
been the occasional overenthusiastic visitor who had flirted
lightly with her. These she had handled with her usual good
humor. But this, this offer that Rainer had made, was an insult
that left her feeling cheap and nasty.

And he'd done it with the slyness of the serpent that he reminded her of. He'd stood there offering her money and heaping scorn upon all the values that she held dear, and all the time nodding and smiling as if nothing was amiss. In full view of his wife!

For the first time in her career, she felt the urge to abandon a tour. She wanted to pick up the phone and call Ian, tell him anything, tell him she was desperately ill and needed another of the guides to take over her group. Then maybe he'd send someone else up, it wouldn't take more than a day, and she'd tell them all "good-bye, nice having you, thanks for coming, enjoy Trinidad," and get into a taxi and drive off. She could leave them all behind: sweet, friendly Fred and Trudy; disturbing Marcus; darling Jodelle; aloof Dahlia; and that evil, evil Rainer. She could go home to her empty apartment and take her phone off the hook so that nobody, not even Brent, who did not love her, could call. Then, surely, she would find peace.

She reached out and picked up the phone. What was Ian's number again? It was almost laughable. She couldn't seem to remember her own office number. She twisted her face into a grimace and stared upward at the ceiling, hoping to find it written there by some accommodating hand.

The sharp, imperious knock on the door startled her. Were the maids trying to clean her room already? They weren't due to check out before noon.

"Yes?" Although she called out, the person on the other side of the door did not identify themselves. Sighing, she uncurled her legs and set the phone down. "Yes?" she asked again, and wrenched open the door. Dahlia stood there, her pale face unsmiling behind a mask of carefully applied makeup.

Maybe she wanted some kind of clarification on the day's itinerary, maybe there was a complaint about breakfast, or about the room. Rhea couldn't imagine any other reason for the woman's presence. She tried to put a smile on her face, and, failing miserably, abandoned it as a bad job. "Good morning, Dahlia, can I help you?"

"I'd rather not stand around here in the open corridor, if you don't mind." Dahlia brushed aside Rhea's attempt at civility.

Perplexed, Rhea stood aside to allow the woman to sweep past her into her room. Usually, she didn't make it a habit of allowing guests into her bedroom, as she always felt the need to keep one little private place for herself, but Dahlia did not seem open to any such admonitions. She stood in the middle of the small room facing Rhea. For a small, slender woman, she suddenly seemed to be taking up a whole lot of space.

"Yes, Dahlia." Rhea didn't like where this was going, and was determined to get whatever it was out in the open and be done with it. Was there a roach in their room or something?

"What were you speaking to my husband about last night?" Dahlia began without preliminaries.

Rhea's heart fell. God, the woman had seen them. And she'd hoped that Dahlia would have been too engrossed in her drawing! "I beg your pardon?"

"I asked you," for the first time, Rhea noticed how mean those fawnlike eyes could become, "what you were discussing with my husband. You hardly seemed interested in the *wildlife!*"

The change in the woman was almost more than Rhea was prepared to believe. All of a sudden, the pale, wilting woman who didn't seem to have enough spunk in her to hold her own against her overbearing husband was transformed into a bristling, snarling creature. On any other day, Rhea would have been happy to see her show a little spine, but she was tired and she'd had a lousy night. Enough was enough. In the past twenty-four hours she had been pushed around, threatened, and insulted by two of her guests. She wasn't about to let it happen to her a third time. Rhea drew herself up to her full height, which was several inches taller than the other woman.

"Listen. First," she counted the points off on her long fingers, "I am not in the habit of inviting guests to my room. If there is a problem, there are other neutral places in the hotel where this could be discussed. Second, don't address me in that tone of voice. If you have something to say to me, you can speak in a civil manner. Third . . ." How do you tell a woman, a paying guest, that you found her husband repugnant?

"Third . . ." Dahlia was mad enough to be unperturbed by Rhea's response. "You and my husband have been having far too many private conversations lately. I want to know what you were talking about last night."

"So why don't you ask him?" She was gambling here. She would have been mortified if anyone found out what had passed between them last night, but she was willing to bet that Rainer had more to lose by a revelation than she, and he would therefore keep his mouth shut. Rhea was sure the man didn't even dream that his wife was speaking to her right now.

Dahlia snorted. "You obviously don't understand men. Do you think that I'd get the truth, what with the way you two have been making eyes at each other?"

Rhea's mouth hung open with shock. The woman was deluded! *She* was making eyes at *him?* She'd rather tangle with a boa constrictor. "Oh," this was a ludicrous allegation, "I can assure you, Dahlia, that the last thing I would do is make eyes at your husband. The last thing I would dream of doing would be to . . ."

"You just stay away from him!" The shriek was loud enough to be heard through the door, Rhea was certain of it. She looked around in fear. All their rooms were adjoining. There was Marcus on one side, and Fred and Trudy on the other. *Please, God, let them still be eating, or out strolling in the garden, anywhere. Just keep them out of earshot.*

Now it was Rhea's turn to snort with contempt. "Believe me, I want no part of him." Before she could go on, the woman's fine, eggshell face seemed to shatter, and then she was weeping with her small well-manicured hands up over her face, shoulders heaving in anguish.

Rhea was horrified. The woman was ill, or mad! Her sudden anger dwindled as quickly as it had come, and she stood in front of the broken woman, perplexed, anxious to help, but not knowing how. She held out her hand, but let it drop to her side.

"Dahlia?" She called her name softly, but Dahlia was too

deeply buried under an avalanche of pain and grief to hear. The sobs went agonizingly on and on, until their high-pitched sounds tore at Rhea's core. Tossing aside the resentment of a few moments ago, she stepped forward and put her arms gingerly around the narrow shoulders.

"You d—d—d—don't understand!" She was struggling to regain control of herself, suddenly embarrassed by this sudden display, but she did not move away from Rhea's comforting arms. "I l—l—l—love him. I love him and still he hurts me so much!"

It was amazing to Rhea that such a swine, such a cruel, heartless, self-centered man could be deserving of any love at all. It only reminded her how love could strike anyone, and hold them in its grip regardless of whether it brought them pleasure or pain.

"I do understand," she assured her softly. Somehow, she did. She stroked the heavily lacquered black hair, hardly comfortable with the idea of coming into such close contact with the unstable, unpredictable woman, yet too moved by compassion not to.

Dahlia pulled away eventually, and stepped back as if the sudden intimacy had been too much of a breach of her normal cultured demeanor. "God, I'm so sorry. I'm so stupid and clumsy." She looked around wildly for something to dab her eyes with, until Rhea hooked a towel up from off the back of a chair and offered it to her.

"It's okay." Still, she watched her sharply for any indication that she would not regain her equilibrium. This was a woman on the edge. After a while, the sobs subsided, and Dahlia stood there, wringing the towel between her fingers. Rhea couldn't think of what to do next. "Sit down, Dahlia," she said at last, and pointed at the bed.

Dahlia declined the offer of the bed but took the small hard-backed chair next to it. She sat hunched over, staring at the smudges that her make-up had left on the thick white towel. Rhea was unsure whether to sit or stand, and eventually opted for the bed that Dahlia had rejected.

"I don't want your husband," she said finally. "I assure you that there is no . . ."

Dahlia gave a small embarrassed laugh. "I know. Not many women *would!*"

Rhea decided that there was no sense in denying what was, to her, an incontestable truth, just for the sake of good manners. She said nothing.

Dahlia looked as if she had been waiting on a response, and, not getting one, went on. "Don't think I'm blind to his faults. I've been putting up with them and trying to change them for years. I know what he can be like." Dahlia sounded defensive. "But still . . ." she trailed off, and sighed.

Rhea waited patiently for Dahlia to go on. All of the distaste she had felt for her was gone now, and her woman's heart was prepared to reach out to another woman in pain.

"Rainer and I, well, we came here to try again. It's been hard. I really haven't been everything he wants me to be. I've tried, you know, but he just isn't satisfied."

Rhea's eyebrows shot up. *"You're* trying to satisfy *his* needs?" The idea was ridiculous.

Dahlia nodded. "It's very difficult for him, running the business, we have a jewelry business, you know?"

"Yes."

"And he really relies on me to be there for him. He wasn't happy with me working. At first, he was really proud of me, and my work was winning a lot of acclaim. But it started to take away from our time together, so we decided I should close down the studio and that I'd just give him a hand when he needed me."

"You decided that? Both of you?"

"Well, it was his idea, but he was right."

She couldn't believe what she was hearing. Rhea felt an indignant remark rise to her lips, but she clamped her mouth tightly shut to keep it inside. Somehow, she sensed that what Dahlia wanted most from her was an attentive ear.

"And I sort of miss working. I do a little of it, for myself, but it's hard to stop wishing I was back out on the art circuit again. So," she sighed, "I've been getting a little depressed, and it's been a little hard on Rainer. We haven't been very happy, so we've come here to make it work.''

Rhea had seen it so many times before, the desperate wish that a change of scenery would make the difference in a marriage. She wondered how much futile time and money were spent each year by couples hoping to get on a plane and fly away from their problems, only to discover that the problems had stowed away in the luggage compartment, and were there waiting when they arrived at their destination, still as painful and damaging as before.

She decided she could hold her peace no more. "Look, Dahlia. You can want it to work all you like, but unless *he* wants it to work, you'll go nowhere. A Caribbean vacation isn't worth a thing, unless you both agree to really try at it.''

"He does want it to work!'' She raised her head and looked plaintively at Rhea. "And he *is* trying!''

Rhea remembered the awful sound of money rustling in Rainier's pockets as he propositioned her last night, and hesitated. Funny how love made you capable of seeing some good in even the worst people. She didn't like to show any disrespect to the man; he was still a client of hers, whether she liked it or not, but it was her responsibility as a woman to speak her mind.

"Dahlia, listen. I feel for you, and I hope everything works out all right. I really do. But you have got to stop taking the whole burden onto your shoulders. And you have to find some time and space for yourself. Don't let him take away your life. Don't let him take your art from you. You have to claim it back. It's the only way you're going to stay sane.''

Suddenly, Dahlia was not listening. It was as if her self-protective instincts were rebelling against the prospect of too much introspection, and her attention began to waver. She got to her feet and tossed the towel back at Rhea without so much as a "thank you'' and moved to the bathroom where she began to carefully wash her face free of any trace of tears.

Rhea got up and followed, standing in the doorway and looked at the woman's reflection in the mirror. She was peering deeply into her own eyes, not for any wisdom or strength that she might find there, but for redness and swelling.

"I wish I had some ice," the other woman said. "My face is a mess. I wish I could bring some of the swelling down. I can't go out in public looking like this!"

Rhea was floored. Had any of this really happened? One moment this beautiful creature had been snarling and spitting at her like a feral cat, the next she was sobbing brokenly over her ill-treatment at the hands of a selfish and uncaring husband, and now she was babbling on about her appearance, like they were two girlfriends trying on makeup they'd just brought home from the department store.

"A pity your foundation is nowhere near my shade . . ." Dahlia was muttering, more to herself than to Rhea. "I guess I'll just have to make it to my room looking like this!" She turned suddenly, and there was a bright smile on her face. "Well," she said in her fragile, high voice, sounding like they'd just shared a polite round of coffee and biscuits, "thank you so much, Rhea." She moved toward the door. "I'm sorry if I've caused you any . . . embarrassment. I think I'll be on my way now."

Before Rhea could say anymore, Dahlia wrenched open the door, stepped out into the corridor . . . and barreled straight into Marcus, who was standing there with one arm upraised, about to knock. As he blustered his apologies, she threw him a bright, brittle smile, waved away his "I'm sorry" and made her way airily down the corridor to her room.

Rhea watched Dahlia's back as it disappeared, truly too stunned to speak. There went a woman who was unable to face the truth, content to remain in an unhappy relationship simply because she was too afraid or too lethargic to try to make things change. She shook her dazed head. This trip was growing more and more bizarre by the day.

"What was that about?" Marcus snapped her back to the present. He was already in her open doorway, and seemed prepared to step inside.

Moving quickly, Rhea blocked him with her body. This was ridiculous. What, did her room suddenly become a thoroughfare for anyone and everyone who was in need of some company? "Yes, Marcus?"

"What was she doing here?" The man placed his body where it most successfully prevented her from shutting her own door. He was in his ever-present jeans, jeans that knew the shape of his body a little too well, and his concession to the heat was a short-sleeved olive-coloured cotton shirt that was buttoned down a little too low for comfort. And God, she could smell him. . . .

"Girl talk," she said curtly. What business was it of his?

"Girl talk? You two?" He didn't believe her for a second. "What, you were talking makeup or something?" he suggested sarcastically.

"Actually, yes." She wished he would go to his room and stop tormenting her hormones at this early hour. "What do you want?"

"That's a fine way to speak to someone who's so concerned about your non-appearance that he came all the way in from the breakfast table to look for you." The fool was smiling at her like he expected her to fall all over herself with gratitude.

She wasn't about to let him sweet-talk her, not on an empty stomach. "Uh-huh? Well, I'm alive. Satisfied?"

"Satisfied?" He let his eyes linger on her lips for a ridiculously long time before allowing his gaze to move lower, down the curve of her chin, and down to her breasts which, she realised, were still covered only in the T-shirt in which she had slept—and nothing else. She tried to raise an arm as unobtrusively as possible to cover her nipples, which were zanily calling attention to themselves. "Satisfied? No, not yet."

"Marcus, look . . ."

He held out a package wrapped in cellophane. "I brought you breakfast. It's a sandwich," he added, just in case she was unable to figure it out herself.

"Thanks," she said dryly. "But if I'd wanted breakfast, I'd have come for it. I know my way to the breakfast hall."

He chose to ignore her unfortunate lack of gratitude. "It's roast beef," he said with the eagerness of a child, "I made it for you."

Him, the sworn vegetarian, sullying himself by coming into contact with meat—for her. It must have been a supreme sacrifice. "Thanks." She opened a small corner and sniffed tentatively at it.

"You don't have to sniff it. It isn't poison, you know." He gestured pointedly at the slab of beef in the middle and added, "not that *I* would eat it."

She looked at his bright smiling boyish face and was perplexed. Her world was a little too full of schizophrenic behavior, of people veering rapidly between nasty threats and actually being nice to her. Last night he was assuring her that they would "talk," whether she liked it or not. This morning, he didn't look as if he had any such chat on the agenda. For this she was grateful, and decided to take his gesture at face value.

She smiled and bit off a corner of the sandwich, realizing to her surprise that she was starving after all. "Thanks, Marcus. This is really good."

"Well, it had better be. My six-year-old supervisor would be very upset if you didn't like it."

She smiled at that. Jodelle really could be domineering when she wanted to be. "Where is she?"

"She's down by the pool with Fred and Trudy. They're just dipping their feet in the shallows, trying to cool off. But," he fished around in the deep canvas bag that he had slung around his shoulder. "She wanted me to make sure that I gave you this." He held out a ripe sapodilla.

Rhea took it with glee. Sapodillas were her favourite fruits. The spicy brown peel of the fruit was as fine as human skin, and the soft sweet flesh inside always reminded her of pink custard. She gave him a grateful smile.

"That's better. You'd be surprised how much that smile lit up your face. I was beginning to get worried about you. You look terrible this morning."

His directness took her by surprise. She pursed her lips at him. "I think you better rephrase that, Mark," she said humorously. It was the first time she'd used the more intimate, shortened version of his name—that is, the first time she'd used it while she was in full possession of her faculties, when she wasn't too engrossed in kissing him to manage to gasp out the longer version. She wondered if he'd noticed.

"Uh, sorry," he apologized for his indelicacy. "I mean, you look . . . tired. Didn't you sleep last night?"

"Not very well," she confessed.

His brow creased. "Why not? Did it have anything to do with that Rainer pulling you aside out there?"

Her face lost some of its colour. He'd seen them, too! She feigned ignorance. "What? Oh, that. No, don't be ridiculous."

He wasn't giving in so easily. He pressed closer. "So, what *were* you talking about?"

What, was *everybody* suddenly interested in every conversation she had? "Nothing," she said crisply. "Turtles."

He obviously didn't believe her. "In private? Listen, Rhea, if he's troubling you, all you have to do is say so."

She would die rather than admit that Rainer was indeed being a problem. "And what, you'll go charging in on your white horse and banish him from the kingdom? Please, Marcus, there is no problem."

He watched her soberly, still not entirely believing her, but nodded. "Okay, fine. But just remember that I'm there when you need me, okay?" He reached out and stroked her cheek. His voice grew seductive. "And if there's anything I can do to help you sleep, will you let me know?"

She didn't need this. She didn't need him touching her like this, not after the night she had had, filled with the faces of two men who were polar opposites, filled with the jumbled emotions of loathing and torment and doubt and wanting. She was sure that one day his gentleness and kindness would prove her own undoing. She had to be strong, and resist him on every front. She backed away from him, into her room, with her breakfast clutched in either hand, and said crisply. "Thanks for breakfast. We'll meet out front at the van at eleven."

He accepted his dismissal with good grace. "Okay. Can Jodie and I sit with you on the way back?" He sounded like a boy begging his mama for a favour.

"I'm sitting up front with Banner," she said tartly, and shut the door in his face.

* * *

They arrived back at the beach house in the middle of the afternoon; too late to plan any major activity, but with enough time to catch a few hours of lazing about on the beach before the sun went down. Somewhere along the road that paralleled the Mayaro beach, Marcus had come up with the brilliant idea that everyone was eating Cajun tonight.

"Rhea's tired," he announced to everyone in the van. "So maybe we should relieve her of cooking duties tonight. So this ole Louisiana boy is going to treat you all to some of my fine Cajun specialties. . . ."

"Oh boy!" Jodelle squealed with delight. "My daddy can cook great!" she announce to Rhea, poking her in the shoulder from her seat just behind her and Banner. " 'Cept he burns it, most of the time."

Marcus yanked playfully on her braids. "That's why they call it 'blackened,' baby. I'll have you know some people like it like that!"

No one seemed to mind; in fact, the prospect seemed to excite them. Trudy pounced on the idea, and elaborated on it with her usual sense of romance. "Oh, you know what? We can play dress-up. We can treat it like a night on the town, and we girls can wear something nice and feminine and flouncy instead of jeans all the time. How's about that?"

The idea went down well, so Rhea surrendered her cooking duties without protest.

As they unloaded their bags, Marcus called out to Banner over the top of the van. "Hey, man, I have to go back into town and get a few things for dinner, but you've done enough driving for the day, and I don't want you to have to go back out again. Can I borrow your keys?"

Normally, guests were not allowed to use the van, but Banner obviously had grown to like and trust Marcus; he didn't hesitate for a second. He tossed the keys over the roof of the van, and Marcus caught them neatly.

"Don't get me fired, man," Banner said jokingly.

Marcus laughed. "Would I do that to a brother?" He hopped

into the driver's seat and adjusted it to his significantly longer legs. He stuck his head out and called out to his daughter. "Hey, shortstuff, you coming for the ride?"

He didn't have to ask her twice. With the flashing of her bare brown legs, Jodelle was round to the other side and settled down in the seat beside him. "Rhea! Rhea! You come, too!"

Before Rhea could beg off, Marcus let her off the hook. "Rhea's tired, honey. Let's give her a chance to take a little nap, okay?"

Jodelle's face twisted. "But I want her to come with us!"

Marcus was about to insert the keys into the ignition, but stopped with his hand outstretched. "Baby, she can't come with us. She needs her rest. Aren't we giving her the afternoon off? It wouldn't be very nice to promise her a rest and then turn around and make her work again, would it?"

"But I waaaant herrrr!" The crumpled mouth let out a wail, and then the tears began to flow.

Rhea was horrified. "Jodie," she began, and stepped forward, but Marcus held up a hand to stop her.

"I'll take care of this."

The girl was screaming shrilly now, kicking against the dashboard in rage, and lashing out at her daddy with her fists. "I want her! I want her!"

Desperate to avert a potentially nasty situation, Rhea was ready to climb into the van to satisfy the child, but Marcus was adamant. "You can't let her manipulate you like that, Rhea. She has to learn that she can't always have what she wants." To Jodelle, he turned and said, "That's it, young lady, out we go. This little trip is canceled."

Rhea protested. "But you were so looking forward to going into town, Marcus. Leave her with me, and you go ahead alone."

Marcus shook his head. "No, then you wouldn't be resting. We gave you the afternoon off, remember? Take a nap. Read a book. Do something else for a change, rather than spend it looking after us."

Trudy, who had gone in to put her things away, had returned in time to see the scene play itself out. She stepped forward and held her open arms out to the child, who was by now hysterically pummeling her father about the head and shoulders. "Why don't you let this old schoolteacher take her off your hands for a few hours? Then you can both get some free time."

Marcus handed her over gratefully, and as Jodelle's screams began to subside, more from exhaustion than from anything else, he planted a kiss on the older woman's cheek. "Thanks, Trudy. I owe you one."

She waved him away. "Nonsense! You just hurry up and get those groceries. I haven't had Cajun cooking in a long, long time, so I hope your cooking is as good as your daughter says it is!"

He smiled at her. "I promise you, you won't be disappointed." Trudy waved away his cocky response with a smile, and Marcus hopped back up into the driver's seat and started the engine. "See you in a while, ladies," he said, and was off with a wave of his hand.

"Stay on the left side of the road!" Rhea yelled behind him, in case he forgot that driving in the West Indies wasn't *exactly* the same as it is in the States. He tooted his horn in acknowledgment and disappeared out the drive.

Trudy held a now-quiet Jodelle in her arms and stood next to Rhea as she watched him go. Then she turned her warm blue eyes to her and said, "She'll be asleep in no time, don't you worry. Tantrums like that just wear them out. Poor little thing. I've seen this happen in my school before, you know. The motherless ones sometimes go and fall in love with somebody who they think will make them a good mommy. Children this age always need a woman around." She pursed her lips and shook her head in a way that said *what a shame*. "Really, Marcus has got to do something about that. For the child's sake, if nothing else."

Rhea felt a lump in her throat. Trudy was right. The child did need a woman around, and it hadn't escaped her that of late, she'd been putting herself into that place, even though it was only in fantasies to which she wouldn't admit, not even to herself. But fantasy had nothing to do with reality, and maybe her feelings for the little girl had more to do with her confusion over the father than anything else.

It was unfair that such a small creature should be suffering the same painful tensions that were enveloping her father and Rhea, though. *This must stop,* she vowed to herself, *this is affecting more than just the two of us.* It couldn't go on.

Unable to answer Trudy's observations without causing herself pain, Rhea murmured something unintelligible and then added, "I think I really will go and lie down now."

Trudy agreed wholeheartedly, and led the way into the house.

The man was clattering around the kitchen like he had something against the dishes. Rhea tossed about on her bed for a while, but in the stifling heat of the afternoon, she was unable to catch a moment's sleep. Reading also proved impossible, as the smell of simmering onions and browning flour began to pervade even the bedrooms. Eventually, curiosity got the better of her, and she drifted out to the kitchen under the pretext of getting herself a glass of cold water from the fridge.

There were vegetables everywhere: peppers, onions, celery, corn, okra, tomatoes, carrots, wherever she looked was a burst of colour. Marcus was suitably attired in her big white cotton apron, and was stirring a pot on the stove, which seemed to contain only burning oil and flour.

"It's a roux," he said helpfully, with the pride of a little boy helping Mother in the kitchen. He obviously fancied himself a master chef. "That's a kind of sauce."

"I know what a roux is," she informed him, "and yours is burning."

He seemed unperturbed. "It's a *dark* roux." He turned to look at her as she wandered about the kitchen and poked into his many bags and boxes. "I thought you were resting."

She shrugged. "My room is hot. I figured you might need some help."

"You mean, you just popped out to make sure I don't burn the house down?" He was smiling.

She didn't answer. She peered into the sink; there was a

huge fresh redfish lying there, waiting to be sliced. "Fish?" she was surprised. First he was making her roast beef sandwiches, now he was cooking fish. Next, it would be on the end of his fork.

"I said I don't eat the stuff, I never said I can't cook it. Like I told you, I'm not here to force my values on anyone. You eat what you like, I eat what I like. If I cook for you, I'll accommodate what you like to eat. It's no skin off my nose."

Rhea was done fiddling around with his things, and couldn't prolong the pretense of needing any more water to drink, or she'd spring a leak. Still, she wasn't ready to go back to her room.

He seemed to notice her hesitation. He took a knife from the rack and handed it to her, holding it by the blade. "Here, you workaholic. If you refuse to let people be nice to you and let you take the afternoon off, and if you really insist on doing something, how about chopping up some of those veggies over there."

After he showed her what to do, she set to work, glad just for the excuse to be with him in the empty house. Everyone was still way out on the beach, catching the last rays of the day, and with Jodelle still sleeping off her outburst, the kitchen was cosy and intimate.

"So what's on the menu?"

He stopped and pointed out the ingredients on the counter. "There's okra gumbo, blackened redfish, tempura-battered vegetables, Cajun-smothered potatoes, corn bread, and red beans." He looked mighty proud of himself, and seemed to be awaiting applause.

"And this is all going to be ready for dinner tonight?" She was impressed by his ambition, but doubtful.

He gave her a mock scowl. "It will be, if you get to cutting those vegetables, missy."

She smiled and shut up. They cut, chopped, roasted, and sautéed in silence for a while, both agreeing to simply enjoy each other's company without any expectations or pressure on either side. For Rhea, it was the most peaceful moment she had spent since she began this bedeviled tour a week and a half ago—had it only been ten days? Such a short time, she mused, to have your whole life thrown into havoc.

Marcus broke the pleasant silence. "Tell me about yourself, Rhea." He didn't look up from what he was doing.

She was puzzled. "What do you mean? What do you want to know?"

"Anything," his voice was soft. "I want to know you. Who you are."

She was pleasantly flattered that he was curious to know who she really was, not the hostess, but the woman behind the hostess face. His request made her smile. "I really don't know where to begin."

"Tell me about your family. How many kids are there?"

"Two brothers, both older . . ." she began.

"You're the spoiled one, then."

She went on without rising to that particular bait, ". . . and my parents are both teachers and both still alive. What else?"

"When's your birthday?"

"May first."

"God," he muttered to no one in particular, "she's a Taurus. I'm not surprised. She's a stubborn, tempestuous one."

"What else?" although she pretended to be a little put upon, she was enjoying his attention.

"Who took you to your prom? Or do you have proms here? And what did you wear? What did you want to be when you grew up?"

"A boy in my class who I haven't seen since graduation; yes, we do have proms but we don't call them proms; I was kind of plump, so I had to wear this awful thing without a waist; and I wanted to be a flight attendant."

"Why?"

"Because I can speak three foreign languages, and besides, I thought it was a pretty glamorous life. When I found out about all those hours on your feet, pouring coffee, I changed my mind."

"What languages?"

"Spanish, French, Portuguese. The languages of the region, basically."

"I'm impressed." He looked as if he truly was impressed, and proud of her, too. That made her feel warm inside.

"Yeah, well, don't start giving out any gold stars yet, okay?"

They went on in this vein for quite some time, with him asking questions seemingly at random, but which, when all her responses were laid out together in a fixed pattern in his sharp mind, gave him a pretty good picture of who she really was. The smile that he wore on his face as he watched her made her face hot.

Then the conversation took a different turn, and the temperature of the room suddenly plunged. "Rhea?" Marcus wasn't looking at her now. He was concentrating harder than was necessary on the fresh salad that he was preparing.

She stopped what she was doing and turned to him, her chest suddenly tighter. His tone had changed dramatically from the light, amused interrogation of a few moments ago. Something told her that what he was about to say was serious, and very important to him.

"Can I tell you something?" He still couldn't look at her.

"What?" she licked her lips, wanting to hear but yet hoping that he was not about to launch into that "talk" he'd been threatening her with, the one that was going to be about "them."

"Since you've been so kind as to tell me so much about you, I think . . . I was wondering if I could tell you something. Something about me and Jodelle."

She waited intently but silently. So it wasn't going to be the talk, it was something else, but something just as serious.

He misunderstood her silence for unwillingness. "Please," he pleaded. "It's important. I need you to know this."

It took some effort for her tongue to become unstuck from the roof of her mouth. What in the name of God could he possibly have to tell her? "Go ahead, Mark. I'm listening."

Her more familiar use of his name seemed to give him the courage to begin. "I think I married too young. Yvette and I were both still in college. . . ."

"Yes, I remember. You told me."

"And I don't think we knew what we really wanted. We

were in love, that's for sure, but it was the young, foolish love that makes you do really dumb things.''

''Uh-huh'' she encouraged him gently. He was still carefully washing a head of lettuce that didn't need any more washing.

''Like getting married before you're ready for it. Well, like I told you, Yvette wanted to dance, and she was a very good dancer. When I met her, she was fresh from the islands, and it was her first time in America, and she was impressed by just about everything. Even me. She was eager to see things, and glad to have me to show her around.

''But by the year we left college, she was spending more time with her fellow dancers, and with the whole entourage—the musicians, the stage people—than she did with me. I just loved my books, and my animals, and soon she decided I was boring.'' He managed a bitter laugh. ''We writers can be pretty boring people, let me warn you. We're all covered in dust and ink, full of our own imaginations.''

I don't think you're boring, she wanted to tell him. *I think you're the most intoxicating man I've ever met. The way you talk. The way you think. The way you touch me . . .* But she let him continue.

''I was idealistic. She was a realist, a sensualist. I wanted to save the world; she wanted to *own* the world. I just wasn't living up to her expectations. I didn't have the kind of ruthless ambition she thought we needed to make it to the top. She got tired of my company. She stayed out all night, went to her parties and recitals, and was always traveling up and down the countryside, performing, and soaking up her rave reviews. Every now and then, she came home to me, but then she got bored again, and missed her bright-light friends, and wandered off again.'' He took a deep breath. ''Then she told me she was pregnant.''

Marcus finally finished washing the lettuce to death and put the leaves into a large salad bowl. He moved from where he was standing and went over to the counter, where he began fiddling with a range of sauces and spices, putting together some kind of salad dressing. In so doing, he had effectively turned his back to Rhea. But she could still hear his voice.

"She said she was pregnant, but, you know, somehow, the math didn't add up. She'd been veering between home and the road for a long time, and there were men. Quite a few of them. Some whom I knew about, and some, I guess, that I didn't. But we were still sleeping together. I mean, in spite of all the bad times, I still loved her. But the math didn't add up."

Rhea was horrified. Could he really be saying what she thought he was saying? She moved over to the counter and prized the little bottles of spices from his tense grip. "Marcus, do you mean . . . ?"

He turned onto her face eyes more full of pain than she had ever thought possible. The golden glow that usually warmed her face with every glance had been eclipsed by huge black circles, widened by years of hurt. "Jodelle isn't mine, Rhea."

Her head was humming sharply with that sudden hot vibration that signaled a migraine. She put a defensive hand to her forehead. "Are you sure?"

"Oh, sure enough. Have you looked at her? Have you looked closely? Do you see any of me in her?"

"No, but I just assumed that she looks like her mother."

"She does," he said harshly, "and somebody else."

"Who?" she felt his pain as if it were her own.

Marcus shrugged and looked away "I don't know. I don't care."

"And Yvette? What did she do? What did she say?"

"I don't even think she knew for sure herself, if you can believe that. But to her credit, she never tried to convince me that the baby was mine. Not even to save face. Maybe it just wasn't important enough to her. The only circumstance surrounding the pregnancy that was of concern to her was how soon she'd be able to dance again. Everything else, including my sanity, including our marriage, was just secondary."

What kind of woman could do something like that to a young man who obviously loved her so much? Rhea felt a wave of anger against this unknown woman. She could only imagine the emasculating doubt, anger and hurt that Marcus must have suffered at her uncaring hands. The self-serving witch had a lot to answer for.

Rhea persisted. "But do you know for sure that she's not yours? Are you positive? There are ways of finding out, Mark. There are tests."

"I know all about the tests, Rhea. I'm not as stupid as you and Yvette both seem to think I am."

She flinched. "That was unfair!"

He was immediately penitent. "I'm sorry. I'm sorry. I didn't mean to lash out at you." He reached up to cup her face in both his hands. "Forgive me."

"Of course." She reached up with one hand to lightly touch the fingers that cradled her face. "I just can't understand why you haven't tried to find out once and for all if you really *are* her father."

"I *am* her father. For all intents and purposes, that little girl asleep inside there is mine. I love her, and every decision that I make in my life, I make with her best interests in mind. So help me, Rhea, I am the only father that my daughter has ever known. She may not be the child of my body, but she is the child of my heart, and that's something that a few drops of blood will never change."

She felt tears rise to her eyes. God, she loved this man! All the admiration and respect that she felt for his integrity and intelligence and generousity of spirit increased tenfold. That he could look at a child who was living proof of the cruelty and deceptiveness of a woman who had once claimed to love him, and hold this child as close to his heart as he did! It made him a very special man indeed.

She could hear the quickening of the breath in his chest as he struggled to bring himself under control, and she wanted to pull him closer, right there in the kitchen, and hold him against her breasts and offer him a safe harbor from the storm that had tossed his life these past six years.

"Are you crying?" he asked softly.

"No," she lied fiercely as her vision began to blur.

The meal was forgotten and he was pulling her against him and she was reaching up to pull his head close to hers and whispering that she was so, so sorry.

He let his little finger run lightly along the soft skin under her eyelid, and as it encountered a tear, he held it up before his face, staring at the tiny droplet in wonder. "Don't feel sorry for me, Rhea. I can't stand that." He lowered his head and brushed his lips against the moist smear on her cheek.

"But I do. I can't help it. This is so wrong! How could anyone do something like that to you?"

"I have a wonderful little girl who loves me and depends on me for everything. What's so wrong about that? Besides, Yvette didn't do anything to *me*. She didn't deliberately set out to hurt me or to humiliate me. It just happened. We both made a mistake."

She couldn't believe what this man was saying. He had spilled out his years of pain and hurt before her, and now here he was defending the woman who had been the cause of it all! It was too much. His refusal to accept her loyal indignation rankled. She'd shown him her support, and he'd brushed it away—in defense of a woman who had made him a cuckold. More angry than compassionate now, Rhea tried to wriggle out of his grasp, but he held her fast.

"What's wrong?" It was incredible; he was truly puzzled! He stopped the rhythmic caressing of her cheek with his lips and stared at her.

The compassion that had been stirring within her began suddenly to wane. "What's wrong," she said cuttingly, "is that you're defending that *witch!* Do you actually believe that she never meant to hurt you? Are you that naive?"

She was still struggling to escape from the tight prison that his arms had made around her, and suddenly he seemed to change his mind about resisting, and let her go. She was unprepared, and had to fight to maintain her balance.

"My wife is not a wicked person." Marcus was angry now. His fine nostrils flared lightly, and his eyes were bright. "She may be selfish and childish, but she doesn't warrant . . ."

"Your *ex*-wife, Mark! You're divorced. It's *over!* There *is* no wife!" Damn him, How could he be so stupid? She grabbed his left hand and held it up in front of his face. "Look at this! Look at yourself! Your marriage has been over for eighteen months . . . no, from what you tell me, it's been over for years, and you're still wearing this woman's ring. You're still wearing your wedding band, Mark! Why?''

He stared at his own hand in surprise, as if he had never even noticed the ring, and seemed at a loss for an answer. Then the look of anger on her face convinced him that she needed a response, and he licked his lips and began so speak. ''You don't understand about the ring, Rhea. You have no idea what that ring does for me.''

''So tell me! Tell me what this woman's ring does for you. Why do you still wear the thing, like you're a grieving widower, or like you honestly believe that this woman is still at home in California, waiting for you when you get back. Go ahead. Tell me.''

''It's for Jodelle ...'' he began, but he didn't sound too convinced.

She snorted ''Right. For Jodelle. And how do you figure that?''

''She knows what it is, and she thinks it binds me to her mother in some way. It reassures her somehow, makes her feel like she still has a family to belong to.''

Rhea wasn't buying. ''Oh, come on! You wear a wedding ring to comfort a six-year-old? Please, Marcus. Don't bother trying to convince me, okay? There must be more than that!''

If anything, he was angrier than she was. ''You want more? Okay! This ring,'' he waved his hand threateningly before her, just in case the object wasn't already stamped in her memory, ''this ring is my fire wall. This ring keeps me safe. It helps me to keep things uncomplicated where women are concerned. I meet an attractive woman, she thinks I'm married, she steers clear of me. Then there's no problem. No complications. This ring lets me get through my life in one piece.''

This reason was probably a lot closer to the truth than the last piece of baloney he was trying to give her. But still it sounded weak. Surely a man like Marcus didn't need a small band of gold to help him keep control his affairs! And besides, the ring was obviously not doing its job; it hadn't kept her from loving him. She pressed him for more information.

"What else? I don't believe that's all the reason there is, Marcus. There must be more."

His face was closed tight and angry. He'd shut her completely off from him now. After the experience of having him open up his secret self just a few moments ago, and sharing his hurt with her, the sudden refusal to share with her was like a wall of cold air.

"Nothing." His eyes were half-closed as he hid their light from her. "There's no other reason. What more do you want?"

Rhea knew that she had a rival for this man's heart, even if the rival had no intention of vying for the prize. It was infuriating. "What about her? Yvette? Isn't she your reason? Tell me you aren't still wearing the ring because of her. You can't forget her."

Marcus gave her a lethal look that in one of her saner moments would have caused her to back down immediately. "Let's not go there, Rhea," he said dangerously.

"No, Marcus. Let's go there. That's *exactly* where I want to go."

Refusing to answer, he went back to his cooking, stirring a boiling pot of rice with quick, angry strokes.

She knew she wasn't getting anything more from this man. His entire demeanor told her to step down, and to leave him alone, even though he hadn't told her the entire truth. As she watched the stiff way that he held his back upright, like an angry cat that didn't want to be touched, she knew what the entire truth was; he still wore his wedding ring because he was still in love with his wife. Even after what she had done to him, even after all those years trapped in a marriage that must have been hell, he still loved her.

The knowledge made Rhea's stomach churn. That she could be right there, close to him, loving him and wanting him as she did, needing him, even, and yet this Yvette, all the way in Moscow, could still have this hold over his emotions. Divorce notwithstanding, he couldn't let her go.

She turned without another word and walked rapidly, head down, out of the kitchen and moved quickly in the direction of the bedrooms—and slammed straight into Rainer. The force of the impact with his pudgy chest knocked the wind out of her already quite deflated sails. She drew her breath in sharply and managed to gasp out: "Rainer! What are you doing here?"

She'd thought that the house was empty. Rainer must have come in through the other way; they'd certainly not heard any movement on the porch. She glanced quickly around: the glass doors that led to the porch were still firmly shut.

The man was grinning hugely. "What am I doing here? I live here. For the time being, at least." His silly little quip seemed to amuse him.

She was appalled to think that he could have been skulking around near the kitchen, listening to all that had gone on in there! Just how long had this repugnant man been in the house? How much had he heard?

Surely he knew what she was thinking. He just seemed to enjoy prolonging her anxiety. "Oh, I came in for a glass of water," he said nonchalantly, and shoved his hands deep into the pockets of his large khaki shorts. "But then, it seemed that you and Lucien were having, ah, a conversation, and, well, far be it from me to interrupt." He gave her his snake-smirk and began walking toward the kitchen. "But now that you two seem to be done, maybe I will have that drink."

The beast was speaking loud enough to be heard in the kitchen. His gambit had the desired effect. Marcus appeared in the kitchen doorway, with a large spoon in one hand. His face was grey with shock. He was as anxious as she was to find out just how much of the conversation Rainer had heard.

Rainer knew this, and obviously had decided to make them wait. Whistling nonchalantly, he slowly and deliberately chose a glass from the cabinet, poured himself some water, and leaned against the closed fridge door, sipping with almost effeminate delicacy. When he'd had enough of dangling them both on the end of his line, he coolly turned his blue eyes on Marcus' ashen face and said "Well, who'd have thought, Lucien, that you've been nurturing a little cuckoo in your nest all these years?"

The effect on Marcus was galvanic. The spoon landed in the sink with a clatter that shredded Rhea's already tight-as-a-bowstring nerves, and then the taller man confronted his tormentor, one large dark hand holding him by the collar of his expensive, pretentious blue polo shirt. Rainer gasped at the swiftness and the ferocity of the attack, and seemed to be fighting for air as Marcus' hand pulled tighter. Ripples of pale fat spilled over the top of the shirt collar.

"What did you say?" Rhea could never have imagined that Marcus' voice could become so deadly.

Rainer was frightened, but still had enough bravado to drive him to taunt the angry man even further. "I said," he managed to say in spite of the pressure on his throat, "that I didn't realize your wife had been giving it up for other men. What's the matter? Were you so busy spending time saving your precious animals that you neglected your duties? Or were you just not man enough to satisfy her in the first place?"

The sound of Rainer's body slamming against the fridge cracked through the still afternoon. Although it was one of those huge, sturdy family models, it seemed to rock on its base, and the air was expelled from Rainer's fat lips in a whoosh.

Rhea hastened to intervene. The man was odious, but she couldn't have two of her guests beating each other up! "Mark!" she pleaded.

Rainer took advantage of Marcus' momentary distraction to squirm free of his grasp and danced away. His bright eyes revealed his fear of the much fitter, stronger man, but still his perverse sense of fun got the better of him. This time, Rhea bore the brunt of his taunts.

"As for you, babe, you should have listened to me all along. Why are you wasting your time chasing after someone who obviously can't be that much of a prize, if he can't keep his own wife in line? I told you there were, ah, better deals to be had."

On hearing this, Marcus took a step toward him, eyes afire, face taut with deadly rage. "What does that mean?" Marcus' hand darted out, taking hold of Rainer once again, and he shook Rainer on the end of his tightly curled fist. "What do you mean by that?" His enraged shaking made Rainer's head snap back and forth with a rapidity that almost threatened to snap it.

This time, Rhea decided that it would be wiser to circumvent any trouble on her own, rather than risk allowing her virtue to be defended. Facing up to this viper had to be better than standing on the sideline like a damsel in distress while the two of them slugged it out. She slipped in between the two men forcing them apart, and leaned into Rainer's face.

"You listen. I'm warning you. I've had enough. I don't want to hear another word out of you about what you heard today, and I especially don't want to have to listen to another of your odious propositions. I am not interested in you, I am not part of the tour package, and I am *not* for sale!"

The man was shocked at the force of her reply. Obviously, he had expected her to be as easily frightened as she had been on the last few occasions that he had accosted her. The biter had been bitten, and he didn't like it one bit. With one hand rubbing his throat where Marcus had grabbed him, he gave her a nasty smile that told her that it wasn't over, and stalked out of the kitchen. A few seconds later, they heard the door of his bedroom slam.

She let her breath out in a sigh and turned to face a still-furious Marcus. Her head hurt, and she rubbed the back of her hand across eyes that burned with fatigue.

"What did he mean by that?" Marcus roared.

Rhea sighed. Obviously, this sudden ordeal wasn't over. Not by a long shot. "By what, Marcus?" she asked in a low, defeated voice.

"You know what I'm talking about. Has he accosted you?" The rage and un-depleted violence within him had his body coiled and tense. He didn't need much else to push him over the edge, and Rhea certainly was not prepared to test him any further.

"He hasn't *accosted* me. He said some things, but it is nothing I can't handle. I can deal with it. I'm a professional. Let me do my job, okay?" Not that she felt very professional after what had just gone on in the kitchen. Parting a fight between two raging bulls certainly didn't come out of the tour guide manuals!

"What did he say?" Marcus insisted.

"Marcus, I don't think it's any of your business." She'd

had enough. It was time to draw the line. "I won't discuss other guests with you. . . ."

"There you go again, you and your control hang-up. You can't always be on top of every situation you meet, Rhea. Sometimes you have to let someone else step in and help you. And this is not a question of 'other guests' anymore. You and I have gone long past our business relationship. I want to know, and I have a right to know. Tell me."

She knew that what he was saying about control was true: it was the Achilles' heel that was plaguing any chance that they might have at a making something grow between them. But the fact that he was right didn't make her any less angry. "I don't need you to ride in and save me. You want to save someone? Go ahead, save the turtles. But don't try to rescue me. And as for our relationship, I think you'd be better off thinking of it as just that: business. Okay?"

Rhea was out of the kitchen and halfway up the hall before Marcus had chance to answer. That kitchen was the last place she wanted to be. Luckily (disappointingly?), he didn't follow her, and as she slipped into the sanctuary of her room, she could hear him banging about as he finished the meal that had begun amidst an atmosphere of warmth and camaraderie, but which had ended in enmity and disaster.

To his credit, Marcus managed to serve the meal with forced good humor, primarily to avoid spoiling the evening for Jodelle, Dahlia, Trudy, and Fred. As promised, they all dressed for the occasion, that is, those who turned up for the meal. Obviously deciding that he was in no mood to face them so soon, Rainer declined dinner, saying that he hadn't come all the way to the Caribbean to be obliged to eat American food, and hid in his room with two cheese sandwiches and a few bananas.

It was painful. Obliged to keep up at least a pretense of enjoying the evening, Rhea wore the only dress that she had packed. The simple black cotton dress was splashed all over with bright yellow and white daisies and barely came down to her knee. The fact that Marcus had never seen her in a dress had crossed her mind while she put it on, but she'd dismissed it, remembering how mad she was at him. She indulged in silk stockings and high heels, dusted on light makeup and a shade of lipstick that made her mouth look as if the blood of arousal had risen to it. Damned if she let the man's foul mood prevent her from raising her spirits with a nice outfit.

Trudy was characteristically resplendent in her lavender chiffon muumuu, and Fred escorted her to the table with an old-world gallantry that made Trudy beam. In spite of her husband's churlish behavior, Dahlia seemed determined to enjoy the evening. Rhea wondered if the conversation that she and Dahlia had had earlier had anything to do with the woman's decision to not to let her husband's sulkiness prevent her from having a good time. It was doubtful, though, that Dahlia knew the real reason for her husband's absence. Rhea hoped to keep it that way.

Dahlia was spared the discomfort of being without an escort by Banner, who seemed, with his uncanny knack for understanding undercurrents, to realize that there were forces at work that threatened to spoil the evening. The older man did his best to entertain Dahlia while filling in the numerous gaps in the strained conversation that accompanied the meal.

Rhea avoided any eye contact with Marcus. She was sure that those eyes of gold, so warm and teasing a mere few hours ago, would hold nothing but venom for her. Throughout the meal, she looked anywhere but at him, only commenting on how great the food looked and tasted because good manners dictated that she do so. From time to time, she stared steadfastly at the centerpiece of red, magenta, and white bougainvillea that Trudy had collected and placed in a large glass bowl.

Across from her, Jodelle sat, dressed with care by her father in a midnight blue velvet dress trimmed with lace. He had lovingly drawn her numerous braids off her face and tied them back with white ribbon. The girl was refreshed from her long nap and seemed to have put her tantrum completely behind her. She sat next to Marcus, beaming with pride as he received accolades for his cooking.

Rhea took the opportunity to examine the girl's face, and saw in her things that she simply hadn't seen before: a complete absence of Marcus. Sure, she had his loud, uninhibited laugh, his sense of fun, his habit of holding the eyes of persons with whom he was speaking. She had his keen sense of observation, and his hunger for knowledge. But these were acquired traits. Any child spending enough time with Marcus would have adopted these mannerisms.

What Rhea couldn't see was any trace of the physical. There was nothing in the nose, the bright black eyes, the shape of the mouth, ears, fingers. Marcus was right. The child looked like her mother—and someone else.

After the first chilling shudder that rushed through her, Rhea tried to examine how this new knowledge made her feel. The child's paternity did not, after all, change who she was. It did not make her any less loving or any less lovable. It made her no less deserving of a father, a mother, a happy family to whom she could belong.

With sudden pain, Rhea was given the answer to her fear that her love for the little girl was merely a reflection or an extension of her feelings for Marcus. She realised that she loved the child, whoever she was, however she had come into this world, and that this precious feeling was not dependent on her love for Marcus; each separate emotion only made the other more glorious, more life-affirming. The realisation made Rhea's chest hurt.

As if in response to her unspoken emotion, Jodelle looked up, her small mouth full of fish that her father had cooked. The bright black eyes met and held hers, and despite the pain that gripped Rhea, she smiled.

CHAPTER THIRTEEN

Mayaro beach looked like an oil painting. The trees leaned out toward the sea but looked lifeless, as their fine feathery leaves hung limply down, undisturbed by wind. The sea was dull, like murky glass, reflecting the sky almost reluctantly. The sky looked like galvanized sheeting stretched over the sea to protect it from the sun. The stillness and the heat were getting to Rhea. She was restless, and a sense of foreboding weighed on her.

It was all Marcus' fault, of course, this discomfort that she felt. He was making no attempt to approach her, and spoke to her only when necessary, with politeness that held just the slightest hint of rancor. He hadn't forgiven her for the angry words they had exchanged before Rainer had made his odious presence known, nor for her refusal to tell him more about what had gone on between Rainer and herself. Whether he was more angry about her refusal to allow him to stand up and fight for her, or about her disparaging remarks about his ex-wife, Rhea couldn't tell. If she was forced to make a choice, though she knew her money would be on Yvette.

And yet in spite of his calm, he seemed to be thinking hard. Over the two or three days that followed that disastrous afternoon in the kitchen, she often caught him staring into open space, pensive, as if he were weighing something in his mind. On the rare occasions that their eyes did meet, he would acknowledge her with a slight nod, and then drift once again into his fugue.

Rainer barely addressed her, and lurked morosely in the rear seat of the van during their short trips around the area. He made no allusion to the scene that had played out, which wasn't surprising, considering the embarrassment that he could have suffered at Marcus' hands if their skirmish had gotten out of hand.

Still, Rhea was sure that the trouble with Rainer wasn't over. He frightened her. Once or twice she looked around and caught him regarding her with deadly pale eyes, which held nothing but malevolence. He'd warned her that he would retaliate if she ever tried to make things difficult for him. She had no doubt that he would at least try. The only question that remained was what he would do, and how he would set about doing it.

Would he be crazy enough to try to force himself on her? As paranoid and as melodramatic as it might sound, it was certainly a possibility. But where would he find the opportunity? The house was always full of people, and she went nowhere by herself. But even if he tried anything, his bulky form was soft and weak, and possessed nothing resembling Marcus' tensile power. She would be able to fight him off on her own ... wouldn't she?

Failing the threat of violence, there was her career to consider. Images of him regaling Ian with stories of her practicing something akin to prostitution rose up before her eyes, and it took a force of will to beat them down again. He was the one who had suggested the exchange of sexual favours for money, not she. He was the guilty one. Yet all her self-protective instincts told her that Rainer wasn't half finished.

She consoled herself with the thought that in three days they would be leaving Mayaro for their brief tour of the north, and in a week the group would all be back on the plane to the States, and out of her hair. Every last one of them. Then maybe she would put in for a vacation, leave the island, perhaps. Visit

Curaçao or the Bahamas or Martinique; be on the other end of the tourist experience for a change. Then things would be simple again, she would forget all about Marcus, and her life would once again be normal.

"Talk to you, Rhea?" Banner stood just behind her, speaking softly and discreetly. The guests were sprawled on the porch sipping iced tea and fanning themselves, complaining about the heat that seemed to press in on all sides, keeping the sea creatures away. Even the gulls seemed reluctant to stray far from home.

Rhea turned to him, eyes wide. There was a note in his voice that rang a warning in her ears.

"Walk with me," he said casually. "Let's go down to the wall."

Curious, yet a little fearful, she followed him out to the wall and they sat, facing the still sea. Banner lit a cigarette and flicked the match onto the sand. They both watched it as it went out. He took one or two long drags, holding the smoke in contemplatively for several seconds before exhaling in a whoosh. Rhea watched the smoke hang in the air, undispersed. She waited.

"Hot," he said, and sucked on the cigarette.

"Yeah." What did he want?

"And so still," he said.

"Banner?" She turned fully toward him and looked into his eyes, searching.

"It's getting hotter and hotter, these past few days. And quieter and quieter. The air's so thick, you can reach out and break off a piece." Gray cigarette smoke enshrouded his head. There was no wind to chase it away. "I don't like it," he said.

There was a gnawing in her gut as the realisation hit her. "Hurricane," she said.

He shook his head. "Not quite. Not yet. Tropical storm. Her name's Hazel. I picked it up on the radio a few minutes ago. It's brewing in the Atlantic, but it's still almost two days away from the Caribbean. They expect it to head northwest, up along the Windward Islands. It won't touch us."

"But . . . ?" Tropical storms were unpredictable, and a strong one could be as nasty as a hurricane.

"But we'll almost certainly get some rain. There could be some flooding on the roads, and then we won't be able to get out of Mayaro. And the rivers might come up over the bridges."

She was silent for a moment.

"That's just a worst-case scenario," he told her comfortingly. "But it's your call."

"How much time did you say we have?"

"Forty-eight hours before the rain comes, at the most."

"Is it likely to be bad?"

Banner shrugged. "Like I said, it's just a tropical storm. There isn't any risk of injury. But it could be unpleasant."

She was in charge of the tour. It was her decision. She would have to choose between truncating a tour on the merest threat of bad weather, depriving her guests of two days at the beach, days which they had paid for, or staying silent and hoping the storm swept up along the Caribbean archipelago, as they almost always did. Either way, there would be trouble.

"We leave tomorrow," she said firmly.

Banner smiled admiringly at her. "I knew you'd do the right thing," he said. "Good for you, Rhea."

It was comforting to know she had the support and admiration of the older man. "Should we tell them tonight?"

He shook his head. "Maybe we should wait till breakfast. No sense getting them all worked up for nothing. Let them get a good night's sleep."

"You're right. But I think I'll call Ian tonight, though. Call him at home and let him know there's been a change of plans. We'll have to bring their hotel bookings in Port of Spain forward a few nights."

"You're calling Ian at home? Good luck. You want me with you?"

"No, I'll be fine." She hoped she'd said it with just the right amount of conviction. Just because she couldn't maintain control of her personal life didn't mean she would lose her grip on her professional life. She was in charge of the tour. The decision was hers.

"No," Ian snapped. "You're not going anywhere."

She couldn't believe he was saying this. "Ian," she said patiently, "there's a storm coming."

"What storm? Did anybody say there was a storm coming here, to Trinidad? No. They talked about a storm for two seconds on the TV this evening. A storm that's about a hundred thousand miles east of here, in the Atlantic, headed for the Windwards. As usual, we're all going to have a little scare, everyone's going to panic and run out and stock up on drinking water and batteries. And the storm's going to veer to the north. It'll pass us completely, if it doesn't die down before it gets here. And you know what? Everybody'll be wondering why they'd gone and made a fool of themselves over the storm in the first place."

"Ian, we'll still be getting some rain."

"A little rain never hurt anyone. You think these people come all the way in from the States expecting sun every day? It's the tropics. It rains here, too, remember?" His voice was becoming shrill, as it always did when he was annoyed.

"I'm not worried about a little rain," she tried to explain, "I'm worried about a *lot* of rain."

"Maybe it will blow itself out."

"It's traveling over water. It's gathering speed out there. You know that's how they work." Why was he being so difficult? She couldn't understand it.

"Look, give it a day and see how it goes, okay? Listen to the radio. If it's any worse by Sunday, you can leave a day early. I paid for two beach houses already for this trip, the one you're in and the one you claim you didn't like. No sense booking two extra nights at a hotel for a false alarm."

Realisation dawned. That was it. It was all about money. He was stonewalling over a couple of nights' hotel fees. She should have known it all the time. The memory of his refusal to provide a nurse for her while she was in bed, floored by the jellyfish sting, still rankled. Money was obviously more important to him than anyone's well-being. "Ian," she began, but she knew it was futile.

"Listen to the radio," he said shortly, "monitor the situation. There's no need to panic anybody—just ensure that everyone has a good time. That's what I pay you for." The phone went dead.

"What do you mean, tropical storm? What exactly do you mean by that?" Rainer leaned forward over the breakfast table, glaring at her as if she were responsible for conjuring up the storm herself. His wife looked up at him, thin lips drawn taut, embarrassed by his outburst.

Rhea tried to remain calm. She and Banner had discussed Ian's directive, and agreed that although they would have to stick to what he said, and remain a day and monitor the situation, they would let the others know where they stood. She cleared her throat and tried to put as much authority as possible into her voice. "There is no indication that it will ever hit Trinidad. I've been on the phone with the weather people this morning, and they have told me that it will turn and head toward the northwest as it reaches Caribbean waters. We're in no danger of being hit head-on."

"So why do we have to leave a day early? We paid for two weeks on the beach, we should get two weeks on the beach. We're entitled to it."

"Yes," she agreed with him, "I understand. But it's only one day, and you will be given accommodation at a hotel in Port of Spain at the company's expense. It's all in the interest of safety."

"But you just said there was no threat, young lady."

She put her hands up before her face, partly in an effort to calm him, partly because of her continuing need to protect herself from him. "There's no threat, but with tropical weather, you always have to be careful. We will almost certainly have heavy rain—the heat and stillness we have been experiencing are a forewarning of that. There might be flooding on the roads.

It won't make it impossible to get out of here if we leave as scheduled on Monday, but it will make it unpleasant.''

"So you're quitting just on a hunch?''

He was impossible. Rhea held her breath, trying her best to hold the sharp retort inside. She was a businesswoman, and it was not her role right now to lose her temper and tell the foolish boor off.

Marcus had no such restrictions. "Bainbridge, don't be a fool. The lady has said we're leaving, and we're leaving. It was her judgment call, and she made it.''

"Nobody asked you your opinion, Lucien,'' Rainer's head snapped around on his thick neck to face Marcus. His face had become the colour of his flaming hair. Obviously, he was not used to being contradicted.

Marcus bristled; his spine snapped erect, his face darkened. It was the first time he had addressed Rainer directly since their encounter in the kitchen, and his demeanor now made it quite clear that he had neither forgiven nor forgotten. They looked like two wild pigs squaring off for a fight. "You didn't ask for it, but you're going to get it. The lady has already made a decision.''

Rhea rolled her eyes heavenward. Hadn't she told him she didn't need him fighting her battles? Why was he insisting on leaping into the fray on her behalf? Before she could wrench control of the discussion back out of his grasp, he went on.

"She's obviously made it in our best interest, that's what she's here for. So stop whining about your extra day at the beach. Grow up.'' The nostrils of his long high nose was flaring with anger.

Jodelle had been following the exchange between the two men intently. She was growing more upset. Too late, Rhea realised that she should have asked Marcus to send her outside to play on the porch for a few minutes, while the adults discussed the situation. The enmity between the two men was not a sight for young eyes.

Thinking that her father was under threat, the child leaped up. She clambered onto her chair and stood on the seat so that she could be closer to Rainer's height. "You leave my daddy

alone! You're not a nice man, and I don't like you!'' Her fierce
little face was full of loyal indignation.

Rainer looked down at her in surprise. It was like suddenly
having a sleeping Chihuahua rise up and begin snarling. Irritated
at being challenged by a six-year-old, he threw her a glare that
was full of poison. The hatred and anger that had so far been
focused on Marcus swerved and fell upon the shoulders of the
child, as brilliantly visible as a searchlight in the foggy darkness.

The malevolent power of the look startled Rhea. How could
anyone look at a harmless child like that? In an instant, she
realised that her misgivings about Rainer were right—he was
capable of anything. The discovery also struck her that his
vengeance could not only be directed at her, but at anyone else
involved. With the instincts of a mother tiger, Rhea ran around
to the other side of the table and swept Jodelle up into her
protective arms.

The child's attack in front of everyone had embarrassed
Rainer, though, and he began to defend his assertion. ''I just
don't want to have to run away for nothing,'' he blustered. ''I
mean, suppose we run out of here like scared rabbits, and then
the storm blows out? We'd have wasted a whole day. I just
want to know if we'll be compensated for the loss of a day.''

Rhea thought it was time she regained control of the conversation. It was her playing field, after all. She was referee and
chief judge. Both men needed to remember that. She set Jodelle
down on the ground a safe distance away from Rainer. ''You
won't be losing a day. Port of Spain is the capital city; there's
lots to do there. And if the weather is fair, we can arrange to visit
one of the northern beaches, which are extremely beautiful.''

''Well,'' he snorted contemptuously, ''I hope that at least
the hotel is clean. I hope we won't be asked to sleep with any
rats this time!'' He turned to Rhea with a triumphant smile,
knowing that his last dig cut deep into a spot where she was
still very tender: her embarrassment over that horrendous night
in the first beach house.

Rhea squirmed, but having achieved her objective of gaining
everyone's agreement to leave a day early, she decided to leave
well enough alone, and let the conversation end there.

* * *

"Hurricane," Banner said solemnly. Everyone in the living room stared. He had not joined them for dinner, and instead had remained in his room, listening anxiously to the radio. "It's been upgraded."

"What does that mean?" Trudy said.

"It means it's no longer a storm. It means it's a lot more serious than that, and it's headed directly for us."

"What do you mean, directly for us? What's that supposed to mean? Huh?" Rainer demanded.

"The storm," Banner said coldly, "is gathering speed and strength in the Atlantic. It has been upgraded to a hurricane, and it is expected to hit the coast, this coast, by midday tomorrow." His voice was very low. Rhea had never seen him look so concerned. "What this means is that I will personally be waking everyone up at five in the morning. You will have your belongings packed tonight. At exactly five-thirty we will be leaving." He turned to face the entire group. "I want all of you to be dressed and waiting. I want your bags placed in the van tonight, and please make sure that you don't forget anything. Whatever you forget to pack will get left behind."

Rainer's throat muscles contorted with rage at being spoken to in such decisive tones, but the look in Banner's eye, and the sheer bulk of the man, were enough to make Rainer swallow his anger. "I don't have to listen to this," he retorted, as he stalked toward his bedroom. "If this thing was really serious, you should have had us out of here long ago." The door slammed, vibrating through the house. There was a palpable release of tension in the room.

Dahlia got up and walked through the open glass doors, obviously embarrassed by her husband's piggish attitude. "I'll be back in a while," she threw over her shoulder. "Just going for a stroll."

"I think we'll go get our things packed," Fred said mildly. Trudy rose and followed him out.

There was an uneasy silence. Banner got up, looking from one of them to the other, and said quietly, "I'll be inside, listening to the weather updates. If there is anything new, I'll call you.'' He left quietly and pulled his door in with a soft click.

Marcus smiled. ''Well, that was discreet of him,'' he said.

Her cheeks grew hot. *Don't tell me,* she groaned inwardly, *don't tell me that Banner has figured things out.* The embarrassment would be too much. Somehow, Marcus seemed to find the idea amusing. ''That leaves us,'' he told her softly and offered her a hand. ''It's time to talk. Just give me twenty minutes, I'll get Jodie showered and ready for bed. Okay?''

She nodded. She wished there were an excuse, a reason not to go, but she'd always known that the impending conversation was inevitable.

''Bedtime, honey,'' Marcus beckoned to Jodelle, who jumped up and trotted obediently toward him. As they passed the chair in which Rhea sat, Jodelle opened her arms and threw them around Rhea's neck.

'' 'Night, Rhea,'' she said with a huge smile.

Rhea hugged her back tightly. The child smelled of sea salt and the coconut ice cream they had had for dessert. The press of the tiny body in Rhea's arms made her inexplicably sad. ''Good night, sweetheart.''

''I love you.'' Jodelle held Rhea's face between her small hands and kissed her lightly on the tip of her nose.

She had resolved to fight this attachment. It could only lead to hurt. But Jodelle's simple declaration of love demanded an honest answer. ''Me, too, honey.'' It took an act of will to release her into her father's waiting arms.

As Marcus led her off, he turned to take one last look at Rhea. She caught his heavy-lidded eyes, and they held something that she did not recognise. Sighing, she settled down onto the couch to wait for his return.

Almost half an hour later, Marcus was back, and for the first time in days, his pre-occupied look was replaced by one of determination, as if he had settled something in his own mind. The transformation was astounding. He looked almost relaxed, and smiled as Rhea turned in her chair and looked up at him.

"Well, I've put her to bed. She should be alright while we're out." He stopped next to her chair and held out his hand to her. "Come, now. Come outside with me."

Rhea stood without taking it. She didn't need his hand, she told herself, to get to her feet. Reluctantly, she followed him outside into the still, night air.

"I don't see why we have to go out," she protested weakly, although it was more of a symbolic gesture than anything else, as they had already fallen into step. Marcus chose to ignore her. As they passed the seawall they could see the dark outline of Dahlia. She was standing close to the water a few hundred yards from them, staring out at the oil rigs glittering in the distance.

"She has a lot to work out, I guess," Marcus observed sympathetically. Rhea murmured an answer, but was truly beyond worrying about those two. Dahlia needed to come to the right decisions on her own, and as for Rhea herself, well, she had enough of her own problems to worry about. They set off in the opposite direction from where Dahlia stood.

Marcus put an arm lightly around her, letting his thumb idly stroke her shoulder. She searched wildly for a reason to tell him to remove it, then realised that she didn't want him to. In the midst of the worry she was feeling over Rainer's behaviour and the coming bad weather, his touch was comforting. She leaned into him, and her entire body seemed to sigh.

"Don't worry," he said gently, "it'll all work out." She almost believed him.

They were walking in the direction that they had gone that first time, when he'd kissed her in the water. It was ridiculous, she thought, that they would gravitate toward the area as if it were "their" spot, as if there were a "they" to begin with.

Even so, it was good for just that one night. She'd indulge her fantasy, walk next to him on this dark, silent beach and let herself truly feel this love of hers for a while, instead of smothering it or fighting it or pretending it didn't exist. It was only for this one short night; at five-thirty in the morning she would be up in front in the van next to Banner, safe, and when they were back in the busy city, there would be no beaches to influence her, and no long walks under a bright starry sky. Then in a week or so he would be back on a plane, far away in California where he could do no harm, and she could go back to her life, and see if she could get it back on stream, mend the holes so that it would be just the way she left it. Only it could never be just the way it was before, her rational self tormented her, because she was in love with him, and that was that. Distance couldn't change it. If she were lucky, time just might.

"Look at all the houses," he said to her, interrupting her dark thoughts. "Look at how quiet they all are."

He was right. The brightly lit beachfront houses were shuttered and silent. Some were completely dark, suggesting that their inhabitants had fled the storm. In others, light escaped from the cracks around closed windows, as if the families inside had been too awed by the eerie quiet, and the sense that all of nature was poised, waiting for calamity.

"Is this what you call the calm before the storm?"

How could he be chatting so conversationally, when her own emotions threatened to cut off the air in her lungs? She sought and found her voice. "Yes, I guess that's what you call it."

"Awe inspiring, isn't it?"

"It is, yes." Her voice was as listless as the air around them.

"Are you afraid?" They had reached the spot where they had bathed that night. As they drew up alongside of the low, sloping coconut tree whose trunk ran parallel to the ground, he stopped. She wanted urgently to sit so that her legs wouldn't betray her. She sat heavily on the low trunk.

Afraid? He was joking. She was more afraid than she had ever been, but not of any freakish storm. Rain could never hurt her as much as he could. She wondered what he wanted, really. What could he ask for, with just a few days left here? If it was sex, he could forget it. She wasn't interested, in spite of what her body was screaming. If he made any allusion to such a need, she would cut him dead, send him packing. What did he think she was?

"Rhea?" He was sitting next to her, his face close, looking concerned. She'd gone off into a fugue. How embarrassing!

She shook her head. "No, I'm not afraid." She hoped she sounded convincing.

"Good," he said. "I'm glad to hear that." He took one of her hands in both of his and began stroking it lightly, almost as if he were not aware that he was doing it. His fingers ran along her slim wrist, along each finger, outlining every bone and crease. He brought her hand to his mouth and pressed his lips into her palm. The action made her shiver. Afraid? Definitely.

"Rhea?"

"Yes?" her breath could barely escape the tight vise that her lungs had become.

"I'm sorry about the way I behaved in the kitchen. I was wrong to treat you the way I did. We were doing so well for a moment there, and then suddenly everything just got out of hand, and I lost my cool. But I don't have any excuses. I'm just sorry."

She nodded her acceptance of his apology and waited timorously for him to go on.

"I just wish you'd told me about Rainer. Did he hurt you?" She shook her head vigorously.

"Did he offend you? What has he said to you? What has he been doing?"

She pulled her hand out of his grasp and threw it up in protest. Why did he keep harping on about the same tired old issue? "Mark, please, leave it alone. I don't want to talk about it. It was embarrassing, humiliating, but I'm a grown woman and I can deal with my own problems. Okay?"

"Why? Why can't you share your troubles with me? Why can't you let me help you fight your battles? I want to stand up for you. I want to defend you."

"Why, Mark? You're crusading again. I'm not one of your causes. I don't need you to fight my battles."

He shook his head, as if he were trying to get rid of a mosquito in his ear. "I don't want to be your crusader. I'm not making you into one of my causes. All I want is for you to let me be a man for you. I want to stand up for you and fight for you. I want to protect you. If someone hurts you, I want you to allow me to defend you.''

''Why?''

''For us.'' He took hold of her hand again, and she simply didn't have the strength to pull it away a second time.

Still, she managed to deny him. ''There's no 'us.' '' If she said it firmly enough, she herself would believe it.

He continued his rhythmic stroking of her hand, rubbing her knuckles gently against his lips. ''You know that's not true. You know there is an us. We both know it.''

Rhea snatched her hand away. ''Don't be stupid.''

''What's so stupid about it?''

''It's ridiculous. It's just one of those things. Since when do two little kisses make an us?''

''Those weren't two little kisses. And there's more to what's going on between us than those kisses. You felt it the first night we met. So did I. Jodelle knew it, too. I think she saw, even before we did, that there would be something special happening between us. Remember that first night, when you brought her that moth? She let you under her skin then. I did, too''

''No,'' she insisted, but still she almost smiled with the memory of that moment when she'd given that huge brown moth to Jodelle. She remembered that it had swirls in it that were the colour of Marcus' eyes. At that moment, something inside the girl had opened up wide and allowed Rhea inside. But she mustn't let her feelings for the little girl confound the issue. The man knew how much she cared for his daughter, and he was using her to manipulate her feelings. It was blackmail, and she wouldn't stand for it. So she said ''no'' a second time.

''Don't lie to me, Rhea. You felt it.''

''No, I felt nothing. Nothing real. It's only attraction. That's all it is.''

He released her hand, and for the first time did not look so sure of himself. ''Attraction? Are you serious? I know you're not serious.'' His voice sounded more full of doubt than certainty. It gave Rhea the advantage.

"Yes, that's all it was." She waited for her words of bravado to get through to him. "Don't tell me you thought there was more to it than that?" She forced a laugh. "Really, I would have thought you were more sophisticated than that, Marcus."

Score one. He released her hand and stood, rubbing his neck in puzzlement. "That's not what your eyes have been saying, Rhea. You're lying."

"I'm not lying. And I think you've put too much stock in what you see going on between Jodelle and me. Yes, I love your daughter. I can't deny that. But I think that seeing her respond to me as she does has influenced you. I think that you let her test me, and when she decided I was acceptable, I became acceptable to you, too."

"That's unfair. And stupid. I don't allow a six-year-old girl to choose my women for me. . . ."

"I'm not one of your women!"

"You know what I mean. I don't allow her to dictate what goes on in my personal life. She and I may have been on our own a long time, but I'm still a man, and I make those decisions myself."

"And you've *decided* that you want me, so I'm just supposed to fall in with your plans? Where did you get your ego?" She was fighting dirty now, but it was the only way she knew to retain her ground.

"You're denying me with your mouth when you know that everything else in you has been telling me otherwise, all week. Is it your boyfriend? Do you love him, too?"

Too? Who gave him permission to be so presumptuous? She decided to put him in his place at once. "My relationship is none of your business, Marcus," she informed him primly. "I don't think you have the right to ask."

"That's where you're wrong." He came to sit by her side again. "I *do* have the right."

"What gives you the right?" she was becoming angry, and scared that if he only pushed a little harder, her resistance would crack. "What could possibly give you the right to interfere in my private life?"

He was solemn for a while. She found herself pinned down by his glowing eyes. "Love does," he said.

She was blown away. She'd expected confessions of lust or desire, allusions to her own frantic need of him that evening on the cliffside, all arguments that she was prepared to win. But not this. He loved her? There hadn't been time for that. Love came slowly. It couldn't possibly be true. "Don't be stupid, Marcus."

He looked hurt. "What's so stupid about it?"

"You can't love me. You couldn't possibly."

"Why not?"

"Because you don't know me. You only met me a week ago."

"What I know of you, I love. And I want to know the rest of you."

"Marcus, it makes no sense! It just doesn't happen this way."

"I didn't think so either." He reached up to run a finger lightly across her lips. His touch was like a kiss. Rhea struggled to resist. "I thought this instant madness was for kids, until now," he told her.

She wished he would take his hand away, let her maintain control. "Look," she said softly, "Marcus, it's just attraction. It's just desire, those kisses we shared. I enjoyed them, too." She took his hand away from her face and he let it drop to his side.

"I loved you before the kisses. There were just so many things about you that held my attention. The way you spoke, the way you walked. All that wonderful knowledge you carry around inside of you. The way you look when you're mad at me. Your hostess face. You intrigued me. I wanted to know all about you. I felt like a big clumsy overgrown teenager. I wanted to swim with you, dance with you, sit in the van next to you. I loved the way your hair smelled whenever you passed close to me."

This last made her flush. She remembered herself standing

in the shower inhaling the scent of the aftershave that he left behind each morning. She'd have died of embarrassment if he ever caught her, but all along he'd been just as intrigued by the way she smelled as she was by him!

He went on, "Those days, when you were sick, you scared me so badly. I'd hardly known you a few days, and I hadn't fully realised how much I wanted you then, but I was still crazy with worry, and fear. I stayed up at night, watching you writhe in pain, even in your sleep, and I was more frightened that I thought I could be for a stranger. I wanted to do everything for you. . . ."

And she'd treated him so badly over that. Her and her injured pride . . .

He let his breath out in a rush. "I didn't just 'enjoy' the kisses. They were rebirth for me. I've been tired and alone and empty for a long, long time. You soothed away all that weariness. You filled me up."

"Not true," she protested. Her eyes were stinging with the effort to resist.

"Yes, Rhea. True."

"Well," she was completely flustered. This confession was more than she was prepared to deal with. In spite of her love, she hated him at that moment, because he'd upped the stakes. It was hard enough trying to extricate herself from this terrible tangle without his having complicated it all by loving her back. Did he really? His face and his eyes and his voice told her he was serious. But it couldn't be true. She didn't want it to be.

"Thank you," she told him politely, as if he'd paid her a simple compliment about her hair or her cooking. "But really, I think you're mistaken."

He was incredulous. "Mistaken?"

She went on in a rush. "Yes. You came on vacation, to a beautiful island, it's all part of the mystique, exoticism. Falling in love with a native girl. It's a fantasy, that's all."

"First of all, I am not on vacation. Second, I think your island is beautiful, but I've traveled all my life, and I think I've become immune to all this nonsense about exotic romanticism. I don't see you as a fantasy. You're reality, and I want to keep on making you part of *my* reality. Third, I don't buy the island girl myth. I may have once, but that was a long time ago, and I was a stupid boy and I made a mistake. Yvette's gone. She's out of my life and she isn't coming back. That's all over now."

Grateful for a loophole, she pounced. "All over? Do you call *that*," she pointed aggressively to the ring which, in spite of everything, still rested on the fourth finger of his left hand, "you call that 'over'?"

He looked down at his hand, stared at it, and she watched him as ghosts of the past flitted before his eyes. There was a battle going on in there, and it was tremendous. The waiting was agony for Rhea. Then slowly and deliberately he grasped the ring with his right hand and twisted it off his finger. "This hasn't come off since the day I married," he said hoarsely, as if something was being dragged out of his gut, with great pain. He held the small gold band out to her with a hand that shook.

When she refused to take it, he pressed it into her palm and forced her fingers closed over it. Rhea opened her hand and stared at the object that had been so important to him. She knew just how much it must have meant to him to do what he had done, but the ring was not for her to dispose of. That was his responsibility.

"No, Mark, this isn't for me to do." She returned it to him.

He took it, almost giddy, then stood and walked down to the edge of the water. In the darkness, she could see his arm as it drew back, like a pitcher at the mound, and then he flung it forcefully forward. The tiny ring made no sound as it hit the water.

When he returned to her side, he was panting as if he had been running. He dropped to his knees next to her in the sand and turned his face upward. "See? It's over *now*." He held out his hands like a boy showing his mother that he'd washed them properly, and he was ready for dessert.

For a moment, she almost relented in the light of his sincerity. He was truly trying. But still, this could only end in hurt, for both of them. For the three of them, as Jodelle would surely be affected. Admitting that she loved him would solve nothing. The odds against their survival were still overwhelming.

Baring her need to him might mean one or two nights of sweetness and pleasure; she glanced around at the soft sand that surrounded them and wondered what it would be like to sink into it a second time and feel the pressure of his body on top of hers . . . but at the end of it all, there would be only pain and good-byes. In a week he would be on his way home again. Had he forgotten the vast distance between his home and hers? She steeled herself. "I'm sorry."

He looked so crestfallen that she felt guilty. "So you don't love me?"

She was amazed that she was able to answer in a steady voice. "No."

"And you don't think you can?"

She shook her head, unwilling to risk speaking.

"Do you love him?"

"Who?"

"You know who," he grated. "Don't be stupid."

"Of course," she realised with some surprise that she was lying. She didn't love Brent. She didn't think she ever had. This is what it took for her to finally realise that? To fall—to crash—into love with another man? "Why are you asking me such stupid questions?"

He ignored her last comment. "Does he love you?"

"Yes." She looked away so that he would not see the lie reflected in her eyes. The admission, to herself, that Brent did not love her stung her pride, but to her surprise, hurt little else. Although there was a sense of loss, she realised that the illusion that she had fostered about herself and Brent had been nothing but a comforting charade. She hadn't lost that much, really. It was nothing compared to what she was deliberately throwing away right now. She was painfully aware of that fact, but she could not stop herself.

Marcus looked so wounded that she longed to confess that she was lying, and that in all her life she'd loved only one man—him. The urge to make this confession in order to put an end to the hurt she was causing him was almost too much to resist. She sought another tack.

"Mark?" she was gentle now, not wanting to inflict any further pain. "Are you sure this isn't about Jodie?"

He was puzzled. "What about Jodie? What about her?"

"Are you sure you aren't just mommy hunting? She loves me and I love her, and maybe you just thought that it would be good to have me in your life to provide her with a mother. Maybe you've just forced yourself, or lulled yourself, into thinking that you . . ." she swallowed hard, "you love me. So you could provide for her."

He snorted. "Mommy hunting! It would take you to come up with an expression like that! No, Rhea, I am not looking for a mother for my child. I have no ulterior motive, I'm not using you to feed any fantasy, any neurosis, any need other than the needs a man usually feels for a woman. All I want is you, and I only want you for yourself, nothing else."

"So it isn't a custody thing?"

He threw his hands up. "Why are you so suspicious? Why can't you trust me? Listen, I have full custody of Jodelle. That's not likely to change. Yvette doesn't want her. She never has. As a matter of fact, she abdicated her responsibility when Jodelle was a baby. She couldn't even hold her without breaking into a cold sweat. I fed her. I changed her. I saw her through her first teeth, her first words, and her first steps. I don't need to set you up as a smoke screen for any judge. All I want is you, for yourself."

Now she felt like a rat. She was questioning his integrity. She decided to plead her way out of this one before she gave in to her weakness. "Can we go back in? It's getting late."

He stared hard at her, than nodded slowly. "Okay, Rhea. We'll stop. I'll stop talking about it. For now. Because as far as I'm concerned, I still have a day or two left. And I'm going to do all I can to change your mind. I'm not giving up on you."

Of one accord they rose and began walking solemnly back to the house. The night was so quiet she could hear the sand squeaking under their feet.

"I'm sorry," she told him meekly.

''It isn't over yet.'' He said curtly. He didn't look at her again.

There wasn't another soul on the beach. All of the fishermen's boats had been pulled well off the sand, almost on the edge of the road, in an effort to save them from the onslaught of the coming storm. They'd been turned over facedown, reminding Rhea of the little game that street hustlers played at bazaars, with the pea hidden under three shells, and they switched the shells round and round, so you couldn't tell which one the pea was hidden under. All the fishing nets that were usually spread out on the beach to dry had been rolled up and put away. The effect was eerie.

They were just within sight of the house when Marcus stopped abruptly.

''What?'' she peered up at him in the darkness, and then looked nervously around for what could have made him halt.

''This.'' He grabbed hold of her upper arms and yanked her close. Before she could protest, his mouth was on hers. Rhea was furious, and tried to wriggle free but he held her even closer, pressing hard against her, and for the first time, she felt fear—she had never before been aware of just how strong he was.

Still, although she fought frantically to get away, she found that her mouth (that traitor!) was kissing him back even as she struggled. Her blood was singing in her ears. The kiss was like a cruel collision, nothing close to the tender sweet seductive kisses of their previous encounters. It was all hard teeth and brutality, he demanded that she give him her tongue, forced his way in, insistent. Violently, he sucked the air from deep within her lungs, taking it all into himself, causing her oxygen-starved brain to cloud.

In spite of his near-savagery, her mouth and her body ached for more. The insistent prodding of his erection against the softness of her belly brought brilliant flashes of colour to the insides of her closed eyelids. His coaxing brought a flood of wet heat between her legs that she was sure, in his heightened state of awareness, he could feel or smell. The thought brought not embarrassment but excitement. When she finally stopped struggling and wound her arms around his neck, whispering his name urgently against his cheek, he pushed her away so roughly that she had to flail her arms about to regain her balance.

"Lesson number one," he said shortly, "we've proven that you're not indifferent. That gives me a place to start. I've got just a few more days, Rhea, and I intend to make the most of them. Stand warned."

"You vicious, brutal lout," she raged, "don't ever touch me again! Don't ever kiss me again! You have no rights where I'm concerned, do you hear?"

"The next time I kiss you, Rhea," he grated, "it will be because you beg me to."

"Don't be absurd."

"I'm not joking. This is a warning. I'll have you begging me, like you did on the side of that cliff . . ." the reminder made her flush madly, "only next time, it will be for a simple kiss. Just a kiss. When you want one, you tell me. I'll be glad to oblige."

She wanted to wipe that sneer off his face, but, too confused by the sharp painful yearning of her body to find a suitable retort, she stepped ahead of him and stormed into the house. Her room seemed to be at the end of a long tunnel; the effort to reach it seemed so tremendous. When she was finally there, she heaved the door shut with enough force to send an echo through the house like a gunshot.

Immediately, she was remorseful. She'd probably woken everyone in the house. Whatever happened to her notorious cool? She wished she could go to the bathroom to splash some cold water onto her heated face, but the fear of encountering Marcus there made her stay put. Instead she splashed a little tepid water from the glass on her bedside table and patted it onto her cheeks with a towel. She heard Marcus' heavy, angry footsteps up the corridor, and tensed. But then there was the sound of his door opening, and her body went limp again. Obviously he was not prepared to pursue it further tonight.

She was just trying to determine why this realisation had

left her with a sinking disappointment when his door was thrown open again, and there were anxious footsteps past her door. The door of the bathroom was thrown open, and then there was a heavy rapping on her own door. She sighed and rose to her feet. It was bad enough that her own noisy entrance had probably jarred everyone out of their sleep, but here he was, demanding that she open her door, hanging their dirty linen out for anyone who cared to listen!

She wrenched the door open and began irritably, ''Marcus, listen. I told you . . .''

He brushed her admonitions aside and stepped into the room. ''Have you seen my daughter?'' His voice was loud, still angry . . . and tinged with something else.

Rhea looked confusedly around, as if she expected the child to materialise from under her bed. ''What?'' She peered at him, still not sure of what was going on.

''I'm looking for Jodelle. Where is she?'' He was beyond patience now, speaking to her as he would to an idiot.

''I don't know,'' she began, then her mouth fell open. ''You mean, she's not in bed?''

Marcus gave her an exasperated look, and stalked out of the room. He moved out to the living room, and began turning on lights, calling her name, first softly, then more and more stridently. Rhea followed him out, anxiety growing within her. They moved around the peripheries of the beach house, calling, but in the pre-storm silence there was no answer.

''Where could she have gone?'' There was no residual animosity from their recent encounter, only shared anxiety. Rhea looked at Marcus' handsome face with concern. His face was grey, lips taut, eyes wide and distressed. Her own fear leaped in recognition of his own.

Leaving him there, she raced inside and banged on Banner's door. It opened before she could knock a second time.

''Rhea?'' With a swift response born of experience, the man was alert, eyes inquiring, ready to respond to whatever situation she had brought to him.

"It's Jodelle. She's missing."

Banner took in the alarm on her face and didn't bother to waste time with stupid questions. Quickly, he stepped outside and knocked on the Steins' and Bainbridges' doors in turn. In seconds they were all standing outside the rooms, listening as Banner quickly explained the situation. "She couldn't have gone far," he said, "Come on. Let's go outside."

They found Marcus outside, coming from the direction of the van. "She's not in the van," he said tightly. "Not under it, either."

Banner turned to Rhea. "You were walking along the beach just now. Did you see anything?"

She shook her head. "No, we haven't seen any sign of her. Nothing. There was no one out there but us."

Banner looked at Marcus. "How far did you walk?"

"A mile or two," Marcus answered.

"What could have made her leave the house?"

Marcus shook his head dazedly. "I have no idea. She was asleep when I left her." He paused. "Why? You think she might have run away? She had no need. She was fine when she went to bed. I don't understand."

Rhea's eyes moved from Marcus' frightened face to the shore, and she shuddered. There was a whole lot of sea out there.

"Listen to me," Marcus said in a voice that had all eyes turned on him. His grey face held an authority that rebuked resistance.

"I want my daughter back right now. Do you hear me? There's a storm coming. We're going to break up into teams and go out and look for her." It was not a heartening prospect; the beach stretched on endlessly on either side, and there were miles of coconut estate to cover as well, if Jodelle had decided to turn inland.

Marcus spoke again. He had his hands on his hips, and he looked even taller than usual. In spite of his obvious fear, his voice was one of firm authority. "Banner, take the van and go up the street. Start with the tracks leading into the estates nearby before you go along the main roads. She might have gone off the road. Fred and Bainbridge, you go south. Comb the beach in a zigzag motion, between the water and the edge of the beach. Take your flashlights, and carry sticks so you can beat down the bushes if you have to.''

Rhea gave him a furious look. He was taking over. What did he think he was doing? She was in charge here. ''Marcus . . .'' she began firmly, but he went on without even turning to her.

''She can swim, but not that well. And I don't think she'd be going toward the water. . . .'' He paused, and seemed to be fighting to draw his next breath. Immediately, Rhea was ashamed. There was a storm coming, and this man had lost his daughter, but here she was worrying about who was in control! She was overwhelmed by guilt. At once, she relinquished her control of the situation to Marcus.

There was a low snort behind her. ''Pity you were more concerned about your *walk* along the beach,'' the nasal voice, undoubtedly Rainer's, penetrated the tension. ''If you'd been looking after the girl like you were supposed to, we'd all still be asleep.'' His pale freckled face held a sneer that, to Rhea's horrified realisation, was coming damn close to being knocked off by the enraged man who turned to face him.

Instead of lashing out as she'd expected, Marcus struggled to control himself. He inhaled deeply and took one step toward him. Even Rainer realised that he had overstepped the bounds of human decency, and cringed.

''Look, Bainbridge,'' Marcus' voice was clipped but controlled. ''I've had enough of you. If you don't want anything to do with the search, get out of my way.'' With an abrupt flick of the head, he dismissed the fat, unpleasant man.

Chastised by the tone of Marcus' voice and the disgusted stares of the others, Rainer turned and stalked into the house. It seemed that not even the threat of all the dangers that could befall a child in the still night could surmount his wounded pride. It was one hand less that they could count on.

''The rest of you,'' Marcus continued, not even looking at Rainer's receding back, ''we don't have much time. It's after midnight and we have a hurricane coming in less than twelve hours. Maybe sooner, if it picks up speed. It's a little dark on the beach, but we have a full moon, so that's a lot of help. Fred, go in and get all the flashlights. Trudy, you turn on all the lights in the house, and open all the doors and windows so that my daughter can find her way home. And you stay there and wait. If Jodelle comes in on her own, somebody should be there.''

He began to look around him, hands on hips and brow furrowed. ''I'm going to make a pile of coconut branches right here in the centre of the beach. Trudy, I want you to bring out all those charcoal briquettes from the barbecue and the lighter fluid and set them down here next to the branches. If Jodelle comes home,'' he paused and his voice seemed to be forced out of his throat only through supreme effort, *''when* she comes home, Trudy can set it all alight. We'll know to come back when we see it.'' Fred nodded and went into the house.

''Banner,'' Marcus continued, ''You can't see the fire from the road, so I want you to check back at the house every hour on the hour, so that you'll know when we've called off the search. Okay?''

''Okay,'' Banner said. The two men shook hands briefly and Banner went to retrieve the van.

Marcus turned to Rhea. ''Let's get this pile of branches going. And please, let me handle this. I don't care if you're in charge. I don't care about your feminist sensibilities. I just want my daughter back.''

She was about to protest. Did he really think she was that petty? Then she remembered her earlier reaction and held her tongue. They set to work quickly.

Together they dragged the deceptively feathery-looking fallen coconut branches to a clear area on the sand and began to pile them up. After weeks of no rain, the branches were brittle as tinder, and would burn marvelously. By the time Fred returned with the flashlights, they had accumulated a pile of branches that was easily five feet wide and three feet high.

Trudy came out with her arms full of briquettes and lighter fluid. She laid them in a pile next to the branches and showed them the box of matches in her pocket.

"You be careful with that lighter fluid, Trudy." Marcus said protectively.

Trudy smiled. "Don't worry, young man. I've been lighting barbecues since before you were born!"

Grateful for a little relief to the tension, Marcus almost managed a smile. He hugged Trudy quickly. With whispers of "good luck" all round, they parted company and began the search.

CHAPTER FOURTEEN

At around four o'clock in the morning, the group returned to the house, tired, disheartened, and empty-handed. The pile of branches in the middle of the beach remained unlit. They'd covered as much territory as they could, even risking trouble with the law by scaling walls and searching private property. Everyone except Marcus sat in the living room glumly sipping hot coffee, each looking to the other for some sort of new suggestion, some idea.

Alone on the porch, in a corner against a wall, Marcus sat with a coffee mug cradled in his hands, his face exhausted and drawn. They were reluctant to intrude on his thoughts, but watched the outline of his dejected form as he contemplated his next move.

Banner rose to his feet and walked out to speak to him. Anxious to be of some comfort, Rhea followed. "We'll have to wait till daylight," Banner was telling Marcus. "There's nothing more we can do now."

"I'm not waiting until daylight," Marcus replied hoarsely. "My daughter is out there." He looked ready to go staggering back out into the night, in spite of his fatigue.

"I know," Banner said firmly, "but it's just too dark. We

tried. We all tried. We can't do anything more right now. We have to wait for a little more light. She's smart, Marcus, she won't allow any harm to come to herself. She probably wandered into one of the other beach houses. Most of them are empty because of the storm. Maybe she's locked herself in, and isn't hearing us because she's asleep.''

Marcus' shoulders sagged. "I know. It's just that, if we stop, it seems like we gave up. I just don't want her to feel that we gave up on her, that's all. Wherever she is, I just want her to wake up to the sound of our voices, and to know we want her back.''

His distraught face drew Rhea closer to him. She squatted at his feet, prized the cup of coffee from his cold hands and stroked his forearms lightly. "We'll get her back, Mark. I promise you.'' She reached up and gently touched his cheek. She felt the dampness against her fingers and wished that there was some way that she could take some of his pain and bear it on her own shoulders.

Banner asked softly, "Was there anything she wanted to see or do before she left? Catch crabs? Gather flowers? There must be some clue as to where she might have gone.''

Marcus threw up his hands in a gesture that said *I have no idea.*

"You didn't have an argument with her at all?''

Marcus shook his head. "No. Nothing.''

Rhea finally voiced the anxious thought that had been nagging at her all night. "Mark, do you think it was because of us? Do you think she knew that . . .'' she trailed off and glanced up at Banner, reluctant to expose herself like this, but it was important to know what had been going on in the girl's head in order to bring her safely back home. Besides, Banner already suspected that their relationship had gone beyond the professional. She began again. "Do you think that she knew that there is, that there *was* something going on between us?''

Marcus turned his harrowed eyes upon her face. "Of course she knew, Rhea. She isn't stupid.''

"And would she be jealous? Would she run away because

of . . . me?'' The idea was just too awful to contemplate. She felt guilty even voicing the idea.

Marcus was incredulous. ''Jealous? No, no, she loves you. I told you so.''

It made no sense. ''Then what . . . ?'' A hideous, impossible idea entered her mind, rattling her to the bone, and refusing to go away. A host of garbled images came tumbling across her field of vision, Rainer in the kitchen taunting Marcus beyond endurance, Rainer with those insolent blue eyes that let her know without a doubt that her rejection of him wouldn't rest there, and today at breakfast, Jodelle standing on her chair, spitting fire at him in defense of her daddy.

It wasn't possible. It didn't even bear consideration. Surely the man wasn't cruel enough to have turned his rage against a little girl? But then she remembered his sneering contempt when the search began, and his refusal to join in. She glanced involuntarily across the room to the place where Rainer sat, stone-faced, his back against a wall. His vacant eyes told her nothing.

The question was, did she dare voice her fears to Marcus and risk seeing his wrath leap out at the other man? She knew from experience just how dangerous Marcus could be when he was angry. What if she was wrong, and he had had nothing to do with the girl's disappearance? What if Marcus pounced, and discovered too late that Rainer was innocent?

Her dilemma was solved without her needing to make a decision. Marcus' sharp eyes followed the direction of her gaze, and with a single cognitive leap, deciphered her suspicions.

He bounded out of his chair and pounced on the soft, fat man with the ferocity of a killer cat. ''Bainbridge . . .'' The growl in his throat brooked no evasion.

Rainer cringed, pressing backward into the upholstery. ''I never touched her,'' he began, holding his hands up to his face, partly as a shield, partly in a feeble attempt at a defensive parry. ''I never touched the child. I only . . .''

His words were cut off by the sudden force of Marcus' large right hand, closing around his throat. ''Where is she?''

Then Marcus had the good sense to loosen his grip, not out

of sympathy or concern, but to allow Rainer sufficient air to pant out an answer. "I don't know. I don't know. I had no idea it would come to this."

"You had no idea *what* would come to this?"

"I . . ." Rainer floundered, the oppressive presence of the powerful man, poised over him like an angry black puma, had him almost tongue-tied.

"Did you touch her?" Marcus had no need to raise his voice; the danger within it was apparent even in his whisper.

"No! No! I haven't hurt her. I don't know where she is! I just . . ."

"Just *what?*" Rhea bristled protectively. She moved swiftly to Marcus' side. What had the bastard done to the child? "What, Rainer?"

The formerly cocky man cringed. He turned to Rhea, preferring to suffer her angry stare rather than Marcus' lethal one. "I told her that Lucien wasn't her father. After you two left this evening, she came out to get a drink of water, and I met her in the kitchen. And I told her. I didn't mean to make her run away. Honestly, I just . . ."

"Why?" Dahlia's horrified voice was a scratchy whisper.

"I owed him. I owed him for the last time he put his hand on me. Him, pretending the little bastard was his, and strutting around like the cock of the walk, sniffing round that stuck up, icy little . . ."

No one ever found out what else Rainer intended to say, as actions removed the need for words and Marcus tore Rainer up out of his seat and slammed his thick body against the porch wall.

"Mark, no!" Rhea begged as the first blow landed on Rainer's jaw. The fierce animal that had possessed the man that she loved hit Rainer a second time, and was about to land a third fearsome punch when Banner caught hold of the upraised fist.

"Enough, Marcus," The muscles on Banner's thick arm bulged with the effort to keep Marcus from making contact with his cowering target.

"Marcus, please," Dahlia's plea was barely audible, but it was enough to bring Marcus back to his senses. He shook his arm free of Banner's grasp and stepped back. The craven whimpers made him sick. He walked out of the house and onto the sand.

"If anything happens to my daughter," he pointed a long finger at Rainer, "you'll have to answer to me." He turned to Rhea, eyes still on fire. "We just have a few hours left. We've got to find her long before the hurricane hits. Are you coming?"

She stepped from the porch and put her hand on his arm. "Let's go out again. It's getting lighter now. We'll find her."

He cringed and nodded, but did not speak.

The sun was rising over the water, and the sky began to take on the appearance of a sheet of lead—dull, matte, reflecting nothing. They set out a second time, legs heavy from the exhausting, sleepless night, hating the eerie quiet that surrounded them. Banner left for town to gather what emergency supplies he could: candles, bleach for sterilizing drinking water, bread, crackers, and canned goods. They were not fooling themselves; they were stuck in Mayaro for the duration of the storm, and, depending on the infrastructural damage that the village suffered, they might be forced to stay where they were for at least a few days.

They trudged along the beach, fanning out. This time they did what they had been loath to do before, search the water itself. They walked along the banks at the mouth of the river, prodding the mud flats with sticks, and followed the sluggish waves of the ocean, looking for the frill of a tiny nightgown.

Rhea stayed close to Marcus. She was surprised at the depth of the pain and fear that she felt. That a child was at risk was one thing, but this child, *his* child, was entwined in everything that she felt for him. She was part of the love she had for him and the yearning she felt to be with him. This feeling involved three of them, not two, and she felt his terror and dread as acutely as if it were here own.

She watched him keenly as he searched the shore, and the memory of how she had treated him last night made her feel less than nothing. Last night, this man who had had everything except a woman to love had been asking her to be a part of his life, and she'd turned him down because of her own selfish

fears. Now he was at risk of losing everything, and ιτ
suddenly clear to her how fast things could change. She need
to grab on to what life offered her, whether or not it made her
afraid.

Lord, she prayed fervently, *just bring her back. You bring
her back and I'll do my best for both of them. I'm not afraid
anymore. I want him. I want them both, and if You give us
another chance, I'll make it work.*

A shout from up the beach interrupted her prayer. The cry
traveled far in all that silence. Holding their fear in check, they
rushed out to see what was the matter.

Three small fishing boats lay on the ground a small distance
away. They were fragile open pirogues, the kind that could be
tossed quite a distance by a good gale, and therefore had been
dragged well past the high water mark and laid facedown.
Two fishermen stood by one of their boats in ragged shorts,
scratching their heads. They'd turned it over again, for what
reason Rhea could not grasp, and had found a beached mermaid
lying underneath.

Jodelle slept on the ground, stretched out on her front with
her arms up and around her head. She did not even hear the
shouts of relief and bewilderment of the people around her.
Somehow, she had crawled under a small space between the
curve of the boat's hull and the ground. She was dry, obviously
never having ventured near the water. She was sleeping as
deeply as if she were in her own bed, with her dark braids
splayed, and the pink tip of her tongue just visible between her
lips.

It was so ironic; they'd searched for miles, and the missing
child had been just a hundred yards from their doorstep. With
a cry of joy and anguish, Marcus rushed forward and gathered
her into his arms. She awoke at the sound of his voice calling
her name. The relief and love on his face was reflected in
Rhea's own heart. Silently, she thanked the Lord for his swift
answer to her petition.

Marcus kissed Jodelle's cheeks and hair, clutching her tight
against his chest. Her eyes flew open, and her first words were

words of protest. "Daddy, you're hugging me too hard! I can't breathe!"

Marcus laughed and squeezed her again. "Honey, I'm going to be hugging you so hard today, you're gonna think I'm a boa constrictor!"

Rhea followed as he took her into the house, past Rainer and Dahlia, who had stayed inside to tend to his grotesquely swollen jaw. Rainer looked relieved that Jodelle was okay. At least Rhea had to give him that. Still, they crossed paths without a word being exchanged. What could they possibly have said?

She followed father and daughter to their room, and watched as Marcus laid Jodelle out onto the bed.

"Why are you putting me to bed?" Jodelle scowled impatiently. "It's *morning*. I've been sleeping all night!"

Marcus' tired face was creased with smiles. "You've been sleeping in the wrong place. If I followed my mind and give you the spanking you deserve, little miss, you'll be sleeping for the rest of the *year*."

Jodelle grinned up at him from her pillows, secure in the knowledge that there was no spanking in the offing. Rhea and Marcus sat on the edge of the bed, one on either side. For a while, no words were exchanged, and none were necessary. There was just the hedge of warmth and love that sprang up around the three of them, keeping everyone and everything else outside.

Then Marcus spoke. "You scared me, little darlin'."

Me, too, Rhea thought silently.

Jodelle was unable to look directly into her father's face. "I'm sorry I runned away. I won't do it again. Promise."

He gently nudged her face upward so that she could look him in the eye. "I know you won't, sweetheart. But why did you do it last night?"

Rhea held her breath as Jodelle hesitated. "You can tell us," she urged softly.

The black eyes were full of confusion and hurt. "The fat man told me you weren't my daddy!" she finally blurted. "He said you're not my daddy but you just keep me because nobody else wants me!"

I'll kill Rainer myself, Rhea thought, outraged. How could anyone say such callous things to a child? That bastard has a lot to answer for!

Although he already knew that this was the reason, hearing her say it made Marcus visibly flinch. He leaned closer to the girl on the bed. "That's not true, baby. It could never be true. No matter what anybody says, you'll always be my little girl, and I'll always be the only real Daddy you'll ever need."

She protested. "Then why did that man say you weren't my Daddy? What did he mean when he said you weren't. . . .''

"Jodie, listen. That's a long story and I'll tell you one day, okay? But not today. Until then, you'll just have to trust me on this. You *are* my daughter. I have you because I want you, not because somebody else doesn't want you. You're the most important thing in my life,'' he glanced at Rhea, making her flush, *"one* of them, and I love you. Okay?"

Shadows of doubt still flicked across her face. Marcus went on. "Think about it Jodie. We walk the same way, don't we? We have the same big, loud laugh. And we both like to keep the house at the same temperature in the winter. We both hate jelly doughnuts, we like strawberry syrup in our milk, we like to go for long drives on a Sunday afternoon. We like to stay up late on weekends to catch the basketball games on TV. We like to stretch out on the floor on the back porch and colour in your little books. We like to read ghost stories until you fall asleep on my lap. When you're sick, I sit next to your bed all night, till I'm sure you're better. Doesn't all this make me your daddy?"

The remaining doubt had been replaced by a beaming smile. "Yes! Yes!"

"So what do you have to be afraid of, then?"

"Nothing."

He kissed her on her forehead and stood up. "Good. Now you be good and get some rest. I'll wake you up when the storm comes so we can watch the houses fly past the window."

"Daddy, that's silly!" she squealed, but looked excited at the prospect. "Will you come and get me too, Rhea?"

Rhea kissed her and stood, too. "We'll both come," she

promised. She realised that she was thinking as Marcus' coun-
terpart, as if they were a unit. The thought made her nervous,
but happy. She was thinking, feeling, and reacting as if she
were the child's mother, but Marcus had proven that parental
love transcended the boundaries set by flesh and blood. She
was determined to do whatever was necessary to make something work between the three of them, even in the face of
the huge emotional and geographical challenges that love had
chosen to toss in their path.

As they left the room, Rhea touched Marcus lightly on the
arm, hoping to convey to him the enormity of the decision that
she had made. He looked down at her and smiled. "Thanks
for being there for me last night, Rhea. It meant a lot to me."

"You're welcome," she smiled. *I'd like to be there for you
for as long as you want me,* she thought but did not say.

They joined the others in the kitchen.

"Is she okay?" Dahlia asked anxiously.

"She's just fine," Rhea answered. "She'll probably just go
back to sleep. She had a hard night. But now," she surveyed
the sleepy group, "we have a hurricane to deal with. Let's get
busy."

They all wished they could crawl into their beds after a night
of fear, anxiety, and physical stress, but there was still work
to be done. Banner returned with the supplies, and they moved
about the house hurriedly as, with his wealth of experience, he
showed them how to make the house as secure as possible.

By eleven o'clock, the windows had all been nailed shut,
with the exception of one on the leeward side, which was
thrown wide open. The effect of this was to reduce any buildup
of pressure in the house, pressure which might otherwise tear
the roof off the entire building. They filled every available
container with water, including the vases, soda bottles and the
bathtub in the Steins' bathroom. They tied all of their candles,
matches, and flashlights into sturdy bags, and wrapped the radio
in sheets of plastic to keep everything dry in case of flooding.
At eleven-thirty, they began cooking all the meat that they had
in large pots and in the oven, as the probable loss of electricity

would have rendered their uncooked food supply unsafe for consumption within a day.

At twelve-fifteen, Hazel struck. She came with stealth, deceptively. The leaden sky became black, like the gathering of wings overhead. The fine but steady rain that followed this sudden darkening was almost anticlimactic in its normalcy. But when the sky eventually opened, even Banner was awed by her force. The house was under assault from all sides. The wind screamed, clawing at the windows, furious at them for having nailed them shut. It tested the roof again and again, trying to tear it off and toss it into the gale. It failed there, too.

As promised, Marcus and Rhea woke Jodelle so that she could experience the excitement. She sat on her father's lap and applauded whenever lightning lit up the sky, which was often.

Rainer seemed content to remain confined to his room; everyone, including his wife, was content to allow him to do so. Nobody was willing to look into the face of the man who, through his own malicious desire for revenge, had endangered the life of a child while forcing them to remain on the coast to face the storm. The group gathered in the kitchen, away from the big glass doors that they hadn't been able to protect. They were afraid to pass anywhere near the doors, as any large airborne object could have come smashing through, sending shards of glass flying. In the more sheltered kitchen, they drank large cups of coffee, which in no way alleviated their exhaustion. They consumed some of the hot meat with yesterday's bread, preferring to reserve their fresh rations for later.

Outside, the greyness swirled, with flying trees, branches, and debris, being tossed about like kindling. "I would give my eyeteeth to be able to go out in that and take some photographs," Marcus said longingly. "Maybe if I tie myself down with a rope, just outside the door . . ."

"You'll do no such thing!" Rhea was horrified.

He smiled at her. "Why? Are you worried about my safety?"

She scowled at him. In spite of his exhaustion, he was still baiting her. "No, I'm worried about the company's insurance."

"Pity," he said, but he was still smiling.

A large branch from an almond tree made a mockery of his frivolous suggestion as it was thrown against the porch, settling against the glass doors like a police barrier. The glass shuddered against the sudden impact, but mercifully, it did not shatter.

They sat for a long time, listening to the frightful unidentifiable shrieks and bangs around them, unable to imagine the destruction that was going on outside. As the day drew to a close, the novelty wore off and they became bored and irritable from being confined indoors. Wrapped in blankets and sheets to ward off the chill that seemed so startling after the days of silent heat, they began a desultory game of cards in an effort to pass the time. Trying to rouse their own spirits, they played poker for candy. The game came to an abrupt end when the power lines came down, and the lights guttered out. They sat in stunned silence, cards in hand.

"Well," Fred volunteered, "at least we're dry."

The spontaneous laughter was cathartic. Suddenly the hurricane seemed to be almost beautiful, a demonstration of Nature's majesty. They found their emergency candles easily, and filled the house with them. They set aside their misgivings and listened to the howling and crashing and imagined it to be music. By nightfall, the hurricane had worked its relentless way inland, away from the coast. As the night drew on, there was a noticeable decrease in the force of the winds, and the slashing rain was reduced to a steady downpour. Completely exhausted from the previous night's activities and from the undeniable thrill of storm-watching, they went to their rooms.

Rhea pulled off her jeans and socks and lay across the bed in her T-shirt. She hadn't had a shower, and even though she knew it would be to her advantage to do so while there was still water in the pipes, she was too depleted to move. The past twenty-four hours had been a tour guide's nightmare. "One for the books, Ri-ri," she whispered to herself. She settled down, glad to put an end to the day.

Still, sleep did not come. She lay on her back with the covers up around her, shivering, but her shivers did not arise out of cold, but out of fear. She finally admitted it to herself—she was terrified. Marcus frightened her. Loving him frightened her. She remembered the fervent deal she had tried to make with God that morning, promising that if Jodelle was found safe and sound, she would try to make it work between her and Marcus. Now that the crisis was over, the fear was back. The conviction that a relationship between them would never work was back.

Love was, to her, uncharted waters, and although those waters were sparkling and bright, tempting her, she couldn't shake from her head the memory of medieval maps she'd seen. These maps showed known land in detail, but as for the areas beyond, where explorers had not yet traveled, they had scrawled in a large bold hand, *Here Be Dragons.*

Here Be Dragons. She was a stranger to love, but she knew that apart from offering warmth and passion and joy, it would also threaten pain, hurt, uncertainty, and doubt, all dragons that Rhea feared. She realised that Brent had been a safe harbour for her, not taking her anywhere near to the heights of love but, still, not taking her to the depths, either. She was safe with him. Why crawl out of that safe place? Just how much did she stand to gain?

Apart from her fears, there were the practicalities to consider. Marcus was an American, and lived in a city five thousand miles away. What kind of love was that? He had a job that took him all over the world for extended periods, and which consumed him, a private passion. So what was he going to do, promise to visit her twice a year, and call her on Christmas and New Year's Day? She'd be no better off than she was with Brent, in spite of the depth of their feelings for each other.

And then there was Yvette. He'd tossed away her ring— was it only last night?— as a demonstration of his commitment to move forward. But there was still the memory of the woman, the presence of the woman, which would always threaten to intrude. What if she decided one day that she wanted to play a greater role in Jodelle's life? What if she decided that she wanted Marcus back? She'd loved him once, and maybe when she was tired of all the lights and the glitter, or maybe when she realised just what she'd given up, she would be back. Rhea wasn't sure that she could contend with the ghost of an ex-wife.

Then there was Marcus' passion for his work. Yvette had lived with Marcus, maybe she had known something that Rhea didn't. Maybe she was tired of spending all those nights alone, while he rushed off in search of a story. He loved what he did for a living, it was a calling rather than a job. Could she handle that? She was not prepared to come to a point where he would have to choose. She knew deep in her belly what choice he would make if called upon.

And of course she had her own career. If he thought for a moment that she would be willing to give it up, and follow him meekly, like a sheep, he was wrong. She loved what she did, loved her country and loved showing it off to others. It gave her the chance to share. No, giving up what she loved so that he could pursue what *he* loved was no solution at all.

She'd have to maintain her self-hood, her ''I-ness.'' Rhea must continue to exist as an individual, not be swallowed up to become another creature, Rhea and Marcus, who was not an individual or two separate individuals but a couple, an entirely different sort of animal. Her I-ness was safe and comfortable. It was what she'd been all her life. Venturing into another state was too much of a risk.

Rhea tossed on the bed in frustration. Next door in Marcus' room, all was quiet. She guessed that he had fallen blithely asleep, comfortable with whatever plans he had made to forge a relationship that did not exist. She couldn't allow it to exist. She gave up all attempts at sleeping and instead lay miserably among the twisted sheets, waiting out the night, aching for the sun to come up and chase away the darkness.

The doorknob turned. In the dim light of her single candle, she peered at the door, wondering who it could be. Yet, somehow, she didn't need to ask. Marcus slipped in quietly and shut the door behind him. As the door clicked, she felt her heart leap with fear.

''What are you doing?'' she asked. Her voice was too high for her liking.

''Rhea, please,'' he said tiredly. He spoke barely above a

whisper, not in an effort to remain undetected, but through sheer fatigue. "Please, don't fight me." His shadow danced across the walls of the small room as he moved toward her.

"But what are you doing here?" The veil of sleep had been snatched from her eyes, and she sat up with the sheets around her waist, tense.

"That's a stupid question." He sat on the edge of the bed, giving it a huge sink that caused her to roll toward him. He began untying the laces of his shoes.

Rhea rolled away from him and scowled. "It's not a stupid question. It's a perfectly legitimate question. This is my room."

He pulled off his socks and stood to unbuckle his jeans. "Rhea, please, it's been a hard day. I just want to sleep, okay?"

"So sleep in your own room! What about Jodelle?"

"She's out like a candle. She isn't going anywhere. And I don't want to go to my own room. I want to sleep here, with you." He sounded like a little boy who'd had a nightmare, and wanted to crawl into bed with his mother. Rhea almost relented. The exhausted, vulnerable look that he cast in her direction, added to the fact that he had now stripped to his shorts, and that his body glowed like a fine sculpture in the light of the candle, was causing her resistance to soften.

"I don't want you sleeping here." She said petulantly, not taking her eyes off his smooth chest. She'd been lying there, telling herself all the reasons she shouldn't succumb to him, but then in he walked, shucking off his clothes, and all of a sudden she wasn't so determined anymore. Damn, he looked good.

He climbed into bed next to her. "Scoot over."

"Don't be ridiculous. It's a single bed. There's only room in it for one person. If you have to sleep in here, there's another bed in this room. Use it."

"The other bed doesn't have you in it." He shifted around next to her like a huge dog trying to find a comfortable spot.

She shoved him hard with an elbow. "Marcus . . . !"

He shoved her back over. It was a tight fit. "Come on, we'll both fit if we sleep like spoons," he said smartly. He turned onto his side and tried to pull her against him. "Rhea," he said softly, "I'm not here to molest you. If you want the truth, I'm too tired to molest you. I'm only here to sleep. But it's been a long day and my body aches all over. I nearly lost my whole life last night. All I want is the comfort of lying next to you as I fall asleep. For God's sake, don't deny me that."

His body stretched out warm and vital next to hers, and in spite of herself, she realised that she wanted to stretch out against him and go to sleep. Still, she resisted. "I haven't had a shower all day," she protested irrationally.

"Neither have I. But I'm sure we both smell just fine. Go to sleep."

"What if the others see you coming out of here in the morning? I'm a businesswoman. Do you have any idea what it would do to my image?"

"I'll be up early and back in my room before anyone else is awake. You won't even hear me leave." He hoisted himself up on one elbow, stretched over her, and blew out the candle. Then he settled back against her body with a contented sigh and slid a proprietary arm around her waist. "Good night, sweetheart." His breath fanned softly against the nape of her neck. He was asleep before she could answer.

She lay in the dark, with her back against his chest. Playing spoons, he'd called it. She lay immobile, listening in spite of herself to her body as it hummed softly against his, contented. She settled against him, feeling him, enjoying every curve and plane of him, until her breathing took on his own rhythm, and she sank slowly beneath the surface of sleep.

Rhea awoke to light but steady rainfall. The sensation of finding herself stretched out against a man's chest jarred her. As her sleep-numbed mind realised that he was still clasping her tightly around the waist, with his chin jutting into the curve of her shoulder, she panicked. Her memory of the previous night was a blur. Had they made love last night? If they had, would she have forgotten? The recollection that he had just fallen exhausted into her bed and dropped off to sleep came as a relief to her.

The next problem, as far as she could see it, would be to extricate herself from his possessive grasp without waking him. She put her hand down to grasp the offending arm. It closed tighter, sliding further around her waist like the coils of a large snake. She tried prizing up the long fingers that adhered to her hipbone, but they continued to cling.

She was wide awake now, her senses sharp and alert. She remembered that this man was definitely not supposed to be here, and that it would be best for all concerned if he would return to his room before anyone could discover them together. She began wrestling out of his grasp more frantically, but his arm was immovable. To her horror she realised that she could feel evidence of his early-morning arousal against her back. She gave a startled yelp.

"Good morning," he said in a voice full of smiles.

"Do you have any idea what you're doing?" She was deeply embarrassed by his physical condition.

"Oh, yes, of course I do. I'm carrying out my threat. I told you I'd make you come to me, and I'm going to do just that."

"Like this? Are you crazy?"

"Just relax and enjoy it, Rhea."

"I thought you said you were going to leave early before anyone else gets up." She was wriggling to escape, but when it dawned on her that her movements were only serving to excite him even more, she became completely still.

"I lied. Don't worry, it's barely light out. They'll all be asleep for some time. Everyone was wasted when they went in last night. They won't be up till lunch."

"You were wasted, too, and you're up at the crack."

"Yes, but I had the regenerative power of a fair maiden on my side."

"Don't be absurd," she snapped. The last thing she needed right now was to listen to his rubbish.

"I'm not being absurd." He began rubbing his stubble seductively against the back of her neck. "Does this feel absurd?"

Actually, Rhea thought, it felt pretty good, but he didn't need to know that. After he'd thoroughly devastated the back of her neck with his rough, pointed chin, he began tugging gently at her hair with his teeth. With her body racing ahead of her mind, Rhea decided that her best line of defense was to remain absolutely silent. The assault on her senses continued as Marcus slid his hand up from her waist, so slowly that she felt like screaming, until it reached its final resting position on her breast.

"I love you, Rhea," he said softly.

She lay quietly against him, all resistance hobbled by the awe-inspiring experience of hearing those words directed at her.

"It wouldn't work," was all she could blurt in response.

"That's not the socially accepted reply. Try again."

"I can't. It's the only reply I can give you." She wished he would stop touching her. It was awfully hard to fight back when all she wanted to do was roll over and kiss him fully on the mouth.

"Well, why then? Why won't it work?"

"Because . . . there's just too much in the way."

"Like what?"

"Like Brent. You've forgotten Brent." She felt no qualms about bringing him into this, even though she already knew that their situation was not about him at all.

"I haven't forgotten him for a second. As a matter of fact, he's the only reason that I've been trying to get you off my mind. It's just that there's something about your relationship that doesn't ring true. Something tells me you're not getting everything you need from him. And if that's the case, well, then I think I have every right to butt in."

All she could say in her own defense was that she cared a lot about Brent.

"Yes," he agreed. "I know you do. But do you love him?"

She had known that she didn't for some time now, but was only now able to admit this to someone else. She expected to feel a great sense of loss, but instead felt just a small sadness over the death of what had always been only an illusion. Marcus tugged at her insistently until she turned around to face him. In this new position, pressed close together as they were, Rhea felt the last of her defenses crumble and fall away. He saw the wall collapse, or sensed it, she never knew which, but instead of triumph showed only concern.

"Does it hurt really badly? Realising that you don't love him?"

She shook her head in bewilderment. "It's not nearly as bad as I expected. I'm sad, yes, but I'm kind of relieved. It's good to face the truth in the light of day, you know?"

"Yes, I know." Then after a while, "And speaking of facing the truth," he held her chin steady so that she couldn't look away, "do you love me?"

She hesitated. In saying that she did, she would be stepping into unknown territory. She would be opening herself up to great joy, which would lift her existence up out of the ordinary to the realms of something glorious, but which would also lay her wide open to all the pain and anxiety that came with love. The raw emotion, so much more sharp and clear than the counterfeit with which she had lived for so long, was so vivid and real that she didn't know if she would have the courage to live in it and with it every day.

Then again, she thought, lying was an option. She could look him dead in the eye, lie, say no, and then as a gentleman, he would have to withdraw, leave her in peace. He'd have to concede defeat with dignity, get out of her bed. And when the rain was over and they could make their way out of this treacherously romantic beach, she would deposit him at the hotel. In a week's time, she would be rid of him. She'd go back to her home, put in for some time off, sleep for a week, then get on with her life.

Still, the clean fresh warmth of the love that she felt for him, and the humbling knowledge that he loved her back made the mere idea of lying about it sacrilegious. The umbrella of love that surrounded them was a holy place, a cathedral in which lying would be the ultimate offense, and merit as punishment the loss of her tongue.

"Rhea?" His voice broke into her thoughts, patient but anxious. Her eyes flew up to his. His entire body was tense, even the rise and fall of his chest against hers had stilled.

She opened her mouth to answer and her courage failed her.

"Rhea, please," his voice was soft.

"Yes."

It was out. She waited for the roof to come caving in but it didn't. Instead, he asked her anxiously, "Yes, what, Rhea?"

She was bewildered. She'd confessed. What more could he possibly want from her? "What do you mean?"

"Yes, what? I need to hear you say it."

"I can't. Don't make me."

"Why not?" he insisted. His long fingers were stroking her chin, running along her lips in a rhythm that didn't help the situation one bit.

"You've heard what you want to hear," she protested miserably. "Leave me in peace."

"I haven't heard what I want to hear. I want to hear more. If you don't say it, it's not worth anything."

"That's not true!" She protested. "It's still worth everything. It's worth everything I've got."

He looked as though he was about to say more, to insist upon her response, but the pain and fear on her face caused him to relent. He took one of her hands and kissed it by way of apology. "I'm sorry. I didn't mean to belittle what you feel. I just need to hear you say it. My heart knows it's real, it's just that my ears need to know it, too."

She felt tears of frustration gather in a hard knot in her throat. "I can't," she told him.

His eyebrows rose. "Why not? Why is it so hard? I love you. I love you. It only brings me joy to say it. Why can't you say it, too?"

"I don't know how!" The humiliating admission ripped out of her.

Marcus was taken aback. "What do you mean, you don't know how? How come? Haven't you ever said it to anyone?"

She shook her head, afraid to risk speech.

"Haven't you ever been in love?"

She shook her head.

"Hasn't anyone ever been in love with you?"

She shook her head again. It was as humiliating as being

sixteen and having to admit to your friends that you'd never been kissed.

His face was a mixture of horror and compassion. "Oh, Rhea, I'm so sorry."

"Don't say you're sorry like that," she said, her irritation masking her hurt. "It's not a disease!"

He smiled at that, and small creases formed around his cheeks and eyes. "No, it's not. But I'm honoured. I'm glad you told me." He ran his finger lightly along her lips. "I'll ease up on the pressure, okay? I'm just content to know that you do love me. We'll work from there."

It was his gentleness that caused the dam to burst. Funny, she thought irrationally as the tears spilled, how easy it is to struggle against might and force, but how hard it is to hold up against kindness. It wasn't right. It didn't make sense. He held her as she cried, not saying anything, not even trying to comfort her or shush her into stopping, as if he knew that it had been welling up inside of her for a long time, and needed to get out.

She pulled his face down to hers, covering him with kisses until his face was as wet as hers. Her lips sought out his, and it was like soothing balm to her spirit. The kisses of grieving gave way to kisses of hunger, growing deeper and more intense. The catharsis of confession made her bold; her tongue probed his mouth with curiosity, growing more and more daring. She tasted him, feeling the soft sweetness of the inside of his mouth, and the deft flicks of his tongue, which reached up to meet hers, sinuous, like a serpent. She luxuriated in the sharpness of his early-morning beard as it tormented her swollen lips. Marcus let her take the lead, enjoying her exploration.

When they finally broke the kiss, they gasped at the force that was pulling them down into the crazy spiral. As soon as he filled his lungs deeply with air, he let out a boyish cry of delight. "I knew you'd come to me! I just knew you would!"

She was taken aback, embarrassed.

He saw the look of uncertainty and hastened to reassure her. "Oh, no, no Rhea, I wasn't gloating. Honest. I just needed to know that you wanted me as much as I want you. Unless you came to me, I couldn't be sure. Do you understand?"

She nodded.

"Now, come closer." He rolled onto his back and lifted her without effort onto him. She stretched out against the length of him, reveling in his smoothness and strength. He attempted the impossible trick of pulling up her short green T-shirt over her head while their lips were crushed against each other's. Even the few seconds' interruption from their kissing, time enough to yank the offending garment off and toss it onto the floor, was agonizing.

After a while, he eased her up off his chest. "Let me look at you." While she sat astride him, looking down into his smiling face, he had ample opportunity to take in her smooth sapodilla skin, the flatness of her belly, and the roundness of her breasts. His hands followed the trail of his eyes, light but insistent, drawing soft kitten grunts in response.

"You're so beautiful," he groaned, "I don't know what to say." He stared, unashamed, and where his eyes roamed, her skin tingled.

"My turn now," she told him. The wine of his kisses had made her bold. Their bodies had not yet become accustomed to each other, and there was some fumbling, but at last she managed to pull off his shorts, which were tossed onto the floor next to her T-shirt and joined almost immediately by her own underwear. For a brief moment she was shocked by her own behaviour, but the seditious thought was squelched by the pleasure of seeing him stretched out naked before her. Excited and curious, she reached out toward him with both hands, letting her fingers trace the corrugations of his chest, the hard roughness of his nipples, and the coarse hair that covered him. Her fingers searched as though they wanted to commit every inch of him to tactile memory.

"You don't know what you're doing," he gasped as she stroked him insistently. "You have *no idea!*"

Now she was the one that was laughing in triumph. He protested. "Rhea, have mercy, please, don't." He squirmed, struggling to regain control of the situation, and their lovemaking took on a deeper, more earnest quality. He pinned her against the bed and slipped his leg between both of hers, hands on her hips, pulling her against him, whispering urgently in her ear, "Tell me what you want. Tell me what you like."

She began to say "Anything. Everything. Just do it *now!*"

She felt the purposeful probing of his fingers as they slipped between her legs, gently spreading her folds, preparing her for his entry. That simple touch alone set a violent wave of vibrations coursing through her. She wanted to shout "Hurry! Hurry!" but her quivering mouth was unable to form the words.

When he pulled away from her as if he'd been stung.

"Oh, my God, Marcus! Did I hurt you?" She sat up with a suddenness that made her dizzy, and watched him, eyes wild with confusion. What had she done?

He sat on the edge of the bed, back turned to her, breath coming in gulps. His shoulders were heaving. Rhea remained where she was, transfixed and uncomprehending. When his shoulders stopped shaking she ventured to touch him lightly on the arm.

"Marcus? What is it?"

"I'm sorry." He turned to face her. His eyes were black. "I'm sorry. I couldn't. We couldn't. I had to stop."

"But why?" She still couldn't understand. She wanted him so much!

"We haven't got anything. No protection. Understand?"

She understood. How stupid of her to have let all thoughts of caution be driven out of her mind like that. It could have been disastrous. Her heart sank, while her body raged, clamouring that it didn't matter, it didn't matter. She tried to silence its hungry cries.

His face was dark with frustration. The pupils of his eyes were like black holes that seemed to go on forever. One look at his face told her that he was suffering the same agony that she was. In spite of her physical pain, she was grateful to him for having found strength and courage enough for both of them. "Thank you."

"For what?"

"I forgot about that. I wouldn't have been able to stop." She was embarrassed. Hadn't life taught her anything?

"I damn near didn't, either." He looked toward the window.

Copious rain was still running down the glass. "For the first time since I've been here, I miss the city."

"Why?"

"Because then there'd be a drugstore on the corner, that's why. I didn't exactly come here prepared for this eventuality, you know."

"Neither did I."

It was almost funny. They both stared at each other, sitting naked and frustrated on the edge of the bed. It was an undeniably nineties predicament.

"I wonder where Banner keeps the keys to the van," he joked, and the tension popped like a bubble. They both laughed heartily. What else was there to do but laugh? He reached down to the floor and retrieved their hastily discarded garments and handed hers to her.

"Oh yes, I'm sure driving ten miles to the nearest store in post-hurricane flooding is just what we need to crank the excitement up a notch," she teased.

He looked almost serious. "For you, my dear, anything."

She hit him with the pillow. "Get out before I decide to throw caution to the wind."

He pulled on his jeans and T-shirt and held his shoes by their laces and hung them over his shoulder. "I think I'll make the dash to my room barefoot," he grinned. "All in the interest of discretion."

"You'd better," she told him. She was quite serious.

He stood, surveying her contemplatively for quite some time before bending down and kissing her on the cheek. "This reprieve won't last long, Rhea. I'll figure out a way for us to be together." His eyes glittered, "Soon."

"Out, out," she told him. "It's the middle of the morning." She sounded irritable, but she was smiling.

He put his hand on the door, and eased it open with only the smallest creak. He looked at her, still naked on the bed, for what seemed like a long time. "I love you," he told her.

"Yes," she said.

CHAPTER FIFTEEN

In the late afternoon the group ventured outside to survey the damage. The rain had petered out, but the sky and sea were still a uniform, dismal shade of grey. They left by the back entrance, as the front was blocked by the huge almond branch that had been tossed against the door.

Rhea and Marcus, surrounded by the others, stole shy, surreptitious glances at each other, slightly embarrassed by the events of the morning. For a brief second, he'd passed her in the corridor and slyly whispered that they'd be alone again soon. Rhea grinned and said nothing.

Now, all together on the cold, damp sand, the group looked around them, amazed. The beach had been wrecked. The sea had come up as high as the seawall, pounding it in vain, and, frustrated, unable to reach the house, had gone off in search of other victims. These it found in the boats where Jodelle had hidden. Although they had appeared to be on safe ground, it was not to be so. The boats had been snatched up from their resting places and dashed against the ground. They lay there, broken. One had been tossed as far as fifty feet. The group found three fishermen standing dazed around the debris, watching their entire livelihood taken away from them.

They were unable to offer any form of consolation to these men, who were now faced with the impossible task of repairing or replacing the boats. Unwilling to intrude upon their privacy and pain, they withdrew to their backyard.

The shrubbery that had surrounded the house looked like it had been torn out of the ground by a gardener gone mad. They were up to their ankles in mud and debris. At the far end of the yard, they saw an unbelievable phenomenon. A small sapling, about as thick around as a man's arm, had been pulled up out of the ground and tossed like a javelin across the garden. It had hit a target—a thick old coconut tree. Unbelievably, the sapling had pierced the tree through its heart, and was stuck there, with its end protruding a full three feet out of the other side of the trunk.

They moved wordlessly to the garage to see how the van had fared. It was festooned with stray twigs and clumps of bush, and a single sheet of galvanized roofing, which had apparently been carried on the wind from some distant house, had slapped into the grillwork in the front. There were long, deep grooves in the paint, some cutting all the way down to the bare metal. Banner shook his head in grief. His precious van had been hurt, and he hurt right along with it.

When they had had their fill of the damage, they trooped inside. Emotional exhaustion began to manifest itself physically, and although it was not yet dark, everyone was willing to have a quick dinner and an early bed.

"I just want to take a short drive up the road to see what the flooding is like," Banner told them, as he left through the back door. "I'll see if the roads are safe, then we'll know how soon we can get out of here."

Rhea prepared the last of the meat from yesterday's cooking spree. The refrigerator had a good seal, and after a day without electricity, its contents remained cool. Still, it would eventually lose its ability to keep anything cold, and Rhea knew that what did not get eaten tonight would have to be discarded by morning.

The candlelit kitchen was soothing; the weak flickering lights lit the walls with a soft orange glow. As she cooked, her shadow danced on the wall. The damp air and the chill that hung about the room did nothing to diminish the warm glow that she carried around within her. She was in love, and the man she was in love with had confessed that he was in love with her.

Throughout dinner, her eyes kept searching out and finding Marcus', and each time she looked up, his eyes were on her. Even Rainer's silent and surprising reappearance at the dinner table couldn't dull the edge of her contentment.

After they had eaten, Marcus met her in the kitchen and began helping with the washing up.

"You don't have to do this," she reminded him. "It's my job."

"Don't be silly. I want to help. Stop hiding behind your job all the time."

Instead of answering, she let him help, excited by his presence even during this mundane task. She stacked the dishes, and to hide her confusion, she chattered away, commenting on how lucky they were that there was still water in the pipes, and that it was still clear and unmuddied. She talked about everything that wasn't personal, and had nothing to do with them.

He let her babble on, more out of a need to listen to the sound of her voice than because he was interested in the content of the conversation. When the dishes were done, they stood by the empty sink, which no longer provided her with an excuse to keep her hands busy and her attention away from him. In the quiet darkness of the kitchen, she felt totally alone with him, even though the house was full of people.

"Rainer apologized to me this morning."

She had been wondering if the man would ever have the courage to do anything so decent, and was happy to know that Marcus had apparently had the courtesy to accept the apology. "I'm glad. I don't think the tour can be salvaged, though."

"What do you mean?"

"Well, I've never had a situation like this before, but there seems to be no way that we can go on for the rest of the tour. When I get back, I'm going to recommend that we cancel the Bainbridges' tour, and refund their money. Ian won't like it, but he'll just have to understand."

"And the Steins and myself?"

"Well, I think it would be best to hand you over to another guide. This has just gotten too complicated for me to remain professional about it."

He laid a hand on her neck, massaging her lightly. "And us?"

"There'll be time to talk. We'll make the time."

He brushed the tip of her ear with his lips. "We'll have to make time to do more than that," he said suggestively.

How she wished the time was right now! But in order to prolong the delicious agony, she feigned ignorance. "Things like what?"

"I have a few ideas." With one hand on the curve of her bottom (oh, the shiver that went through her when he touched her there!), he nudged her closer. The hard ridge in the front of his jeans pressing against the swell of her belly, told her just where his ideas were headed. His next words only served to reinforce the notion that his body had adequately communicated. "We're stuck here for at least another day. Banner's lending me the van tomorrow, so I think I'll just take a drive into town and see if I can solve the little problem we had this morning. Would that suit you?"

She was blushing crazily in the flickering orange candlelight. "You're crazy. The house is full of people!"

His lips were warm against her ear as he whispered softly, "Don't worry. I've got it all figured out. Trust me. Okay?"

She trusted him.

The tap on her door the next night was so soft, that first she thought she must have imagined it. It came again, and then a third time. Rhea sat up in the darkness, feeling around for her flashlight. Her watch told her it was well after midnight. She stepped quickly to the door and opened it a crack. "Yes?"

"It's me."

The voice was enough to send thrills into the pit of her stomach. She threw open the door. "Marcus!" she exclaimed, a little too loudly in her joy.

He shushed her with a light kiss. "Shhhh, baby. Sound travels in all this quiet." He put a finger lightly on her lips.

"What are you doing here?" She peered at him in the thick darkness, realizing that he was fully dressed.

"I've come to get you. Get your clothes." He pushed her gently back into her room and began searching for her jeans in the beam of his flashlight.

"Get me for what? Are you crazy? It's after midnight!"

"Sweetness," he tugged her affectionately to him. "Didn't I promise you we'd be together before we left? Didn't I promise you we'd fix things so we could be alone together, and finish what we started?"

The rapid sequence of images that his words brought to her mind made her face flare.

"Get dressed. We're not staying here." He picked up a pair of her sneakers and handed them to her. "Put these on."

"Where are we going?" She was mystified.

"Didn't I tell you to trust me? I promised you I'd arrange everything, didn't I?"

Excited now, Rhea dressed quickly. Marcus certainly knew how to throw a little excitement into everything. She pulled a light cotton jacket on over her T-shirt, as the evening had promised to be cool, and was ready to go. "Is Jodelle okay?"

"Are you kidding? She must have spent six hours in the water. She's out like a candle. She'll sleep right through till morning."

Rhea nodded. "Good. Lead on, then."

She followed him out of the room, and they tiptoed along the corridor like spies in a bad movie, careful not to wake anyone.

They pushed the back door gently on its hinges and were out in the cool, clear night. Rhea sniffed the crisp, salty air. "It smells so good tonight."

"You smell good tonight," was the response.

Rhea's first instinct was to look away, but her excitement and love for this man made her brazen. "I might taste even better than I smell," she said throatily, causing him to drop his head toward hers in a long, thoughtful kiss. When he finally broke it, he ran his tongue along his lips as if he were taste-testing a new flavor of ice cream. "Hmmm. You know what? I think you do!"

What began deep inside her as a laugh escaped as a purr. "I think we'd better get out of here before we don't have the willpower to move any further."

"I think you're right." He shouldered the large canvas bag that he was carrying and stepped out into the moonlight.

She eyed the bag curiously. "What you got in there?"

"Secret," he smiled, and made his way around the house to the beach.

Even in her excitement, she was irritated. "Where are we going?"

"Secret," he said again, and she had to restrain herself from thumping him. Instead, she fell into stride next to him. He linked his fingers with hers.

"Nervous?" he asked softly.

She had to admit that she was. The magnitude of her love for Marcus made her desire for him even more frightening. Tonight, they would be making love, and it would not only be the first time for the two of them, but the first time that she would experience how soul-tearing this physical union between two people who were really in love could be. The anticipation was almost daunting. She shivered.

He felt the tremor rush through her and squeezed her fingers comfortingly. "Don't be afraid, love. I'm a little scared myself, actually."

She glanced at him in surprise. *"You?* Really?" She was sure he could never be as afraid as she was. He'd been in love before, with his wife. The anticipated onrushing emotions that she feared would be no stranger to him. "Why?"

He stopped and turned to face her. "Rhea, it's been a long time for me. What, did you think I've spent the last few years jumping into bed with every woman I meet? This means as much to me as it does to you. This thing between us frightens me, too. And I hope . . ." He paused to gather his thoughts, and then began again, choosing his words carefully. "I just want it to be good for us. Sometimes, it takes a while for two people to get used to each other, to know what the other needs or wants. And I just don't want to disappoint you.''

She was moved. It had never occurred to her that this man, self-confident to the point of arrogance, was actually worried that he wouldn't please her. She touched his chest lightly. "You couldn't possibly disappoint me, Mark."

He seemed relieved, but tried to pass it off as a joke. "Thank you for your vote of confidence."

She smiled, and they resumed walking. "My pleasure."

They had only gone a few hundred more yards when Marcus stopped short. "We're here."

Rhea looked around her in the darkness. They ware standing in front of a row of beach houses that were usually filled with holidaymakers. Tonight they stood black and silent. She let the beam of her flashlight play over the front of the nearest house. In the absence of any electricity, the building was shrouded in shadows. She could barely hide her misgivings. "Here?"

"When we get back to Port of Spain, I promise you an evening out in a city restaurant—Chinese, French, Italian, whatever you like—and a night at the best hotel in town. But for now," he shrugged apologetically, "this will have to do."

"You rented a house?" she hurried to keep up with him as he led the way up the front stairs.

He looked sheepish. "Not exactly." He shone his light on the porch doors. The beautiful stained-glass French doors had been shattered by what looked like a hail of coconuts. Shards of coloured glass, glittering like muted jewels, crunched underfoot. Realisation dawned.

"You're not serious!" She gaped as he stepped through the huge gap in the door and waited for her to follow. "Marcus, this is breaking and entering! We could go to jail for this!"

He was smiling. "Well, just entering, actually. It was pretty much broken before we got here." He took in the look of consternation on her face. "Oh, come on, Ri-ri. Be a sport. There's no one around for miles. The tourists who were staying here packed up and left days ago. There's no one to disturb us. Besides, where's your sense of adventure? Didn't you play hooky and camp out in abandoned buildings when you were a kid?''

She smiled at this, and had to admit that she had. In spite of herself, the prospect of sneaking around like two naughty children excited her. She stepped through the doorway behind him.

''And we won't go any farther than the living room, okay?''

''Okay.''

She watched as he let the heavy canvas bag he was carrying drop to the ground with a thud. Finally, the mystery of the bag would be solved. She tiptoed to look over his shoulder as he began to tug items from it. A large blanket came first. He shook it out vigorously and spread it out into the center of the living room.

''I came in earlier and swept up all the broken glass in here,'' he informed her.

''You think of everything,'' she teased. She watched as he withdrew a pack of eight candles and a small stack of saucers that she recognised from their kitchen. He went about carefully sticking the candles onto the saucers, lighting them, and placing them about the room. By their flickering light, the walls of the room danced cheerily.

Rhea lost the last of her misgivings and threw herself into the fun. ''All we need now is wine and three fiddlers.''

''As Madame requests,'' Marcus said with a chivalrous bow, and tugged his CD player from the bag. In minutes, the strains of a mean tenor sax filled the room. Next came a bottle and two teacups.

''Not wine!'' she gasped. ''I'm impressed!''

He shrugged modestly. ''It's a brand I've never heard of before. It's even got a screw top instead of a cork, and it's at room temperature, so I can't vouch for the quality. But any wine in a storm, I always say.'' He laid the treasures in the centre of the blanket and pulled her gently next to him. ''Behold, our banquet of love.'' He was smiling broadly.

''It's wonderful,'' she said truthfully. The man had gone through great lengths to make sure that they would have comfort

and privacy. The thought of that warmed her through and
through. "Thank you."

He stared at her in the candlelight for ages before looking
down at the bottle in his hands. He cracked the seal and poured
it out into the two teacups before saying anything. "You're
beautiful." He handed her the cup almost reverently.

She could find no answer to that, and instead held her cup
out in a toast. "To our night together."

He clinked his cup against hers. "To us."

They both took a sip, and watched each other, waiting for
a reaction. Finally, Marcus broke. "God, this is terrible!" He
set the cup down with a grimace.

She had to struggle to swallow her wine without choking
on her own laughter. "Awful! What's the main ingredient?
Antifreeze?"

Marcus reached out and took the cup from her, setting them
both far from reach. "That's okay. We don't need it. We've
got all we need right here." He inched over to her and cupped
her face. "Come, sweetheart. Come closer."

There was no wine that he could possibly have brought that
could have tasted better than his mouth. He began playfully,
teasingly, lips light and gentle. Then without warning, there
arose a force within him that was not satisfied with those light
kisses, and that demanded more.

She struggled to meet those demands, breath rising in her
throat, pausing for a few seconds to draw air deeply into her
lungs before surrendering herself to be drowned once again in
the warm desire that rose around them. It was a while before
she became aware of his frustrated tugging at her jacket. She
stopped and drew back to let him pull it off and toss it aside.

It was joined immediately by her T-shirt and bra. Now her
bare breasts glowed in the orange light until the flames were
eclipsed by his shadow as he bent forward to flick a taunting
tongue across the taut peak of her nipple. As the swift, sharp
pleasure hit her like a lightning bolt, Rhea struggled to cry out
his name, but no words came, only a rough, hoarse sound,
which she could not recognise as her own voice, and which
seemed to go on and on.

He was greedy. He drew the hard dark knot of pleasure fully into his mouth like a man who had not known the taste of a woman in a long time. His big hands slid under the curve of her breasts, cupping them, nails lightly scratching her along her rib cage until the heart that lay beneath them sang.

When at last he lifted his head, she thought he was having mercy on her, because she was sure that if he went on, she would die from pleasure and pain, but her respite was only momentary, as he shifted to the other nipple and began his assault anew.

She found her voice in a rush. "Mark, please!"

"Honey, I need this . . ." he managed to gasp.

Her hands betrayed her in her moment of protest, grasping the back of his head and forcing him even closer, if such a thing were possible. Then to her own astonishment, she found herself pulling at the buttons on *his* shirt. It wasn't fair, she decided. She was just as hungry for a taste of him. He stopped to allow her to tear the shirt off him and toss it away.

"Just don't let it fall on a candle," he managed to gasp, still holding on to his sense of humor in spite of their urgency.

She punished him with a sharp bite on his exposed chest. *"Arrgh!"* he writhed, trying to escape, but it was now her turn to make him plead for mercy. She ran her tongue lightly across the sprinkling of dark hair until she found the hard, small nipple hidden in it. It gave her great pleasure to return his torture measure for measure.

When she was satisfied with his groaning pleas for her to *stop, stop at once, Rhea baby, please,* she let him up.

"You'll pay for that," he threatened, and pounced. In seconds, her jeans and panties were lost somewhere in the darkness. As she lay back on the thick blanket and observed the gleam in his eye, she began to wish she'd never challenged him to this duel of caresses.

He swooped down upon her like a huge bird, and the first contact of his sly, hot tongue between her slippery thighs brought a scream to her lips. He laughed throatily, lifting his head to watch her, golden eyes now black pools. "Scream all you like. There's no one around to hear you."

The threat made her shiver, but there was no time for a rejoinder. He lowered his head once again, and the sheer force of his contact made her thighs jolt upward as if a current had run through them. One of his hands slid under her trembling bottom, pulling her hungrily closer, while the other slid upward until his fingers were entwined with hers.

Brightly coloured ribbons of pleasure rippled through her, and by the time he finally stopped and crawled upward to face her, there were tears coursing down the sides of her cheeks and into her hair. "Like honey," he gasped against her lips. As she kissed him, she could taste her own lushness on his mouth. Her excitement climbed to an even greater height.

"Better this way," he told her, sniffing deeply at the warm scent that he had rubbed onto her mouth and cheeks. "I can be inside of you, kiss you, smell you, taste you, all at the same time."

"Hurry," was all she managed to reply.

He tore his jeans off as if they offended him. She heard a rustle of foil as he tore open their protection, and within seconds, he was stretched fully on top of her. She waited for his sharp thrust, but to her surprise, he did not move.

"Mark?" she was puzzled.

She could feel his chest heaving against hers. "In a bit, sweetheart. I just want to savor this. Are you okay?"

She nodded.

"Scared?"

"A little."

"Me, too." He stroked her hair. "I've wanted you since the first night I met you. I've wanted you so much, some nights I couldn't sleep."

She thought of the nights that she, too, had lain awake, tormented by thoughts and images of him, and almost laughed at the irony of it. Then she slipped an arm around his broad, hard shoulders. "You've got me now."

In response, he hoisted himself up onto his powerful arms and spread her thighs with one determined knee, and then he was nudging his way in, gently but insistently, and all

conversation was replaced by the astonished gasps of two people pushed beyond the limits of pleasure.

The CD had long stopped playing but they moved to their
own private rhythm as the sound of a sax that only they could
hear flowed around them. He was a large man, but the weight of
him rising and falling against her only intensified the powerful
sensations that raced through her. In an effort to accommodate
him, she threw her legs up around his hips, locking her ankles
high across his wet, slippery back. Her hands roamed, first over
his neck, then across the straining muscles of his torso, then
down to clutch his hips, digging her fingers into the taut muscles,
egging him on.

The awareness that there was so much more going on in that
little half lit room than the joining of their physical selves was
almost excruciating. She could feel their spirits reach out to
each other, enmeshed, dancing, swooping, flying, joined. This
is the union of two people in love, she thought. This is the
crossroads at which sex and love meet.

Then her tongue was loosened, and the words, once so reluctant, tumbled out. "I love you! I love you!" She was shouting
her love for him, over and over, and his body answered with
a power that left her shaking.

It was a while before she realised that he had stopped moving
above her, and was instead holding her tight against his chest,
rocking her like a small child, whispering soothing words into
her hair. He held her close until their breathing returned to
normal, and then he kissed her eyelids one by one.

"My sweet little girl. You don't know how much I wanted
to hear you say that." His face was all smiles. "I love the
sound of it. Say it for me, one more time."

"I love you." It pleased her that she could say it in a moment
of sobriety, rather than in heated insanity. Limbs and body
heavy, she laid her head against his shoulder. His skin was
misted with a fine sweat.

The candles were burning low. Some of them were guttering
out, leaving the room even darker than before. They talked
softly for a while, about things that Rhea knew she wouldn't
remember in the morning. They seemed to be talking more out

of a desire to maintain the flow of current between them, and when they discovered they didn't need conversation, they fell silent.

She fell asleep, her head heavy on his shoulder, and dreamed that she was a little girl again, at the mouth of a river, chasing crabs with her brothers.

CHAPTER SIXTEEN

Rhea awoke to find Marcus leaning over her, staring down into her face. It was still dark, but there was a faint glow to the night that told her it wouldn't stay dark much longer. She stretched, shifting from her cramped position, and smiled up at him.

"Hey," she said. She reached out to touch his chest lightly.

At first, he didn't answer, but continued staring as if her face were a puzzle he was trying to decipher. Perhaps because his silence brought a bemused frown to her face, he hastened to answer her. "Hey, Rhea."

She got to her knees and faced him. He was already dressed. She wondered how long he had been awake. Without a word, he handed her the small pile of clothes that he had folded and laid neatly next to her, and she let him help her put them on.

"Didn't realise how much that blanket scratched," he joked weakly as he folded it and packed it into the canvas bag.

Rhea stared at him. This wasn't the man who had been stretched out above her, licking away the drops of sweat from the hollow of her throat, suffering her frenzied scratches without flinching. This was a man who was avoiding her gaze, acting like a teenager who, after the embers had cooled, was just hoping to find his way back into the house before his mother found out he'd been fooling around with the wrong girl.

What on earth could be wrong? They had been wrapped around each other, giving, taking all the other had to offer, just . . . what was it, a few hours ago? And now she was waking to careful politeness and feeble humor. What had she done? She was assailed by a series of rapid, explicit flashbacks of her response to him, legs twined around his back like a snake, and at the end, God, how humiliating, she'd been screaming that she loved him, over and over. Maybe she'd gone too far too fast.

She pulled on her sneakers and stood. Marcus had packed all evidence of their presence—the candles, the saucers, the awful wine—into the huge bag as she had slept. He'd done it silently and efficiently, like a thief, while she, wrapped in warm cotton-candy clouds of their lovemaking, had heard nothing. All they had to do was sneak back through the way they had entered, and no one would know they had ever been there. There was nothing to indicate that two people had recently made love right there on the living room floor. And except for the soreness of her muscles and the slight burning between her legs, she was beginning to wonder if anything had happened at all.

"Mark?"

"Love?" he answered softly, but the eyes that met hers were carefully hooded.

"Are you okay?" Wasn't this supposed to be different? Wasn't there supposed to be more caresses, endearments, soft words? She was disoriented, as if she had fallen asleep in the middle of one movie and awoken in the middle of an entirely different one, except that it was played out by the same actors.

"Of course." This time there was conviction in his voice. "Everything's fine." He set down the canvas bag and put his arm around her shoulders. This time the touch was Marcus', the kiss that fell on her wrinkled brow was Marcus', and Rhea began to think that her uncertainty was a product of her own imagination. "You were wonderful. Thank you."

"Thank you? It wasn't a favour. I mean, it . . ."

"I know what you mean. Don't take it like that. It was truly wonderful. But I'm thanking you for what you said to me. About how you feel about me."

"Okay." Still, her uneasiness was not fully laid to rest.

"Sweetheart, we'd better get going. It's almost morning, and I want to be with my daughter when she wakes up." He shouldered the bag again, and moved to the doorway, where he stood, waiting.

Of course. That was it. He was concerned about his daughter. How stupid of her. And how selfish of her to have expected to awaken to a prolonged afterglow, here in a borrowed beach house, where they didn't even belong, when he had a little girl at home who would be frightened if she woke up and found him missing!

She felt like an idiot. That was just another lesson in parenting that she needed to learn if she was going to be a part of Marcus' life. Sometimes, Jodelle would come first. That was just and right, and she would have to learn to work with that, if the three of them would be a team, or even, if she dared to dream about it, a family.

As she followed Marcus out into the greying pre-dawn, that one little word spun round in her head. *Family.* Why not? Why *shouldn't* they be a family? They loved each other, and they both loved the little girl terribly. And this little girl needed a woman in her life, one who was willing to teach and nurture and care for her. *I'm not just willing,* Rhea thought, *I'm eager. This is what I want. I want them both in my life, all my life.*

Warmed by her convictions, she turned to smile up at Marcus, but he never noticed, much less returned, her smile. He was staring ahead, face serious; he seemed deep in thought, and suddenly she was glad for the thin cotton jacket she wore because the air around them abruptly became a few degrees cooler.

With the coastal road finally cleared of post-storm debris, the group was able to leave by early afternoon. The return trip was a dreary affair. Her guests were fed up after the days of enforced stasis, and Rhea herself was tired, having managed to catch only two hours' sleep before she had to get up to make breakfast. Wasn't lovemaking supposed to suffuse you with a glow that lasted all day?

Maybe, she thought wryly, if you had the luxury of spending that day alone in the company of your lover, letting your mind run lazily over the events of the night, punctuating your warm thoughts with soft, wet kisses, maybe even seeking to re-enact the scene in some other tantalizing way. Still, in spite of the letdown brought on by business as usual, she could do little to suppress the sharp spikes of joy that leaped up inside her at the least opportune moments, causing her to grin idiotically to herself, and making Banner have to ask her, more than once, if she was sure she was okay.

"Oh, fine," she always answered vaguely, willing her wayward glance not to flick across to the spot where Marcus sat. "Great." And Banner would give her the amused, knowing look of a man who'd been there and done that, and she would flush and avoid his gimlet gaze.

As for Marcus, for that entire day and the night that followed, he seemed deeply engrossed in looking after his daughter. There was little opportunity for her to manage a word to him, and none whatsoever for them to be alone, even for a moment. Rhea hid her disappointment; business was, after all, business, and her work had to be done. But yet she tried wherever possible to catch his glance, telegraph silent endearments over the oblivious head of the young child. Sometimes, it seemed that her messages missed their mark, as the dark head did not lift, and the golden eyes did not meet hers.

Other times, she turned to catch *him* looking at *her*, and his eyes held the studious intensity of a man deep in thought, whose eyes just happened to have settled upon her face, when he could just as well have been staring at the wall or a vase of flowers or a coatrack.

The intense but distant gaze frightened her a little, and puzzled her a lot. Where were the smiles that had arced between them during their post-hurricane confinement at the beach house? Where were the sly glances, and the wordless promises that they'd be alone together, soon, soon, soon, and then they could fall into each other and taste and touch and smell as they had done on the floor of that barely lit, abandoned house? She shrugged away the questions, balled up the puzzlement and hurt, and hid them somewhere she was sure she wouldn't find them. There was business to attend to, and she was glad for the excuse to concentrate on serious and mundane details instead of allowing it to spin round and round until she got dizzy.

She spent the next day sorting out the tour that had gone so woefully wrong. She made arrangements with one of her colleagues for the Steins and Marcus and Jodelle to join another group for the four days that remained for their tour. With the number of mishaps that had plagued them since the beginning, it seemed the fair and logical thing to do. Besides, she wouldn't have a full complement without the Bainbridges, and therefore continuing with just the others would be uneconomical.

There was no way that she could continue to work with Rainer, and she had no guarantee that he would not be a disturbing element if she were to transfer them to another group. The Bainbridges accepted her reasons for canceling the rest of their tour, and accepted their refund meekly.

Ian was less accommodating. "Bad enough you wasted my money on a *second* beach house, then got the van damaged because *you* stayed in Mayaro too late to escape the hurricane," he stormed. (As if he wasn't the person who had ordered her to stay behind in the first place!) "But refunding money to a guest! You trying to ruin me?"

As she sat in his office, listening to him rail, she consoled herself with the thought that soon he would be all cussed out, and let her go. Then she could make her way over to Marcus and seek shelter in his arms. It was the only thought that kept her from doing more damage to her career than she could afford.

Finally, he let her leave, but not without docking her pay for the four days she would lose by handing over her group. Tired and beaten, she made her way to Marcus' hotel. Two days had passed since they were alone together, and since they had not been able to exchange so much as a light kiss. Two days, she decided, was long enough.

The Hilton at Port of Spain was unique in that it was probably the only hotel in the world in which the lobby was at the top floor of the building, and where guests went down, instead of up, to their rooms. Rhea had been to the hotel on business numerous times, but never before had the building seemed so brilliantly lit.

She asked discreetly for Marcus at the desk, and flashed her Tours With A Difference ID. The desk clerk clacked on her keyboard for a few moments. "There's a note here that says you're to be sent through to his room, no matter what hour you come or call," the clerk said. "You go on ahead, I'll call and let him know you're on your way." Rhea smiled gratefully at the clerk and walked toward the elevators.

Jodelle answered her knock at the door. "Rhea!" with a squeal, she was clambering onto her with the energy of a rock-climber. Rhea lifted her happily into her arms and kissed the small dark face. "Hi, li'l girl. How you doing?"

"Oh, I like this hotel! It's got a pool and a garden and there's this boy downstairs, he taught me how to play cricket, it's just like baseball only with a big bat, and you can play tennis, too, and then we went for a swim. Right, Daddy?"

Marcus was standing behind her, smiling. "Hi, Rhea."

The sight of him made the awful taste that the day had left in her mouth just disappear. She longed to touch him, but was still a little shy in front of Jodelle. Soon, it wouldn't matter, though, because they would work something out, the three of them. Marcus and Jodelle might be scheduled to leave in a few days, but he'd be back as soon as he could. That, she trusted him on. And when everything was all sorted out, she could let her love for him fly in all its glorious colour, and Jodelle would be happy for them both.

The astute little girl seemed to read her mind. "Daddy, aren't you glad to see Rhea? I know *I* am." She cocked her head to one side and looked up at him, her black gleaming eyes full of feminine wiles.

Marcus sighed heavily and took in Rhea's face for the first

time in what seemed like ages. "Yes, I'm very glad to see her." He let his eyes rest on her mouth, and her lips swelled in answer.

"So why come you're not kissing her?" Jodelle's smile was sly, and held a knowledge way beyond her years.

"How come," Marcus corrected automatically.

"Yeah," Jodelle nodded.

"Rhea, my daughter thinks I should kiss you," he said gravely. "What do you think?"

"Listen to the child." Rhea couldn't resist a grin.

To the delight of both females in the room, Marcus leaned forward and kissed Rhea, first lightly, then lingeringly, before pulling away with a sigh of something that Rhea knew at once was too sad to be pleasure or longing. She looked up at him, trying to read his face, but it was inscrutable, closed off to her as she had never seen it before. She remembered the chill that had run through her that morning as they made their way back home after making love, and felt that chill once again. It was then that she realised that something was terribly and frighteningly wrong.

"Mark?" Her voice was not her own. It was thin, and higher than she liked. She couldn't seem to catch the downcast golden eyes with her own gaze.

Instead of answering, he strode across to the bedside and dialed a three-digit number on the phone. As he spoke, his shoulders seemed to droop. "Trudy? It's Mark. Can you take Jodelle for a half hour? I'd really appreciate it." Rhea could hear the familiar high-pitched buzzing of Trudy's voice on the other end of the line, and then she heard Marcus say, "Thanks, I owe you. She's on her way over."

He laid the handset gently onto its cradle and spoke to his daughter without looking at Rhea. "Honey, do you remember the way to the Steins' room?"

Jodelle scoffed. "What do I look like? A *baby?* It's right across the hall!"

"Well, then, honey, could you run across to Trudy for a little bit? Daddy and Rhea have to talk."

She pouted. "I wanna talk, too."

Marcus was firm. "No, honey. This is grown-up talk. You and I can talk later."

She brightened at that. "Promise?"

"Promise."

Jodelle opened her arms wide to Rhea, begging for a kiss. "See you later, Rhea!"

"See you later, Jodie," Rhea agreed, although something somewhere whispered that, perhaps, later wouldn't come for them. It was this knowing little voice, this bringer of bad news, that made her hold on to the little girl even tighter than she intended.

"Ouch!" Jodelle protested, and Rhea let her go. She watched as the girl let herself out and padded across the hall to the Steins'. When she was safely inside, Marcus shut the door—and locked it. The sharp click cut into Rhea like a jagged metal edge.

They stood at opposite sides of the bed for ages, in that beautiful room with the matching furniture and demure pastel curtains and the bright bowl of flowers on the side table, and Rhea realised she would rather be back in the damp beach house with no electricity with Mark looking at her with all that love, than be right here, right now, in all this quiet luxury, and have him watch her like he was going to end her world.

He fidgeted, shifted his weight to his other foot, and then restlessly shifted it back again, sighed heavily once again and rubbed the back of his neck as if it hurt. The golden eyes were dull and clouded, the full, sensuous mouth drawn taut, as if it were shutting itself tight against words it didn't want to utter.

He didn't need to speak. Rhea wasn't a child, and she had seen enough of life to know just what lay in the silence between them. Without speaking a word, he told her all that she feared.

"Why?" she was stunned. She stared at him. "Why, Mark?"

Behind him, brilliant sunshine streamed past the curtains. There were muted sounds of traffic passing in the street far below.

So that nagging unease, that little feeling that something wasn't okay had proven to be right after all. The time for excuses and evasions was over. She folded her arms across her breasts in an effort to protect the heart that was now clenching and unclenching inside her chest like a fist. She looked up at him with puzzled eyes. "Why?"

"It just doesn't make any sense," he mumbled, still looking down.

"Why doesn't it make any sense, Mark? We love each other. Isn't that sense enough?"

He held his hands out to her in an effort to placate. "We have our own lives to lead, and we have our own careers. I'm never home. Neither are you. We live in two different countries, for God's sake. With a day's flying between us. Does that make any sense to you?"

"We can work it out," she said tightly. "Love is always worth working things out for." It had taken her a long time to figure that out for herself, but now that she could see it so clearly, it amazed her to realise that somehow he could not.

"Rhea, we were on a lovely romantic beach, with a big, silver moon, and a sky full of stars. We had all this excitement, riding out a hurricane together, facing death, and living. It was wild and scary and exciting and romantic. Things like this happen all the time. When you get back to the city and you can't smell the salt anymore, you come to your senses."

She couldn't, wouldn't believe he was actually saying this. *"You* were the one that denied all that! You were the one who said you didn't buy the island girl thing, and that the beach and the moon had nothing to do with what you felt for me! You said it wasn't so. So why are you changing your story now?"

"I know I said that, Rhea. I know. Maybe I believed it at the time. It might have been true when I said it, or it might have *felt* true, but when I think about it . . ."

"You said you loved me!" Her protest tore from her louder than she expected, but her hurt had begun to fuel her anger, and she didn't care if she could be heard beyond the walls.

"I did. I thought I did. But now, maybe . . ." He floundered, inhaled deeply, and tried again. "Maybe I was wrong." He was rubbing his neck again, and in her anger Rhea hoped his neck really hurt him, badly.

"How could you be wrong? How could you make a mistake? You're a grown man. You loved me from the start. You said that yourself. You said that, didn't you? Didn't you?"

He had no choice but to concede, but still protested. "What I felt was strong, but it's still a mistake."

"It wasn't a mistake that night when you were making love to me," she grated. On top of all the hurt, her pride chafed at the memories that taunted her now, of her lying on the blanket that he had spread for them, naked, panting, begging, surrounded by the smell of their two heated bodies. . . . Propelled by anger, she snatched up the bunch of flowers from the bowl beside her, bright, sturdy tropical flowers whose cheerfulness had no place in the dense hurt that closed in around them, and threw them at him as hard as she could. They hit him full in the face and exploded in a shower of petals and bruised blossoms. Spots of water darkened the light blue shirt that he wore, but he never noticed.

"Rhea, the last thing I want you to think is that I used you that night. Believe me, I never lied to get you to sleep with me. I wanted you so badly. . . ."

"And then what happened? What happened, Mark? We were in love and desperate to make love, and then as soon as we did, something changed. Something happened. Was it because . . ."

She stopped in mid-thought. A humiliating idea sprang at her out of nowhere. Could she have been such a lousy lover that he chose not to continue on those grounds? Was she so insensitive to his needs that she had been unable to fulfill him?

He saw her thoughts as if they were written on the wall above her head. "Don't even think what I know you're thinking. Don't do that to yourself. You satisfied me. You know you did. You did more than that. It was just that . . ." he inhaled sharply.

"Well?" she demanded.

"I've been feeling ever since that I've been here before."

"What?" She had no time for riddles; she was simply not in the mood. Damn him, he'd better explain himself, and his answer had better be good.

He had the grace to look ashamed. "I've been here before. In the arms of a beautiful West Indian woman, from a far-off island, with her voice full of music and spices. And it didn't work."

How stupid could she be! It was that bitch Yvette! It was her all along. The woman was poison. Marcus had thrown away her ring, but he hadn't managed to get the woman out of his heart. The next time she spoke, there was contempt in her voice. She spoke clearly and cuttingly, as if he were a particularly irritating moron. "Different island, Mark. Different accent. *Different woman.*"

"I know, but . . ."

"I'm not Yvette."

"I know, but . . ."

"But you let her screw you up so badly, that you can't even let go. You're *divorced*, Mark. You aren't married anymore. There's no more Yvette. You're divorced because she didn't want you." In her pain, she was cruel. Marcus winced. "But you just can't let go. You're willing to scuttle what you have because you're afraid you'll have to go through all that again. If I were an American woman, with an accent like yours, and a lifestyle and history like yours, would you trust me more? Would I still remind you so much of Yvette?"

He shrugged, too miserable to speak.

Rhea threw up her hands in frustration, too drained and exhausted to say or do anymore. She laughed harshly. "You know what? You're a coward. You're full of big words, fat talk about saving the world, but you're too much of a coward to save yourself from your own loneliness. Go ahead. Wear that woman's ring around your heart for the rest of your life, if you like. I hope it tightens and tightens until it chokes you. If you can't tell the difference between her and me, then maybe it *is* best that you don't love me!"

She turned and moved toward the door. She was crying, and she made no effort to hide it. "Tell Jodie I had to go. Tell her I love her but something came up and I had to leave without saying good-bye."

She was eager to leave, just to get out and be in a place

where she could breathe again. She fought with the lock on the door, tugging at it with sweaty hands. Just her luck, the handle seemed to have stuck. Her humiliation at not even being able to make a clean exit made her vicious. She threw one last shot over her shoulder, hoping it would hit him like a cannonball. "Maybe you're right, Mark. Maybe it wouldn't work out. I could never love a coward."

He moved instinctively to help her with the lock but she got it open without his help and stepped past him quickly, almost expecting him to strike out at her for that last remark. But he seemed exhausted, almost indifferent, and let her go without protest. She walked to the elevator and pressed the button for the lobby. As the flashing lights indicated to her that the elevator was descending at her command, she turned for one last look at him, even though she knew it would tear her up inside. The gesture was wasted: the door was already closed.

CHAPTER SEVENTEEN

Brent took the news that she no longer wanted to be with him with ego-bruising equanimity. In spite of the fact that she was now completely and entirely alone, she knew that she could not go on with him. She had known from her first encounter with Mark that the dull, companionable relationship that she'd had with Brent would never be anything more. There was no sense in forcing it or trying to make it anything more than a lukewarm friendship, which, by comparison with her brief encounter with Mark, was like drinking a slightly flat soda: not unpleasant, but hardly thrilling, either.

She broached the subject of a breakup the morning that Mark and Jodelle flew out. Brent reacted with the resignation of a man who had known for a long time that it was over.

"Have you got someone else?" he asked in a tone that suggested more curiosity than jealousy.

"No," she said truthfully, feeling pangs deep within her belly. "Nobody. I haven't got anybody."

He accepted this without challenge. "All right, Rhea," he said mildly. "If that's the way you want it."

What a change, she thought, staring at him. What a change from the man who was calling her up at every opportunity, insisting that she speak to him even when she was working! This was a man who called her if she was an hour late getting in touch with him, demanding an explanation. It was all about attention, she realised. She'd given him all her attention, and he'd thrived on that. Once she had begun to assert her right to her own life, to living within her own time frame, he had lost interest. All the time, she'd been thinking that she was breaking up with him, and now she realised that Brent had lost interest long ago, perhaps even before her own dissatisfaction had become a reality.

With some embarrassment, she realised that his unwillingness to even challenge her left her piqued, but deep inside, she was happy that it hadn't ended with any bitterness. She left his house with one or two of her CDs and other trinkets, which he insisted that she take back, wondering if that was all their two years together had added up to.

Rhea buried herself in her work, glad for the constant stream of new foreign faces who would help her take her mind off her soul-destroying encounter with that tall, dark man from Louisiana. She tried to avoid touring the southeast, concentrating on the small scattered islands off the northwest tip of the island, taking visitors to the golf courses, hiking in the Northern Range or down into the swamps in search of Scarlet Ibis and other elusive birds. She just wasn't sure whether she would be up to facing the memories that she had left scattered across the Mayaro sand.

Banner treated her with exceptional consideration. He was like a father who knew that his daughter was grieving, but couldn't do anything about it. With five full-time drivers on staff, he somehow always managed to get himself assigned to her, and Rhea knew that he was using every method of persuasion at his disposal to ensure that Ian kept them together as a team. *The better to watch over me,* Rhea thought wryly. She was glad that in all of this torment she had found a friend on whom she knew she could rely to look out for her.

She heard from Dahlia. She told her that Rainer had finally agreed to accept counseling. Rhea was glad for the poor woman; she really had a battle on her hands. Fred and Trudy sent her a

lovely thank-you card, promising that they would visit Trinidad
again, perhaps in March, to witness the Carnival.

A copy of the travel magazine with Marcus' article in it
arrived for her at the office. There was a plain white card
stapled to the cover with the words *Rhea, compliments, Marcus*
scrawled curtly across it in black. She read the article three
times, first in the privacy of her office, a second time with the
magazine propped up against her steering wheel while she was
stuck in traffic, and a third, in bed, crying softly.

The article that she held in her hands was the magazine's
feature story, running eight pages. She scrutinized the photographs; each one was a punctuation mark along the story of
their brief encounter. There were the gas platforms and oil rigs,
Mark's "little sisters," huddled together on the grey horizon
with their skirts above their knees, shots that he'd taken on
that first morning that they had sat out in the dew. There were
shots of the river that Marcus had dragged them all to, a few
days after her encounter with the jellyfish, and of the colorful
Mayaro market. There were photos of the curious grey mud
volcanoes, which he'd taken on the morning before everything
in her life had gone out of control, the morning before he'd
first kissed her. There was Dahlia, standing over the blowhole
on the rock face at Toco, skirt billowing in the wind; shots of
fishermen with their solid black skin and sun-reddened hair,
dragging in their net full of fish. Finally, there were photos of
the devastation after the storm had struck, shots he'd taken on
the morning after he'd said he loved her.

The article was written with integrity and compassion, born,
as he had promised, out of a need to set things right, rather
than from any desire to embarrass or destroy. She was deeply
ashamed of having doubted him; Marcus had written with the
passion of a man who had fallen in love with her island. He
was able to love her island, she thought bitterly, but couldn't
see his way clear to loving her. What an unkind cut!

Rhea folded the magazine and put it away in a drawer,
promising herself that she wouldn't look at it again.

* * *

Late November was the beginning of peak tourist season, at least, as far as the influx of tourists from the North was concerned. As the temperature in North America and Europe dropped, the residents who could afford it became intent upon seeking out warmer climes. The colder it became in the North, was of course the warmer it became in the Caribbean, and those in the know lost no time in shunting aside their woolens in exchange for swimsuits and suntan oil.

The heightened tourist traffic kept Rhea busy. For this she was grateful. Physical exhaustion had that mind-numbing quality that allowed her to fall asleep in a tired heap every night, preventing her from dwelling on the fact that the space beside her on the bed was empty.

Her present group was quite fun to be with. They were a group of twelve American women from the deep south, members of a retired women's support group. Rhea loved their sense of fun and eagerness to explore. They were all over the age of sixty, all anxious to plunge into a life of adventure after years of being tied to the office, to their husbands, children, and homes. They were determined that their three weeks in the Caribbean would make up for all the years of routine and boredom that they had faced in the past, and would once again encounter upon their return home.

Rhea had discovered that they were avid bird-watchers, and for the past two days they had been camped out close to the peak of the highest mountain on the island, El Cerro Del Aripo, a noble green mass of lush forest, wide rushing rivers and of course, a startling array of wildlife that included birds that nestled in the trees like bright blossoms, monkeys that hooted loudly to each other across the forest canopy, ferocious wild pigs, which Rhea would rather avoid, and snakes that could grow as long as twenty feet.

They women were a dream group, the kind every tour guide prayed for. They were eager to learn, and fell upon each new discovery with the curiosity of excited children. They had returned to camp just before sunset on the day before they were due to return to Port of Spain. Rhea was standing close to the tents, watching as three of the women whipped up a hot dinner on some camp stoves.

She was chatting with one of the more gregarious of the bunch, a woman called Bernadine, who was a retired lawyer, only recently widowed. Bernadine was nearing seventy, but tramped through the forests with the vitality of a Boy Scout. Bernadine was enthusiastically describing a spider that she had come across in the forest, a huge member of the bird-eating variety that Rhea found more repulsive than interesting, when she stopped in midsentence.

Rhea frowned. "What is it?"

Bernadine lifted her hand and pointed toward the base of their peak, to the area where the accessible roadway ended and a footpath began. "There. It's a van. Do you see it?"

Rhea squinted. Bernadine was right. A tiny four-wheel drive was tackling the mountain with a vengeance. It bounced up and down on the rugged road with no apparent regard for the vehicle's suspension.

"What's that fool trying to do," Bernadine said disapprovingly, "break his neck?"

"Question is," Rhea added, "why is he here?" She hoped it wasn't a hunter. If there was one thing she disliked, it was the sound of gunshots echoing through the forest. Besides, the person seemed intent on coming toward this particular spot, and although the area was accessible to all, she felt a pang of territorial jealousy. There was a whole mountain out there, so why was this person so bent on coming toward their campsite?

The two women watched as the vehicle reached the end of the road. The sole occupant, who was still just a stick figure in the distance, leaped out and slammed the door, and made his way toward the footpath with unusual rapidity.

"Fool doesn't have any camping gear on his back. It'll be dark in an hour. What's wrong with him?"

Rhea was wondering that herself. The two women stared, fascinated, as the man plodded up the path without pausing for a breath. Rhea's fascination turned to horrified amazement when, as the man came closer, she recognised the determined gait. It was Marcus.

No, she corrected herself. It was someone who *walked* like Marcus. Marcus was still in the States. He had gone back because he didn't want her. No, he'd gone back because he was still in love with his ex-wife, and didn't have the courage to shake that obsession long enough to fight for what he'd had with Rhea. She pursed her lips.

Bernadine, quick on the draw as ever, saw the gesture and looked at her sharply. "You know him?"

Rhea shook her head. "No, he just reminded me of someone, that's all."

But as they watched, the man got closer, and it wasn't long before Rhea's first suspicions were confirmed. Her sharp indrawn breath drew Bernadine's curious eyes to her face again.

"Uh-huh," the other woman drawled, not accepting her denial one bit. The two watched until he had crested the incline and was drawing near. By this time, Banner had also noticed the intruder, and had come to stand at Rhea's side in an instinctively protective gesture. Rhea was glad to be flanked by two such strong people; they prevented her from turning tail and running for the forest.

By the time Marcus was close enough for them to see his face, Bernadine was grinning hugely. "Mmmm-hmmm, girl. I hope you *do* know the brother, because if you don't, I sure as hell am gonna go on there and get to know him myself."

In spite of her turmoil, Rhea smiled back. But this was a serious situation, so she schooled her face into a sober expression. What could he possibly be doing here?

The other women had noticed his presence at the edge of their camp, and there was a murmur that was half curiosity, half shameless appreciation. These women might have been well past middle age, but they weren't blind!

Banner was the first to approach Marcus and speak. He held out a hand to be shaken, then pulled Marcus closer and embraced him warmly like a brother. "How you doing, man?" They broke the embrace and stood grinning at each other.

Marcus inhaled deeply, trying to get his breath regular once

again. "Hot. I've been driving around out there for hours."
His handsome face was dripping with sweat from the exertion
of the climb, but he looked triumphant, like a man who had
set his mind against the mountain and had come out a winner.

"You look like you could do with a beer," Banner said.
"How about a Carib?"

"I wouldn't drink anything else," Marcus answered, and
Banner ambled off toward the battery-powered refrigerator they
kept in the supply tent.

Marcus mopped his brow and panted out his gratitude. "I
must be out of condition," he said apologetically. Rhea dis-
agreed silently. With his light denim shirt clinging to his damp
chest, he looked in fine form, dammit. A glance at Bernadine
told her that the older woman agreed with her unspoken
appraisal.

With courtly politeness, Marcus introduced himself to Bernadine and saluted the curious group of women who now seemed
more interested in the newcomer than in ensuring that dinner
would not burn. Rhea observed as Marcus held the eyes of all
around in his thrall, and seethed. Trust him to make a spectacular
entry and have all female eyes on him. She was sure he enjoyed
that.

She had not spoken to him, even after he gulped down the
cold Trinidadian beer that he had grown to appreciate so much
during his last visit. She answered with an incredulous glare
when Marcus asked, politely, if the ladies would excuse him
and Rhea for a few moments.

"You go, girl," Bernadine exulted, and walked immediately
back toward the circle of gaping women, shouting at them in
the voice of one who was used to exercising authority. "What's
wrong with y'all? What y'all staring at? Don't you have dinner
to make? You're burning it!" All heads snapped obediently
toward the business at hand, leaving Rhea, Marcus, and Banner
alone at the edge of the camp.

Marcus turned to Banner as if Rhea wasn't even there. "I've
come to take Rhea away for the night. I'll bring her back
tomorrow. *Late* tomorrow."

Rhea felt her mouth go slack with incredulity. Was he serious? She stared at him, eyes agog.

"Yeah?" Banner was smiling like he found nothing surprising in the proposition.

"Yeah. Can you handle things here for the evening alone?"

Banner gave a belly laugh. "Are you kidding? We're all buttoned down for the night. No problem. Y'all go ahead. Just make sure you're good to my friend, here," he warned Marcus with mock seriousness.

Marcus gave Banner the boyish grin that she had loved—still loved—so much. The grin irritated her. The two of them smiling and slapping each other on the back like they weren't a day out of school got on her nerves.

Rhea could keep silent no longer. The brotherhood of men had struck again: even Banner was turning against her. "Hello? Has everybody forgotten that I'm here? Can I have a say in all this?"

Marcus turned his deep golden gaze upon her face. "I haven't forgotten that you're here for a minute, Rhea. I haven't forgotten you're here in the past three *months*. You're the reason I came back. Don't you know that?"

"I think this would be the appropriate time for me to go help the ladies with dinner, or something. See you tomorrow, hon, and take care, okay?" Banner kissed Rhea lightly on the cheek, asking forgiveness for his treachery, and strode away without waiting for an answer.

Rhea turned to Marcus, not caring if her clients were watching while she blew him out of the water.

"What do you think you're doing?" she demanded.

He looked at her in all seriousness. "I came to get you. I told you."

"How could you come to get me? I'm working. This is my job, remember?" She was seething. He never ceased to amaze her.

"Don't worry." Marcus waved her protests away like an irritating mosquito. "I called your boss up and told him you had a family emergency. It was an uphill climb, but he gave you twenty-four hours' leave."

Rhea opened her mouth, found that there was nothing she could say to express her shock, and shut it again.

"Without pay, of course," he added almost sheepishly. "But I'll make it up to you. I promise."

She looked at his determined face and knew then that there was no sense in fighting him. "How did you find me?" she asked resignedly.

"Your very obliging secretary gave me precise directions. She was concerned, but I told her that everything was under control." He looked so proud of his persuasive skills that Rhea made a note to let Charlotte have the sharp side of her tongue when she got back into the office. Under control? *His* control!

"Well?" she folded her arms and waited impatiently for him to begin. "You have half an hour before sunset. . . ."

"Precisely." He grasped her arm. "It's a long, dark, lonely road down there, and we're taking it tonight."

She followed him grudgingly to her tent, where Banner already had her kit bag packed and waiting. She took it without a word. Better to just get the whole nightmare over with. She remembered a line from a dozen bad war movies that she had seen as a child, "Surrender; all resistance is useless."

Ignoring the unabashed stares from the women around the campfire, Rhea muttered her apologies for her hasty exit, wished them all a good night, and began following Marcus down the track toward the vehicle.

"Hey, no problem," Bernadine yelled at their receding backs. "In your position, I'd be gone in a flash, too!" The good-humored ribbing made Rhea's ears burn.

Rhea sat next to Marcus in silence as he eased his way out onto the country road, staring out of the window, determined not to speak. He seemed to appreciate her need for quiet, and let her be.

After an uncomfortable hour of driving, he pulled into the parking lot of a small hotel, leaped out, and ran round the other side to open her door. She got out wordlessly and let him carry her bag up to his room. If he thought she would be staying any length of time, he had another think coming. But as he closed the door behind them, her heart stepped up its pace.

"Thirsty?" he asked like a polite host.

Rhea shook her head.

"There's a shower," he pointed in the approximate direction.

"I assume there would be," she answered mirthlessly. Why didn't he just say what he had to say and let her leave?

Marcus sighed and looked at her taut, noncommittal face for a long time before he spoke again. "I thought you would be glad to see me."

"You thought wrong. Begin." She folded her arms, partly in defiance, partly to protect herself.

"Uh," he was thrown off his equilibrium, and looked a little flustered. "Um . . ."

Rhea rolled her eyes, and turned abruptly toward the door. She had no time for this. She had no time for this man and his stupid games, when all she wanted was to touch him and see if he was real and not some elaborate hallucination conjured up by her own loneliness. He stopped her with a strong hand on her shoulder.

"Don't go. Rhea, please."

She stopped, but glared balefully at him, still waiting. If he expected her to be overwhelmed with joy, he expected plenty.

"My daughter . . ." he began, and Rhea felt a stab of fear.

"Is she all right? Is something wrong with Jodie?" God, if something was wrong with the child, and there she was, giving Marcus a hard time, she wouldn't forgive herself.

"No," he comforted her. "Jodie's fine. I left her with her grandmother for a few days. It's just that, she's sent me on a mission."

"What mission?" her eyes narrowed.

Marcus was smiling sheepishly. "I'm to get you to agree to marry me, or else."

Her face registered her astonishment, then disdain. "Oh, so your *daughter* sent you."

Marcus seemed oblivious to her tone. "She hasn't stopped nagging since we left the island in August. You'd be surprised how insistent a six-year-old can be, once she makes up her mind. She can be as manipulative as a grown woman."

Rhea held up a hand to stop him. "Marcus, look, that's very

nice and all, but if you're just here because your daughter wanted you to come, then I don't think we have anything to say to each other. How dare you come here to interrupt my business, drag me off like a big ape, and then stand there handing me such a ham-handed proposal of. . . ."

He interrupted, aghast. "No! Rhea, no, it's not like that. I'm not here because of her."

"But you just said . . ."

"I'm sorry. I just didn't know what to say. I didn't know how to broach the subject. You were just standing there glaring at me, and I was beginning to think I'd made a mistake. So I just said the first thing that came into my head. Jodelle wants you, Rhea, but she isn't the reason I'm here. I'm here because I want to be. I'm here because I love you."

She refused to back down an inch. "I've heard *that* before!"

He protested. "It's true!" When he saw that she wasn't buying, he went on, "It was true the last time, too," he admitted.

"But you said it wasn't! You said it was an illusion. You said . . ."

"Rhea, please," he put both hands on her shoulders and tried to hold her agitated gaze with his own. "I know what I said. I've been tormented by those words over and over since I left. I was wrong. I was wrong to send you away. I don't have any excuse for that."

"Well, why, then?" Her eyes held a plea for him to explain what had made him hurt her so deeply. She was almost afraid to hear the truth.

"You frightened me. The size of what I felt for you, the hugeness of it, scared me. So I backed away. I said all that just to keep you away. You were right. I was a coward. I'll never forget hearing you call me that. You were so right."

"And Yvette? You're still carrying her around in you."

He shook his head vehemently. "No. Not anymore. Yvette is over. I just couldn't see that. She hurt me so deeply, that I couldn't get her out of my system. That's what scared me so much. It wasn't your origins or your accent or the island. It was knowing what a woman had done to me before, how she tied me up in knots and made my heart her slave. And falling

in love for the second time in my life was even more te[...]
because this time I fell even harder than before. The n[...]
made love in that beach house, I realised that what I was [...]
for you was stronger and deeper than anything I ever felt for
her, even when things were going well, and we were happy.
And that scared me, because if my wife could hurt me so
deeply, there was no telling how much you could do to me if
things ever went wrong between us.''

"So you ran," she snorted contemptuously. "You panicked
and you ran. You didn't even trust me enough to tell me about
how you felt. You shut me out and left me wondering for two
days what was wrong, if I had done anything wrong, and then
you just cut me loose. You were such a . . .''

"Coward. I know. But not anymore. It's been damn long
and hard, but I've worked it through, and I've put that behind
me now. I'm sorry I didn't trust you. I'm willing to try again,
if you are. Whatever it takes, I'll do it, if you only say you'll
give me a second chance.''

Through her misted vision, she realised he was waiting. She
drew a deep breath to steady her voice before she answered.
"But Yvette . . .''

"I told you, that's over. I don't need her ring or her memory.
I don't need her insults or her lies. She's over. She gave me
one thing I will love and treasure until I die, and that's my
daughter. But apart from that, there's nothing. She can't hurt
me anymore. And all that space she took up inside of me is
cleaned out and empty, and there for you. If you want it.''

He was getting to her. Her love was making it hard to remain
angry, and hard to keep protesting. "But there's still the distance. You're thousands of miles away, Mark. I don't want to
give up my job to follow you. It might be good at first, but
eventually I'll miss the work I love to do, and my island, and
I'll start to resent you, and that could make me bitter.''

He grinned, realising he was getting through to her. "Don't
worry. I've already thought about that. You don't have to follow
me. Jodie and I can follow you. I've spoken to the editor of
that magazine, and he's willing to let me do a whole Caribbean
series, roam up and down along the islands like a pirate. I can

still travel, and I can still write. And I'll always come home to you.''

He grasped her by the arms. "Listen, don't worry about all that yet. We can talk about it later. We have all the time we need to work those details out. We *will* work them out, I promise. All I want to know right now is if you can forgive me for hurting you, and if you're willing to give us a try.''

He was right, they'd work things out. The details were easy, once you got the love part down. The simplicity of it made her laugh.

He gave her a scowl that was only half serious. "You find my anguish amusing, Miss?''

"No, no. I think it must be joy. I *know* it's joy. And relief. Marcus, I missed you so much.''

"I missed you. You don't know how!''

She reached out for him and was shocked at how good he felt under her hands, even better than her memory had led her to believe. They began snatching kisses that got longer and longer. Standing in her sturdy hiking boots, she was as tall as he, and the sensation of being face to face, pressed hard against him, shoulder to shoulder, hip to hip, as they would be if they were lying against each other in bed, was delicious. He managed to lift his mouth from hers long enough to ask her if she was tired being on her feet.

"Maybe, but if I sit next to you, I might never want to get up!''

"Sit all the same,'' he urged, his broad hands doing a number on her spine that she didn't even want to think about. They plopped down together on a dark green couch, side by side, and the hungry kisses began again.

"I love you, Mark.''

He smiled widely. "I've only heard those words playing over and over in my memory these past few months, but all they did was cause me hurt and bring regrets. It's good to hear them again. This time, they even sound different. They make me happy.''

Kneeling before her, he tugged the heavy leather boots off her feet and began stroking her, starting at the ankles and working his way slowly upward along her denim-covered legs until his hands skirted along the tops of her thighs.

"How's your leg, sweetness?" He let his fingers run back down along the place where he knew her jellyfish sting lay.

"Better," she answered, feeling the puckered skin under his fingertips contract. "Scarred a little, but not so bad."

"I'll kiss those scars away, you wait and see." He pressed his lips to her jeans-covered thigh in promise.

Rhea writhed, biting her lip in an attempt to keep from crying out loud. She was dressed to do battle with any mountain, in clothes that were rugged to the point of being masculine, but under his hands, she felt as feminine as if she were wearing stockings and fine lace.

With his hands moving up to grasp her hips and pull her toward him, he leaned forward with a contented sigh and laid his head in her lap. He reveled in her warm scent. His hands never ceased their movement, kneading at the curve of her bottom, lightly squeezing the warm flesh. Rhea heard him whispering something softly against the thick material of her jeans, and when she leaned forward she discovered it was her name, being repeated over and over.

"Oh," she said, as if a thought had just struck her.

He looked up from her lap, eyes huge and dark. "What?"

"I just realised . . . there's a bed in this room."

He turned to look at the huge king-size bed that dominated the room. "So there is," he agreed.

"Not a little guest-house cot."

"No."

"Or a blanket thrown across the floor in someone else's living room."

"No." He had a huge smile on his face.

They never knew who got there first, or how they managed to free themselves of their tight, heavy hiking outfits so fast, but the next thing they remembered was being on the bed, fully stretched out on the clean, crisp sheets, arms and legs locked around each other.

He was all fingers, all tongue, touching, rediscovering, tugging on something deep inside her that caused her hips to rise toward his hungry mouth. She forced the back of her hand against her mouth to keep back her frenzied cries, but he urged her to let go. "Let me hear you. Come on, Rhea, open up for me."

She opened up, with wails of sheer delirium that went on and on until he covered her mouth, taking the sound deep inside him, inhaling her cries for more.

"It's been so long. I haven't had a good night's sleep ever since I left, thinking of doing this to you. Rhea . . ."

"Don't talk, touch!" she demanded. "I need you. Hurry! Hurry!"

He needed no more encouragement. He slipped into her heat with the sigh of a man in intense pain, and her legs drew up around him, locking him in tight. Her arms echoed the shape of her thighs, wrapping around his smooth, hard chocolate shoulders. They came together and separated again and again, in a fierce ritual whose only objective was to stem the pained need that they had both suffered during their separation.

When their heated encounter came to its inevitable conclusion, they lay together, slippery but still locked into place, stunned by the force and power of their lovemaking.

"My God," he gasped in wonder.

"Yes," she agreed. Her muscles ached as if she had been shooting the rapids.

They let the silence envelop them, listening to each other's breathing as it slowly became normal again.

After a long while, Marcus broke the silence. "You haven't said if you'll marry me yet, you know."

"Huh," she joked. "I'll think about it."

"I'll take that as a yes."

"You'll take it as nothing, until I'm good and ready," she said tartly, and snatched a quick kiss.

"Well, let me know fast, madam, because I have to phone in a report to the little lady of the house to let her know that my assignment here is done." He was rewarded with a punch in the arm.

"Alright, alright. Take all the time you need. Take until Tuesday, if you like."

She looked at him, curious. "What happens Tuesday?"

"That's about when I expect my patience to run out," he smiled.

"Alright, Tuesday, then." She reached out and tugged mischievously on his damp chest hairs. "Or maybe tomorrow, if you're good," she teased.

"We'll have lots of tomorrows," he promised, and kissed her lightly. "All the tomorrows you want."

She snuggled against his solid chest, feeling the warmth and reassurance of his arms around her and the rhythm of his breathing. As they both fell into exhausted, contented sleep, the last thing they heard was the soft hum of the air-conditioning unit, the hooting of an owl, and the joyous chirping of crickets as the night came alive outside.

Dear Reader

As a Trinidadian myself, I share Rhea's pride in her country and her delight in showing off the amazing beauty of Trinidad and Tobago to others. As a passionate defender of animals, I also share Marcus' indignation at the ecological ills that are foisted upon helpless creatures by uncaring humans. I hasten to explain, however, that while we are, as a nation, struggling to right ecological wrongs, thus restoring to Nature the balance that is rightfully hers, these islands are much more than this.

These islands are intrigue, wonder, talent, music, song, dance and creativity. They are sophisticated, literate, and developed, providing a level of comfort and service that any visitor could desire. An open invitation therefore stands: don't take Rhea's word for it; come see for yourself just how enticing a holiday spot these islands can be.

I hope you enjoyed reading Night Heat as much as I enjoyed writing it, and look forward eagerly to your feedback. And yes, I do answer all correspondence!

Simona

ABOUT THE AUTHOR

Roslyn Carrington, who also writes as Simona Taylor, believes that the lush multicultural Caribbean islands of her native Trinidad and Tobago provide the ideal setting for nurturing the creativity of a young writer. There she juggles a hectic career in Public Relations, a weekly op/ed column in the country's most established newspaper and a blossoming career as a novelist.

Her extensive travels and avid curiosity combine with her passion for the delights of the English language to lend wings to her writing. During the many late night hours that she spends writing, she is encouraged by the company of her cat, Simona, from whom she borrows her pen-name.

She would be delighted to hear from her readers, and can be reached at:

Roslyn Carrington
4405 N.W. 73rd Avenue
Suite #011-1241
Miami
Florida 33166-6400

Or visit her website at www.roslyncarrington.com or e-mail her at
simona@roslyncarrington.com

COMING IN AUGUST . . .

UNTIL THERE WAS YOU   (1-58314-028-X, $4.99/$6.50)
by Francis Ray
Best-selling author Catherine Stewart, renowned for helping troubled children, retreated to a friend's mountain cabin in Santa Fe after a traumatic assault. Once there, she couldn't resist helping others. She never thought they'd come to her aid, and she never dreamed that her roommate, Luke Grayson, would help her overcome her past and lead her to love.

A TASTE OF LOVE   (1-58314-029-8, $4.99/$6.50)
by Louré Bussey
Nia Lashon took a position as a maid at Roland Davenport's chain of Caribbean resorts in St. Croix. Roland's never believed that he could run his business and have a serious relationship. Until Nia. Now Roland is determined to give Nia the inspiration to reach her goals and the passion she's always yearned for.

FANTASY   (1-58314-030-1, $4.99/$6.50)
by Raynetta Mañees
Struggling singer Sameerah Clark landed a job on the Fantasy cruise liner, but she hadn't realized it was as back-up vocalist for singing idol Tony Harmon. She blurts out her frustration, but the fiery beauty with the melodious voice only intrigues Tony. After his invitation to sing a duet ends with a bold kiss, desire courses through Sameerah's blood.

WHEN LOVE CALLS   (1-58314-031-X, $4.99/$6.50)
by Gail A. McFarland
Thirty-something Marcus Benton had forsaken all for his career. Then, when phone lines accidentally crossed in a vicious storm, fate brought him to Davida Lawrence, a forty-year-old widowed mother. The possibility of becoming a husband and father challenged everything Marcus struggled for. Their age difference made Davida doubtful of a future together. Only by trusting in each other can two uncertain people find a forever kind of love.

Available wherever paperbacks are sold, or order direct from the Publisher. Send cover price plus 50¢ per copy for mailing and handling to BET Books, c/o Kensington Publishing Corp., Consumer Orders, or call (toll free) 888-345-BOOK, to place your order using Mastercard or Visa. Residents of New York, Washington D.C. and Tennessee must include sales tax. DO NOT SEND CASH.

SPICE UP YOUR LIFE
WITH ARABESQUE ROMANCES

AFTER HOURS, by Anna Larence   (0-7860-0277-8, $4.99/$6.50)
Vice president of a Fort Worth company, Nachelle Oliver was used to things
her own way. Until she got a new boss. Steven DuCloux was ruthless—and the
most exciting man she had ever known. He knew that she was the perfect VP,
and that she would be the perfect wife. She tried to keep things strictly professional, but the passion between them was too strong.

CHOICES, by Maria Corley   (0-7860-0245-X, $4.95/$6.50)
Chaney just ended with Taurique when she met Lawrence. The rising young
singer swept her off her feet. After nine years of marriage, with Lawrence away
for months on end, Chaney feels lonely and vulnerable. Purely by chance, she
meets Taurique again, and has to decide if she wants to risk it all for love.

DECEPTION, by Donna Hill   (0-7860-0287-5, $4.99/$6.50)
An unhappy marriage taught owner of a successful New York advertising
agency, Terri Powers, never to trust in love again. Then she meets businessman
Clinton Steele. She can't fight the attraction between them—or the sensual
hunger that fires her deepest passions.

DEVOTED, by Francine Craft   (0-7860-0094-5, $4.99/$6.50)
When Valerie Thomas and Delano Carter were young lovers each knew it
wouldn't last. Val, now a photojournalist, meets Del at a high-society wedding.
Del takes her to Alaska for the assignment of her career. In the icy wilderness
he warms her with a passion too long denied. This time not even Del's desperate
secret will keep them from reclaiming their lost love.

FOR THE LOVE OF YOU, by Felicia Mason   (0-7860-0071-6, $4.99/$6.50
Seven years ago, Kendra Edwards found herself pregnant and alone. Now she
has a secure life for her twins and a chance to finish her college education. A
long unhappy marriage had taught attorney Malcolm Hightower the danger of
passion. But Kendra taught him the sensual magic of love. Now they must each
give true love a chance.

ALL THE RIGHT REASONS, by Janice Sims   (0-7860-0405-3, $4.99/$6.50)
Public defender, Georgie Shaw, returns to New Orleans and meets reporter Clay
Knight. He's determined to uncover secrets between Georgie and her celebrity
twin, and protect Georgie from someone who wants both sisters dead. Dangerous secrets are found in a secluded mansion, leaving Georgie with no one to
trust but the man who stirs her desires.

*Available wherever paperbacks are sold, or order direct from the
Publisher. Send cover price plus 50¢ per copy for mailing and
handling to Kensington Publishing Corp., Consumer Orders,
or call (toll free) 888-345-BOOK, to place your order using
Mastercard or Visa. Residents of New York and Tennessee
must include sales tax. DO NOT SEND CASH.*

LOOK FOR THESE ARABESQUE ROMANCES

AFTER ALL, by Lynn Emery   (0-7860-0325-1, $4.99/$6.50)
News reporter Michelle Toussaint only focused on her dream of becoming an anchorwoman. Then contractor Anthony Hilliard returned. For five years, Michelle had reminsced about the passions they shared. But happiness turned to heartbreak when Anthony's cruel betrayal led to her father's financial ruin. He returned for one reason only: to win Michelle back.

THE ART OF LOVE, by Crystal Wilson-Harris   (0-7860-0418-5, $4.99/$6.50)
Dakota Bennington's heritage is apparent from her African clothing to her sculptures. To her, attorney Pierce Ellis is just another uptight professional stuck in the American mainstream. Pierce worked hard and is proud of his success. An art purchase by his firm has made Dakota a major part of his life. And love bridges their different worlds.

CHANGE OF HEART   (0-7860-0103-8, $4.99/$6.50)
by Adrienne Ellis Reeves
Not one to take risks or stray far from her South Carolina hometown, Emily Brooks, a recently widowed mother, felt it was time for a change. On a business venture she meets author David Walker who is conducting research for his new book. But when he finds undying passion, he wants Emily for keeps. Wary of her newfound passion, all Emily has to do is follow her heart.

ECSTACY, by Gwynne Forster   (0-7860-0416-9, $4.99/$6.50)
Schoolteacher Jeannetta Rollins had a tumor that was about to cost her her eyesight. Her persistence led her to follow Mason Fenwick, the only surgeon talented enough to perform the surgery, on a trip around the world. After getting to know her, Mason wants her whole . . . body and soul. Now he must put behind a tragedy in his career and trust himself and his heart.

KEEPING SECRETS, by Carmen Green   (0-7860-0494-0, $4.99/$6.50)
Jade Houston worked alone. But a dear deceased friend left clues to a two-year-old mystery and Jade had to accept working alongside Marine Captain Nick Crawford. As they enter a relationship that runs deeper than business, each must learn how to trust each other in all aspects.

MOST OF ALL, by Louré Bussey   (0-7860-0456-8, $4.99/$6.50)
After another heartbreak, New York secretary Elandra Lloyd is off to the Bahamas to visit her sister. Her sister is nowhere to be found. Instead she runs into Nassau's richest, self-made millionaire Bradley Davenport. She is lucky to have made the acquaintance with this sexy islander as she searches for her sister and her trust in the opposite sex.

Available wherever paperbacks are sold, or order direct from the Publisher. Send cover price plus 50¢ per copy for mailing and handling to Kensington Publishing Corp., Consumer Orders, or call (toll free) 888-345-BOOK, to place your order using Mastercard or Visa. Residents of New York and Tennessee must include sales tax. DO NOT SEND CASH.

ROMANCES THAT SIZZLE
FROM ARABESQUE

AFTER DARK, by Bette Ford   (0-7860-0442-8, $4.99/$6.50)
Taylor Hendricks' brother is the top NBA draft choice. She wants to protect him from the lure of fame and wealth, but meets basketball superstar Donald Williams in an exclusive Detroit restaurant. Donald is determined to prove that she is wrong about him. In this game all is at stake . . . including Taylor's heart.

BEGUILED, by Eboni Snoe   (0-7860-0046-5, $4.99/$6.50)
When Raquel Mason agrees to impersonate a missing heiress for just one night and plans go awry, a daring abduction makes her the captive of seductive Nate Bowman. Together on a journey across exotic Caribbean seas to the perilous wilds of Central America, desire looms in their hearts. But when the masquerade is over, will their love end?

CONSPIRACY, by Margie Walker   (0-7860-0385-5, $4.99/$6.50)
Pauline Sinclair and Marcellus Cavanaugh had the love of a lifetime. Until Pauline had to leave everything behind. Now she's back and their love is as strong as ever. But when the President of Marcellus's company turns up dead and Pauline is the prime suspect, they must risk all to their love.

FIRE AND ICE, by Carla Fredd   (0-7860-0190-9, $4.99/$6.50)
Years of being in the spotlight and a recent scandal regarding her ex-fianceé and a supermodel, the daughter of a Georgia politician, Holly Aimes has turned cold. But when work takes her to the home of late-night talk show host Michael Williams, his relentless determination melts her cool.

HIDDEN AGENDA, by Rochelle Alers   (0-7860-0384-7, $4.99/$6.50)
To regain her son from a vengeful father, Eve Blackwell places her trust in dangerous and irresistible Matt Sterling to rescue her abducted son. He accepts this last job before he turns a new leaf and becomes an honest rancher. As they journey from Virginia to Mexico they must enter a charade of marriage. But temptation is too strong for this to remain a sham.

INTIMATE BETRAYAL, by Donna Hill   (0-7860-0396-0, $4.99/$6.50)
Investigative reporter, Reese Delaware, and millionaire computer wizard, Maxwell Knight are both running from their pasts. When Reese is assigned to profile Maxwell, they enter a steamy love affair. But when Reese begins to piece her memory, she stumbles upon secrets that link her and Maxwell, and threaten to destroy their newfound love.

Available wherever paperbacks are sold, or order direct from the Publisher. Send cover price plus 50¢ per copy for mailing and handling to Kensington Publishing Corp., Consumer Orders, or call (toll free) 888-345-BOOK, to place your order using Mastercard or Visa. Residents of New York and Tennessee must include sales tax. DO NOT SEND CASH.